P9-DXS-758

Jury Rigged

OTHER FIVE STAR BOOKS BY LAURIE MOORE

Constable's Run (2002)
The Lady Godiva Murder (2002)
Constable's Apprehension (2003)
The Wild Orchid Society (2004)
Constable's Wedding (2005)

Jury Rigged

Laurie Moore

FIVE STAR
A part of Gale, Cengage Learning

Detroit • New York • San Francisco • New Haven, Conn • Waterville, Maine • London

Set in 11 pt. Plantin.
Printed on permanent paper.

LIBRARY OF CONGRESS CATALOGING-IN-PUBLICATION DATA

Moore, Laurie.
Jury rigged / by Laurie Moore. — 1st ed.
p. cm.
ISBN-13: 978-1-59414-710-4 (alk. paper)
ISBN-10: 1-59414-710-8 (alk. paper)
1. Women lawyers—Fiction. 2. Fort Worth (Tex.)—Fiction. 3. Inheritance and succession—Fiction. 4. Murder—Investigation—Fiction. I. Title.
PS3613.O564J87 2008
813'.6—dc22 2008037092

Published in 2008 in conjunction with Tekno Books and Ed Gorman.

Printed in the United States of America
2 3 4 5 6 7 12 11 10 09 08

ACKNOWLEDGMENTS

Many thanks to editors Mary Smith and Tiffany Schofield and the fine folks at Five Star Publishing and Tekno Books and to the friends and fans who inspire me to write, especially the two Jims who truly are two gems.

To my daughter Laura and in memory of my dad,
Judge Howard M. Fender

PROLOGUE

When Sheriff Bobby Noah carried a washing-machine box into Cézanne Martin's bungalow on Christmas day, she tried to conceal her disappointment. As she opened a succession of cartons in graduated sizes, her excitement mounted in inverse proportion to the dwindling sizes of the containers. By the time she unwrapped the little blue gift box with Tiffany written on the lid, he'd dropped to one knee and proposed.

The police detective accepted.

They had a lot in common, starting with their backgrounds in law enforcement—his as the sheriff of Johnson County; hers as a homicide detective with the Fort Worth Police Department in Tarrant County. So she understood when his cell phone rang, cutting short their celebration. A complainant in a residential burglary reported an arsenal of weapons missing. The victim wasn't just any old man; he was blind. And he was Bobby Noah's father.

As she closed the door behind her tall, lanky lawman with ocean-blue eyes and rugged, cowboy good looks, she couldn't help believing that her life had finally jumped back on track.

The past month had been hell. She'd solved the Lady Godiva murder, along with an eight-year-old cold case the media dubbed the Great Dane murder. She'd managed to convince the brass at the PD to grant her a ninety-day leave of absence from the homicide unit, enough time to get her law office up and running. If things worked out, she'd quit the department for good. If it looked like she wouldn't be able to make a decent living in private practice, she could return to the PD and pull in a steady income until another one of those coveted prosecutor jobs opened up at the District Attorney's Office.

She shimmied out of her black cocktail dress, shucked off her Ferragamos, and shrugged into a silk kimono. As she lifted her hand to admire the gorgeous diamond, the red light on her answering machine snared her attention. It blinked with a new message.

Now what?

She glided over and pressed the play button.

A man claiming to be a Seattle lawyer named Mitch Roselli wanted to know if she was related to his client, Bob Martin; if she was, could she return his call?

Bob Martin?

She knew the skunk, all right. Sorry swine ducked out on his wife and three kids and never looked back. After a twenty-year absence, why would the man pop up like a jack-in-the-box on Christmas, for God's sake?

Maybe he'd been in WITSEC—the witness protection program.

She listened to the message three times before copying down the number. For a long time, she stood perfectly still with her internal loran vibrating.

Working up enough nerve to dial that number called for a shot of liquid courage. She uncorked Bobby's bottle of leftover champagne and downed it. If the attorney told her where to find old Bob, would she call him? What would she say to the most hated man in her life?

"Hey, dirtbag, why'd you run out on us?"

By now, the trim, handsome guy she'd once called Daddy probably turned into a doddering geezer in need of financial help. If he wanted to juice her for money, she had two words for him: Go fish.

Flopped in a tufted leather wingback with her feet propped up on a matching ottoman, she let her gaze drift over the living room. The sight of a tabloid magazine, opened to a grisly tale of murder, prickled the hair on her arms.

She didn't read tabloids.

Neither did Bobby.

Neither did Deuteronomy Devilrow, the black handyman's niece who'd dropped by earlier to inform her she'd be moving in for several months.

Her vision sharpened. For no good reason, the painting above the fireplace hung off-center. The ficus tree near the front door had been moved closer to the windows. Her ears pricked. Something's not right. The drone of a leaf blower came from Mrs. Pietrowski's side yard next door.

By the time she dialed Seattle, her head buzzed.

On the third ring, a man answered. His jolly baritone brimmed with holiday cheer. "Ho-ho-ho, Merry Christmas." Joyous squeals of children at play echoed in the background. His attempt to muffle the mouthpiece failed. "Hold it down, munchkins, Daddy's on the phone. Hello? Sorry about that."

Cézanne cleared her throat. Emotions roiled in her gut. "I was out when you called about Bob Martin. I used to be his daughter."

"Oh, boy." A deep breath, slow to exhale. "Look, I'm sorry to call you on Christmas."

"He's in trouble, isn't he?" Without awaiting a reply, she used the vilest tone she could muster. "He probably left out a few details when he hired you to do his dirty work, so let me set the record straight." A rush of childhood memories flooded back, none of them good. Her fist stiffened against her hip. "Did he tell you my sister Monet died the night he abandoned us? Bet he failed to mention that part since he didn't even have the decency to show up for the funeral."

"He thought your sister was alive until a month ago."

Words exploded from her mouth. "Monet's been dead twenty years."

"I'm sorry for your loss."

"Well don't be."

Christmas music played in the background. José Feliciano sang "Feliz Navidad."

The Seattle attorney muffled the mouthpiece. "That's beautiful, Gabe. Did you make that all by yourself? Mommy helped? Okay, I'll be there in a minute." He raised his voice. "For God's sake, Gloria, would you wipe the icing off his mouth before he gets cookie all over the couch?" The daddy disappeared, and the professional returned. "Look, Miss Martin, it's not my intention to dredge up bad memories on Christmas. This can wait. Why don't you call me in a few days? We can talk then."

"I think we should talk now." Hostility fueled sarcasm. "Just so you know, I got along fine without him. My mother went off the deep end; my grandmother had to step in and finish raising me. Then she died, and my life went to hell."

And where was Bob? Sitting in a tavern, swilling down well drinks and flirting with barflies?

Tears blistered behind her eyeballs. Holiday smells that cheered her earlier suddenly made the air cloying and unbreathable. She didn't like the empty feeling draining the joy out of the engagement ring. This should've been the happiest time of her life.

And yet she'd secretly suspected the old man would return one day.

"Let me give you a message to pass on. Tell him I said to drop dead."

Long pause. "You don't really mean that."

"Oh, but I do." Said nastily.

Only she didn't.

Deep down, she wanted an explanation. And she wanted her daddy back.

"Merry Christmas. You get your wish."

Chapter One

The most jarring sensation that pulled Cézanne Martin out of a deep, Technicolor sleep wasn't the bone-cracking echo of a cocked hammer in her ear but the size of the cannon pointed in her face when the intruder flicked on the lamp next to the bed. Mind-numbing fear gripped her throat. Her heart went dead then thunked back to life in the unnatural rhythm of the damned.

It took a couple of dedicated eye blinks before the gun barrel shrank in size. The woman pointing the weapon came into sharp focus. Her fingers whitened against the pistol grips. She stepped back and smirked.

Darlene Driskoll.

Soon-to-be convicted murderess and estranged wife of Fort Worth police detective Doug Driskoll.

Estranged, because Darlene had been locked in the Tarrant County jail ever since her arrest in the killing of Fort Worth police rookie Carri Crane. The carnage didn't stop there. By the time a grand jury convened to hear grisly details of a homicide dubbed the Lady Godiva murder by the press, she'd been charged in the deaths of three other young women.

Only Darlene wasn't incarcerated at the moment. She waited near the foot of the bed close enough to hear the thud of Cézanne's erratic heartbeat.

"Hello, Cézanne. Long time, no see." The greeting of a madwoman, infused with mock cheer.

"Darlene." It was the best she could do at midnight. Especially with her five-shot Chief Special beyond the lunge area, resting at the bottom of her purse.

The homicide detective frowned in the hurling confusion. The DA's Office had promised to warn her if Driskoll's wife got out on a writ of habeas corpus. As she choked down the lump forming in her throat, she drank in the sight of her captor.

Weapon of choice—a .357 Magnum. Government issue, like the ones carried by deputies of the Tarrant County Sheriff's Office.

Home-invasionwear—a Tarrant County jailer's uniform.

Her mind sharpened. A skin-crawling realization snared her in its grip.

Darlene had escaped.

Cézanne's heart raced. "When did you get out?"

The unbalanced woman paused in serene reflection. "Five, maybe six hours ago."

Odd occurrences instantly made sense. The tabloid that didn't belong in the house. The unexplained repositioning of plants and furniture. Cracker crumbs on the kitchen countertop. A knife in the sink with remnants of peanut butter. The milk carton in the fridge with only a few heady gulps remaining.

Cézanne's skin crawled. The outlaw had lost weight. The *Danger: High-Voltage* hairdo that once framed doughy cheeks now hung around a slimmer face. Dark roots contrasted sharply with dry, processed blonde hair. Eyes, shockingly catlike, barely blinked.

Darlene's yellow irises glittered. "Bet you're wondering why I'm here, aren't you?"

But the detective knew. She was more curious about how the deranged woman got inside. The set of Yale locks installed on the front door of the brick bungalow should've held the Screaming Eagles at bay. Cézanne fisted the eiderdown comforter to her chest as if it were a bulletproof shield.

"Get up." Darlene wagged the revolver. "Put your clothes on. We're going for a drive."

Cézanne climbed out of bed on shaky legs. She stumbled to the highboy blaming Doug Driskoll.

Philandering bastard swore he was single.

Never would've done the hokey-pokey with him if he hadn't lied about his marital status.

Now I have a crazy woman after me.

Her stomach clenched. She moved with the sluggishness of a zombie.

"Speed it up." Darlene used the gun as a pointer, wiggling it in the direction of an antique dresser. "Grab the first thing. It's not like you're going on a date."

She tried to keep calm as she slid open the drawer. She needed to coax out the truth. To gauge the demented killer's level of desperation.

Morbid curiosity, steeped in denial, strengthened her resolve to ferret out details. She wanted to believe Darlene had been made a Trusty. Trusties had wandering privileges. She envisioned Darlene dressed in bright orange coveralls, sweeping bird droppings off the sidewalk outside the jail. Imagined her pausing long enough to suck in the sweet breath of freedom, then propping the push broom against the salmon-colored brick exterior and walking away.

When the big iron door slams shut, you want to be the one on the outside.

The clothes told a different story.

"How'd you manage to get released?" She sucked in a breath and held it.

"Let's just say I borrowed a uniform off one of the jailers and leave it at that."

Cézanne plucked a UT Longhorn sweatshirt off the stack.

"Put it back." Darlene motioned with the barrel. "Pick something dark."

"Maybe you'd rather choose?" Cézanne backed away from the drawer.

Maybe let me get behind you. Take you down with a choke hold.

"This'll do." Darlene snatched up a black T-shirt draped over the arm of a nearby rocking chair and thrust it at her.

"It's dirty. I did housework last night."

Darlene took a whiff and wrinkled her nose. She pitched it over, then sailed a pair of raggedy cut-offs through the air. A faint smile thinned her lips. "In three days, a sweaty T-shirt will *not* be the overpowering smell making people gag."

Inwardly, Cézanne predicted her own future. This uninvited houseguest wasn't referring to civilians. She meant Crime Scene detectives.

"I'd like to change in the bathroom. For privacy." The request had nothing to do with modesty. Or about keeping the lunatic from comparing cup sizes.

"In the bathroom?" The intruder's gaze went glassy. Remote, cool detachment filled her tone. "Where you keep a spare pistol in the drawer next to the hair-dryer? No, I don't suppose you will."

Cézanne shuddered. Darlene must've creepy-crawled the house like the Manson Family did before they slaughtered Sharon Tate and the rest of her guests. She mentally whipped herself for not noticing the subtle differences after Bobby brought her home from the Christmas party at the Petroleum Club. Should've realized after he snacked on leftover turkey and suddenly felt queasy that it had nothing to do with an afternoon of gorging on holiday treats. Should've seen her abrupt need for a nap after eating a slice of pumpkin pie as a warning sign.

Her gut sank.

"I have to use the bathroom." The request fell on deaf ears. "C'mon, Darlene, be a sport."

"Go ahead." With an ice pick glare, Driskoll's wife eased over and blocked the door leading into the hall. She expected her to go right there on her grandmother's Persian rug.

Instead, Cézanne hiked up the cutoffs beneath her nightgown, then slipped the tee over her head and wrestled out of the bedclothes. In her haste, a prong on her solitaire caught a thread. As she worked it loose, the princess-cut diamond caught Darlene's attention.

"What's that?"

"I'm engaged." Her voice trailed. She wasn't sure how much information to disclose.

"Is this one married? Or did you bother to check?"

"Single. Unattached. A nice guy."

"How lovely." Driskoll's wife drooled sarcasm. "I'll bet he gave it to you for Christmas, didn't he? Want to know what I got? Twenty bucks to buy Oreos through the jail commissary."

"Oreos are good." Said hopefully.

Darlene snorted in disgust. "Another cop?"

"The sheriff of Johnson County."

"Sheriff," Darlene said, testing the word. "He looked pretty good in a Marlboro Man sort of way. At least what I could see from my hidey-hole in your closet. I kept waiting for the sheet to slide off. Damned the luck. Is he hung like Doug?"

The spurned wife had a way of ratcheting up the discomfort.

"Where are we going?" She hated the waver in her voice.

"You'll see." Gold-flecked irises gleamed stubbornly.

Cézanne's cell phone shrilled. Her eyes slewed over to the nightstand. A scenario played out in her head as the second ring brought the caller one step closer to voice mail. If Darlene let her answer . . . if she heard Bobby on the other end there might be an opportunity to drop a hint. Maybe scream, "Darlene

Driskoll's holding me at gunpoint. Get an ambulance en-route to pick up what's left of me."

Followed by an orange blast exploding from the muzzle of the Magnum.

She inwardly winced.

"Pick it up." Darlene motioned with the gun barrel. "No tricks, understand? Or you'll leak like a sieve."

She opened the wireless clamshell with a curious mixture of dread and hope. "Hello?"

The voice at the other end belonged to her best friend, Raven, a deputy with Tarrant County Constable Jinx Porter's office.

"Zan. I've been trying to call. Your landline's out of order."

She pressed her knees together to keep from shaking. Put her fingertips on the bed's hand-sewn antique quilt to steady herself. Across the room, Darlene studied her with the passion of a junkyard dog.

"I suppose the phone company cut off my services." She spoke in code. "I guess I forgot to pay my bill again. You know what a ditz I can be."

That should be enough of a hint. Raven knew how neurotic she was about not owing money.

Darlene flashed a knowing smirk. She made a little hand-sign, forming her fingers into scissors, and snipped the air in front of her.

"Have you heard the news?" In her excitement, Raven didn't wait for an answer. "Darlene Driskoll broke out of jail."

"How nice. Who told you I got engaged?"

"What?"

Cézanne could almost visualize the dark-haired beauty yanking the phone from her ear, staring at it like a cobra in a basket.

"It's pretty. Bobby picked it out himself."

"Did you hear what I just said? Darlene Driskoll killed a jailer and busted out of lock-up a few hours ago." She amended her announcement. "They haven't exactly pulled the plug yet, but Jinx said the poor woman flat-lined. That's as good as dead."

"That's wonderful. What'd Jinx give you for Christmas?"

"What Jinx gives every woman, sooner or later. A raging case of the clap. Only I'm not accepting those kinds of gifts from that serial philanderer anymore, so he pawned off a gift certificate to a third rate restaurant. Figures, doesn't it? Same thing the two-timer gave the rest of his employees. You'd think all those years of putting up with his bad behavior would've counted for something, wouldn't you? Cheap bastard." Frustration strained Raven's voice. "Are you listening to me?"

"Of course. You say they released Darlene from jail?"

Driskoll's wife arched one brow. Tiger-eyes narrowed into the shrewd glint of a predator. Full lips thinned into an angry, crimson thread.

Raven went on, annoyed. "I did not say they released her. She released herself. Ohmygod." Jinx's deputy alerted with the intensity of a scent canine. "Is she there with you?" Raven sucked air. "She's there, isn't she?"

"Yes."

"Jinx called. He said to suit up and go get you. To take you to my house. Every agency in the county's been called in to help with the search. Hold on. I've punched nine-one-one on my cell phone. Does she have a gun?"

"Yes, I hope you two have a lovely time. Thanks for the invitation, but I won't be able to make it," Cézanne said to the mouthpiece. Downy hairs on her arms stood straight up. In the background, Raven relayed information to the dispatcher. "By the way, did I mention my father died?"

Raven came back on the line. "They have units on the way. She said they sent an officer by your house as soon as Darlene escaped, only you weren't home. She said he left a business card. Hang on, Zan. Help's on the way."

"Perhaps we can get together and celebrate once the holiday madness is over."

"They called for SWAT."

With her free hand, Darlene made a cutthroat motion with her index finger and sliced it across her neck in the universal *Time's up* gesture.

"I have to go now," Cézanne muttered without enthusiasm.

"Don't hang up. Stay on the line."

"It's good to hear your voice."

Over Raven's protests, she snapped the clamshell shut. The central heat shuddered on, forcing a blast of warm air from an overhead vent. It wouldn't keep the dement from hearing police sirens close in on them, but it might buy a few extra seconds before Darlene turned her head into a saltshaker.

"This belongs to you." Driskoll's wife reached into her pocket, pulled out the patrolman's card and danced it through the air. "Although you won't be needing it. Let's go. We're taking your Mercedes."

"It's out of gas."

"I hope not for your sake." Her mouth took a downward tilt. She motioned toward the back door, to the garage. "I carjacked an old junker from a couple of high school kids at the Taco Hell. I'm sure they reported it stolen—although I probably did them an unintended favor. Pitch me your cell phone."

Cézanne followed orders. Her mind spun with ideas, none of them usable. The .38 Smith & Wesson snub nose hidden in the box with her grandmother's scarves, top drawer. A wicked-looking survival knife with serrated edges taped to the wastebasket in the guest bath. A Taser nestled in a plastic shoe pouch hanging in the closet. All these precautions taken in anticipation of just such an occasion.

"Where're your car keys?" Darlene's ice pick glare narrowed.

"In my purse."

"Okay, smart ass, where's your purse?"

"In the closet." Cézanne gestured to a mirrored door.

Driskoll's wife took a couple of sidelong steps, knelt without averting her eyes and rummaged through the handbag until she came out with a set of keys.

"Let's go."

"Can I put on makeup first?"

"Beauty queens. You're all alike."

"You've got it all wrong," Cézanne said, but her protests lost effect.

"You don't need to fix your face. Besides . . . ," eyes like amber ice glimmered in their sockets, "in three days, all the cosmetics in the world won't do you any good. Your skin'll be sliding off your bones like a cooked chicken. A fatty, putrefied chicken with green mold fluffing up all over it. What the coyotes don't drag away, that is."

"Stop it. This is beyond what you're capable of."

"Is it? You'd be surprised. Day after day, sitting in a cell with nothing to do but let my imagination run wild. Would you believe—in my mind—I've chopped off your head, packed it in dry ice and mailed it to your mother at the insane asylum? I've choked you into unconsciousness a million times, revived you, and choked you all over again. Each time, I imagined you'd react a different way. A couple of times, I even imagined forcing sex on you. Practice makes perfect."

"Enough." She might have to die, but she sure as hell didn't have to put up with verbal torture.

"Does that bother you?" her captor asked, feigning sympathy. "I'm sorry. I just thought you should know I mean business."

Cézanne glanced around. "Do you see my shoes?"

"You won't need those, either."

Her eyes blinked in astonishment. "Darlene, it's freezing outside."

"Really?" she said airily. "After awhile, I doubt you'll even notice."

"You're going to kill me no matter what, aren't you?"

"I'm afraid so." Almost as an afterthought, Darlene asked, "Are you going to cry?"

"No." But the quiver in Cézanne's chin suggested otherwise.

"Good. Because if you do, I'll use this little gizmo." She dug an index finger into the shirt pocket of the slain jailer's uniform, then pulled out a micro-cassette recorder and held it aloft. "That way, I can play it back and listen to it whenever I get bummed out. If I have to resort to this, do me a favor. I want to hear plenty of begging. Got it?"

Cézanne's gut roiled. After the sudden wave of nausea passed she willed herself into contrition. But while her mouth was saying the right things in an effort to buy time, the tiny voice of survival screamed a warning inside her head.

Fight for your life right here.

Chapter Two

On their way to the back door, Darlene pitched the cell phone into the commode. As the hall clock softly ticked away another second, every breath became precious, every minute stolen.

Where were the patrol cars Raven promised? Cézanne's heart hammered.

"Can I get a drink of water before we leave?" Bottles of champagne cooled inside the refrigerator door. Cézanne imagined bashing Darlene's skull in with one of them. As she plotted, a flicker of alarm registered in her captor's eyes.

"Out of the tap. Not the fridge." Her gaze coolly narrowed. "Wait a minute. What're you trying to pull?"

"I'm thirsty, that's all." But that was a lie. Cézanne wanted a chance at the cutlery drawer.

Darlene's jaw hardened. She vetoed the request. "Do without."

"You'd refuse a condemned woman a glass of water?"

"Believe me, thirst is the least of your worries."

"What kind of monster are you?"

"You haven't even scratched the surface."

Inside the garage, Darlene dangled a set of handcuffs in her outstretched hand. "Put these on."

Her heart thundered. She knew from working homicide cases that victims who were bound rarely survived. Once a killer tied you up, he could do anything he wanted. Especially torture. Statistics bore that out.

Frantic, she took a backward step and shook her head. "I'm not wearing those."

"Sure you are. Now be a good little captive."

If she did as ordered, she was as good as dead. If she didn't, she'd be dead sooner.

Thoughts turned to her late partner, Roby Tyson. What would Roby do? He wouldn't shackle himself with his own handcuffs, that's for damned sure.

"Darlene . . ." she appealed in a pleading voice. The woman's glare hardened into ball bearings. Cézanne tried logic. "Who's going to drive?"

"You are."

"I can't wear handcuffs and drive."

"Sure you can."

"What if someone sees me and dials nine-one-one? You wouldn't want that, now would you?"

Darlene seemed to be mulling over possibilities.

"Maybe not both hands together," she mused. "Fine. We'll do it your way. Snap one cuff on your left wrist and the other to the steering wheel."

She wished she'd kept her mouth shut. Might've been able to jump out of a moving car. Shackling her hands Darlene's way actually worsened her chances for survival.

Cézanne loosely ratcheted one cuff on—maybe Darlene wouldn't notice—and hooked the other to the steering wheel. Her abductor apparently hadn't seen the handcuff pick sandwiched between all the keys on the key fob. If she couldn't slide out of the cuff, maybe she'd get a chance to pick it.

With Darlene in the passenger seat menacing her with the Magnum, they rode the Mercedes Kompressor down Interstate 30, past car dealerships and industrial parts of Fort Worth, toward the town of Weatherford thirty miles away. As civilization played out, and oak trees dotted the countryside, Cézanne plotted escape. First chance she got, she'd swerve in front of the next driver. If she jerked the steering wheel, hard right, the impact would ram the passenger side, she'd defeat the handcuffs and bail.

No one pulled up beside her.

The madwoman jiggled the gun barrel like it was an extension of her own finger. "Get in the slow lane. Set the cruise control at fifty and lock it in. And don't try any shit."

The last of the street lamps twinkled in the rearview mirror. Nothing ahead but a black velvet sky to contemplate her fate and an interstate that stretched clear to El Paso.

With her hands clenching the steering wheel and her heart beating wildly, Cézanne asked a favor. "Could you maybe let the hammer down on that thing?"

"Afraid it'll go off?"

Don't want to take a bullet wrenching it away.

"If it did accidentally go off," she reasoned, "we'd both end up deaf."

"Now there's a thought." Darlene appeared to be considering the consequences. She slid a wistful glance sideways before cutting her eyes to the speedometer. "Think that might put a stop to the voices?"

"You hear voices in your head?"

"I'm just messing with you." Darlene let loose a cackle. She leaned in and swatted Cézanne's arm in the way of old friends. "I don't hear voices." Teeth glinted in the dim glow of the electric dash panel. Without warning, her expression hardened. Her lips thinned into an ugly gash. "When's the last time you saw my husband?"

"When I made Captain, I transferred him out of Homicide. I didn't see him after that." Close, but not the whole story. After shipping Driskoll off to no-man's-land, she'd driven out to the auto pound to grill him about the supplemental reports he wrote on the Great Dane murder. Instead of answers, the son-of-a-bitch locked her in the trunk of a junked car, unzipped his fly and urinated on her through the rust holes. Cézanne set her jaw.

"That was pretty funny, you transferring him to the pound. What a sucky job," she laughed. "Bet he wasn't thinking about diddling you after that. Reckon he still wanted to play hide-the-salami once you fucked up his job?"

"Darlene, please don't."

"You're right. I shouldn't talk that way. It would be mean." She seemed uncomfortable wedged into the buttery soft leather of the passenger seat. But she held tight to the gun, often resting it on the fleshy overhang above her waistband while staring into space.

"My feet are freezing."

"Is that so?" Spoken with fake sympathy. "What do you think we ought to do about that?"

"I have a gym bag in the trunk. If I could get my socks . . ."

. . . and my .22.

"Don't think so."

Darlene appeared to slip into the abyss of her thoughts. Unexpectedly, she broke into a lullaby. Her voice rang with the clarity and tenderness of a mother soothing a child to sleep. A psychotic mother. Corkscrewed in the seat, her gaze shifted from the windshield and settled on the speedometer.

Cézanne tightened her grip on the wheel. "You have a nice voice. Do you go to church?" Flesh rippled. Chills fanned over her body. "Do you sing in the choir? Because you have a really pretty soprano."

Darlene looked over expectantly. "Want to hear the next part? I made up my own verse."

Cézanne didn't think so. She suspected it might have something to do with shallow graves and dismembered body parts and a fat lady standing over her corpse, poking sticks into intimate orifices. "We could listen to the radio."

"No radio. I wanna sing you my song."

Sweet Jesus. Let it be nice.

A shudder went through her. "Please do."

"Good." Deep breath. The creepy melody floated between them.

When Darlene rhymed cry with die, Cézanne's chin corrugated. The rest of the song was drowned out by the screaming inside her head.

Panic set in. A tear leaked out. Her kidnapper leaned in and caught it at the jaw line. With her back nestled against the door, Darlene licked it off her finger. Cézanne squeezed the wheel in a death grip. The escape plan fizzled. She was going to die.

"Stop whimpering. Don't make me turn on the recorder."

God help me.

A hush fell over them. Fifteen miles west of Fort Worth and halfway to Weatherford, Darlene perked up.

"Slow down. There's an off-ramp up ahead. Take it. When we get to the top, there's a dirt road to the right. Turn in. The gate's already open."

A tap to the brake disengaged the cruise control. Gooseflesh zipped up her legs and thighs. Being in the trajectory of Darlene's bullets tended to affect her that way.

Cézanne made ready to bargain. "I resigned from the PD last month." A half-truth.

Melodic and taunting, the outlaw said, "How nice. What, pray tell, is your current occupation? Whore?"

"Attorney."

"Same thing." She laughed at her own joke. "Then again, you don't have to sink that low; you'd make a fairly decent whore."

Cézanne swallowed hard. She knew crazy people. She'd met

plenty of crackpots during her stint with the Fort Worth PD—some of them members of the force. But trying to reason with Darlene Driskoll had all the characteristics of dealing with a suicide bomber.

"I'm a solo practitioner. I've been working out of my house until I find workspace I can afford. Since the tornado wrecked a lot of high rises, office space is hard to come by." Her voice trembled with the effort of speech. "I could help you out of this mess."

"Just drive," Darlene said dully.

Cézanne's pulse thudded. In the deafening silence, she contemplated the remaining escape hatches. She wrenched her hand into a claw and pulled against the handcuff. Nothing happened. She'd need the use of the other hand to force it through. At the hilltop, a tree line did a little can-can on the horizon. Things looked grim.

Crashing the car into a fixed object could kill them both. Even bailing out of a moving vehicle didn't ensure Darlene wouldn't take the wheel and run her down—assuming she survived the impact. Apparently all the drunks had arrived home safely. God only knew how many times she scouted the highway for one to swerve into. Clearly, she was running out of options.

Darlene motioned toward the side road.

Cézanne's blood pressure slipped into the danger zone. Carnal panic seeped from every pore. She found herself blubbering. Grasping at gossamer threads of reason.

"It was always you. Doug never cared about me. Never talked about marriage or kids." *Liar, liar, pants on fire.* "I couldn't hold a candle to you." Not very convincing, considering she was about to hyperventilate. Tears streamed down her face.

"Slow down."

Darlene stared through the windshield with such intensity she'd either convened a Board of Directors meeting inside her head or she was trying to make out shapes through the stand of trees. She pressed the electric window button and lowered the glass a few inches. The steady crunch of gravel poured in like white noise. A waning moon provided a sliver of light in an overcast sky.

Gauzy air hung in the headlights so thick that each breath pulled in a bad taste. An unfamiliar stench filled Cézanne's nostrils, enveloping their close space with the overwhelming stink of fear. In an effort to play on her abductor's sympathy—to humanize herself to her kidnapper like she'd been taught in the police academy—Cézanne pulled out all the stops.

"Today I found out my father died."

"I'm so sorry." Darlene twisted in her seat. The sociopath had the gall to give her a reassuring pat on the knee. "I overheard you telling your friend. Look at it this way—you'll be seeing him very soon."

Cézanne hoped not. Wherever Bob Martin ended up, she suspected she'd be heading in the opposite direction.

"Cut the lights." Outlaw sympathy came to a snappish halt. "Stop the car."

Her heart leapt to her throat. It stuck like a golf ball lodged in her esophagus. Up ahead, a huge tree loomed. She fought back sobs.

Cézanne made a pivotal decision and floored the accelerator.

She reached across the steering wheel, folded her clammy hand and forced it through the handcuff until she thought she'd pass out. Before Darlene realized she'd freed herself, she whipped the Kompressor, hard right. Popped the door. Hit the resume button on the cruise control. Spilled onto the packed dirt with such force she almost blacked out from the impact. For several seconds, she lay facedown unable to breathe. Blades of dead grass zoomed into sharp focus. Insects buzzed. Nightlife moved in the shadows. Something slithered past her ear.

The Mercedes exploded against the tree.

Cézanne sucked in great intakes of air. Stunned and disoriented, she rose on all fours spitting out dirt. She looked over her shoulder half expecting to see the boogieman. A smoky veil spewed up from the hood. A jolt of pain shot through her left foot. It had to be broken. For what seemed like an eternity, she stared at the car. No movement came from inside.

On wobbly legs, she limped toward the vehicle, fixated on getting the vintage cell phone stored in the console. Darlene had to be dead or unconscious. The mighty oak had a sports car wrapped around it, for God's sake.

Fifty feet from the car, brake lights flashed.

Her heart revved.

Rear tires churned up a cloud of dust. In an ear-splitting rip of crunched metal, the car pulled free of the tree trunk.

Cézanne whirled around. With gravel punishing her bare feet, she hobbled down the road. Couldn't run barefooted through the prickly pear and stickers. Each time her injured foot smacked the ground she blinked back tears. Limping toward the highway, she chanced a backward look. A lone beacon swept over the high grass. The engine whined with climbing RPMs.

The mangled Mercedes whipped onto the path.

A shot of adrenaline whipped through her. Running blind in unbearable pain, she veered onto the grass into a stand of oaks. Better to hurt for a while than to be dead forever.

She glanced back over her shoulder and took a header into a hole.

Stunned and disoriented, she spit out muck. Moist leaves suffused with mold stuck to her chin. The cold ground around her felt damp to the touch. As she shook off her stupor, the scent of decay hit her nose. She'd fallen into a shallow grave.

Her grave.

Slippery deadfall as silky and smooth as coffin crepe stuck to the sides of the pit. She made a desperate scramble to claw her way out. Darlene didn't have time to dig this tonight. She must have done this before she got arrested. She'd put a lot of effort into premeditating this murder. Badly shaken, Cézanne pushed up on all fours, then rose to a crouch and staggered further into the thicket of trees.

As she stumbled through the darkness, a lance-like object penetrated her bum foot.

Down she went in a crumpled heap. She clutched her heel; her hand came away wet and sticky.

The growl of the Kompressor's engine filled the night. Cézanne burrowed deeper into the foliage. Brambles and grass burrs scored her flesh. Nearby, the car stalled out. A snakelike hiss carried on the breeze. The engine whirred with each crank of the ignition, but the car wouldn't budge.

The door hinge creaked.

Cézanne lay still, barely breathing. Leaves rustled a few feet away.

Dear God, not snakes.

She stifled a scream and forced herself to listen. Snakes hibernated in winter, but Fort Worth had just come off a couple of unseasonably hot days.

"Come out, come out, wherever you are." Darlene's singsong voice carried in the chill. Footfalls padded against the road. "I know you're out there. You can't get away."

Cézanne clapped a hand to her mouth to squelch a whimper. She could hear Driskoll's wife drawing near and glanced around for a stick. For anything she could use as a weapon. Nothing. Sobs caught in her throat.

"Rattlers'll get you." The killer's words projected from the opposite direction. "Rattlesnake venom affects the respiratory system."

From the sound of her fading taunts, the lunatic seemed to

be walking away.

"It paralyzes you. Your lungs shut down."

Leaves rustled overhead. An acorn hit the ground. Cézanne froze in terror. Darlene must've heard it, too. She walked toward the sound.

"You can't breathe so you suffocate. It's a slow, agonizing death. You don't want to die that way, do you?"

The wind picked up. Several more acorns fell to the ground. One thudded onto the road.

Calm exploded in gunfire. Darlene gave a derisive growl. "Shit."

Blood whooshed between Cézanne's ears.

"I'll find you, bitch." She pounded the car. Kicked the tire and howled. "Goddam slut. I'll kill you."

Ahead and to the right, Darlene rampaged through the high grass shouting profanities as she beat back reeds of tall grass.

Thundering heartbeats filled Cézanne's head. The need to flee was overwhelming. Driskoll's schizoid wife could return anytime. She lifted herself up on one elbow. Her surroundings took shape in monochromatic shades of midnight blue and charcoal gray. Darlene's diatribe tapered off.

Cézanne pushed herself up on shaky arms and crawled to the road. She did a visual inventory of the crumpled Mercedes, fixating on the door. Its lone headlight illuminated fifty feet of dirt; she needed to kill the glow before making a run for it. And she wanted the .22. Upon impact, a low velocity round like the hollow-point stingers she loaded into the cylinder of the little North American Arms would open up like fan blades, chewing up a person's guts with the precision of a meat grinder.

On her feet, she stumbled to the Kompressor. She extinguished the light and pressed a button. The trunk floated open with a *pfft.*

She grabbed her gym bag and staggered to the passenger side

of the car. The door, accordioned into a corrugated mass of metal, refused to budge. She reached through the fractured glass and tried the glove compartment. Locked. Unable to retrieve the vintage cell phone, she abandoned the notion and stumbled into the underbrush with the gym bag in her grip. A wave of nausea passed through her. She tried to run on her lame foot. With every footfall, her heart hammered.

Left in her wake, Darlene raged. "Don't you dare leave me."

Cézanne groped through the gym bag and palmed the .22. The little North American Arms with collapsible grips wasn't all that accurate, long-range. It wasn't all that effective either since the hammer had to be cocked each time you fired it. But up close and personal, it gave her the confidence of a sniper.

She loped along, panting for breath until the interstate came into view. With a glance to the right, then back to the left and over the shoulder, her options came to a snapping halt. She spread the bag wide open and sat on it. Her heels dug into the turf. She propelled herself forward and rode the incline down the bumpy embankment with her haunches on fire.

Nearly out of her mind with pain, Cézanne came to rest on the highway's shoulder. She rolled off the asphalt, took cover in the grass and flattened herself against the slope.

In the distance, the low beams of an oncoming vehicle glowed like lemon drops in the haze. Thirty feet above, Darlene's shoes hammered the dirt. Cézanne waited in the weeds with her heart beating double-time.

Please, please, please. Stop for me.

"Come back, Cézanne. I'm not mad anymore. I just wanted to scare you." Snappish irritation carried on the breeze. Without warning, she howled with laughter.

On the brink of tears, Cézanne prayed.

Please, please, please.

The oncoming automobile closed in at a steady pace. The big

V-8 engine emitted the erratic drone of a missing spark plug. Not to mention its owner was all over the highway. She'd asked God to save her, and He sent a drunk driver. Go figure.

She waited, knowing as soon as she leapt out and showed herself, Driskoll's wife would open fire.

Breathless, Darlene shouted, "Don't do it, Cézanne. I mean it."

She could feel that creepy smile cracking and did a panicky review of her options. The DWI won out. Her stomach clenched. Blood pounded in her ears. Pain flared in her foot.

What the hell? She'd probably be picking her teeth out of the grillwork before Darlene cranked off the first round.

Fifty feet away the bulbous outline of an old pickup bore down on her. Then twenty feet and closing in. Circa fifties. A tank.

She jumped onto the pavement with a Banshee shriek. Frantically flapping her arms, she loped into the Chevy's path. Tires screamed against the asphalt.

Darlene's first round zinged into the blacktop six inches from her bum foot. Another whistled past her right ear. Caught in the golden wash of headlights, Cézanne staggered to the driver's door screaming, "Hit the deck." A bullet ricocheted off the front fender and grooved the median. The next gun blast moved a gust of hot air past her cheek. She ciphered in her head—four spent shells—five counting the stray round Darlene fired off into the dirt road. That left one bullet in the chamber.

Cézanne yanked open the door handle and saw the driver flopped over in the seat. She took cover behind the bed of the pickup, cocked the hammer and popped up long enough to crank off a shot.

The shell didn't pack much firepower, but it probably got Darlene's attention. Either that or it pissed her off more. For good measure—in case her abductor stopped to reload—she fired another round.

She yelled, "Scoot over, pops, we're outta here," and the man crawled into the floorboard. As she pulled herself in, the truck rolled forward. She grabbed the gearshift and slipped it from neutral into first.

The wizened face of an old black man stared up at her, wide-eyed. "Are we back in Nam?"

The old Chevy had a column shift like the one Cézanne learned on as a child. When she dropped it into fourth gear and goosed it, she caught the shadowy specter of Darlene Driskoll receding in the rearview mirror.

"I'm Cézanne Martin." With a grip on the steering wheel's ten o'clock position, she reached out to shake a hand calloused by years of manual labor. "Glad to meet you."

"Asia Polk." He raised his head above the dashboard like an alligator peering over a log. "What the hell was that all about?"

"A crazy woman tried to kill me." She managed a wobbly smile. "You saved my life."

The man cowering in the passenger seat had a couple of days' growth of whiskers and the bill of a Ranger baseball cap snapped low over his forehead. The inside of his truck smelled of motor oil, Vick's VapoRub, and happy hour; Asia Polk reeked of cheap tobacco and rancid whiskey.

She fanned her hand in front of her face.

"I know what you mean." He removed his cap and ran a hand over his bald head. "It's the humidity."

She scanned the road looking for the highway patrol. Asia Polk's voice faded to a droning buzz. She couldn't go back home, and she needed to file a police report. Darlene was still out there lying in wait. For all she knew, the woman could hitch a ride back into town and be hiding in the attic.

Asia Polk pulled a box of Swisher Sweets from the pocket of his overalls. Before he got a chance to light up, Cézanne jumped the bloated Chevy onto the median and completed a U-turn across the divided highway with her hijacked host clutching the door handle.

"We're going to the police department." She adjusted the rearview mirror and pressed the accelerator all the way to the floor.

"I'm on probation for my second DWI, and I'm drunker'n Cooter Brown. Last place I need to show my face is the calaboose."

"A crazy woman tried to kill me."

"They'll arrest me for drunk."

"I need to file that report."

"Hmmm." Asia Polk stroked his chin. "Reckon if you insist, that would give me the opportunity to file my own report. On account of a crazy woman carjacked me."

Chapter Three

From the porch of a two-story Tudor in the Berkeley addition of Fort Worth, Cézanne waved so long to Asia Polk and turned her attention to the doorbell. After several rings, she limped to the edge of the wraparound and craned her neck for a view of the upstairs windows. When the lights didn't come on, she hobbled back to the entry and jabbed the button like she was tapping out Morse code. For good measure, she pounded the doorframe before inching back for another look-see. A gold wash of light appeared in a corner room on the second level; a chandelier lit up three stained-glass windows staggered along the staircase. The audible shuffle of slippers scuffing the floor could be heard over the homeowner's colorful expletives. Seconds later, she sensed movement behind the door. The peephole clouded over.

A gruff voice bellowed, "Oh, hell. Not again."

She suspected Marvin Krivnek might still be studying her through the aperture, so she wiggled her fingers in a half-hearted wave. He yanked open the door, and she was treated to a view of the Assistant Medical Examiner in his gray wool bathrobe. Thinning hair the color and sheen of stainless steel spiked up from his head like a currycomb. He unfolded his wire spectacles and seated them onto the permanent dents of an eagle beak nose. He peered out from behind a stub of gray eyelashes and regarded her with a healthy degree of censure.

"Why me?" He stiffened.

"Hi, Marvin." Said softly, with a sheepish duck of the head. "I was hoping you could take a look at my foot. I think I sprained it."

His gaze dipped. "It's broken. Why aren't you at the hospital?"

"Because they have police there, and the guy who dropped me off is DWI."

He shook his head in disgust. For a moment, she thought his eyes crossed.

"Look, Marvin, I know you're still stewed about the time I woke you up at three in the morning asking you to test me for GHB. But it wasn't my fault those hedonistic crazies from the Wild Orchid Society drugged me into unconsciousness, and you were the only one I could turn to." Her eyes cut to Krivnek's grandfather clock. "At least this time I waited until five."

He regarded her with contempt. Stepped aside to let her pass, unable to keep the bite out of his tone. "May as well come in. No sense letting all the hot air out."

She hopped over the threshold onto polished hardwood planks and trailed him into an opulent parlor filled with reproductions of period furniture.

He led her to a Rococo settee and motioned her to sit.

"Do you have insurance? Because I'm not setting that foot if that's what you came here for."

She understood he was still steamed. "I need a ride to the ER and then to my house. I didn't want to go home on account of Darlene Driskoll might be waiting to finish me off. You were the only one I could think of who might drive me to the hospital and wait with me until the police came."

"At what point in our business dealings did you get the idea we'd crossed the boundary to friendship?"

She grinned in spite of the jagged pain knifing through her foot. "Come on, Marvin. You like me. You know you do. You think I'm a little avant-garde, but you appreciate my grit."

He heaved a great sigh, as if he'd known he'd lost the battle the moment he viewed her through the peephole.

"Start at the beginning," he said, and she did. Before she reached the part about Asia Polk, he got up from the Rococo settee and headed for the stairs. He came back dressed, carrying a down-filled jacket, a pair of argyle socks, and a cordless phone.

"I'll drive you to the ER," he said, opening a hall closet. While she slipped on the socks and jacket, he wrapped a wool scarf around his neck and shrugged into his overcoat. Then he dialed nine-one-one. "Dr. Krivnek, here. I've got one of your detectives—"

"Former detective. I'm on leave."

"—and we're headed for the county hospital. Have a Major Crimes investigator meet us. Attempted murder." He tapped the off-button and placed the cordless phone on a marble-topped coffee table. "First things first. They'll set the break, you can give the investigator a written statement, and then we'll get Crime Scene to meet us at your house."

"You'll stay at the hospital with me?"

"I suppose." He moved to her side and offered his arm for support.

The small concession choked her up. "I don't know, Marvin. That sounds like the kind of thing a friend would do. Since we're not actually friends . . ."

"You talk too much." Followed by a sideways glance and a soft, "I'm glad you're alive."

Two hours passed before the ER doctors took X-rays, diagnosed her with a hairline fracture, and released her with a prescription for pain medication. She decided not to take it; she'd need her wits about her in case Darlene returned.

"I'll bring a set of crutches by later." Krivnek measured her with a glance. "What are you . . . about five feet eight?"

"Five-seven."

"Same as me."

Maybe if you stood on a couple of phone books . . .

As he dropped her off at the brick bungalow on Western, Wolfgang "Slash" Vaughn rolled up to the curb in the Crime Scene van. It thrilled her to see him on duty. Everyone in Tarrant County law enforcement circles knew Slash beat the rest of the investigators hands-down. So what if he'd gotten his nickname after cutting a priceless painting while gathering evidence at the homicide scene of a dead art dealer. The dispatcher had sent the best crime scene detective in the state—the country—the world.

Toting a tackle box filled with fingerprint powder, brushes, and other tools of the trade, the tall, rusty-haired detective met Cézanne on the front porch. While she fumbled under the flowerpot for the spare key, Slash unsnapped his holster and scoured the surroundings with a series of furtive glances.

"I heard what happened. You must've been climbing the walls."

"Darlene Driskoll won't let up until bagpipes are playing at my gravesite."

The deadbolt snapped open and they stepped inside.

Slash drew his gun. He set the kit on the floor, glanced around and sniffed the air. "Somebody wears *Toujours Moi.*"

"Not me. I hate the stuff."

"Me, too." He grinned big. Turquoise eyes lit up with boyish charm. "Wait here. I'll check out the rest of the house." He slid the Maglite from the waistband of his jeans and held it aloft.

She watched him disappear into the dark recesses of her home, illuminating small areas with a beacon of white. Room by room, lights flicked on. When he returned to the living room, he asked for a hat and a broom.

"What kind of hat?"

"Doesn't matter," he whispered.

"What'll you do with it?"

"I can tell you didn't check out many attics while you were on patrol."

Moments later, Slash tugged on a cord dangling from a trap door in the ceiling. He tugged at a set of pull-down stairs, unfolded them, then stuck the hat on the tip of the broom. As he climbed onto the first rung and shoved the decoy through the opening, Cézanne flinched, expecting gunfire to erupt.

Nothing happened. Slash climbed a couple of steps, raised his Maglite and flashed it around. "Somebody's been living up here. No kidding. There's an Oreo cookie wrapper and a couple of empty Whataburger sacks."

Cézanne sucked air.

Slash backed down the rungs. A thin film of dust coated his rust-tinged hair. "I need my camera. This psycho bitch is over the top."

He left the room and returned with a high-dollar digital and the fingerprint kit and ascended the ladder.

Cézanne was scouring the pantry looking for the marshmallow sack to put the finishing touches on two cups of hot cocoa when Slash called out with startling urgency.

"Don't eat anything."

"What?"

"Don't drink anything either." This time his voice projected much stronger. He'd thrust his head through the opening to make himself heard. "Don't use your dishes or utensils. I'm coming down."

She took the saucepan of milk off the stove, turned off the burner, and set it in the sink. The spring-loaded hinge that retracted the ladder snapped into place with a loud clunk. Slash joined her in the kitchen still wearing latex gloves. His eyes widened in alarm.

"When did you buy rat poison?"

"I didn't."

"You don't have a rodent problem?"

"Not that I know of."

"What about peanut butter crackers?"

She angled over to the cupboard, to a snack box on the shelf.

He snapped, "I'll get it," before she could touch it. With gloved hands, he inspected the carton carefully, placed it on the countertop and left the room. He returned with a pair of tweezers pinched between his fingers.

Confusion filled Cézanne's head. "I bought them a few days ago. I don't recall opening them."

"There's a cellophane wrapper in the attic." The snacks came in packages of six. He removed each wrapper, one-by-one. She knew by the scowl on his face that he'd found something awry. "This one's been doctored. Seriously, do you have someplace to stay for a few days?"

"Not really. I've been trying to get my law practice off the ground, and I've been working out of my house. My client base is small. I've set appointments and can't just cancel them. I need money."

"I'd bunk with a friend if I were you. And I'd get a cleaning service in here to sanitize this place from top to bottom once I release it back to you. Call that HAZMAT company—the business we recommend when we find a decomposed body in a house."

"You can't be serious."

"Dead serious. You never know where the next booby trap is."

"I can't abandon my home." She stood against the counter with her hands flapping so hard she was close to lift-off. He was asking the impossible. She'd never let Darlene Driskoll run her out even if her heart was beating triple time. "This is my place.

I'm not leaving."

"Then you should call Greenlawn. Maybe look into some sort of pre-need deal."

He meant the cemetery.

Her blood went icy.

"I already checked the doors," he said. "No striation marks. That means your burglar either came in through a window or she has a key."

"No key. And it's an old house. The windows have been painted shut for fifty years or more."

"Did Doug Driskoll ever have a key?"

The mention of the biggest playboy on the force called for a slitty-eyed response. "He did not. He never visited this house."

"I'm only asking because that might explain how she got in." Slash returned to his investigation.

In her bedroom, Cézanne changed into a periwinkle blue angora skirt and sweater. She searched the closet and dug out one right shoe. Its two-inch heel would match the lift on the removable cast. With a few extra clothes draped over one arm, she gathered her make-up pouch, set her things near the door and rejoined him.

"I need to make a phone call. Can I use your wireless? Mine's in the toilet, and Darlene cut the landline."

He fished a cellular out of his pocket and handed it over.

She stabbed out Bobby's home phone number. Poor thing . . . probably climbing the walls since her disappearance. Inwardly, she warmed at the thought.

A recorded message came on. The line wasn't in working order.

She punched out his cell number. It rang four times before rerouting to voicemail.

Next, she telephoned the Johnson County SO. A dispatcher fielded her call.

"No, ma'am, Sheriff's not in. Not gonna be, either."

"Where is he?"

"Don't reckon I can say."

"I'm his fiancée."

"Don't matter. Can't do it. Love my job. Don't wanna lose it."

"Put me through to someone who can disclose that information," she snapped.

"Well in order to do that, I'd have to put you through to the sheriff. Only he ain't here."

She envisioned a roly-poly farm boy, kicked back in a comfy chair, having a good time at her expense.

"Listen," she said with put-on sweetness, "it's been a bad night. Perhaps you watched the news? I was abducted from my house."

"Yep. Sorry about that. Still can't help you."

She was about to raise her voice when Slash re-entered the living room and peeled off his gloves. "I have to go back to the station. I need thirty-five millimeter film and a better camera." His gaze dipped to the cell phone. "You through?"

She snapped the clamshell shut and grudgingly handed it over.

"This'll take awhile. If you've got any rat-killing to do, now's the time." He apparently picked up on her confusion because he laid out the problem in no uncertain terms. "This could go on for hours. I need to check the food in your refrigerator and your toiletries. You don't know what kind of booby-traps she may've left."

Cézanne gave him a slow blink. "You're kidding."

"I'm dead serious. Do you have an extra house key you can leave with me? I'll need to let myself back in."

He followed her into the kitchen where he pocketed her spare key. He even waited beside her on the porch as she threw the deadbolt and fumbled for her car keys. Memories of the Kompressor, wrapped around a tree, rushed back. She had no transportation.

"This really sucks."

"I know." He gave her shoulder a friendly pat. "Climb in the van. I'll drop you wherever you're going."

She checked her watch. Mitch Roselli, the Seattle lawyer handling her father's estate, insisted she meet with his local contact and had even set up the morning's meeting for her. "I have a nine o'clock appointment at Deakins Williams and Rushmore. They're probate specialists."

Slash grinned. "A bit premature, don't you think? You're not dead yet."

"No, but my father is."

Cézanne accepted Slash's offer of breakfast, and when they finished, his ride to Deakins Williams. The law firm was famous for its penthouse suite in the Bank One Tower until a tornado followed the path of the Trinity River and slammed into downtown. It sucked out the desks and most of the file cabinets, but the leather wingback, folded newspaper, and eyeglasses in old man Deakins's office remained unscathed. This, according to Betty, the receptionist at the firm's new location in a converted storefront on East Belknap Street.

A heavyset man with a fat cigar strolled into the lobby a few minutes after nine. He made eye contact with Betty, whose eyes cut to Cézanne. The man wandered over.

"Hollis Rushmore," he said by way of introduction. He shrugged out of a brown overcoat, revealing a brown suit underneath. He had brown hair, what little there was of it, intelligent brown eyes hidden behind tortoise-shell horn rims, a brown ostrich briefcase, and lizard wingtips to match. In her foul mood, Cézanne half expected him to have matching brown teeth and was pleasantly surprised to be greeted with such an engaging smile.

He spoke in a brandy-smooth voice. "You've come about the house."

Her mouth gaped. "The house?" Maybe there'd been a story about her kidnapping on the early news report. Had Slash talked to the media? Surely not. "How'd you know about the house?"

"It's my job to know about the house. Walk with me."

She followed him into his office, a tastefully decorated room with one wall painted cranberry, hand-knotted rugs layered atop each other, and black lacquer furnishings from the Orient.

"Have a seat. I'll just be a minute." He disappeared into an anteroom. Soon, strains of country music wafted through the intercom. Rushmore returned with a file. She presumed it contained information about Bob Martin.

With the fat cigar still clenched between his teeth, he took his place behind the desk, sank into a huge leather wingback on wheeled feet, and thumbed through the manila folder. "We had a hell of a time finding you." He swiveled his chair in her direction.

"I don't know why. The Seattle lawyer who put me in touch with your office didn't seem to have any trouble contacting me." She appraised him with a suspicious once-over. "Other than four years of undergraduate school at UT Austin, I've always lived in Fort Worth. I have an unlisted phone number, but that shouldn't have stopped you."

"Bob was living in Seattle when he died. He'd been a merchant marine for the last twenty years."

She welcomed the distraction of a scrimshaw tusk displayed next to a glass-encased cork sculpture on Rushmore's credenza. For no reason other than instinct, she shifted her gaze back to the lawyer.

"He remarried," Rushmore said.

Her heart skipped. Hearing that Bob started another family hurt. It really did. "Farmer Brown can't even tend to his own cows yet he goes out and milks somebody else's."

"I take it you weren't close."

She gave him her best *You've gotta be kidding* scowl and rolled her eyes so far back in her head she could almost see her sinus cavities. "What's the bottom line? Why am I here? Because I have no plans to dip into savings to bury that seagoing rum scutch. The state of Washington can dump him into the ocean or stick him in a cardboard box and bury him in a pauper's grave for all I care. And I'm not squaring any debts he might've run up, either."

Hollis Rushmore stubbed out the cigar. "Bob Martin didn't have debts. He had assets."

Her eyes narrowed coolly. "Why tell me?"

"Because Bob died in testate." He tented his hands on the desk. "Without a will, you kids stand to inherit the house."

A sigh popped out before she could restrain it. "Fat-lotta-good a house in Seattle will do me. My roots are here in Cowtown."

Rushmore showed a mouthful of piano-key teeth. "Then you'll really like this. Bob Martin leased a condo near the wharf. What he owned was a house in Fort Worth on South University. What he amassed in the way of funds is six hundred thousand dollars stashed in off-shore accounts."

Cézanne sat erect. Periwinkle eyes darted around the room in furtive glances. "You're telling me that slippery eel had a boatload of money?"

"Not quite the appreciative response I'd expected from you," Rushmore said with a droll shake of the head.

"Let's just agree that my father's abrupt departure left me with serious abandonment issues."

She didn't want to discuss the psychological baggage Bob

Martin caused. Not baggage exactly . . . more like steamer trunks filled with crippled emotions. No, she didn't care to explore her jaded view of men with Hollis Rushmore or disclose how every relationship she'd ever been in failed because Bob Martin walked out of her life.

Every one except for Sheriff Bobby Noah.

The attorney slid open the top drawer, pulled out a leather key fob, and dangled it.

A roguish inflection tinged his voice. "Until we sort out who gets what, I have a fiduciary interest in keeping that house in good repair. It's been vandalized twice in the last three weeks. Kids throwing rocks through the windows, I would imagine. I figure if you elect to put a renter in it until we get things squared away, that'd be fine and dandy with me."

CHAPTER FOUR

From the receptionist's phone, Cézanne ordered a rental car. Then she dialed Bobby.

When he didn't answer his wireless and the SO's dispatcher gave her the runaround again, she wondered what could be so important that he wouldn't even bother to check on her. Surely he'd watched the news. He should've been beating the bushes trying to find her.

She studied the engagement ring. Insecurity set in.

Within a half hour, the rental car agency delivered a sleek Cadillac Catera in a metallic color so deep and green that it appeared to be black when parked in the shade. With the key to the University Drive property in hand, she drove ten miles over the speed limit, anxious to view Bob Martin's digs. Past Texas Christian University near Bluebonnet Circle, an old brownstone with Moorish arches, spiral concrete columns, and a red tile roof rose up from the ground like the crown jewel mounted in a setting of hundred-year-old pecan trees.

Gooseflesh scrambled up Cézanne's thighs. Her mouth gaped. She stared incredulous, only taking her eyes off the property long enough to double-check the address against the one Rushmore provided. Lightheaded, she realized she'd been holding her breath.

Who'd have guessed?

Bob Martin owned the best house in the entire neighborhood.

Not a bad haul for a thirty-two-year-old police detective on sabbatical, practically elbowing her way into the soup line. She parked in the driveway and hobbled up the front steps.

Renter hell.

What a great place for a law office.

Until she got the all-clear sign on moving back into her bungalow, she could camp here. Maybe even move in a futon bed and let it double as a sofa for clients.

She stopped envisioning Bob dancing on hot coals and inserted the key into the lock. She still didn't like him, but at least he'd tried to make up for his transgressions by leaving her this great two-story home.

Okay. So he didn't actually leave it to her outright. A minor point.

But Monet was dead, and nobody had seen her brother Henri since he stormed out of the house on his sixteenth birthday and rode into the night on his motorcycle. An heirship proceeding in Probate court would rectify the problem.

She twisted the key until the bolt slid back. The door opened a few inches before the slack in the security chain snapped to an abrupt halt.

Occupied?

She sensed movement inside. The chain slid along its track and clattered against the wood. The door yanked open.

Cézanne jumped back, tripped over her cast and ended up in a pratfall, staring up a flowered muumuu housedress, past knees like doorknobs, at folds of cellulite and wrinkles.

She viewed the scary sight in stages. An old woman with a five o'clock shadow on her upper lip and pale pink hair the texture of spun cotton candy stared out through the hazel depths of beady irises. Cat-eye glasses with black rims, decorated with rhinestones the size of chigger eyes on the up-swept corners, hung around her neck, secured at each earpiece by a gold metal chain. She stood six inches shorter than Cézanne, had a chest as flat as a tortilla, and clutched a baseball bat positioned a foot above her head.

"What the hell do you mean breaking into my house? I'm buying me a gun tomorrow and using it. How'd you pick the lock? Burglar tools? I know a few things about burglars. I ought to get me a crowbar and split your head open."

This couldn't be happening.

Cézanne stammered, "Who're you?"

"Who'm I?" The shrew raised her two-pack-a-day voice. "Who in the cat hair are you?"

"I own this place."

The woman reared back, looking as tough as the corns on her feet. She readied the bat to swing.

Cézanne drew her legs up. Shielded her face with her hands. "Okay, okay. I don't exactly own it yet. It's my dad's. He's dead. But once the bugs are worked out, the house should pass to me. I'm Cézanne Martin."

Slowly, the bat came to rest at the interloper's side.

"Cézanne, eh?" Hooded lids thinned into a squint. A gnarled finger mashed her eyeglasses into position. "Bernice's kid?"

The detective-turned-lawyer mustered a sick smile of hope. "Guilty as charged."

"I'm Velda."

"Velda?" She searched her memory. Dawning realization hit. The corners of her mouth tipped up in happy remembrance. "Aunt Velda? I thought you were killed by tigers in Sumatra."

"You wish."

According to Bernice, Velda had been dancing on burning embers for years. "My mother used to tell us bedtime stories about how you were captured by natives. Just before they boiled you alive, tigers dragged you off into the jungle—and then ate you."

Velda grinned, exposing a mouthful of nicotine-stained teeth. "That's okay. I told my boys your mother was a prostitute with terminal syphilis who enjoyed being ravaged by drunken sailors. Get up."

After a bit of floundering, Cézanne made it to her feet.

Her aunt's gaze slewed to the Cadillac and back. "What the hell are you doing trying to break into my house?"

"The lawyer said it belonged to us kids. Monet's dead. For all I know Henri's dead, too. It's been years since anyone heard from him. The lawyer gave me the key and said I could move in."

Velda wielded the bat overhead. "Over my dead body."

"Now wait a minute." Cézanne grew a backbone. The prospect of getting a free law office had that effect on her. "No lunatic relative of mine is going to ban me from my own property."

"Possession is nine-tenths of the law."

"Nine points of the law," Cézanne corrected her.

"Points . . . tenths . . . who gives a tinker's damn? Point one is I'm residing here and you're not. Point two, I have a bat and you don't. Point three—and this is the main point—I never liked you."

Cézanne did a double take. "What about Thanksgiving?"

"What about it?"

"You came to our house when we were little. You passed out gifts from your travels. You braided my hair and secured the sides with ivory combs that you brought from Africa. You sent me a hand-carved puppet on my birthday. How can you say you didn't like me?"

"Snot-nosed brats. All of you. Point four . . ."

By the time Velda rattled off the ninth point, she'd already stepped back into the house, slammed the door, and toggled the deadbolt.

Several blocks south of Bob Martin's fabulous estate, where University Drive intersected Bluebonnet Circle, Cézanne could feel the force field of a Mexican food restaurant sucking her in. She whipped the Catera into a space, went inside, and asked to use the telephone.

"We have lunch specials," said the manager, a light-complexioned Hispanic with a full head of dark hair.

Smells of puffy tostadas, chili con carne, and freshly sliced jalapenos filled her nostrils. Just thinking of the possibilities made her mouth water.

"I'm not here to eat. I need to borrow your phone."

"Like I said, we have lunch specials." He held the telephone hostage.

"Fine," she huffed. "Box up something to go. And cut the onions."

He murmured, "I can see why," and handed her the receiver. It wasn't until he walked to the kitchen pass-through and barked commands in Spanish that she realized she stank. She hadn't had a shower since the murder attempt. Slash wouldn't let her use her own facilities until he'd checked the entire house for booby traps.

She dialed Raven's cell phone. The deputy constable answered in her usual chipper lilt.

"Raven, it's me. Zan."

Words tumbled out in a hyperventilating rush. "Ohmygod, where are you? We've been looking all over. Slash told Jinx you went to a lawyer—I think that's a great idea, by the way. Sue that psychopath for all she's worth. I went by the law office, but that guy Rushmore wouldn't give me any information. And you didn't answer your cell phone, so we didn't know where you were. Ohmygod, are you all right?"

"I'm fine." She reached into her handbag and scooped out her wallet.

"Do you need a place to crash? Because you can stay with me. I want exclusive rights to your story. Remember when I wrote that bestseller about Jinx? I actually told everybody it was fiction so he wouldn't sue me, but Jinx went around bragging about how his ex-girlfriend wrote a book about him. Dumb ass. He actually thought the guy in the novel was a stud. Jeez, what kind of Romeo goes around bragging about his conquests? Half the men in this town, that's for sure. So where can I pick you up?"

"I rented a car."

Cézanne let out a shriek. Diners' heads jerked upright. Gazes riveted in a collective shift. She withdrew a crimson hand, complete with a razor blade sticking out from the tip of one finger. Tuning up in a coyote wail, she dislodged it. Blood gushed over the cash register like an arterial spurt.

"What happened?" Panic transcended Raven's concern.

"A rusty razor blade." Cézanne's stomach gave a nasty flip.

They called out the culprit's name in unison. "Darlene."

The restaurant manager grabbed a cloth napkin off the nearest table. He unfurled it like a surrender flag, sent the flatware clattering across the table's Plexiglas protector, and shoved it at her to cap the flow. The mess dotted the floor like spilled paint. Once she got things under control, she tried to pay with blood-speckled cash. Instead of taking her money he pronounced lunch on the house and shoved the sack at her. Then he fanned his hand toward the door in a *Get out* motion.

Cézanne turned her attention to Raven. "Are you mobile?"

"Where do you want to meet?"

"University Drive." She gave her friend the address. "And bring an extra gun. There's a burglar in my new law office."

"Want me to call for backup?"

"Don't bother," she deadpanned, "they're all over at my house working the crime scene."

Fifteen minutes later, Raven arrived in her unmarked constable car.

Cézanne hobbled down the sidewalk as her colleague and confidant rolled up to the curb. As soon as Raven snapped open the electric door locks, she jumped into the passenger seat with the cloth napkin still wrapped around her hand in a crude bandage.

Raven wore western clothes and roper boots. As usual, she'd tucked her long, brunette waves up under a Lady Texas High Roller with only a few tendrils falling below the brim. The hat made her appear taller and lent her a dangerous presence. Nobody would've guessed by looking past the flawless complexion, into huge, gray doe eyes, that the prettiest deputy constable in Tarrant County might also be the best shot.

Enveloped in the vapors of expensive perfume, Raven reached for the mike mounted against the patrol car's dashboard and radioed her location to the dispatcher. When the "Ten-four" acknowledgment came back, she settled her carefully lined eyes on Cézanne. Pewter irises turned into lead slugs.

"Since when did you buy a law office?"

"I inherited it. It's not a law office yet, but it will be. Plus, I'll have a place to stay until Slash pronounces my house clean."

"Honey, you'll need an exorcism to get the bad vibes out." She jutted her chin at Cézanne's injury. "You really think Darlene's responsible for that?"

"Who else would hide a razor blade in my purse?"

Raven nodded knowingly. She whipped off the hat and placed it on the seat between them. Shook out her hair and flicked a stray lock over one shoulder. "There's a statewide dragnet that includes Oklahoma and Louisiana. Jinx thinks she's still in the area, though. That's good news."

"Is it?" A shot of fear lanced her stomach. Darlene could still come after her. The sickening clench moved to her chest.

"Jinx says the farther away she gets, the better her chances are of assimilating into the regular population."

"I suppose that makes sense." Cézanne relaxed. Abruptly, she went ramrod stiff. Jinx Porter happened to be pretty savvy when it came to thinking like a criminal. His latest public showdown included the capture of a satanic kidnapper that he'd tracked clear to Nebraska. No matter what kind of bad press Jinx received that earned him a reputation as the boyfriend from hell, it was inversely proportionate to his reputation as a cunning law enforcement official. Not to mention he'd saved her life in the past—twice in as many months. "What else does Jinx say?"

Raven grimaced. "I don't want to alarm you."

"Out with it."

"Jinx thinks she'll head down to New Orleans and reinvent herself. He says she could become anyone she wanted to, what with the hurricane disaster cleanup going on. Think of all those government records that washed away when the levee broke. Nobody'd even notice . . . or care."

A frightening thought, Darlene assuming someone's identity. She'd already proven she could modify her appearance with hair dye, colored contact lenses, and fashion changes.

Raven continued. "Officers found your car. They towed it, but they didn't find anything else. At least nothing they're making public. You'd think she would've changed clothes, wouldn't you? Pretty conspicuous, if you ask me, trotting around in a TCSO uniform. From here on out, you need to be aware of your surroundings."

"First things first. I need a shower—"

"I wasn't going to mention that." Raven fanned the air in

front of her nose.

"—and that old crank's keeping me from getting inside. Did you bring an extra gun like I asked?"

Raven tensed against the seat. "What're you planning to do with it?"

"Right now, I only intend to shoot the security chain off the door."

"Are you crazy? You can't do that."

"Sure I can. It's my house."

"You can't discharge a firearm inside the city limit. I'd have to arrest you."

"Look the other way."

"That would make me part of the conspiracy."

"Just give me the gun." Cézanne held out her hand, palm-up, in demand.

Raven leaned into the steering wheel and contorted herself enough to pull the .38 five shot from the shaft of her boot. "You're not going to cap anyone with this, are you? Because it's registered to me. I don't want the cops locking it in the evidence vault until it's time to try you; that could take years. Besides, you never know when I might need to use it on Jinx."

"I'm not going to shoot her. I'm just going to nick her."

"Her?"

"My long, lost aunt. Velda."

"Have you taken leave of your senses? As your friend I'm obligated to stop you."

"If you were really my friend, you'd help me haul the body out in a rug under cover of darkness. I'd do it for you," she added, trying to guilt-trip her pal into handing over the snub nose. "Besides," she said cheerily, "it's not like any of her ex-husbands will miss her. And everyone else in the family thinks Velda's already dead."

Chapter Five

Immune to indignity and dripping water on Hollis Rushmore's carpet, Cézanne waited close to an hour before the door to the deposition room opened and the lawyer's eleven o'clock pranced out. As soon as Betty-the-receptionist left her desk to top off her coffee, Cézanne made a beeline for the attorney's office. With her foot throbbing and her blood pressure spiking into the danger zone, she stormed into his domain in a whirlwind of fury and caught him pouring himself a scotch. He regarded her calmly when he saw her framed in the doorway, sopping wet, but his lips still pinched at the corners.

"By the blood in your eye, I see you met Velda. So how'd it go?"

"I just experienced the *trompe l'oiel* of the senses." She carefully modulated her voice in an effort to conceal her outrage. "Just so you know, I shot the chain off the front door, so if I have trouble hearing you, it's because my ears are still ringing." Re-telling it put a strident edge in her tone. "How was I to know the old battleaxe dragged a garden hose into the house? She doused me, as you can plainly see. Now I've got a borrowed .38 full of wet ammo. How do you think it went?"

"That certainly sounds like Velda."

"Why didn't you warn me there was a homicidal maniac living there?"

"You would've called the police." His eyes took on a speculative gleam. "And Velda's not hurting anything. Now that we know you exist, as soon as we locate the whereabouts of your brother and pull up the death record on your sister, we'll resolve any contest over the estate in probate court. Meantime, the old lady agreed to keep an eye on the place."

"She moved in, for God's sake. That's a little more than keeping an eye on the place."

"I told you we had problems with vandals, and Velda suggested—"

"You're on a first-name basis with that circus freak?"

"—I allow her to stay there since there was a good chance she might be Bob's closest surviving relative."

Cézanne seethed. "She's psychotic. You let a mentally unstable person move into my house."

"Don't be so harsh. Velda's really just a sweet old Southern belle."

Her expression went from uninvitingly blank to one of utter disgust. "Just because you're born in the South, doesn't make you a Southerner. If your dog had puppies in a shoe box, that wouldn't make them boots, now would it?"

"You just need to learn how to communicate with her."

"I'd have better odds trying to baptize a cat. Velda's demonically possessed. She took a bat to me."

"She's a good old gal once you get to know her."

"I don't want to get to know her. My mother knew her. She did everything possible to take my mother's kids away from her. The nicest reference my mother ever made to Velda included the term 'bad influence.' "

"You might actually get to like her if you give it a chance. And she's blood kin."

"Bloodsucker, you mean. I want that dement out of my house."

Rushmore downed his drink. "It wasn't your house when Velda moved in. Why can't you just peacefully coexist with her for the time being? She's an interesting character. Did you know she used to live in the Middle East?"

"She's Satan in a muumuu. I saw up her dress. She's got more wrinkles around her knees than a Shar Peis. As for the Middle East, that's probably why people over there are so screwed up."

"You looked up her skirt?" Rushmore contorted his face into a grimace. "That's sick."

"I didn't intend to look up her snatch. It was just there. I only glanced up to see if she'd really bring that bat down on my head. I rolled out of the way in the nick of time."

"I don't know that I want to hear any more."

"You think I'm cold-hearted? I'm not. I know perfectly well Velda can't help being ugly, bless her heart, but she could at least cover herself up. I'm talking underwear, mister. Granny pants. She needs to start wearing them."

He grabbed the liquor bottle off the credenza, poured himself a double, slammed it back, and drew his shirt cuff across his lips with a hefty swipe. Brown eyes glittered. "It's a two story house. Velda can take the upstairs, and you take the downstairs. Until we sort through the mess, why not partition it out?"

It didn't take Cézanne long to examine a hot horseshoe, no siree. "You're Velda's lawyer, aren't you? I knew it." Thoughts of mayhem vibrated off the top of her head. Seething with indignance, she planted her fists on her hips.

"Velda's lawyer works at Cohen Lonstein. I'm the court-appointed Ad Litem."

"Then you're my lawyer."

"I'm an officer of the court."

"Bullshit. You're my lawyer, and you're going to start acting like my lawyer. I want that fishwife out of my house, or I'm calling the cops."

"Fine. Call the law. What'll they do? They'll tell you it's a civil problem—" his voice got suddenly loud "—because it's not your house."

"It will be." Muscles tensed along her back.

"That might not happen for another six months."

"Six months?" she yelled at the top of her lungs. He was watching her with disdain now, still dripping on his Oriental rug.

"If you're lucky. If you're not so lucky, it could take upward of two years."

Cézanne staggered to the door, appalled. "I can assure you it won't take two years because one of us will be dead. I'm thinking it should be Velda."

"You can't kill that old lady."

"She's evil, and she's crazy. The world isn't going to go into a holding pattern if Velda drops off the face of the Earth. It'll be a case of justifiable homicide."

"If you do her in, you won't inherit." His head cocked in thought. "Plus you'll burn in hell."

"I won't burn in hell. I'm already there, and I haven't caught fire yet."

Imagine that: Two fabulous houses, and no place to stay.

Cézanne thought cool-headed reflection worked better seated in the Catera, where she could use the steering wheel to choke Velda's wrinkled old chicken neck in effigy, than in the offices of Deakins Williams.

Dealing with Velda called for guerilla tactics.

She turned the ignition, dropped the Caddy in gear, and drove to the bungalow on Western. The Crime Scene van was still parked in the same spot, front and center.

She let herself inside. Her heart stalled.

"Don't shoot," she cried.

Down the hall, Slash had drawn his .45 and dropped into an

FBI combat stance.

"Sorry." He came out of a crouch and holstered his weapon. "You should've announced your presence. I thought you might be the insane Mrs. Driskoll coming back for seconds."

"I'm here for my law books. You scared the hell out of me."

"Occupational hazard. Makes it hard to get dates."

"No, working permanent nights makes it hard to get dates." Her eyes traveled up Slash's jeans. She tried not to stare, but he was a good-looking man. "How's it going? Find anything? Because I really need my house back."

"Soon. Follow me. I want to show you something." She trailed him into the kitchen where two-dozen paper bags sealed with fragile red evidence tape sat in rows on the floor. Each bore Slash's initials. "Driskoll's wife used a butcher knife on your clothes. And your plants are looking kind of puny, probably from that empty bottle of Drano in your trash. Do you keep rat traps in your lingerie drawer?"

Her eyes widened.

"Because a couple of them went off. They had Post-It notes attached. Childish scrawl. The gist of the messages is, *Next time it's a spring gun.* After I photograph them, I'll Ninhydrin the prints. I figure once the comparisons are made, they'll come back to her. Did you know you have green stuff growing in your refrigerator?"

The nearest chair was in the dining room, and Cézanne headed straight for it. When she sank onto the tapestry seat, Slash's eyes got big.

"Get up."

"What?"

"Get up."

She rocketed up from her place at the table and fled to his side. There, she saw what he saw: horsehair stuffing, drifting to the floor. He pushed her back into the kitchen and went for the chair. In one smooth move, he flipped it over. The lining had been slit. He tugged his Maglite from the waistband of his pants and shined it across the webbing. "Don't stick your hand up there. Razor blades."

Cézanne's heart picked up its pace. Slash checked the bottoms of the other five chairs, all eviscerated.

Her eyes rimmed with tears. "Those are eighteenth century Philadelphia chairs. Heirlooms from my grandmother's estate. Darlene desecrated them."

Slash put the chair back in its place. He reached over and lopped an arm around her. "You're shaking. Everything'll work out fine."

"How do you know?" Her voice crescendoed into the high-pitched whine of a three-year-old.

"When it comes to crime scene evidence I'm the best there is. Now run along and let me do my job."

With Cézanne all cried-out and the Cadillac filled with law books, she headed for the house on University loaded for bear. She got out of the car, slung her purse over one shoulder, grabbed two armloads of litigation books, and kicked the car door closed with her good foot. At the porch, she tramped purposefully up the steps, muttering curses as she climbed. This time, she rang the bell.

"Who is it?"

"Pizza delivery."

Velda opened the door. Eyebrows shot up into peaks.

"Out of the way." Cézanne pushed past, knocking the door into her aunt and plastering the woman against the wall.

"I'm calling the cops."

"Call them." Defiant, she conjured up a lethal glare and stared into a face that had become lined and leathery from years of cigarette smoke and harsh exposure to the sun. "You're trespassing."

"Poppycock. You're the intruder."

"Not me. Squatter."

Cézanne dumped the books in the middle of a large hooked rug and took stock of the house. In a sweeping glance, she surveyed the kingdom over which she presided.

Way to go, Bob.

Twelve-foot ceilings with embossed tin tiles painted white. Crown molding. Plaster walls in a nice shade of Wedgwood pink that matched the old she-devil's hair. A cast iron ceiling fan that looked sturdy enough hold Aunt Velda in the event she came across a coil of rope to loop around her pleated neck. The house had good bones. On the down side, her new digs contained lots of Empire furniture and a Biedermeier sofa—ugly pieces her ancestors probably brought over on the boat.

All in all, the big room had the comforting smell of her grandmother's linen closet and the makings of a great office foyer. Plus she still had a whole 'nother floor to scope out.

She squared off with her nemesis.

"Let's get something straight. I need this house; you need this house. Only you're not going to get this house if I burn it to the ground with you in it. And the only reason I don't set fire to it right now is because I'm moving my stuff in here so I can start taking clients."

"Clients?" Velda gave a derisive grunt. She folded her arms across her chest in displeasure. Behind her, a freestanding radiator furnace shuddered. "What are you, a hooker?"

Cézanne saw red. For the second time in twenty-four hours, she'd been compared to a prostitute. "That rips it." She fished in her purse, pulled out a pair of handcuffs, and backed Velda against the wall.

"I swan. You're one of those whores they talk about on the daytime talk shows. They handcuff men and make them bark like dogs and such."

Cézanne spun the interloper around. She ratcheted one cuff onto a bird-boned wrist, then slammed the other metal crescent against the radiator and snapped it closed.

Velda's chin quivered. Her eyes misted. At once, she seemed almost fragile. "You can't do this to me. My bones're brittle."

"It's the only way to keep you out of my hair until I get the rest of the car unloaded."

"My arm hurts," she whimpered. "I think you broke it."

"Wouldn't that be a tragedy?"

Velda was praying the Twenty-third Psalm when Cézanne hauled in the last of her library. Tears streamed down parchment skin. "In Jesus's holy name, Amen," she said softly, then shot her niece a villainous look.

Cézanne clapped the dust off her hands and strolled over. She narrowed her eyes. "If I take those bracelets off, are you going to behave?"

Velda emitted a pitiful chirp, then nodded. Through the lenses of her glasses, her eyes appeared huge and watery. For a fleeting second, Cézanne felt a pang in her heart. She slotted the handcuff key into the lock, and the steel crescent swung away. Velda came loose.

And delivered a swift kick in the shin with her clodhopper.

"Ow, ow, ow." Now Cézanne had two hurt legs and couldn't hop on either one.

Velda yelled, "Ingrate," and bolted for the kitchen.

"Crazy witch."

"Flesh peddler."

"Grizzleguts."

They continued exchanging insults as the fleet-footed hag scurried out of the room. She returned with a fire extinguisher. Screaming, "Gutter slut," Velda pulled the pin. An avalanche of white rolled across the room.

Hosed in foam, Cézanne covered her nose and scrambled for the front door.

"Kiss my ass," Velda shouted, hot on her heels.

"Kiss mine and cover yours," Cézanne yelled back in a childish taunt.

The deadbolt snapped shut from the inside. The security chain grated along its track.

Velda's cackle filled the air.

In her sarcastic superiority, the wily old woman still had the upper hand.

Chapter Six

Slash took a break from processing the crime scene at the bungalow on Western.

"What in God's name?" He gave her the once-over. "You look like hell."

Still covered in globs of flame retardant froth, Cézanne clomped past with her foot dragging along the hardwoods. She reached her bedroom hoping for sanctuary, but Slash trailed her to the door.

"What happened?"

"You know how some people claim to see Jesus' face in the Shroud of Turin? Or witness stigmata? I had a rendezvous with the devil."

"Whew." Slash wiped his forehead in mock relief, flicking invisible sweat into the air. "That was close. Because for a minute, I thought you went to the gorilla exhibit and excited the alpha male."

Cézanne scrunched her face. "Are you about done?"

"*Well* done." His playful expression turned serious. "I don't think it's a good idea for you to stay here until you get this place re-keyed. And you really should wait until the lab reports come back before you go around touching anything." His forehead lined with concern.

Cézanne pulled her make-up pouch out of her purse and angled off to the bathroom. "I've got to wash my face and take a shower," she said.

"Yeah, I didn't want to mention it, but you smell like my dog's breath."

She gave him another face scrunch, *Thanks a heap,* and said, "Feel free to guard the door."

"I'll be in your kitchen cleaning up after myself. By the way, your buddy Krivnek stopped by with a set of crutches. I sent him to your new address."

Great.

Once the M.E. encountered Velda, he'd probably never speak to her again.

The sting of hot water refreshed her skin. She reached for the shampoo and lathered her hair to a fare-thee-well. When she sensed a warm tingle spreading over her scalp, she finished soaping her head. After a quick rinse, she repeated the treatment and massaged in a dollop of conditioner. The bathroom was still steamy when she stepped out of the tub and dried off. She sifted through the makeup bag until she located a small jar of revitalizing cream, slathered it over her face and waited five minutes for it to work its magic. Hopefully, it would give her the baby's butt skin the label promised.

Slash gave the door a sharp knuckle tap.

She wrapped herself in a towel. With the tickle of face cream melting down her cheeks, she opened the door a sliver.

"Just wanted you to know I'm finished. Here's your key. I thought I'd walk you out."

"In a second." Blue goo slid past her brows on its way toward her eyes. She lifted one corner of the towel and smeared it away. She tried to close the door but Slash blocked it with his hand.

In a voice tight with controlled fury, she said, "Now wait just a minute," and gave him the Heismann.

Cops. Sex perverts, every last one of them.

His brows angled up until they became asymmetrical dashes.

His eyes filled with revulsion. "What's with the eyebrow?"

She blinked in confusion.

"Your eyebrows. One's gone."

"What?"

"It's gone."

She snatched a washcloth from the towel rack and wiped a circle of steam off the mirror. Her left eyebrow was missing.

"Ohmygodohmygod." She turned on the faucet and splashed water over her face as if Darlene's horrible joke could be undone by this small act of reversal.

Instead, the other one came off in her hand.

With hair gobs on her fingertips, she turned to Slash. Instead of words of comfort, he sprinted down the hall and returned with a wooden tongue depressor and paper bag. He pushed her aside and shut off the tap. As the last of the lather circled the drain, he scooped a dollop of foam onto the stick and dropped it into the sack.

Cool air drifted into the bathroom, evaporating the moisture on the mirror. She leaned closer to observe what Slash had seen—a face without expression.

"Oh, for God's sake. I'm Whoopi Goldberg."

"Where'd you get that face cream?"

"I gathered it up along with a few other toiletries before we left for breakfast."

"Didn't I warn you not to touch anything?"

"Did you? I don't remember. I guess I wasn't paying attention," her voice spiraled upward "since I just narrowly escaped being killed by a sociopath."

"Looks like Darlene's trying her hand at product tampering. Now what?"

"I'll have to draw them on." Panic vaporized. Conspiracy took over. She took his arm confidentially. "You have to go to the store for me. You have to buy me an eyebrow pencil."

"No way. That's female stuff. I wouldn't know anything about that. No, ma'am." He gave her a vehement headshake. "Absolutely not."

Slash towered over her by a good six inches. Since she wanted him to understand just how devastating it was to have a face without eyebrows, she grabbed his jacket by the lapels and pulled him close enough to smell her desperation.

"How hard could it be? My hair's brown. Go get me a brown eyebrow pencil."

"I wouldn't do it if you gave me a million in singles."

"Why?" Her hand closed firmly around his wrist. She tightened her fingers until she detected pain. "Why won't you help me?"

"Because if anybody I know ever saw me in a store buying makeup, they'd think I was gay. I don't need that can tied to my tail, no thank you."

She released her grip. "I can't be seen in public without eyebrows." Her eyes misted.

"What're you gonna do for me?"

"How about a . . ." Cézanne thought fast. "Get-Out-Of-Jail-Free card? Now that I'm retooling my career and I'm getting my law office up and running, I can owe you a legal favor."

"Oh, babe." Slash's eyes brightened. His face cracked into a grin. "Are you ever gonna be sorry."

The last of Fort Worth's old time department stores still sat on the West Side in a long, two-story building put together with red bricks. Middle-aged people shopped at Cox's when they wanted personal service; grandmothers could still find a decent selection of support hose. And the owners thought enough of their customers to place overstuffed sofas near the doors so the elderly could sit and visit or watch the street until their ride showed up. For as long as she could remember, Cézanne escaped the mall crowd in favor of Cox's. Now, post-Christmas, she waited in the Crime Scene van while Slash disappeared inside.

He returned with a small silver sack and tossed it across the seat.

She ripped into it like a cheetah on a carcass and scowled. "It's purple."

"It's not purple. It's sable."

"It looks purple." She shoved the paper bag at him. "You'll have to exchange it."

"I'm not taking it back. It's the light. It distorts the color."

"It's purple, I'm telling you. Get chestnut brown. If the color doesn't say brown somewhere on the package, don't get it."

Ten minutes later, Slash returned beet-faced. He flung open her door, tossed in the sack, stalked around the front of the van and climbed into the driver's seat. He started the vehicle, backed out of the parking space, and dropped it into drive.

Cézanne read the label. "This says dark brown. I need light brown. Did they have Chicory? Because that would exactly match my hair."

"Tough."

"I can't use this. It's not the right shade."

"The only other color was black."

"That's impossible."

Slash slammed on the brake so hard she almost grazed the windshield. Reflexively, her arms flew up to buffer the impact. As he corkscrewed himself into the seat, she sensed a showdown coming on.

"You said brown. I got the only color brown they had. If you want something else, get it yourself."

"I can't go in there. I've got no eyebrows."

"Then draw on a couple with your brown eyebrow pencil. I'm not going back inside."

"Why not?"

"They think I'm queer." He gave the rearview mirror a furtive glance, as if a lurker might've overheard. On instinct, he lowered his voice. "Last time I checked out, I felt compelled to introduce myself to the cashier."

"Why would you do something stupid like that?"

"I gave a fake name."

"Whose name?"

"Doug Driskoll." A sporting grin broke across his face.

She raised her hand to high-five him.

Against Slash's advice, Cézanne picked through her clothes closet and sorted out a week's worth of undamaged outfits along with shoes in neutral colors. As a courtesy—or maybe because he thought she shouldn't be allowed out in public unsupervised—he followed her to the *ad hoc* law office to help carry her belongings inside.

In the distance, a step-van pulled away from the curb. It merged with traffic as she wheeled the Catera into the driveway. When she glimpsed a logo depicting a door key on the side panel, a lump formed in her throat. They were out of their vehicles, standing together on the sidewalk, when the upstairs shutters flung open and Velda poked her head through the window.

Cackling wildly, she called down in a hectoring voice. "What's with your face?"

Cézanne curled her fingers into Slash's sleeve. "Pay no attention. She's deranged."

The old woman erupted in a hyena laugh. Her head ducked back in and the window slammed shut.

"Who was that?"

"Leprosy in a Petri dish. She claims to be my aunt."

Slipping from her grasp, he lugged her overnight bag up the

walk at a fast clip. At the door, Cézanne's key jammed halfway into the lock. She let out a rebel yell, hitched her way back down the porch steps and strode into the yard. "Velda, this is my house, you freaky, pink-haired, flamingo-nosed whacko."

The window flew open with a bang. "It's mine, you no-eyebrows, pencil-face, kiss-butt."

Cézanne shook an upraised fist. She cupped her hands to her mouth. "Get your flabby carcass down here."

Passersby reacted with ghastly expressions, like the ones on the faces of Afghani peasants in old newsreels. Neighbors rubbernecked from their verandas while a shadowy specter in the house across the street took a more cautious approach and peered through the slats of old wooden blinds.

"Open the door, puss-boil," she yelled. Slash watched her carefully, taking it all in from the safety of the porch. "Listen, buzzard-bait, don't make me come up there."

Pretty brass-ballsy considering she had no way to make good on her threat.

Velda disappeared back inside.

Sunlight beat down on her face, fueling her anger. Sweat dotted her forehead, and she wiped it away.

After rejoining Slash on the porch, Cézanne's voice dissolved to a whisper. "She's off her chain."

"Is she now?" He took a step sideways the way people around the courthouse did when panhandlers approached. A disturbed look settled over his face. "I'm sure you're aware there's a noise ordinance."

"Well, aren't you the voice of reason?" Here he stood, reminding her of code violations when he should've been loaning her his service weapon. She grasped the front of his police jacket and hauled him close. "Get me a sledgehammer."

The audible click of a neighboring deadbolt carried on the crisp winter breeze.

He pried her fingers loose. "I'm sorry, that's not an instrument we normally carry around in our tool kits. Besides, it's not my nature to break into houses," he said in a voice laced with sarcasm. "See, I'm the guy you call to find the people who commit the break-ins."

A howl of delight filtered past the second story window and into the yard.

"She's making fun of me." Cézanne's blood boiled. "I'm getting a tire tool."

"Can't let you do that either, sweetie. It's not your house."

"It is my house. I just can't produce a deed right this second."

"Sorry, babe."

"Give me your cell phone."

He never had a chance to hand it over. She reached into his pocket and yanked the clamshell out by its antenna. She mashed the keypad for Information and requested the number to a locksmith.

"What're you doing?"

"Pulling a break-in."

"You're on your own." Slash set the suitcase on the porch and bounded down the steps. "If you manage to stay out of jail, call me later. If you don't, call me from jail."

She realized she'd been sharp with him, if not downright nasty. "Wait. You've been a champ." She whipped a new business card out of her purse and wiggled it at him. "If there's anything I can do for you . . . anything at all . . . don't hesitate to ask. If I can ever repay the favor, just let me know."

Slash ventured close enough to snatch the card. He fished out his badge case and tucked it inside. "There is something."

"Name it."

"That Get-Out-Of-Jail-Free card? I'd like to redeem it. Not for me; a guy I know needs some legal work."

"Sure. Have him call me. The initial consultation's on the house."

"It's not that simple. It isn't a matter of an office visit. I want you to represent him. I can't afford much, but I'll see to it you get paid even if I have to send you a check every month for the rest of my life."

She gave him the visual once-over.

Two months before, he cleared her in the stripper murders Darlene Driskoll now stood accused of. A few weeks later, on the QT, he rushed a set of fingerprints through AFIS, the Automated Fingerprint Index System, in time for her to discover the identity of the Wild Orchid Society's ringleader. The member known as The Executioner turned out to be a detective in her own police unit. This time, he went through her house with tweezers and a UV light, gathering enough evidence to support a kidnapping case against Darlene Driskoll. The man didn't just do his job; he did it better than anyone.

She said, "This one's on the house."

"Can't let you do that." A man in a blue Toyota pickup curbed his vehicle in front of the house. The magnetic sign stuck on the side read AAA-Locksmiths, the As standing for Absolute Access Anytime. "This is where I get off. Catch you later." With a wave goodbye, he strode to the Crime Scene van.

"I mean it," she called out after him. She hobbled down the steps in a fruitless attempt to follow. "I'll do it for free. I've got to get in the trenches sometime. It may as well be now."

He climbed into the van, fired up the engine, and powered down the window. "At least let me pick up your expenses."

"Deal." She gave him the thumbs-up sign. "Wait. What'd the guy do?"

Whatever he mouthed, she didn't catch it. She stood, slack-jawed, as he whipped the search unit into traffic.

A blond-haired man with no chin, a gimp leg, and slight

build sauntered up. He wore a light blue shirt with an oval nametag embroidered with Horace above the pocket. Horace took a passive aggressive stance.

"Sorry to bother you," she said sweetly, "but I just got in from a long trip, and I seem to have lost my keys. Be a dear, will you?"

He spoke in a monotone. "Fifty bucks. Cash."

The upstairs window banged open. Velda poked her head out. "I heard that. You're not running a whorehouse in this place, by God."

"Zip it, poison ivy."

Framed in the opening like a faded old watercolor in need of restoration, Velda cut a spooky picture.

The locksmith's eyes narrowed in suspicion.

Cézanne leaned in and touched the sleeve of his blue denim work shirt. "Dementia. She got to be a real handful at the asylum, so we have to keep her locked up for her own protection."

Thirty minutes later, the door to the South University house had new brass hardware, and Cézanne, the only key.

That'll put sand in her gears, she thought smugly.

But Velda had already one-upped her.

Behind an old piece of plywood dragged in from who-knows-where and nailed across the opening, the evil genius had sealed off the top of the landing. Only Velda had access to the entire second story—for now.

A light bulb idea went off in her head.

A battering ram would splinter it into kindling, and she knew just where to get one.

Constable Jinx Porter. Raven's ex-boyfriend never showed up to serve a felony warrant without carrying a "master key" in the trunk. Raven could borrow the Rapid Assault Tool and drop it off on her way home.

For now, with Velda barricaded in upstairs, she could leave for the grocery store free to stock up on provisions.

After all, she exercised complete control over the kitchen.

If push came to shove she'd starve Velda out.

Chapter Seven

Two hours later, Cézanne returned to the property on University Drive with a trunk full of groceries.

A panel truck pulled away from the curb belching a coil of brown exhaust. She watched the brake lights tap on at Bluebonnet Circle and wondered what kind of mischief Velda plotted. When the driver turned, hard right, she read the writing on the side of the van—Kal Kalvin's Karpentry Kloset—and took in the stenciled painting of a board, a hammer, and a jolly fat man wearing a tool belt.

Noooooooo.

She limped to the house, leaving the perishables to defrost. From the base of the stairs she looked up at the landing. The sight of a new door, complete with frame, siphoned the air out of her lungs.

She cupped her hands to her mouth in a makeshift megaphone. "What've you done?"

Laughter erupted behind the closed door.

Fury blistered Cézanne's eyeballs.

She hurried to the phone and punched in Raven's number. "Get over here—quick."

"What's wrong? I don't have to help you bury a body, do I?"

"I need you to pick up Jinx's battering ram and bring it to my law office."

"I don't like the sound of this."

Cézanne could feel Raven frowning at the other end of the

line. "Just get over here, will you?"

"This caper you're planning—it isn't going to land us on the organ donor transplant list, is it?"

"Not if you keep me from tumbling down the stairs."

She disconnected, then went out to the Catera to bring in the frozen food. By the time she finished stocking the refrigerator the doorbell rang.

Cézanne yanked open the door and stepped aside. The excited smile died on her lips.

Raven arrived without Big Bertha.

"Where's the master key?" she said in a voice laced with impatience.

"Jinx has it. He's out with the guys serving a warrant. What's the problem?"

"At the very least, I need a sledgehammer." Cézanne led her to the base of the stairs and finger pointed at the problem. "Or a twenty-pound maul."

"What the—"

"Velda's an evil genius, that's what. I want that battering ram. We're going to march up those steps like the Teutonic invasion."

"The Teutones were defeated in an ambush."

"Don't be so negative. I'd bust down your door if you asked me to."

"Are you sure Darlene didn't hit you over the head? You're not thinking straight." Then Raven clammed up. With her eyes fixed on the landing, she climbed the stairs. At the top, she motioned Cézanne to follow her up. That triggered an eye roll.

"Look," Raven whispered.

"Yes, it's a door. It's locked." Cézanne enunciated each word. "I need a battering ram to get inside. Only you didn't bring one. So now I need—"

"A screwdriver and a hammer."

"I was thinking shotgun."

Raven flashed a beauty pageant smile. Gray eyes crinkled at the corners; her cheeks plumped up pink against perfect, porcelain skin. "What kind of dumb ass installed this?"

"Kal Kalvin's Karpentry Kloset."

"Don't hire him if you need to lock out thieves, burglars, and other intruders." She pointed to the doorframe where the pins holding the hinges in place faced outward . . . just crying to be pried off by anyone with a screwdriver, a hammer, and a yen for a comfortable bedroom.

Tomorrow she'd buy a set of tools.

Velda only thought she had the upper hand.

For the first time in days, Cézanne laughed so hard her face hurt.

The lead off story on the six o'clock news featured a gimlet-eyed mug shot of Darlene Driskoll plastered across the TV screen. Then viewers were treated to a split screen image of an old wedding photo of her sporting a Cheshire grin next to the police photo showcasing her bad attitude, downturned mouth, and ninety extra pounds.

Stretched across the length of couch, Cézanne positioned a pillow on one arm of the sofa and sank her injured foot in the middle of it. From her place on the Beidermeier, she could watch the big screen TV and still have a clear view out the window of most of the front yard and the mouth of the driveway. She was eating soup straight out of the can, marveling at a close-up of Darlene's foot-wide nostrils, when she glanced past the windowsill and glimpsed Krivnek's head bobbing across the lawn.

He'd finally arrived with the crutches.

She made it to the door before the bell chimed.

The M.E. said, "Great seeing you, too. Try not to look so

happy. It's not like I ran over your dog."

She set the soup can on the fireplace mantle and took the crutches, testing them out with a few awkward steps to see if they needed adjusting. "Thanks. You really didn't have to make a trip. I could've come by your office."

"I'd just as soon you didn't. Bad things happen when you show up at my work." His eyes darted around the brickwork, past her shoulder, taking in the living room from his spot on the welcome mat. "Nice place. We're practically neighbors. Don't feel like you need to visit." He leaned in close. Uncharitable thoughts seemed to brim as he peered over his wire rims. "What's wrong with your eyebrows? You singed them, didn't you? You're a danger to yourself."

"I didn't blow up anything if that's what you're asking. This was a gift from Darlenc Driskoll."

"I see." Although clearly, he didn't. "So is an extra-terrestrial expression in vogue these days?"

She didn't care to argue. He'd done something nice for her and she appreciated it even if it came wrapped in sarcasm. "Want to come inside? You really should get to know the layout just in case there's ever a murder here. Otherwise, I'll get back to my can of chunky beef."

Cézanne glanced over his shoulder, out to the street. An ancient Daihatsu hatchback with an illuminated plastic bucket attached to the roof braked to a screeching halt. Pizza delivery. A pimply-faced high schooler jumped out with a large pizza box and started up the sidewalk.

"Hey—you there—where do you think you're going? I didn't order pizza."

"I did." The voice came from above and to the right.

Velda.

Cézanne limped to the edge of the porch and scanned the upstairs wall in time to witness her aunt lowering a rope with a clothes hamper knotted at the end.

"Don't you dare leave that pizza," Cézanne shouted.

The pizza lackey halted in his tracks.

Velda hollered, "Put the damned pizza in the basket, slug dick."

"I'll give you ten dollars if you'll give me that pizza and leave." Cézanne watched, outraged. At the FBI school in Quantico, she'd learned how negotiators wore down hostage takers. First they cut off the utilities. Only that wasn't about to happen since she lived there, too, and didn't relish freezing her ass off. Second, they controlled the food.

And that's how the cow ate the cabbage.

"It costs fifteen." He held the box in a protective clutch.

"Twenty bucks. Twenty bucks and you keep the pizza."

"Fifty," Velda countered.

The boy cut his eyes back to Cézanne. "A hundred?"

"Are you nuts? I'm not giving you a hundred dollars."

Velda yelled for her sausage and mushrooms. "Take the damned money out of the hamper and give me my pizza. I'll send thirty bucks back down."

"Sorry, lady." The delivery guy cut across the dead grass. He scooped up Velda's money and dropped the sixteen-incher into the basket.

Cézanne saluted her aunt with a stiff middle finger. Velda stuck out her tongue and hoisted the container out of sight. She let out a Rebel yell that echoed down the street. "Sucker."

The window banged shut, leaving the boy staring with the sort of dumbfounded confusion you'd expect of a tourist who'd just had his pocket picked.

Krivnek said, "Is that woman an invalid?"

Cézanne shook her head in stunned disbelief. "Why, that pokenose guttersnipe—where's my gun?"

The contours of Krivnek's mouth hardened. "Are you shooting old ladies now?"

"Old lady, hell. She's the Ebola virus with legs. She's like a smallpox carrier. She looks harmless, but she's a menace to society. I'd be doing a public service. I'd be canonized for Sainthood. They'd name a street after me. I'd get the key to the city."

"You'd get five-to-ninety-nine or life." Krivnek watched, disgusted. He screwed up his lips as if he'd just chewed lemon rind.

"Follow me and I'll explain. Maybe you can help me come up with a plan to make her leave." Her mind jumped ahead and landed on the perfect solution. She could almost feel the release of endorphins surging through her veins. "You could swipe me some chemicals from your lab. Maybe something the body metabolizes; something that won't leave any trace evidence? Do you know where I could purchase a couple of bags of lime? Because I discovered an empty cellar in the back yard that's perfect."

"You're a very dangerous woman. I don't want to know what's going on here, and I'd better not get a callback. I'm not a big enough fan of yours to face life in prison."

But Cézanne sensed laughter behind his eyes. "You like me, Marvin. You think I'm cool. And you feel sorry for me because my aunt's bug-fucking nuts, and she's trying to steal my house."

"I suppose I wouldn't want to see you do yourself in. Look, if you're going to stick with those eyebrows, don't smile. Smiling makes your face look creepy with those things drawn like that. My skin's ready to slide off my body."

"Let me explain."

"I'd rather you didn't. There's something unnerving about you. This kind of stuff doesn't happen to other people. Just you. You're conflict-habituated. Seek help."

She sighed and held up the crutches. "Thanks for these." She scrutinized one with the intensity of an engineer, imagining how it would fit around Velda's neck. If properly used, it might make it easier to drag the cadaver outside under cover of night and roll her into the next-door neighbor's flowerbed.

Krivnek was already retracing his steps to the car. By the time she whiffed the aroma of sausage, mushrooms, and jalapeños, she was thinking less about first degree murder and more about her chances of storming the upstairs and raking in Velda's pizza with a crutch. Instead of finishing her soup, she hopped to the bathroom and redrew her eyebrows.

Around seven that evening, as she applied stenciled lettering to the windows, Slash popped in unannounced. She'd gotten as far as LAW OFFICE, C.R. MARTIN, ATTOR when he rang the bell. Nestling a crutch beneath each armpit, she hitched her way across the living room and slid back the chain. She didn't bother inviting him in, just stepped aside and allowed him to enter.

Cradling a large file in both hands, he glanced around for a place to spread out and headed for the Beidermeier. "Nice place. Most burglars just take their chances, but you—you really thought out this burglary." Once seated, his nose wrinkled and his mouth took a fishhook twist. "Holy cow, Zan. What's with your face?"

Reflexively, she touched her mouth feeling for crusty remnants of food.

"SOS. Your eyebrows."

She winced under his disapproval, traipsing to the bathroom on a feeble, "Excuse me." Slash was right. Her eyebrows resembled Morse code. She quickly redrew them before returning to her guest.

"Is the Mommie Dearest look in fashion this year?"

She did a mid-stride U-turn back to the mirror.

When she rejoined him, he said, "You want fries with that? They look like the golden arches."

Another about-face followed by more painstaking attention. Finally, she gave up.

"Nice. The look of permanent surprise." With turquoise eyes crinkling in amusement, Slash patted the cushion. "You can be bored out of your skull and still look interested in what I have to say. Men thrive on that."

She pitched the crutches off to one side and flopped onto the sofa. He gave her knee a fraternal squeeze.

She actually felt a twinge of affection for him. And not just because he excelled at his craft. He looked so much like his younger brother, Teddy, a loyal employee and a true gentleman. Behind keen-eyed, detective personas, the siblings exuded boyish charm and a hint of pure-D friskiness. She caught herself staring and looked away.

Slash wasn't just intelligent and capable; he was hot.

No wonder Raven had a crush on him. After putting the finishing touches on a disastrous wedding ceremony that ended with the deputy constable dumping her groom at the altar, Cézanne set them up on a date. But now, caught up in his hypnotic presence, she wondered whether she'd made a mistake. If she hadn't believed she had a future with Bobby Noah she would've chased him herself.

"What brings you here? Velda called the police, didn't she?"

He shook his head. "I thought I'd drop this off. It's the case I asked you to look into." He sandwiched the accordion folder between them and tugged a checkbook from the back pocket of his jeans. "I can leave five hundred dollars tonight. At the point where you need the transcripts, I'll order and pay for them myself."

"Transcripts?" Uh-oh. Her gut clenched. "What kind of case is it?"

"Homicide."

He may as well have lifted his hind leg on her. She figured

he'd bring her a misdemeanor. Maybe a felony DWI tops.

Startled into honesty, she backpedaled. "I don't have the legal experience necessary to handle a murder."

"I'd be lying if I said you were the first lawyer I'd made a run at. Truth is, I've seen five different attorneys—all heavyweights. Nobody'll touch it."

Barely breathing, she stared at the dangling check, unwilling, for the moment, to take it. "Your friend committed murder?"

"He's not my friend. We went through the police academy at the same time, that's all."

"He's an officer?"

"Ex-cop. The brass thought he had a drinking problem. Internal Affairs gave him an ultimatum: Get rehab or get canned. Erick didn't think he needed help." Slash thumbed over his shoulder. "So out he went on his can."

"Who'd he kill?"

"Allegedly killed. His wife."

"If a jury convicted him, he didn't allegedly kill anyone. He's a convicted killer." As she listened to the logical side of her brain screaming *For the love of God, don't get sucked in,* she watched Slash's jaw muscles flex and tempered her opinion. "Let's say he's wrongfully convicted. What's it to you?"

"He didn't do it."

"How do you know? Were you there?"

"In a manner of speaking. I worked the crime scene. And crime scenes don't lie. People do."

Chapter Eight

Even with her foot immobilized in a removable cast, sleeping on the Beidermeier made it hard to writhe in the midst of a nightmare.

In her dream, the man at the jewelry store pulled the ten-power loupe away from his eye and pronounced her diamond ring a fake. When she tried to convince him Bobby would never give her a CZ, the proprietor pulled out a hammer and smashed it.

The shrill of a thousand demons filled her head. She clutched a throw pillow to her ear but the rusty-hinge cries only got louder. Fully awake, she tossed the pillow aside and hoisted herself up on one elbow.

Velda.

Shrieking to a fare-thee-well.

It sounded like one of those hostage negotiations ploys she'd learned at the FBI academy, back when the Chief of Police used to approve whatever conference she put in for just to be rid of her. One of the most useful tools she'd learned at hostage negotiations school was that continuously blasting obnoxious music or tapes—Tibetan chants, recorded sounds of dying rabbits, "Cattle Call"—over a loudspeaker could encourage a kidnapper to abandon his plan. She suspected playing the background music to the TV show "Cheaters," a complete lecture series on jet propulsion, Barbara Walters or Lou Dobbs tapes and anything by Yoko Ono would work, too.

The frightening peal coming from upstairs was starting to feel like hostage negotiations in reverse. Because she was the one being disrupted, and Velda Martin Steelhammer Wahlberg Wagonseller Francis Barnhart—she numbered all five husbands on her fingers to ensure they'd each been accounted for—was the one raising hell.

Her eyes bulged. She smashed her palms to her ears.

So this was how Velda planned to get rid of her. Sleep deprivation.

She cupped her hands to her mouth. "There's a noise ordinance in this city. You're violating it."

"It's not me. It's the demons. I have demons inside me." Velda resumed keening.

"Stop it. You'll wake the neighbors."

"You don't understand about the demons."

"Oh, I understand, all right. One kidnapped me the other night and tried to kill me."

Velda went suddenly quiet.

After a few minutes of silence, with nothing but her heartbeat and the ticking of the clock, Cézanne reclined against a bolster pillow and concentrated on falling asleep.

Abruptly, Velda tuned up again.

"Knock it off before I call the police."

"It's the demons. They're everywhere."

"Cast them out and go back to bed before I come up there and beat you with a shovel."

Velda expelled a raspy chuckle. "You can't get in."

"You'll know the answer to that soon enough," Cézanne shot back, mentally elevating the tool purchase to the top of tomorrow's to-do list.

Velda fretted. "I can't cast them out because I don't know their names."

"What does that have to do with anything?"

"If you call their names they have to leave."

Cézanne sunk into her thoughts. There had to be a way to get the shrew to button it. "Do you have a computer in your room?"

"What's it to you?"

"Get on the Internet and look up demon names on a search engine."

"I'm not the only one in this family with demons."

"What's that supposed to mean?" But she knew. Mean-spirited Velda had just made reference to her mother, locked in the psychiatric hospital, awaiting another trial for an extended commitment. Tormenting her with reminders of Bernice's mental illness seemed cruel even for Velda.

The silence stretched between them.

"Okay, I'll bite," Cézanne muttered. To Velda, she yelled, "Are you suggesting I have a demon inside me?"

"I'd lay odds on it."

"What do the demons look like?" she asked, dripping sarcasm. "Maybe I have one and don't know it. Do the demons have tails? Pointy tails with little barbs on the tips?"

"I don't appreciate you poking fun at my misery."

This *was* fun. Cézanne sat upright with her back pressed firmly against the Biedermeier and settled in for a howling good time at Velda's expense. "Do they wear clothes?"

"Tutus."

"What?" Surely she'd misheard. She cupped a hand to one ear.

"Pink net tutus."

"What are they, gay? You have gay demons inside you? How messed up is that?"

Velda tuned up shrieking. It was like Chinese torture without the water.

"Okay, okay. You're right," Cézanne yelled. Her aunt stopped keening. "I do have a demon."

This piqued Velda's interest. "What does he look like?"

"I don't know."

"Then how do you know you have one?"

"Because he gets on eBay and buys stuff."

"Like I said, you don't understand about the demons. If you had more compassion the demons might go away."

"I understand about demons. I got this inheritance, and one came with the house."

That dried up the conversation.

Cézanne borrowed an Afghan throw from the arm of an old channelback chair and tried to drift back to sleep.

Each time she flopped over in search of a more comfortable position, the weight of the cast held her in place. Eventually, she settled into slumber gripping Raven's .38 beneath the bolster.

Evening turned into the wee hours of the morning.

In the midst of a dream about the eBay demon she awakened, bolt upright. She'd totally forgotten that Leviticus Devilrow was supposed to drop off his niece, Deuteronomy, at the bungalow on Western.

She ripped off her covers and hobbled into the sunroom.

Poor Duty. Surely Devilrow wouldn't leave her alone.

She thunked her forehead with the heel of her palm.

Of course that con-wise reprobate would abandon her. He'd done it before.

She hiked up sweat pants, grappled with a sweatshirt, grabbed her keys and limped out to the Catera as quietly as she could. No sense waking Velda when she probably had a locksmith on speed-dial who advertised twenty-four hour service. She tried slipping the car into neutral and pushing it down the driveway and out onto the street but the cast and crutches threw her off balance. Finally she started the engine where it sat.

If Velda locked her out she'd call the guy's competition.

With the traffic signals blinking yellow, it took less than ten minutes to reach the bungalow. When she pulled into the drive, her heart broke. Deuteronomy sat shivering on the porch the way she had two months ago when that shiftless conman Leviticus Devilrow dumped her off in the freezing cold wearing nothing but a threadbare dress.

Duty's harlequin Great Dane, Enigma, lay stretched across her lap.

Cézanne yanked up the emergency brake and grappled to get out. "You poor kid, I'm so sorry." Deuteronomy didn't move, just sat there with her teeth chattering like Levar Burton's tap shoes. "Are you all right?"

"Miz Zan, I nearly froze solid."

The dog seconded her with a muted *woof.*

"And 'Nigma? He's so weak from hunger he can't get up."

"It's inertia."

Duty said, "Whatchoo mean?"

"A body at rest tends to stay at rest. Enigma's big, lazy, and unmotivated." Cézanne stooped to pat his head.

"Where's Ruby?" Duty was referring to the red Kompressor.

On the drive back, she filled the girl in. Duty listened, spellbound. The update concluded when they coasted into the drive.

"Crazy Aunt Velda took over the upstairs. We'll have to make do until I figure out a way to get rid of her." Before they went inside, Cézanne briefed the girl on their accommodations. "There's one bathroom downstairs, so courtesy becomes top priority. I have clients with appointments scheduled for tomorrow, so we need to keep things tidy. No wet towels. No dirty clothes thrown in the corner. Apparently the bedrooms are upstairs. But I found blankets in a hall closet, and if we double them, the floor might not seem so hard.

"Whatchoo mean? You makin' me sleep on the floor? We don't

have a sofa?"

"There's a sofa. I'm sleeping on it."

Duty snorted in disdain. "I'm a guest. If anybody sleeps on the floor, it should be you."

"We'll both sleep on the floor. Tomorrow I'll buy a couple of cots."

"Mmmmm-mmmm. So if you and me are sleepin' on the floor, can 'Nigma have the couch?" And then, "Miz Zan, what's wrong with yo' eyebrows?"

Inside, Duty got the grand tour of the first floor. She especially liked the bonnet top of the vintage Frigidaire and the old sea green Chambers stove in the kitchen.

"I can work magic with this stove, Miz Zan."

"You're not planning on whipping up any Voodoo potions, are you? Because if you live with me, you can't go around casting spells on people."

"Don't need to. Unless maybe you want me to take care of that po-liceman's wife for you." Duty gave her a sly smile.

"You don't have any of those little dolls with you, do you? We could find a cotton ball and soak it in Pepto-Bismol."

"Whatchoo want with nasty ol' pink stuff?"

"Aunt Velda's got pink hair."

"Go on." Duty swatted the air. "You got a auntie with pink hair?"

"Yes. And she's freakishly intuitive so stay away from her. If you ever catch her outside, lock the doors and call the police."

"Velda's crazy?"

"She thinks she has demons inside her."

"Demons? Does she know their names? 'Cause if she knows the names of the demons, she can call 'em out and they have to leave."

"What are you—the demon expert?"

"Oh, I been knowin' about demons and spirits and loa for a long time. It's why I wear my gris-gris necklace." She pulled the vile-smelling pouch out from beneath the scoop collar of her shirt and held it by a neck chain. The pungent aroma of nutmeg wafted out, followed by the scent of the grave. "Protection."

Cézanne fanned the air in front of her nose. "Put it back."

Duty went on, "Demons like to stick to certain families."

"Are you suggesting I have a demon?"

"I'm sayin' if they find a family they like, it's easier to stay put than move around. Movin' around—for a demon—takes a lot of work. Take the Royal Family for instance."

Cézanne narrowed her eyes to a squint. "What about the Royal Family?"

"They got 'em. That Paris girl whose video tapes are on the Internet, she got a lot of demons. And that music entertainer fella—the one named after candy—he got one too."

"So you're saying if Velda has demons, I may have a demon?"

"I know you have one. I've seen it take over in rush hour traffic."

"Knock it off. I don't have road rage. Are you hungry?" Cézanne opened the refrigerator. "I bought groceries, so we've got plenty of—" Her mouth dropped open at the sight of the depleted inventory. "She stole the lasagna and green beans."

Her gut sank. If Velda swiped the entrees, she probably rifled through the rest of the groceries.

Cézanne rushed to the pantry. Six cans of chunky soup vanished along with individual servings of heat-and-serve stew and a bag of Cheetos. And what happened to the microwave? Shanghaied, of course.

She yelled at the ceiling. "Damn it, Velda. I know what you did, you harpy."

Hysterical laughter filtered through the plaster.

"That's Velda?" Duty pointed upward. "Want me to take care

of her for you?"

Cézanne took leave of her senses. "Can you do it without actually killing her?"

Duty touched a finger to her lips. Her thoughtful expression settled on the light fixture hanging above them. "I might have just the thing. This'll take a little time."

"Let's get some rest. We'll get started in the morning."

Only Cézanne couldn't sleep.

In the shadows of darkness, Slash's accordion file took on spectral proportions. Blue light cast by the street lamps filtered through a large cherry laurel near the window. With each swaying branch, the murder case on Erick Rackley seemed to pulsate in its corner. Nearby, Duty had turned Enigma into a living pillow and was snoring like a sea lion.

Cézanne yielded to the folder's gravitational pull. She flipped the lamp switch, untied the string and pushed back the file flap. As she leafed through the pleats, she discovered the contents were broken down by manila folders and further organized by date.

The first partition held a typed transcript for an audiotape and was rubber-banded to a small envelope containing a thirty-minute cassette. Both had been stamped FWPD, signed by the interviewer, and tagged with the defendant's name, time, date, and case number.

Erick Rackley's call to nine-one-one came in a few minutes before midnight.

"Get over here now. My wife got hold of a gun, and I can't get the bleeding stopped."

Chills crawled up Cézanne's tenders. She slapped the transcript shut and took long, deep breaths. She wanted to listen to the voice. To hear Rackley's fear—or lack of it. To sense the desperation in his tone—or not. Listening to that tape would help her get a sense of Rackley's innocence.

Or guilt.

She tiptoed to the sunroom with the floor creaking underfoot. The icy glow from the street lamp shimmered through the window enough to illuminate the unopened boxes stacked near the law books. She lifted the lid on one marked Office Supplies and pulled out a small micro-cassette recorder leftover from her rookie days on patrol. After putting in fresh batteries, she slotted the little tape into the machine and turned the volume down low. The scratchy lead cleared up after a few seconds, and the clear voice of a female dispatcher spoke with authority.

"Nine-one-one. What is your emergency?"

"Get over here now. My wife got hold of a gun, and I can't get the bleeding stopped. Tell me what to do. It's coming out all over the place. What do I do? Somebody please tell me what to do."

"Sir, there's an ambulance on the way. I need you to calm down. I'll walk you through."

"I think she's dying. Yvonne, wake up. Wake up!"

"Where is she now?"

"On the bed."

"Where was she shot?"

"In the chest. I think she's dead."

"Is anyone else there who can help you?"

"Just me."

Smooth move, getting him to admit only two people could've done it—and one of them was dead.

"Stop the blood loss. And tuck some pillows under her feet to raise her legs."

"But I put it on her chest. To stop the bleeding."

Immersed in the transcript, Cézanne's heart settled into an erratic beat. Her skin rippled, transported to the scene by the written word. She imagined Erick Rackley slipping into shock in the terror and confusion, powerless to stop his wife's life from ebbing away.

"How did it happen?"

Unintelligible response.

"Sir, I can't understand you if you scream. Can you feel a pulse?"

"No. Thank God. They're here." Rackley's voice went abruptly calm. "What should I do? I have to let them in. I can't leave her."

"Go let them in, Mr. Rackley. I'll stay on the line."

"You know my name? Right . . . my address came up on your computer screen. I used to work at the PD. Is this Sandy? My wife is Yvonne." Loud banging at the door. *"I'll let them in."*

Spoken in a Zombie voice.

A glass of cold orange juice sat on the end table along with a half-eaten granola bar.

Each time Enigma looked beyond Duty's blanket and licked his chops, Cézanne menaced him with a glare. Once, when he made a move to get up, she admonished him with a throaty warning delivered through clenched teeth.

She tabbed through the file until she came to a folder labeled Photographs. She found Rackley's mug shot snapped the night of his arrest, his police cadet photo, and an eight-by-ten glossy taken at a wedding. She assumed the bride was the late Yvonne. The rest were crime scene photos or black-and-whites of the deceased taken at autopsy. Cézanne set the pictures aside and leafed through the tabs, appreciative that a man with an obvious fetish for perfection organized the file.

Offense Reports.

She thumbed through the narratives looking for signatures of cops with friendly faces. It'd be a place to start if she intended to re-interview witnesses.

Many reports came from Slash. At the end of each one he signed his full name: Wolfgang X. Vaughn, scrawled in the penmanship of a deranged physician.

Charles Crane. No way to interview the former captain of

Homicide now that he was deceased.

Her stomach gave a nasty flip. In a fleeting moment, she contemplated the idea that Crane might still be alive. Nobody else thought so. Not the dive team that searched Eagle Mountain Lake for the body, that's for sure. But it just wasn't right, a truck sitting on the lake bottom with the doors closed and the windows rolled up tight and no body inside. Oh sure, the lead diver said he could've gotten out. Could've shut the door on reflex but he couldn't have made it to the top. Not unless he survived a head injury—judging by the circular crack in the windshield—and could hold his breath for five minutes.

Jock Featherston. Forget him. Jock turned out to be the executioner for the Wild Orchid Society, an exclusive BDSM group of ultra-wealthy Westsiders. Fired from the PD after being indicted for the murder of his paramour's husband, the attempted murder of Cézanne, and a host of lesser crimes in case the major ones didn't stick, he could be found cooling his hocks in I-block at the Tarrant County Jail. The "I" in I-block stood for isolation and housed disgraced police officers, baby rapers, and other scumbuckets the general population wanted to beat the shit out of.

Teddy Vaughn. Slash's brother. She broke into a smile. If anybody deserved to make sergeant, the homicide detective did. Teddy didn't know she'd cemented his promotion when she whispered his name into the Chief's ear during her exit interview from the PD. She looked forward to seeing Teddy again.

Doug Driskoll, escargot-dick. Ugh. With an invisible dagger gripped in her fist, she stabbed herself in the heart. Six years ago, Driskoll was the first officer at the Rackley crime scene. The thought of coming face-to-face with him again was enough to make her white corpuscles separate from the red ones.

Krivnek did the autopsy. Good guy, highly competent.

Thorough. Honest. Under cause of death, he entered: Undetermined.

She came to a pocket folder containing several audiotapes. This file contained two ninety-minute cassettes marked Interview. She paused to reflect.

What she needed was a better tape recorder. One with enhancer capabilities that could digitally filter out extraneous sounds and echoes. She wanted to listen to Erick Rackley's nine-one-one tape again to see if she could pick up anything in his tone or inflection. Especially the garbled portion. And she wanted to hear the interview tapes.

With her heart beating fast, she set the file aside and cut the light. Outside, the wind picked up. The cherry laurel near the window moved like a Hula dancer. Her eyes cut to the folder.

What the hell have I gotten myself into?

Chapter Nine

Across the street, behind the neighbors' Tudor-inspired homes, a tangerine sun climbed over the trees. When the morning light slanted through the wooden blinds, Cézanne cracked open her eyes. Fisting sleep from her lids brought the room into sharp focus.

Duty padded out of the bathroom, barefooted, wearing black sweats and towel-drying her hair.

Remembering the tainted shampoo, Cézanne scrambled upright. "Tell me you didn't use my shampoo."

Duty's lower lip protruded. "I didn't even see yo' stuff, Miz Zan. I got my own."

"You misunderstand." She softened her tone. "Darlene Driskoll monkeyed with my things. She could've poisoned that bottle. I meant to turn it over to Slash when he dropped in last night."

The lip retracted. Duty's eyes brightened. "What's for breakfast?"

"Since *Cruella De Velda* rat-holed our food, I say we go for take-out. Only not together. One of us has to stay behind to make sure she doesn't lock us out."

Maroon irises sparkled like garnets. "I think I should be the one to go, Miz Zan. I could drive yo' Caddy."

"You don't have a license."

"That didn't stop you from lettin' me drive Ruby. And yo' patrol car."

Poor Ruby. Best car she ever had, wrapped around a tree.

And the unmarked cruiser? The body shop never did get out that algae smell after Duty parked it on the bottom of the Trinity River.

"I could take yo' Cadillac." Her eyes shifted to the ceiling where the cast iron fan whirred softly overhead. "I would look good behind the wheel of a new car. I could order us pastries, juice, and a sausage biscuit for 'Nigma."

Cézanne's mouth watered.

The upstairs pipes whooshed. Velda had turned on the shower.

Still in pajamas, Cézanne wobbled into the sunroom and grabbed her coat. "There's not much time. Let's go."

They returned twenty-five minutes later with two hot chocolates, a sack of Krispy Kremes, and a speeding ticket. She wanted to ask the officer to extend a little professional courtesy, but motor jocks had nasty temperaments and reputations for citing their own mothers. And since the little Napoleon strutted up to the Catera grimacing like his Hanes had ridden up his rump roast, she decided not to provoke him as he took in her presence in stages: uncombed hair, purple PJs, no eyebrows.

Duty stood five feet six, but her fast-growing puppy could still get his paws on her shoulder when he jumped up to greet her. "Can 'Nigma have a donut?"

"No. Sugar's bad for dogs."

Duty slipped him one under the dining room table and settled into a chair.

Cézanne dressed quickly in a skirt and sweater and joined her. "I've been thinking . . ."

"I knew a man once, did so much thinking he busted a blood vessel in his head."

"Don't get smart. I have a great idea. Now that I have a real law office, you could be my assistant until school starts. Leviticus Devilrow brought you here to improve your education. Since it's important for you to be able to communicate with highly educated people clear down to the lowest common denominator, we should add a new word to your vocabulary each day. That blood vessel that burst in your friend's head? It's called an aneurysm."

"Okay."

"I can give you the word for the day or you can open the dictionary, close your eyes, and point. Which works for you?"

Duty said, "I might cheat."

"Fine. Use it in a sentence five times during the course of the day. That's the only way to brand it into your memory. Today's word is . . ." An ugly visual popped into mind. The image of looking up Velda's housedress, returned. "Obscene. There's a dictionary in the bookshelf. Look it up."

"Don't need no dictionary. Here's my sentence: Obscene a real good dog named 'Nigma, actin' real nize, waitin' for his donut." Duty beamed.

"Wrong. Get the dictionary. It's in a box in the sunroom. Five different sentences."

Duty headed for the stacks singing, "Obscene the Promised Land." As she flipped through the Oxford English Dictionary, the doorbell chimed.

The first client arrived. Cézanne wiped her mouth, then brushed a couple of sugar flecks from her black skirt and cashmere pullover.

Delbert Ray. Misdemeanor probation revocation. His retainer would pay next month's mortgage.

With her crutches in position, she headed for the door.

Shrieks erupted overhead.

"Help me. Call nine-one-one. I'm being held prisoner in my own home."

Velda.

"Save yourself." Velda again, carrying on like a fishwife. "Don't come inside or you'll end up chained to the pipes. Haul ass while there's still time."

Cézanne yanked open the door in time to see Delbert Ray mounting his Kawasaki. He ignored her shouted invitation to come inside and slipped on a black helmet with red and yellow flame decals shooting back from the visor.

Duty laughed so hard hot chocolate spewed out of her nose. She drummed her sneaker-clad feet against the hardwoods. "That Velda. She's downright obscene." And then, "Miz Zan, can we get us a hog? I'd look so fine on a bike. 'Specially one with flames on the tank."

After leaving Duty to mull over the top ten reasons why they couldn't have a Harley, Cézanne crutched her way out into the back yard. She studied the wrought iron staircase spiraling up to the second story. As best she could tell, the house had three, maybe four, bedrooms. Velda must still have a key to the outside door leading into the kitchen. Should've had the locksmith change out all the deadbolts. Even if that crabcake barricaded off the entire upstairs she could still sneak down the back way and re-enter the first floor.

That unpleasant prospect called for a home improvement project.

An hour later, she returned from the hardware store with a hundred-piece tool kit, a monkey wrench, galvanized nails, and a hammer. Back inside the kitchen, Cézanne slanted her crutches against the tile countertop and headed straight for the walk-in cupboard. She dismantled a shelf and nailed it across the door, hammering vengeance into each swing. Upon further inspection, she decided not even a patrol car with push bars could penetrate her handiwork.

Duty walked in as she closed the tool drawer. "That looks obscene."

"You can do better than that."

"So can you. It's crooked."

"It isn't supposed to be pretty. It's supposed to keep out that flesh-eating carrion buzzard."

"Carry-on? Is that like carry-on luggage? 'Cause you keep callin' her an old bag."

"It's a vulture."

Duty hoisted herself onto the countertop and crossed her feet at the ankles. "Seems to me, Miz Zan, Velda got bedrooms, and we got food and cable and a pretty nize hi-fi. I don't like cribbin' on the floor. Seems what we need is to get us a room upstairs in exchange for givin' the old buzzard kitchen privileges."

"Velda doesn't need kitchen privileges. She stole our food and made off with the microwave. She can survive quite well over the next six days. That old crepe hanger will probably gain weight."

"I never heard such obscene talk." Duty grinned. "How 'bout I see if she's willing to trade? I could be the medi . . . media . . ."

"Mediator. And the only way we're mediating with that shrew is with a forcible entry and detainer."

"Say what?"

No time to explain. Somebody was pounding the front door.

Maybe Delbert Ray decided to come back. She needed that retainer.

Cézanne jammed a crutch under each arm and swung out of the kitchen. On the way to the living area, she flipped on the crystal chandelier in the dining room, lighting the place up like the mothership.

She yanked open the door and saw her astonished expression reflected in the mirrored sunglasses of two uniformed patrol officers. Both stood over six feet tall. They lingered, menacingly, with their arms braced across their chests.

She leaned beyond the doorjamb and looked the length of

the porch. "May I help you?"

The beefy one said, "We'd like to step inside."

"Is there a problem, officer?"

"We need to have a look around."

"I didn't call you. Is something wrong?" She measured Duty through slitted eyes. "Do you have warrants?"

"Of all the obscene things to say."

"We're here about the sign." The beefy one again, pointing skyward.

"The sign?" Like seeing Jesus' face in the bark of your favorite pecan tree? She'd read in the paper about an old Mexican man down in the Rio Grande Valley who claimed the image of the Virgin Mary appeared on his penis. "What sign?"

"The sign in the window, ma'am." Said condescendingly.

She propped her crutches against the bricks. With cops trailing her down the steps, she hopped from the sidewalk onto the lawn. Shielding her eyes from the morning glare, she stared at the second floor.

Evil biddy.

Cézanne drew in a sharp intake of air. A piece of cardboard Velda had hand-lettered and propped against the glass read: CALL 911. IMPRISONED BY MADWOMAN. SAVE ME.

The beefy one pointed a finger the size of a Polish link. "Is that your idea of a joke?"

"I didn't know it was up there. I'll take it down."

"We have to check the premises."

She couldn't let them encounter Velda. If the old bat made up a credible-sounding story she could end up in the hoosegow for injury to the elderly or some other trumped up charge.

"Really, officer, it's no trouble. It won't happen again."

The Blue exchanged knowing looks, then skirted her like a couple of basketball forwards. They headed inside with Cézanne hustling to keep up.

In the living room, Duty did some serious eye rolling. "I swanee. Velda's like a booger you can't thump off. Crazy old carrion, what's she thinkin'? Gonna get us thrown in the pokey." She stiffened under the piercing gazes of The Blue. "I confess. I did it. I thought it'd be funny. It was just a joke on account of Miz Zan's so bossy. Like last night, she made me and 'Nigma sleep on the floor, which ain't right. I'm not the maid; I'm a guest."

Beneath the dining room table, Enigma staked out a space on the Karastan rug and horked up donuts.

"Deuteronomy didn't do anything." She limped to Duty's side, slung an arm around her shoulders and gave her a protective squeeze. "Here's the truth. There's an old lady in my house, and I've been trying to get rid of her."

"That's a lie. Miz Zan would never kill anybody."

She dug her fingernails into Duty's skin to silence her. Periwinkle blue eyes shifted from the chatty adolescent to the officers. "I meant I want her to leave. But she won't. She barricaded herself upstairs, and we can't get in. I want her out. Since you're already here, maybe you could flush her out and haul her off?"

Duty shook her head, *woe is me*. "Miz Zan, you don't have to story on account of me." She offered up her wrists. "I confess. I wrote the sign. Take me to the slammer."

Cézanne swatted down her scrawny arms. "You're not taking her anywhere. I'm telling you for real there's a crazy woman in the house."

The Blue exchanged telepathic glances.

"I'll take down my sign," Duty said quickly. And then, "Say, do the po-lice have one of those Explorer Scout programs? 'Cause I'd be real good at that. Ever since that time I borrowed one of yo' po-lice cars, I been thinkin' I wanna become a lady po-lice officer. Do you make enough to pay for digital cable?

How 'bout high-speed Internet? 'Cause I like to surf the net, only Miz Zan, she got a slow connection."

Their faces lined with skepticism. They took the stairs in twos. At the landing, the big one unsnapped his holster, then turned the doorknob.

Cézanne winced. Velda would cook up a lie to get her jailed.

With guns leveled at the hip, the door gave way and they disappeared from view.

She stared, open-mouthed. Her heart beat in cadence with their footsteps as they conducted a room-to-room search. Voices buzzed overhead.

Duty, who'd been holding her breath while she cleaned up after the dog, whispered on exhale, "Do you have bail money? 'Cause if you do, I think you better get it. And you probably ought to leave me the car keys since I'll have shoppin' to do and you won't be around to drive me where I need to go."

"Just where do you need to go while I'm being locked up?"

"Mexico. I'd like to buy one of those stuffed frogs with its lips sewed shut. I think it would look real nize next to my shrunken head and my feather collection. About those keys—I'll be real careful. I'm a good driver."

"You drove an unmarked police car into the Trinity River."

"Not my fault. The road ran out."

One of the troops shouted overhead.

"Oh, fuck." Cézanne clapped a hand to her mouth.

"That's obscene. A highly educated woman like you really should take measures to improve yo' vocabulary. When I feel like cussin' I just whip up a bad spell and cast it."

But Cézanne wasn't listening.

The ship had hit the sand.

The uniforms bounded down the steps. When they reached the bottom they veered off in opposite directions. The crewcut blond headed for the sunroom. The beefy one went for the kitchen.

He hollered, "Can't be boarding up doors, ma'am. It's a code violation. Fire hazard."

Cézanne gave them a feeble, "Okay," but her eyes cut to Duty, and she knew they were sharing a simultaneous thought: *Where's Velda?*

Her mind played a trick. It freeze-framed a Hawaiian beach scene where a hundred thousand geriatric tourists, all dressed in loud, flowery muumuus and Hawaiian print shirts, cavorted by the sea. Like the book about the nerdy guy in the red and white striped knit. Waldo. Yeah. *Where's Waldo?*

The sound of splintering wood put a grimace on Duty's face. She cupped her hands to her mouth. "Are we goin' to jail, Miz Zan?"

"Probably."

"You didn't do Velda in, did you?"

"Can you say it any louder?" Cézanne hissed. "I don't think the next-door neighbors heard you."

But Duty's eyes widened with excitement. "You can trust me, Miz Zan. I just wanna know where you hid the body. She's small and wiry, that Velda. I don't suppose you stuffed her in a drawer? 'Cause if you did, that'd be clever. Only we need to get her out before she bloats up and starts to stink."

"You know I didn't kill Velda. You've been with me the whole time."

Duty put a finger to her lips and frowned. "Let's see, now. Maybe I can alibi you, and maybe I can't. I could probably remember better if you was to let me drive yo' Caddy down West Freeway."

"You're not driving my rental car."

"Too bad." Duty went quiet and sunk into her thoughts. "Could've done her in while I was puttin' shine on my hair in front of the bathroom mirror."

"Oh, for God's sake." Panic set in. She wanted Velda out of the house, not decomposing underneath it. "What if she's really dead? Like those Kamikaze pilots in World War II—only it's a suicide screw job? What if she killed herself to spite me? That would keep me from getting my house. Velda probably figured they'd prosecute me."

Recognizing crazy talk when she heard it spoken from her own lips, she applied the brakes.

Velda needed to show herself, *pronto.*

The officer came out of the sunroom. He stationed himself in the living room where he had a bird's eye view of the kitchen and a clear shot at the open front door. He pulled a hand-held radio from its leather case, keyed the mike, and gave his call sign over the air.

At the dispatcher's response, he reported in. "Looks like a kid's prank. Hold us Ten-eight."

A series of tones sounded, then came the reply. "Ten-four."

Cézanne sighed. The tension in her neck dissolved, but the knots stayed.

The beefy officer carried the mangled cupboard shelf into the dining room. "Don't be blocking doors." He handed Cézanne what resembled kindling.

Her heart beat time-and-a-half. "Where's Velda?"

"Who's Velda?"

"The woman who took over my house. The one who locked herself in and wrote that sign."

He eyed her with cold scrutiny. "There's nobody up there."

Her eyes slewed to Duty.

So did the cop's. He crooked a sausage finger. "You mind stepping over here a second so we can have a word, Miss . . ."

"Devilrow. Deuteronomy Devilrow. Duty for short."

Cézanne's eyes widened. That's how they did it—cops

separating the witnesses, sniffing out holes in their stories. Murmurs filtered over from the corner. She didn't trust the way Duty's eyes kept cutting in her direction, nor the way she lifted her hand and twirled her index finger near her ear in the universal *loco-in-the-coconut* gesture. The officer glanced over several times and nodded.

Duty stuck out her hand for a shake. "Thank you so much Mista Officer, sir. I'll see to it she gets help."

Through a measured squint, Cézanne watched them close in on her.

The cop turned to Duty. "Don't put any more signs in the window."

"I won't."

"If you do, we'll have to haul you to Juvenile. Understand?"

"Yes, Mista Officer, sir. I will not do it again. That I will not. I will not put up any more signs, especially not obscene ones." She clenched her teeth in a forced grin.

The brawny patrolman made eye contact with his partner. They gave each other simultaneous headshakes. "Let's go. Ladies, take it easy."

Cézanne said nothing. Just stood with her fists jammed in her pockets and her mouth agape.

Duty offered up a sincere, " 'Bye now."

On the way out, the lead officer thumbed at Duty. Snippets of conversation filtered their way. "Poor kid . . . owner thinks a ghost lives upstairs . . . haunted house."

Duty hustled to the window. She positioned her knee on a chair seat with her palms suctioned against the pane. Enigma trotted over and slimed the glass with his nose. Behind them, Cézanne folded her arms across her chest and watched the uniforms climb into their shiny new black-and-whites.

She seethed through gritted teeth. "You told them I was crazy?"

"Not crazy. I said you was disturbed because this old house creaks. And sometimes you hear things nobody else can hear. That you have a demon inside. I had to admit I was yo' caretaker on account of you need close watchin'. And I might've said you claim to be psychic."

Convulsive laughter sheared the conversation. They whipped around to see Velda standing near the bottom of the staircase. She doubled over in a fit of amusement with one hand clutching her stomach and the other holding a broom. Tears of mirth streaked her cheeks.

"Lordy mercy. Is this yo' auntie?" Duty's arm shot out reflexively. She grabbed Cézanne's wrist, hauled her close and hissed out a warning. "She's givin' off bad vibes, Miz Zan. The air around her just turned violet . . . well, waves of violet. Like heat snakes on the road."

Enigma stretched his feet in front of him like the Great Sphinx. He gave a little whine and put his head between his paws.

"You see purple air?"

"Not anymore. It's turned black as pitch. I think she's evil. Looks evil to me. I never met anybody with pink hair. And a skinny white neck. Like a paper cone of cotton candy from the circus." Duty covered her ears like the middle chimp. "Miz Velda's frock's so loud I'm 'fraid my ear drum's busted."

The girl had a point. Velda's housedress was bright enough to make a blind man reach for an eye patch. Chartreuse ruffles decorated the hem of a fuchsia A-line, with a red and purple sweater opened to the third button.

"Where've you been? I could've been arrested because of you."

Velda snickered like a cartoon dog. "Think of this as a shot across the bow." She guffawed so hard her shoulders bobbed. Soon, she hee-hawed like a jenny and pointed a crooked finger at Cézanne. "What'n the cat hair happened to your face?"

"What's wrong with my face?" But she knew.

"Miz Zan, I been meanin' to tell you, you should let me draw yo' brows on. I can do it. That, I can. If you was to rat-hole a laundry marker I could show you how. You won't be disappointed. Got a pen with permanent ink? I'm partial to black."

The idea skidded past both ears and kept going. Cézanne turned to Velda. "We need a peace treaty before somebody kills somebody."

Velda's chuckles subsided. "That'd be me doing you in." Glowering, she riveted her attention on Duty. "Who's this?"

"You talkin' to me?" Duty, indignant.

"Pipe down, Miss Low Brow. I'm addressing Miss No Brow."

"Then why you studyin' me?"

"You're in my house. And you're Colored. And I don't recall advertising for a maid. And which one of you fools let that giraffe inside?"

Enigma trotted over and cold-nosed Velda's crotch. She beat him back with the broom. He growled low in his throat and scrambled into the dining room, circling the rug three times before plopping down exhausted.

"Listen, earwax, I ain't no maid," Duty said in a voice tight with controlled fury. "You got the broom. You fixin' to clean house or fly outta here?"

"I'm not taking sass from a Colored."

"Seems to me the only one colored around here is the one with titty-pink hair."

"Then you're a burglar." Velda's eyes darted around. "Where's my bat?"

"I don't steal." Duty's temper flared, along with her nostrils.

Cézanne introduced Deuteronomy Devilrow. "She's my ward for a few months."

"Can she cook?" Velda measured the girl through a squint.

Duty muttered, "Can she cook? Do my kinfolk hail from the Louisiana bayou? I can whip up concoctions you could only dream about . . . only maybe you won't like the ingredients . . . wrinkled old battleaxe. Get myself a owl feather, a crow feather, and a horned toad, you'll be wishin'—"

"That's enough, Duty." Cézanne attended to her aunt. "This situation has gotten completely out of hand."

Velda grinned. Wrinkles shifted like a Chinese roadmap. "I already thought of that. About two o'clock in the morning, while you were down here playing with yourself, I was thinking up ways to fix your little red wagon. Thought up a couple of good ones, too."

A jolt of pain shot past Cézanne's left eye, a reminder to unclench her teeth. Bright blue comets played in her field of vision. "I need this place."

With the panache of a lion-tamer, Velda glided to the dining room table and wrapped her hands around the top rung of a ladderback chair until her knuckles turned white. "I'm not moving."

"That makes you a squatter."

"Squatter." Duty put a finger to her lips. Maroon eyes stared thoughtfully at the pressed tin ceiling. "I like the sound of that. How 'bout we let that be my word for tomorrow? Is that like fly squatter?"

Cézanne silenced her with a glare. Her eyes shifted to Velda. "We both want the house."

"If you want me out of here you'll have to pay me off."

"Don't count on it." Cézanne used her know-it-all voice. "Constable Jinx Porter will set your stuff out on the curb so fast it'll make you dizzy."

"It'll take at least a month to evict me," Velda pointed out with a sinister chuckle. "I know the law. I can get into a lot of mischief in thirty days."

Duty mumbled, "I think we ought to fumigate the house with you in it, you old dung beetle."

Cézanne's aunt leaned across the chair back. She wagged a gnarled finger with oversized knuckles. "Gang up on me all you want. But first you've got to gain control of the house. Don't think I won't be there to contest the proceedings, you hussy. You weren't around when your father took sick. I've got restitution owed me for all the medical I shelled out."

"Fine. Deed any interest you think you have in this house over to me, and I'll cut you a check."

"Hot check, you mean. Why don't you write one out, throw it on the floor, and let's see if it bounces?"

"It isn't hot." Technically, it was practically guaranteed to combust as soon as the ink dried. She eased into a dining chair at the opposite end of the table and positioned her lame foot where nothing would contact it. "Take the money and never look back. Duty, bring me my purse." With the girl looking on, she whipped open her checkbook. "What's it going to take?"

"A hundred and fifty thousand ought to do it."

Velda's extortion demand hit her like a harpoon to the brain. "That's highway robbery."

"I only want what I spent on his upkeep. And maybe a little extra for my trouble."

"Are you talking dollars? Or pesos?"

"I suggest we compromise. Either let me stay here until the judge says I have to go or sell this dung heap, give me my money, and I'll find another house. Makes no difference to me."

"That's what you want? For me to sell it?"

"Or I could just live in it 'til I die. You could give me a life estate. After that, I wouldn't need it anymore. Meantime, you could run your office out of here in the daytime. I'd be able to come and go as I please and at nighttime. I could live upstairs."

Cézanne regarded her with suspicion. "What're you saying?

You want me to share my office with you?"

"No, Swiss cheese brain. I'm offering to give you office space in my house."

"I hate you. Kibitzer."

"Back at ya, harlot," Velda said. "I reckon we've got one of those symbiotic relationships." She showed her teeth. "Host-parasite. Kind of like a tick on a dog."

"Just so we have our roles straight, you're the tick. I'm the dog."

"Remains to be seen." Velda stuck her nose up in the air and sashayed out of the room with a flourish.

Duty walked over to Enigma. She leaned in low and muttered, "Don't much matter who's the tick, who's the dog. Before it's over, I'm gonna be animal control."

Chapter Ten

Having reached a standoff with Velda, Cézanne talked her into returning the old princess phone to the telephone nook in the downstairs hall. While Duty adjourned to the kitchen to whip up lunch and Velda plopped herself down in front of the big screen TV to watch "Judge Judy," Cézanne called the Johnson County Sheriff's Office and asked for Bobby Noah.

She ended up talking to Eunice, Bobby's receptionist, a thick-waisted grandmother with bleached blonde hair and a penchant for hair bows, and from that contact learned that nobody had seen him. She suggested he might have taken the week off. After all, Bobby's father owned dairy cattle. Maybe they were having trouble with the new milk machines.

"I called his house. I must've left twenty messages on the answering machine. Isn't that unusual for him not to call? Did it ever cross your mind that something bad might've happened?"

"Honey," Eunice drawled, "I'm just the right hand. Sheriff Noah's the boss. I do worry, but I report to him, not the other way around."

"If you should hear from him, ask him to call me."

Unexpectedly, Eunice relented. "Look, hon, I know how you're feeling. You're not the first lady I ever met who took a shine to our sheriff. But we did think you might be the one and that made things more pleasant around here because Sheriff Noah's been so chipper the past few months." Silence stretched between them. "Here's what I'll do. You give me your phone number, and if I hear anything, I'll give you a buzz. Fair enough?"

Cézanne rattled off the number to the law office.

Before she hung up, Eunice hatched another idea. "You know me, honey, I'm old-fashioned. I tell my granddaughters nice girls don't chase boys. But Sheriff Noah's not a boy, and you've got something totally different going on. Nothing's stopping you from driving out to his house."

Good point. No reason to stay ostrich-headed.

She tried Bobby's home phone one more time. The sheriff shared the ranch with his legally blind father, so hearing a woman's satiny voice at the other end of the line came as a big surprise.

"May I speak to Bobby?"

"Who's calling?"

"His fiancée. Who's this?"

"His other fiancée." Giggle.

Her stomach knotted. For several seconds, a low-level hum vibrated her sinus cavities until it filled her head like the spooling of a jet engine. Apparently, history repeated itself. She'd chosen badly, again. Thoughts of that lying Doug Driskoll cavorted in her head.

The woman with the schoolgirl voice put her on the spot. "Would you like me to give him a message?"

"Yes," she said, barely able to breathe. The unbidden image of a bleach-blonde bimbo wearing frosted lip balm and a Dairy Queen uniform acted like a punch in the gut. "Tell him I moved. And tell him never to call me." She severed the connection, replaced the receiver in its hook, and stared at her engagement ring in disbelief.

She decided not to give it back.

If he demanded its return, she'd take a meat tenderizer and render it into a thousand chigger-eye chips.

Duty called out from the kitchen. "I was thinkin' maybe tuna noodle casserole might be nize."

"Fine." Shell shocked, she moved into the living room with sluggish steps. "Hot rolls. That's a good idea."

Duty gave her one of her *Whatchoo mean?* looks.

Thoroughly bummed, Cézanne removed the diamond ring. She gave it one last, longing look before dropping it into the bottom of her purse.

"Miz Zan, we got any toothpicks?"

"Next to the sugar caddy."

"Who's got a sugar daddy?"

She slumped into a chair. While Duty banged pans, Velda broke into song. At first, the tune seemed playful. But once she warbled the chorus, the made-up ditty turned ugly. "The double-wide next door to mine just got sold to nig—"

Duty flew out of the kitchen with a cast iron skillet held high.

Velda took flight from the couch. Still spewing out offensive lyrics, she broke for the stairs clutching the TV remote.

Duty stomped through the dining room hot on her heels. "You come down here before I sew a butt-ugly doll and fix your droopy old neck for good."

The slammed door at the top of the steps echoed like a gunshot. A toggle bolt snicked into place. Duty trailed her to the landing and pounded the wood with her fists. Then she used the skillet.

"Open up, Velda. I'm gonna beat you senseless."

Instead of mediating the commotion, Cézanne locked herself in the bathroom for a good cry. After picking the last remnants of tissue from her puffy skin, she rinsed her face and had another go-round with the eyebrow pencil. With her eyes looking like a couple of scalded oysters, she returned to the living room and flopped onto the Biedermeier ready to plunge herself into the Rackley case.

Swelled to capacity, Erick Rackley's file contained a playground of information.

Cézanne sat on the uncomfortable sofa with her head bent in concentration, tabbing through the accordion folder until she came to the photographs.

She took a second look at Rackley's mug shot, assessing him in increments. Dark hair, nice bone structure. Eyes the color and luster of light brown M&Ms. With a look of helplessness and something else—unmitigated fear. She compared the mug shot to Rackley's wedding photo. He wore a tux and sported a grin like he'd just won a one-half interest in the Powerball.

In a way, he had. The bride's income potential soared above his.

Her eyes shifted to Yvonne's picture. Petite, with auburn hair cascading down her shoulders in billowy, highlighted waves. Huge, China blue irises looked even bigger behind the thick, square lenses of eyeglasses in vogue at the time. Perfect lips. Not full, not thin. And that skin. As if she just stepped off the set of a Dove commercial. If Yvonne's squeaky-clean appearance attracted Erick Rackley then she'd gravitated to the dangerous, adventurous spirit of her polar extreme. No mystery as to what caused the mutual attraction between the bad boy and the choirgirl. This was simply a case of positive and negative ions pulling at each other.

And the bride's parents. Oy vey. Peeled off the canvas of American Gothic, each with a hint of dread in their eyes and that pinched, *wish-I-were-anywhere-but-here* look captured in their faces.

She flipped to the pocket folder containing the audiotapes.

Checking her watch, she decided she had enough time to

drive over to her bungalow and pick up the tape machine. By now, the husband-wife police team who ran Cleaning Solutions should've finished sanitizing the house. If she left now, she'd be back in a jiffy.

She never got the chance.

Slash telephoned the house around ten that morning. The Kompressor had been processed for prints. Now the bucket of bolts was parked at the police auto impound yard, incurring a storage fee at a rate of fifty dollars a day. Since the insurance adjuster had already dropped by to evaluate her claim, she was free to have it towed to the Benz dealership for bodywork.

She pulled Duty off to the side, to a place in the kitchen where wretched Aunt Velda would be unlikely to overhear. "I'm heading out to the auto pound. Don't leave the house unless it's on fire."

"Got any matches?" Duty coyly dipped her chin.

"You're not contemplating arson, are you? Because if you decide to go that route, be sure to seal off the exits and get out before Velda does." She mustered a stern look, then winked to show she didn't mean it. Grabbing her purse, she fumbled for the keys.

"Miz Zan, you so bad." The girl ambushed her at the front door. "Miz Zan, maybe you ought to let me go along. Maybe Velda won't change the locks."

"*Ha.* That viper has a locksmith on speed dial."

"Remember the last time you went to the pound?"

How could she forget? Doug Driskoll lured her to the far end of the lot and locked her in the trunk of a Buick classic. If that wasn't enough to make blood coagulate and back up in her veins like a stopped-up sewer, the blanket of rats undulating toward her from the Trinity River was. She didn't even want to think about how he'd urinated on her through the holes in the trunk.

Never again would Driskoll get the upper hand.

She patted Duty's shoulder and told her not to worry.

Now if she only believed it herself.

The police impound yard sat between Main Street and Interstate 35 north of downtown. Railroad tracks laid to the immediate west. To the east, a bridge leading to the freeway. Behind the pound, beyond the perimeter of cyclone fence topped with a continuous coil of razor wire, the Trinity River snaked past. She turned into the lot and parked next to the faded buttercup-yellow portable building with one pressing thought—sign the release so the wrecker driver could pick up the Kompressor and leave. She wrenched herself out of the Catera and fitted the crutches beneath her arms.

The auto pound office reeked. Years of stale cigar and cigarette smoke had been absorbed by the walls and flooring. Her nose snapped shut in self-defense as she looked around for an attendant.

In sauntered Doug Driskoll.

Cézanne's confidence tanked.

Gravity worked its pull on her blood. What didn't clot behind her eyeballs settled in her feet like liquid lead. Instead of pivoting on her good foot and heading for the exit, her crutches turned into tent stakes and anchored her to the floor.

Transfixed, she stood in Driskoll's presence. The stinking sex fiend wasn't supposed to be assigned to day shift. When she took leave from the PD, he'd been relegated to permanent nights. He was lazy and unmotivated and spent the majority of time with a cell phone stuck to his ear. If breathing wasn't an involuntary reflex, Driskoll would be dead.

Windblown hair the color of two parts salt to one part pepper stood up like porcupine quills. Wind burned cheeks made his olive complexion look as if he'd taken sandpaper to them. He tossed a clipboard onto the desk and favored her with a grin, but his green eyes glinted with hostility. When he shrugged out of a sheepskin-lined jacket, her breath caught. Driskoll wore the tartan flannel she'd given him for Christmas the previous year.

He sideswiped her, easing around the desk and into his chair. With booted feet propped up on the desk and his shoulders pressed against the seat back, he swept her with his gaze.

"Lookin' good, Zan." His attention lingered, momentarily, on the cast before traveling up her gabardine slacks and resting on her face. "I've missed you."

"Yeah? I missed you, too, but my aim's getting better." Said nastily.

He squinted. "What's with the brows? They look like corporal chevrons."

She unclenched her jaw. Driskoll had a way of making her feel contaminated. She wished she'd buttoned her charmeuse silk shirt all the way up to the collar now that his gemstone eyes had strayed to her cleavage. "I'm here to sign for my vehicle."

"The Mercedes. Nice wheels but a little banged up. You okay?"

"Better than your wife'll be when I get hold of her."

Driskoll chuckled. "The old ball and chain."

"I don't suppose you've seen her?"

"The detective asked me that, already. The Chief didn't believe me. I had to submit to a polygraph. I passed." He opened a drawer, pulled out a pack of cigarettes and tapped one out. A match hissed against the sole of his ropers; he touched the flame to the cigarette and drew in a deep breath. Smoke snaked out his nostrils. "You've thinned down. I thought you had somebody to buy you dinner. Maybe I heard wrong."

Her heart skipped a beat. Maybe Darlene told him about the engagement to Bobby. "Where'd you hear that?"

"Teddy Vaughn. He and Slash dropped by earlier."

Her breath went shallow. Driskoll wore his wedding ring. If he'd been wearing it while he was conning her into going out with him, she'd have run from him. And now, even though he'd never get any traction with her again—getting shot at by an angry wife could do that to a person—it still hurt. "Where's the paperwork on my Kompressor?"

He pushed the clipboard close, swung his feet off the desk, and planted them on the floor. While she flipped through the log, he went behind the front counter and fumbled through the key locker. After dropping the signed receipt onto the desk and shoving an outstretched palm at him, Driskoll pressed the keys into her hand.

An electric jolt went straight to her—

—God Almighty.

"For what it's worth," he said, "I can't get you out of my mind."

The Captain and Tennille.

Driskoll couldn't even come up with original pickup lines, the masher. He pirated them from songs, movies, or soap operas. She should've whacked him over the head with her crutch and hobbled out the door, but her legs were tingling so much that the floor seemed to vibrate. She wondered if he heard her heart pounding.

"Something else on your mind?" Driskoll's eyes smoldered. Stubbing out the cigarette, he exhaled a contrail of smoke, reached into a drawer and popped a square of mint gum from its plastic seal onto his tongue.

"You were the first line officer on the call to Erick and Yvonne Rackley's." She watched his brow furrow. "I'd like to ask a few questions."

"Sure." He reached under the desk and tipped a wastebasket enough to get rid of the gum. "Have dinner with me."

Chills zipped up her spine. Same old Doug. She leaned on

the crutches with her knee slightly bent. Unexpectedly, he advanced. Hooked an arm around her neck and put a lip lock on her. Ground himself against her.

The air thinned. She sensed a lightheaded rush. The Driskoll charm had returned full force.

He unhinged his jaw. His tongue snaked out and slicked along her mouth. Abruptly, he released his grip. She pulled away, sucking in great gulps of air.

"A little cold in here?" He stared at her nipples. "Or maybe I still do it to you?"

"I don't think about you at all except when I check the Ds in the obituary column each morning."

He whispered, "I still love you," and she thought the top of her head would blow off. "Dinner at eight?"

"The only way I'll come is if I bring my own car."

"That's not the only way you'll come, babe."

He reached out, and she drilled his foot with a crutch. Driskoll hopped back like a Mexican jumping bean. The guy had the capacity to ruin her life.

Outside and coming straight at them, heavy shoe soles pounded the asphalt. The door banged open, and an old man entered. He carried two fast-food sacks and a cardboard tray with two drink cups.

"Here y'go, short timer."

Driskoll grinned big. He caught one of the brown bags midair and opened it up for inspection. The smell of burger and fries wafted out.

Cézanne glanced Driskoll's way. "What did he mean, short timer? Are you quitting the force?"

The idea was enough to make her want to return to Homicide.

Driskoll's face brightened. "You didn't hear? I'm getting my old job back. In Narcotics."

She shook her head in disgust. Narcotics was the perfect place to troll for new victims. Crack whores gave it up at the drop of a rock. Most wouldn't file complaints with Internal Affairs if Driskoll got a little nookie on the side. Even if they did, criminal records and drug habits usually ruled them out as credible witnesses.

"I'll tell you what I remember about Erick Rackley, counselor. Plan to spend three or four hours with me tonight. We've got a lot of catching up to do."

Without comment, Cézanne hitched to the door. As she prepared to descend the steps, she gave him a backward glance and let him know what she thought of his idea with a stiff middle finger.

Chapter Eleven

Duty started warting her the moment she walked into the house. She wanted to shop Cox's sale and claimed to have stockpiled her Christmas money for just such an event. As for Velda, the girl reasoned the old lady would sleep through the afternoon.

"What do you want to buy?"

"Well, I was thinkin' maybe if I'm gonna help you out 'round the office, I might get me some stockings and a pair of nize heels. Make me look taller so I can boss people like you do."

"Who's paying?"

"I can cover the cheap stuff. I figure you can write off the rest as a business expense. Maybe get me some new threads while we're at it."

"What about all those clothes I bought you last time you were here?"

"Ain't new anymore."

They agreed to go mid-afternoon, but Slash dropped by, unannounced, at a quarter past one. The buckskin jacket he wore over his department-issue knit shirt brought out the red in his hair, and Cézanne figured any deer at the salt lick would have gladly given its hide to warm such a fine looking man.

She opened the door and stepped aside. He carried in what appeared to be a scale model of a house pieced together using foam-board and glue.

The first words out of his mouth were a commentary on her eyebrows. "A little stubble. Five o'clock shadow. Definitely an improvement. Maybe drawn a bit long but if you put glasses on nobody should notice."

"I don't need glasses. Besides, Duty drew them on so I wouldn't say anything bad if I were you."

Slash scanned the room. "Who's Duty?"

"My ward for the next few months. She often whips up potions so if you say anything derogatory, you could wake up with shrunken testicles."

He seemed to cringe involuntarily, then headed straight for the dining room table with the murder house. Duty came out of the kitchen with her hands dusted in flour.

They assessed each other through the silence.

Slash said, "I remember you."

"I remember you, too."

"Didn't you swipe a patrol car?"

"Borrowed. I don't steal. Cops were shootin' at me, so I thought it'd be a good idea to clear out."

Slash slid his thumbs into his belt loops. In boots, he towered over them. "It's all coming back to me. You led everyone on a high-speed chase. Drove a brand new car into the Trinity River." He grinned big. "Nice job."

Duty high-fived him. Flour drifted down like tiny snowflakes. She pulled a cup towel from a kangaroo pouch in her chef's apron, wiped her hands, and took a seat at the table. With her legs curled under her and her elbows propped a few inches from the model home, she sank her chin into her hands and started quizzing him.

"Is this what you take to court to show where the dead guy was at the time of the murder? Is that real blood on the wall?"

"Red nail polish."

Pinprick dots speckled the inner partition square where a matchbox-sized bed had been placed. On the flat area outside the L-shaped house was a marine-blue, kidney-shaped outline that Cézanne assumed depicted Erick Rackley's swimming pool.

Duty said, "I could make a little person to go in that bed. I'm good at sewin' cloth people with hair and everything. Like last night, after everybody went to bed, I sewed a scraggly little doll with pink hair. I had to make the hair out of a cotton ball and colored it with Pepto Bismol, but I guess I didn't let it dry enough because the wad of cotton kept fallin' off. You got any SuperGlue?"

Upstairs, Velda unleashed a damning scream.

Slash bounded up the steps in twos. In the time it took Cézanne to follow, Duty rushed into the kitchen, returned with the granddaddy of all meat cleavers and shot past like Cochise. At the top of the landing, Slash stood before the barricaded door trying to talk over Velda's muffled cries.

"Are you hurt? You need an ambulance?"

"Get away from the damned door and let me be. I'm old and naked and my clothes are on the bed, you damned sex pervert."

Slash cut his eyes in Cézanne's direction. "*Dejá vu.* I'm having a flashback. You want to handle this?"

She ordered Duty to put away the meat cleaver, wrangled her way to the top of the stairs, and tried to charm Velda into opening the door.

The bolt snicked back, followed by the slap of bare feet against the hardwoods. With a loud bang, Velda locked herself in the bathroom.

"Sounds like the death throes of a rendering plant in there. You didn't cut an artery shaving, did you?" Cézanne said with strained hope.

Velda sniffled. "You wish."

"What's with the slaughterhouse imitation?"

Velda cracked the door open a sliver. She'd wrapped herself in a blue spa towel and draped a smaller one over her head like a shriveled Madonna. Hair dye leached onto wizened skin, creating apricot stains on her forehead. Her eyes cut in the direction of the stairs. Her chin quivered. "Are they gone?"

Cézanne looked the length of the hall. "No, they're still on the landing, waiting to process the crime scene."

"You don't have to get smart."

She looked past Velda's wrinkled shoulder and saw nothing of interest, then focused her gaze on her aunt's pleated neck. The old lady had enough folds of flesh to upholster a small chair; the idea that they shared the same DNA creeped her out. She fervently hoped she took after her mother's side. The Rosens might be crazier than a rat in a drainpipe, but when it came to skin, theirs had great elasticity. In a world preoccupied with sex appeal, good skin and voluptuous breasts trumped just about everything.

"What's all this caterwauling?"

Tears tracked Velda's face. "My hair."

"What about it?"

"Gone." She peeled back the towel. Other than a few tufts of peach fuzz, her scalp was as slick as a honeydew melon—with the same pale sheen.

"Oh, no." Reflexively, Cézanne clapped a hand over her gaping mouth. Deep down, she felt a pang of guilt.

Duty hollered, "Wassup?"

Slash's hand hovered near his gun butt.

Cézanne leaned in close and whispered, "What happened?"

Between sobs, Velda ran down the problem.

"I washed it, same as yesterday. Only I might've left the lather on too long. But I don't know why that would matter. I left it on last night on account of it was time to put the color enhancer in my hair."

"Hair dye. Say it. You dye your hair."

Velda's eyes went shrewd. "You don't know that for sure."

"Give me a break. How many people do you know who were

born with clown hair?"

"You're hateful. Just like your mother. Never did like her."

"Leave my mother out of this," Cézanne snapped. She pointed at Velda's cue ball scalp. "You were saying?"

"I wanted to make sure the color enhancer took. Next thing I know, I'm rinsing, and it's falling out in clumps and clogging the drain. Why would it do that? It's like it just disintegrated."

Tainted shampoo.

Cézanne's stomach twisted. She warned Duty not to use her toiletries, but she never suspected Velda might slip downstairs and filch them.

"The other night, when you swiped our food, did you take my shampoo?"

Beady eyes hardened. Velda's chin corrugated, drawing several inches of skin back into place. "Stingy. You had plenty."

"Wait here."

"That's the stupidest thing I ever heard. Do you really think I'm going anywhere looking like this?"

Down the hall, Cézanne offered an explanation to Slash. "Darlene struck again."

"Whatchoo mean? Is Velda bald? 'Cause if Velda's a skinhead, I wanna see." Giddy with excitement, Duty thundered down the hall in five strides. Velda slammed the door shut and toggled the bolt. Duty flattened her palms against the doorframe and pressed an ear to the wood. "Let's see yo' head, Velda. I wanna see if you look like E.T." And then, "Miz Zan, if Velda look like E.T., can we put her on the porch and charge people like a sideshow, maybe gimme spendin' money to shop at Cox's 'til I get my real job?"

After Slash collected the shampoo as evidence, Cézanne picked up the tape recorder from the bungalow. The couple from Cleaning Solutions estimated the house would be ready the following morning, but Cézanne was in no hurry to reoccupy it. She wasn't about to let Velda have the run of Bob's place while the probate case was pending.

By late afternoon, a couple of hired hands—students from Texas Christian University—showed up to move her desk, a chair, a couple of file cabinets, and an old oak barrister's bookcase into what had now become the law office lobby. In the midst of the commotion, Velda sneaked downstairs. She wore a mustard-colored felt hat with a peacock plume sticking out of the band.

With Duty loitering within earshot, Cézanne buttonholed Velda and pulled her off to one side. "I've given this some thought."

"Stop the presses."

"I'm serious. Since we have this host-parasite relationship, I've decided there's something you can do for me. A little problem I need help with."

"What makes you think I'd help you?"

"*Quid pro quo.* In exchange for doing something for me, I'm prepared to do something for you."

Velda's eyes glinted. The bright green sweater she'd slung over her back and looped around her neck by the arms caused the gray rims surrounding her hazel eyes to deepen. "I won't help you operate a cathouse."

"I'm not a madam, and I don't operate a brothel. I'm an attorney."

"Lawyering's merely another form of prostitution."

Cézanne huffed out her irritation. "Hear me out. Since I started practicing I can't seem to collect all the money people owe me. If I spend time running it down, I can't take on new clients. I was thinking maybe you wouldn't mind making a few phone calls to the deadbeats, maybe encourage them to come in and settle their bills."

Velda folded her arms where saggy breasts should've been. She'd forgotten her prostheses, and the red hibiscus blossoms on the gold background of her latest muumuu drew attention to her flat chest.

With a haughty air, she said, "And what're you doing for me?"

"You obviously don't have a car. I could drive you to the store from time to time. I could take you to the hairdresser."

"What for? All I've got left is one little Hare Krishna rat-tail sticking out of the back of my head."

Duty piped up. "What's a Hairy Krishna? Oh, I get it. That's his name. Harry Krishna. That's funny. Never heard of him. Is Harry a beautician? Can he get Velda her 'do' back?"

"I look like I've got alopecia. What the hell do I need with a hairdresser?"

Duty moseyed over. She tugged Cézanne's sleeve. "What's alopecia?"

"Baldness," she muttered, and mentally kicked herself for not pointing the girl to the dictionary.

Velda whipped around snarling. "It's mean of you to remind me my hair's gone."

Duty put a finger to her chin. A pensive expression settled over her face. "Alopecia," she said softly. "I think I would like that to be my word for the day. Alopecia."

Velda glowered at Cézanne. "You give her alopecia, and I'll stuff this house shoe up your rump."

"What's wrong with alopecia? It's a perfectly good word."

"Because I don't want to hear it in a sentence five stinking times."

When the movers positioned the last of the furniture, Cézanne settled the bill and hurried to dress for the dinner appointment with Driskoll. She decided on a slinky black cocktail dress with a Chanel jacket in tropical weight wool.

With her elbows on the bathroom counter and her chin resting in her palms, Duty leaned in close, watching as she drew on her brows.

"I could do that for you. That I could. You'd look like Marilyn Monroe when I finished."

Cézanne stared at her reflection and continued to pencil a line along the stubble. "Marilyn Monroe with brown hair and small breasts, you mean. That would make me Olive Oyl."

Duty laughed. "You so funny, Miz Zan. Who you goin' out with? Does Mista Bobby know you like that Slash dude? You axe me, Slash gotta nize booty. And I think he's sweet on you."

She felt a heart pang at the mention of Bobby's name. "Slash is just being attentive because he wants me to take on the Rackley case. And this isn't a date, it's business. I'm meeting Doug Driskoll."

Duty gasped. She straightened to her full height and jammed her fists against her waistless form. "I don't think you ought to go anywhere with Mista Driskoll, you axe me. He's no good, Miz Zan. Gonna be courtin' trouble. That Darlene, she'll come after you."

Cézanne shuddered at the idea.

She surveyed herself in the mirror. As an afterthought, she penciled on a thread of lip liner, filled in her lips with Jezebel-red lipstick, and decided she didn't look half bad.

"Back in awhile." She patted Duty's shoulder and limped to the door.

The girl folded her fingers into her palm a few times in a half-hearted wave. "Hope you know whatchoo doin'."

"I do. Don't feed the dog sweets while I'm gone."

Chapter Twelve

It was a good thing the high-dollar steakhouse had valet parking since Cézanne had removed her cast and rewrapped her injured foot in an ace bandage. Inside the posh restaurant, Driskoll stood near the entrance with a highball glass in one hand and a menu in the other. When he saw her, his eyes sparkled.

"Let me help you." He offered his arm.

"I can do it myself." She didn't trust his roving hands.

The waiter seated them at a table downstairs, behind a partition of varnished wood and glass that overlooked the length of the bar. In low light conditions, Driskoll looked the part of the gentleman in his navy blazer, blue pinpoint oxford, and khaki slacks.

After the waiter left with their drink orders—his, a rum and Coke; hers, a piña colada—Driskoll did a quick lean-in and helped her shrug out of her jacket.

"You look good enough to eat."

She shook out the cloth napkin and let it parachute into her lap. "I'm here for the sole purpose of discussing Erick Rackley. I want to know what happened from the time you were dispatched to the call until you left the station at the end of your shift."

"I mean it, babe, you look hot." He reached for her elbow, but she moved before he made contact. Easing against his chair back, he gave her the eye. "You're not going to let me touch you? Not even a friendly little pat on the arm for old time's sake?"

She locked eyes with him. "Let's go over it once more. You're married. Your wife tried to kill me—numerous times. I'm here to get information on Erick Rackley, not to resurrect a dead relationship."

A lupine grin spread across his face. "Slip your hand under the tablecloth. Let's see if you can resurrect the dead."

A waitress appeared with their drinks, and their waiter presented menus. They left after a quick run-down on the house specials.

Driskoll took a sip from his glass and stared, rheumy-eyed. "I love the way you look in that dress. When I'm in bed thinking about you, I—"

"Don't be thinking about me, especially not in bed." Cézanne scowled. "What I want to know is what you saw at Erick Rackley's. You got to the house. Was your back-up there?"

"Just me. The house sits between two inclines. It's a split-level, and the middle section is built on stilts. The creek actually flows underneath where the living room juts out over it. To get to the front door from the street, you have to take a long sidewalk that meanders down to the house. The Rackleys installed lantern lights on each side of the path so guests wouldn't break their necks. It's tricky navigating."

An image formed in her head. "Describe the front door."

"Solid as a granite slab. You walk inside, and there's a huge, open-concept room with a rock fireplace at one end. Straight ahead, a series of plate glass windows cover the length of the room. When you look out, you see creek water rushing twenty feet below. Hardwood floors. I remember the sound of Rackley's feet thundering across the planks to get to the door. MedStar paramedics charged in behind me."

Their server returned to take their orders. Driskoll selected a New York strip. Cézanne chose tenderloin and let Driskoll select their vegetables *à la carte.* Asparagus. Potatoes. House salad.

Once the waiter left, Driskoll continued.

"Rackley was in his 'Looms. His hair was sticking straight up like somebody'd buzzed his scrotum with a stun gun. He was snockered, but he managed to show us to their bedroom. That's where we found her."

"Did he have on shoes?"

Driskoll took a drink. Ice clinked in his glass. "Don't recall. What difference does it make?"

"Go on."

"I only had a couple of seconds to scan the room before the paramedics rushed in to resuscitate her." He unbuttoned his collar. Loosened his tie. "Speaking of resuscitation, I'd like to take you home, rip off your clothes, and throw you down."

Schmuck.

"I could let Big Doug out to play—"

"That's enough."

"—maybe get you to perform a little CPR magic on him."

She cringed inwardly. Locked her knees together and fought the erotica conjured up by his nasty talk. "What'd you see when you first came into the bedroom?"

"The victim was on the bed in a sheer nightgown."

"Long or short?"

"Ankle-length. I remember because I wanted her to have on one of those skimpy silk teddies. Don't look at me that way. Guys love those things. I still think about that trashy little red number you wore for me that time."

"You're deranged. Victoria's Secret isn't trashy. Stick to the topic."

He relaxed against the chair back. "Except for the GSW to the chest, she looked like Sleeping Beauty waiting to be kissed. And of course, her eyes were half-open and pink froth was coming out of her mouth. Blood on the wall above the headboard."

A waitress appeared with their salads. She placed a basket of homemade rolls center table, and asked if they needed anything. Before Cézanne could mention butter, a waiter zipped by on his way to serve an elderly couple at the next table and deposited a silver dish with a whipped yellow ball in it next to her plate.

Alone again, Cézanne pressed for more details. "What'd she look like?"

"I'd have to say she looked dead. That's fairly accurate since she was dead."

"I'm referring to the color of her skin. How she was placed? Did the crime scene look staged?"

Driskoll ignored her. He spread his napkin across his lap, grabbed his fork, and dug in.

Cézanne prompted him with an under-the-table foot nudge. "Did she have on her glasses?"

"I don't remember. Who cares? She was pretty much dead and didn't need them."

It matters.

"What were you doing while the paramedics worked on her?"

"Mainly keeping Rackley out of the way."

According to Driskoll, Erick Rackley kept trying to edge around him to oversee the resuscitation efforts. His job was to cut down on Rackley's interference, to ask what happened, and to make sure he didn't taint the crime scene any more than he already had.

"Did Rackley say anything?"

"Claimed it was a break-in."

The intruder theory. Only Driskoll's written report noted that the doors and windows were locked from the inside.

"How many paramedics?" She envisioned the emergency medical technicians taking a pulse, listening through stethoscopes, stringing IVs, and giving the ER doctor a rundown. "What were the EMTs doing to her?"

"Ogling her tits. ShitifIknow." Driskoll slammed back the last of his drink and assessed her through glazed eyes. "They had to cut the pillowcase off her neck—"

"What?"

Her reaction sheared conversations at nearby tables. She gave a weak smile and refocused her attention on her dinner companion. Two servers returned. While one whisked away their salad plates, the other presented their steaks.

Driskoll grabbed his knife, sawed off a hunk, and scarfed it down.

Cézanne pronounced hers perfect. She ordered another piña colada and continued the probe.

"Tell me about the pillowcase."

"Rackley said he tied it around her neck while he was talking to the dispatcher. Said the dispatcher told him to make a tourniquet to slow the blood flow. Where I come from, a tourniquet around the neck's called a noose."

It made no sense. Unless Rackley wanted to finish her off.

"How'd he act?"

Driskoll did an exaggerated eye roll. "He was pig drunk. And he was a basket case. Hopping around from one foot to the other . . ." Abruptly, he clammed up.

"You remembered something." Her voice resonated with excitement.

"Barefooted. He didn't have shoes on. I remember looking at his feet. We were standing on the carpet, but he was hopping around like the floor was cold."

"Probably nervous. His wife was dying. Did you Mirandize him?"

Driskoll wagged his steak knife and called a halt to the interrogation. "I'm paying good money for this, Zan. The least you can do is eat it while it's hot."

Reluctantly, she stopped grilling him. As she ate, she slipped into her thoughts and wondered what Bobby Noah was doing.

Well, hell. Not what he was doing, more like who he was doing. She sipped her sissy drink and felt some of the tension leave her shoulders.

"I could take you there," Driskoll said, "to the murder house. Let you see the layout for yourself."

He had flecks of asparagus stuck between his teeth. She took a sharp mental picture in case she ever felt weak-kneed around him. And she decided not to tell him.

"What about the owners?"

Driskoll smiled. His eyes crinkled at the corners. "It's for sale. Tomorrow morning, assuming you can still walk, we could get the realtor to meet us there. Introduce ourselves as Mr. and Mrs. Doug looking for the perfect home." His grin drooped. "I know what you're thinking, Zan. I can tell by the way you're chewing the inside of your mouth. You're plotting. You're thinking you'll take my idea and go it alone."

Mind reader.

"Only you need me. If I go along, I can point out where things were. You never know what I might remember once we get inside that house."

Limiting her time with Driskoll seemed wise, but this made sense. Reluctantly, she accepted the offer.

He pushed his empty plate away. "How's business? You rich yet? Because I've always wanted to be married to a rich woman."

"I'm hanging on by the skin of my teeth."

He held out his hand, palm-up. "Gimme your business cards. I know people. I can drum up a few clients for you while you're waiting to settle Pennzoil-Texaco."

He appeared sincere.

Against her better judgment, she dug out a handful of cards. On the back of one, she wrote the number of the house on South University. "This is where I'm conducting my law business."

The server appeared long enough for Driskoll to decline dessert and coffee and left a leather folder containing the check on the table.

Driskoll opened the flap. His eyes widened. He squirmed in his seat, removed his wallet, pulled out a credit card, and tucked it inside. The waiter breezed by, scooped it up with a flourish, and practically arabesqued from the room.

Cézanne was slipping into her jacket when the man returned, stern-faced. He whispered in Driskoll's ear. Whatever he said made Driskoll drop his napkin on the tablecloth. A grotesque expression formed on his face.

"Phone call," he said. "Be right back."

Her mind free-associated in his absence. Maybe someday they'd be friends again. If his wife stumbled into quicksand, and the Earth didn't burp her back up, that is.

She noticed the waiter lingering behind the partition. Driskoll walked toward the table with a tight expression straining his face.

He slid into his seat. "Don't know how to tell you this, babe, but dinner's on you. My credit card's maxed out."

She stared in stricken silence, aware of her eyes scalding in their sockets. Gradually, she became aware of her gaping mouth. She wanted to pick up her steak knife and plunge it into his dead, black heart, but the server had already removed the flatware.

"What makes you think I brought any money?" she said through clenched teeth. "You invited me as your guest, remember?"

"You don't have any cash on you? That sucks. Looks like somebody's gonna have to do dishes."

"I'm not doing dishes you egotistical little prick. And I'm not buying your dinner."

"Write it off as a business expense."

She opened her handbag, pulled out two twenties and a five, and signaled the waiter with a crook of a finger. "Here y'go. Split the ticket. This covers my dinner, drinks, and tip."

She pushed back from the table, stood on wobbly legs, and asked a favor of their server. "Would you be a prince and assist me to the door? I need to retrieve my car from valet parking."

With the shades lowered over the second floor windows and the glass on the first floor uncovered like a slack-jawed, lazy giant, the old house appeared to be asleep when Cézanne arrived home from the Driskoll disaster. One glaring change became obvious as soon as she flicked on the lamp switch and entered the front room.

Duty hadn't made their beds on the floor. As a matter of fact, the girl and her dog were nowhere in sight. Halfway up the steps, she heard Enigma's raspy wheeze clacking like a spoon drawn over a washboard. A locomotive whistle followed each intake of breath. It brought such joy to hear the racket coming from inside of the bedrooms that she could barely contain her excitement.

Like the West Bank and the Gaza Strip, Velda relinquished a portion of territory. But at what price?

Whatever the old biddy wanted was probably worth it. And to think it had taken Deuteronomy Devilrow to talk her into it.

At the top of the landing, Cézanne gave the doorknob a twist. It gave way, allowing her unguided access. She counted five doors in all. Which meant at least one bathroom and probably four bedrooms. The one closest to the landing appeared to be Velda's. When turned, the crystal knob refused to give.

She crept down the hall, atop an Oriental runner, past the bathroom to an open door. Moonlight slanted through a large window, reflecting the patina of two Jenny Lind beds. Each had been butted against a wall, beckoning houseguests with their satiny glow. Duty lay beneath the covers of one, her dark corn-rows barely visible with the blankets pulled over her chin. In the opposite bed, Enigma opened his eyes, guarding his mistress like the great Sphinx. Cézanne pulled the door to and made her way further down the hall.

The next room must've been Bob's.

White chenille bedspread. Wool tartan blanket on top. Fluffy pillows piled at the head of the mission-style bed. Comfy looking. A man's haven.

A walnut spinet desk near the window contained a display of nautical maps and personal papers browned from age and rubber-banded together in neat bundles. In the center of the ceiling, an ornate light fixture with eight butterscotch shades overhung a Hamadan rug. Tomorrow she'd study the book titles lined up on the shelves of an ancient bureau bookcase with wavy glass panels on the doors. See what kind of literature the old man read.

She took a long breath and closed her eyes, inhaling the lingering scent of pipe tobacco. She opened her lids, switched off the light, and made her way down the hall to the next room.

A flick of the wall switch illuminated a crystal fixture. It hung from a plaster ceiling medallion and resembled a huge glass pineapple accented in bronze. Prisms of light danced on pink wallpaper, playing across the pale blue ceiling like a sky full of comets. A canopy bed with a white crocheted coverlet complemented its sheer fabric skirt in a tea rose print; gauzy swags of material linking each mahogany poster cascaded to the floor like a bridal train.

The patina of a fall-front desk positioned near the window had been polished to a high luster. In the far corner of the room, an old steamer trunk served as a coffee table for a handful of magazines fanned across its top. Drawn into the room by an arrangement of silver-framed pictures hanging from the walls, she inwardly thanked Duty for not commandeering the room made for a princess.

She kicked off her shoe and loosened the ace bandage on her injured foot. The plan to ease onto the bed long enough to figure out if the mattress was lumpy vanished like a genie. The moment her body sank into the featherbed and her head hit the down-filled pillow, her last conscious thought concerned this magical transport to Candyland . . .

. . . where a weary player could rest on a marshmallow cloud.

Chapter Thirteen

The telephone's persistent ring shrilled out a little after nine the next morning, shearing Cézanne's dream-filled slumber. She could use a jolt from a cattle prod to get started. With her robe loosely cinched, she trudged down the staircase, unable to intercept Duty as she bolted from her place at the dining room table to answer it.

"Who's callin'? Doug Driskoll? I thought I told you to stay away from Miz Zan." Long pause. "She cannot be disturbed."

Cézanne waved her hands in a no motion, but Duty continued her rant.

"Take a message? I will not. I'm a guest. I'm not the housekeeper. If you want to talk to her you can just get off yo' rusty-dusty and drive over here."

Cézanne wrenched the phone away. Casting a slanty-eyed glare, Duty slinked back to her breakfast.

According to Driskoll, he wrangled an appointment to meet the realtor at eleven. She'd barely have enough time to shower, grab a bowl of Cheerios, and meet him in the parking lot by Texas Christian University's football stadium.

Before leaving, she turned over a list of clients for Velda to dun for money and left instructions with Duty on what to cook for lunch. Dressed in a black cashmere turtleneck and black tropical wool slacks with the left leg gathered up enough to accommodate her cast, she grabbed a matching boiled wool jacket and her purse and headed out the door.

Duty trotted up with the crutches. "My Unca Ezra's got a sayin': You can't shine a sneaker. That Mista Driskoll, he hasn't changed a bit. Gonna getchoo killed." Huge maroon eyes misted with worry. Her chin corrugated. "Why not go with Slash? He's nize. I like Mista Slash."

Cézanne patted the girl's shoulder. "I know what I'm doing."

"You gotta gun? Because I think you should take a gun. If Mista Driskoll pulls a fast one you can brain him with the butt."

"If it'll make you feel any better, we'll go to Cox's and buy those shoes when I get back."

Duty brightened. "Can I get stockings, too? I don't like pantyhose. Black women have trouble with pantyhose. Pantyhose rub the hair on our legs wrong. I think I would like silk stockings and a garter belt. My momma, Thessalonia Devilrow, she bought a pair of those stockings from Victoria's Secret with the rubber grips on 'em. Only she was walkin' outside a bar on Galveston Island with that no-account Jerome and those hose rolled down around her ankles. Can I have a garter belt?" A sheepish grin played across her lips. "I think garter belts are nize."

Cézanne left her on the porch with a cheery wave and a "We'll see."

She drove less than a mile to the football stadium. Driskoll had parked his white pickup at the mouth of the parking lot next to an empty space. She whipped the Catera into the slot beside him and hit the electric window button, powering the tinted glass halfway down.

"Get in before we're late," he said.

In no time, they were headed for Erick Rackley's former address.

The realtor, a trim, sixtyish, high-octane, chain smoker introduced herself as Claudia Toomey. She beckoned them to follow, warning of the treacherous descent down the path to the split-level house. Railroad ties shored up each flagstone step, but the narrow path remained steep. On rainy days or before the sun burned off the dew, the rocks could be as slick and dangerous as black ice.

Cézanne's stomach fluttered at the notion.

Driskoll read her mind. "I have an idea." He took her crutches and passed them to Mrs. Toomey. By the time Cézanne snapped to the plan, he'd already scooped her up in his arms. "Lead the way."

As she stared evil directly in the eye, the realtor navigated ahead of them. If she overheard Driskoll's lewd suggestions, she didn't let on.

"Your legs are nice and firm, babe. You've been working out." He copped a cheap feel. "I was thinking maybe later we could go to my place."

"Fat chance." Unexpectedly, his footing wobbled. She tightened her grip on his neck and held on for dear life. "You do this about as well as a cow dances."

"You miss me, Zan."

"Like a brain misses a tumor. Stop talking and watch where you're going."

"I love the way you smell. Coconut's my favorite." He sniffed her neck.

"It's hairspray. And if you do that again I'll slap you so hard you'll miss quail season. I'm not kidding. You'll be missing teeth."

Mrs. Toomey reached the front door. She opened the lock box, removed the key, and waited for them to catch up. Less than twenty feet from a wooden deck that ran the length of the house, Driskoll nuzzled her neck. Breath scented with mouthwash warmed her skin.

"When we get inside, ask to use the bathroom. Take off all your clothes, and I'll excuse myself to check on you. The things

I could do—"

"Drop dead."

"—to make you sing high 'C'."

The front door swung open. He flashed the realtor a broad smile. "This is great. Lots of privacy. Just what we're looking for. Can you walk by yourself, sweetheart?"

"Don't call me that."

Mrs. Toomey regarded them with curiosity. Driskoll chuckled.

Unceremoniously, he deposited Cézanne across the threshold, onto the maple plank flooring. "She hates public displays of affection, don't you sweetie?"

She showed him her fist.

Inside, Driskoll set the ground rules. He wanted to get the feel of the place, so would Mrs. Toomey mind waiting outside while they scoped it out on their own? The disclosure that they were cash buyers shored up his credibility. Their guide excused herself to the rear balcony for a smoke. Driskoll gave Cézanne a bow at the waist and a swashbuckling hand-swipe through the air.

She now had the run of the place.

He slung an arm around her shoulders. "Let's do it. I'll keep a lookout while you—"

"Do you ever think of anything besides sex?"

"You make me crazy. I want you."

She thought back to their last horrible encounter. "You locked me in the trunk of a car and took a leak on me."

"You pulled a gun on me."

"I should've shot you between the eyes."

"I was frustrated, babe. When I think about you my dick gets hard. When my dick gets hard I think about you."

"We're here to reconstruct events the night Yvonne Rackley died."

"Gimme some." Driskoll went for his zipper.

She grabbed a hunk of skin near his ear and pinched, adding a corkscrew twist to double the pain. With his attention instantly redirected, his memory returned. In the spirit of cooperation, he recalled additional details about the night he rolled up at the murder call.

Before they left the property with Mrs. Toomey's business card in hand, Cézanne had a clear picture of the layout. She knew what kind of furniture the Rackleys owned and where they positioned it. Even better, she had a chance to check the windows for replaced glass and screens.

There were none. Even the doors bore no striation marks from having been jimmied.

Which put one theory to rest.

The night Yvonne Rackley died there was no intruder.

Unless one was already present when the couple arrived home.

An odd thing happened when Cézanne returned to the house on South University. Besides the faint smell of gas from the space heaters turned up high, she whiffed the spicy aroma of Cajun-seasoned poultry baking in the oven. Since she'd declined Driskoll's lunch invitation, her growling stomach signaled her brain to feed her.

Velda and Duty were sitting at the dining room table playing cards for matchsticks. Judging by the growing pyramid in front of Duty, the girl had the winning touch.

Cézanne balanced the crutches against the inside wall of the sunroom and tossed her jacket and purse onto a chair.

She limped across the room and stood next to Duty. "What's going on?"

Velda sat with her elbow on the table and her chin in hand. She snorted in disgust. "We're playing Spades."

"Would've played Old Maid, but I didn't want yo' auntie to

have the advantage." Duty grinned so big her teeth shined, bright white against her pink tongue. Seated in her chair, she did a little victory dance while raking in matches.

Velda shuffled the deck. "You don't have to gloat."

"I know I'm winning, but I'm not the type to rest on my morals."

"You mean laurels," Cézanne corrected her.

"No, morals. I cheat." And then, "Miz Zan, when can we go to Cox's? I won enough money off yo' auntie to buy me some nize toilet water. Do they have good smellin' stuff at Cox's?"

Cézanne shot Velda a wicked glare. "Whose idea was it to play for money?"

The cardsharps answered "Hers" in stereo, each finger pointing at the other.

"You're the grown-up. You shouldn't be corrupting her by teaching her to gamble."

Velda sniffed. She avoided Cézanne's stare and returned the cards to their plastic container.

"Soon as Velda pays me, can we go? I want to get my silk stockings."

Duty was counting matches at a rate of a dollar per stick when the front door swung open. Silhouetted against the light, a hulking male filled the entrance.

Cézanne shielded her eyes from the slant of the afternoon sun. "Can I help you?"

The man introduced himself as Mack Four Eagles, and he'd dressed for the occasion in a powder blue seersucker suit. When he shed his jacket, they viewed colorful suspenders holding up his pants. He claimed to be Native American; the gray-streaked braid that fell to the middle of his back seemed to bolster his assertion. When he smiled, berry-colored lips angled up the left side of his face in a sneer.

Doug Driskoll had referred him.

According to his court paperwork, a hearing on the felony charge of aggravated sexual assault of a child had been scheduled the following month. The indictment alleged he raped a thirteen-year-old girl after enticing her to use peyote during a religious ceremony.

It took less than ten minutes of conversation to decide she wanted nothing to do with Mack Four Eagles. She told him he needed a more experienced lawyer, shook his hand, and sent him packing.

When the door closed him off from view, Velda, ever the fashion plate in her blue floral housecoat with red hibiscus and fuzzy pink bunny slippers, piped up. "What kind of nincompoop wears a seersucker suit in the dead of winter?"

Cézanne gave her a squinty-eyed stare. "I'm not sure you're in a position to poke fun."

"Nobody wears seersucker anymore. Except maybe ice cream vendors." Her laughter tickled her so much she doubled over in a fit.

"That's enough. Duty's an impressionable young lady. I don't want her thinking it's okay to ridicule people less fortunate."

"Quit trying to act like such a goody-goody." Velda chuckled so hard her teeth shifted.

Cézanne inwardly flinched. Not only did the Martin side of the family have bad skin, they wore partial plates. She reminded herself to floss.

Duty came out of the kitchen licking a spoon thick with brownie batter. "What's a seersucker suit?"

Velda howled with laughter. "A suit from Sears, and he's the sucker who bought it." Tears streamed down her pleated face.

For a moment, Duty seemed lost in thought. She turned to her caretaker, eyes brimming with curiosity. "Miz Zan, if you get seersucker suits from Sears, what kind do you get from Cox's?"

Cézanne's bedroom made a peaceful hideaway.

Mid-afternoon, while studying the Rackley file after she and Duty returned from Cox's, she discovered the defendant's court-appointed defense attorney never polled the jury after trial. She decided to telephone the jury's foreman. In the middle of the phone call, a disruptive cadence broke her concentration. From her position at her desk, she eyed Duty's dog clumsily scratching behind his ear.

Fleas. Just what she needed. More parasites.

She jotted down directions to Gary Oakes's North Side office, then disconnected and yelled for Duty. The girl hustled in with her hair as wild as a Plains Indian.

"What in God's name are you doing?"

"Moussing my 'do'."

"Why?"

"So I'll look pretty."

Deep sigh. She decided not to tell her it wasn't working. "Enigma has fleas."

Duty's eyes cut to the dog. " 'Nigma don't have fleas."

"If only that were true. I want you to take him outdoors and bathe him. He smells like an athletic supporter."

"What?"

"A jock strap."

"What's a jock strap?"

"Your dog smells like a boys' locker room. Would you please take him outside and bathe him?"

"No dog shampoo."

"Buy some."

Maroon eyes sparkled like garnets. "Can I borrow yo' car?"

The request fell on deaf ears. "I'll drive you. I need to swing by the bank and deposit a couple of retainers."

"Is that what fits in your mouth when you get braces on your teeth?"

"Money. A retainer is pre-payment for legal work."

Doretta Beaudoin had an appointment that afternoon but had sent a check the week before to cover a set of mom-and-pop wills. Doretta, a dog breeder, intended to leave on a week-long cruise with her husband as soon as they sold off the last of their puppies.

Cézanne deposited the three hundred dollar check at the bank's drive-through window. As she dropped Duty off at the nearest shopping center with enough money to pick up a burger on the walk back home, random thoughts of Bobby popped into mind. Her stomach gave a violent twist; she switched the radio station to classic rock and concentrated on song lyrics to drive his memory from her head.

She met Oakes at his place of business, an insurance agency located in an eight-story building two miles north of the courthouse. The man's commanding telephone voice belied his appearance. Through the earpiece, he seemed ten feet tall. In person, dressed in an argyle vest and navy slacks, he measured a few inches shorter than Cézanne and wore his thinning brown hair styled in a comb-over. After announcing he could spare ten minutes, no more, he offered her coffee, a chair, and a view from his seventh floor window.

"You called about Erick Rackley. I don't know what to tell you except that we heard the evidence, deliberated, and reached a verdict." He checked his watch.

"Tell me about the first round of deliberations. Was it unanimous?"

"Hardly. We had four women. Women go soft. It's up to us men to keep 'em in line."

She blinked. "You don't think women can make up their own minds?"

"Look, counselor, the prosecutor passed the gun around during the trial. A couple of gals on the jury tried to dry-fire it and couldn't. One of them was pretty hefty. We were asked to believe Mrs. Rackley pulled the trigger herself. Myself and eight others weren't convinced she had the strength."

Cézanne leaned back, incredulous. "That's what you based your decision on? That she wasn't so furious with her drunken husband that a shot of adrenaline coursing through her veins couldn't give her the strength of ten men?"

He checked his watch, tapped the crystal and stood. "I'm afraid that's all the time I have."

"Can I ask you one more thing?"

He moved around the desk and waited beside her. "I'm sorry. I really must ask you to leave. Appointments, you know."

She got to her feet. Placed the half-empty coffee cup on his desk. Peered through the plate glass partition into the main office where the receptionist sat reading a dog-eared paperback. "What about the crime scene detective's testimony? Wolfgang Vaughn. He said Erick Rackley didn't do it. Detective Vaughn called it an impulse suicide."

"Mistakes happen all the time. I admire the guy's spunk, but the expert witness said he did it. That's what swayed us. That and the gun." He moved to the door and opened it. "Thanks for dropping by. Say, do you need insurance?"

"No."

"Everybody needs insurance."

"Not me. I'm single, no kids, and I'd rather see my money escheat to the state than go to anybody in my family. Besides," she said cheerfully, "I plan to die broke or in debt. Anything else, the blood-sucking IRS can pick clean."

"I wasn't suggesting life insurance unless you have a dangerous job. I was thinking more along the lines of malpractice insurance."

Elizabeth Fielding, juror number two, wasn't much help. At her small boutique in the mid-cities area where she sold Southwestern jewelry made by Zunis and Navajos, she spoke freely.

"I didn't want to be on a jury. I was absolutely sure they'd strike me." She hooked a lock of dark, chin-length hair behind each ear and smiled. A sterling silver medallion of Koko Pele hung from a necklace, complementing a long, loosely woven dress made of hand-loomed wool threads in earth tones. "I had a three-year-old to care for, so I went to jury duty fully intending to invoke my waiver. Once I learned we were being picked to hear a homicide, I decided not to use my kiddo as an escape hatch. We had to make a terrible decision, but I'm glad I heard the evidence. I felt so sorry for Yvonne Rackley. You could tell at one time she really loved him."

The boutique owner asked to be called Liz. She sat behind her desk tagging pieces of turquoise jewelry while she talked.

"I picked this piece out for myself on my last trip to the Reservation. The artist signed it on the back. What do you think?" She handed over a small Zuni brooch made of inlaid, colored stones set in a geometric pattern and edged in sterling.

"Very nice." Cézanne turned it over in her hand, checked the price and handed it back. "Were you one of the women who tried to fire the weapon?"

"All four of us tried."

"But you couldn't do it?"

Liz scrunched her eyebrows. "Says who? Pearlie Gray and I didn't have any trouble pulling the trigger. Pearlie's father taught her to shoot when she was little. They lived on a farm, and she grew up with guns. I was able to fire it. I have a permit to carry a concealed weapon, so I have to qualify at the pistol range. I take a thirty-eight with me when I go on buying trips." She opened a drawer, pulled out a coil of wire with grips attached, and squeezed it a couple of times before tossing it aside. "I use this little gizmo to strengthen my hands."

"What about the ladies who didn't have enough hand strength to pull the trigger?"

Liz's huge blue eyes widened. "Who told you that? The thing had a hair trigger."

Hair trigger? Could've gone off with a good sneeze.

"What was the vote when you first went back to deliberate?"

"Six for guilty, six not guilty."

"What changed your mind?"

"You're assuming I was one of the ones who originally voted not guilty. I wasn't. All the women thought he did it, except for Pearlie Gray."

"Why?"

"Because the expert said he did it. And because we were sick and tired of having family dinners spoiled by reports of domestic violence on the evening news."

Chapter Fourteen

Cézanne arrived home to find that Doretta Beaudoin had arrived fifteen minutes early to pick up the wills. The client appeared to be in her early fifties, with graying hair slicked back from her face in a thick ponytail. She waited on the Biedermeier, thumbing through a two-year old *Reader's Digest,* when Cézanne crossed the room with an outstretched hand and introduced herself. The woman jumped to her feet and smoothed the slacks of her muted blue pantsuit.

"I'm Doretta Beaudoin." She pronounced it, Bo-dwin. "Forget about the wills for now. I have a bigger problem. I spoke to your receptionist about the puppies."

Receptionist?

From the kitchen, Duty gave her the thumbs-up sign. Enigma was sitting at her side lashing his tail against the floor in strong, deliberate whacks.

"I'm pretty sure I can help." Cézanne dropped her handbag onto a chair in the sunroom, propped her crutches against the wall, and limped back over to the sofa. She took a seat and patted the spot next to her. "Let's chat a few minutes before we decide what to do about this."

The woman sat down and laid out the situation in concise terms. She bred Shar Peis puppies and sold a pair for twelve hundred dollars the week before. The buyer, a thirtish, reed-thin female with frosted blonde hair, black roots, and a perpetually runny nose, paid by check. Three days later, the bank returned the instrument with Stop Payment stamped on its face. No dogs. No money. No extra cash for the weeklong cruise.

Doretta Beaudoin wanted blood.

"Tell me more about the lady who bought the dogs."

"Stole. Stole the dogs." The client took a deep breath and did a five second exhale. "She wore jeans and a Stanford University sweatshirt. I'm guessing the hair was shoulder length because she could barely get it into a ponytail without strings of it coming down in the back. Anyway, I asked why she wanted two pups since they're so expensive. She said they'd keep each other company."

"Did you watch her write the check?"

"Sure did."

"Why don't you see if the District Attorney's Office will file a theft case?"

"I did." A serious eye roll paired with a loud huff of breath spoke volumes. "They said they couldn't do anything. If you ask me, what the DA needs is a worthy opponent in the next election."

"Do you have the returned check?"

"Right here." She patted her purse. Exasperation in her face turned to worry. "Ms. Martin, I don't run a puppy mill. I love each and every one of my dogs. I can't imagine why somebody dressed so slovenly would want to steal my animals. It takes a lot of money to raise a puppy so it doesn't make sense that she'd want two when she couldn't even make herself presentable."

A motive flashed into mind. "Duty, bring me the newspaper." To Doretta Beaudoin, she said, "A hunch."

With her own puppy on her heels, Duty sashayed in carrying copies of the local paper and the *Dallas Morning News.* Cézanne checked the classifieds while the unblinking Enigma appraised her client through luminous brown eyes.

Cézanne skimmed the pet section and spotted two listings for Shar Peis. She compared the phone numbers to the one on the check. Bingo.

"Crooks are stupid. That's why they get caught." She folded the Dallas paper and passed it across the sofa. "Here's the motive: She buys them from you, cancels payment, and re-sells them. Pure profit. Or so she thinks."

Duty folded her arms across her chest. "Miz Zan, we need to go get those puppies."

"Make a police report. See if they'll accompany you to get the dogs back." Cézanne locked eyes with Mrs. Beaudoin, but the client was shaking her head no. "Then we'll need a writ of sequestration to have the Constable pick them up."

"Whatever it takes." Doretta Beaudoin opened her purse and pulled out her checkbook. She uncapped a pen and poised it to write. "How much extra?"

Deep breath. Here came the deal breaker. "You have to put up a bond. It's usually twice the value of whatever you're sequestering. That's twenty-four hundred dollars for the bond—"

The dog breeder gasped.

"—plus a flat fee for me. And we have to identify the location where the dogs will be kept until the hearing."

"I don't have that kind of money. Why so much?" Tears teetered along the rims of her eyes like ball bearings.

"It's in the code." Cézanne gave Doretta Beaudoin's knee a consolation pat. "The judge sets the bond."

Teardrops sluiced down the woman's cheeks. Enigma let out a plaintive whine. He sank to the floor with his head between his paws. Cézanne glanced over at Duty. Her chin quaked like an aspen.

Words tumbled out in a rush. "Maybe we could get the judge to lower the bond."

"She stole my babies. She probably isn't feeding them. They may not have clean water to drink." Doretta Beaudoin's eyes became huge spheres. Her voice corkscrewed upward. "What if they're a nuisance, and she yells at them or kicks them?"

Cézanne stared helplessly at the two blubbering females.

Then Velda entered the room in her feather hat and muumuu. "What's all this racket?"

Duty moaned, "There's puppies out there that need savin', and Miz Beaudoin don't have enough money, and now they're gonna die, and it's all Miz Zan's fault 'cause she won't go get 'em back."

Doretta Beaudoin let out an eerie wail and buried her face in the palms of her hands. Her shoulders wracked with sobs.

Velda's voice went strident. Her eyes rimmed red. "What the hell're you waiting for? Let's go get them. Where's my bat?" She pivoted on one foot and stomped out of the room.

"Ohmygod. Would everybody just please stop unraveling so I can think?"

The waterworks abruptly turned off. Duty sniffed. Enigma whimpered.

What Velda suggested actually had a legal term for it. It was called "self-help," and it often turned out to be a good way to get shot.

Doretta Beaudoin pleaded, "Will you help me?"

"Leave a check to cover my fee. I'll talk to the judge about lowering the bond."

But she was thinking, Oh hell, why me?

Slash worked dogwatch, a pejorative term FWPD insiders used when referring to the eleven-to-seven shift. Dogwatch described the wee morning hours when the only movement came from roaming packs of canines. Even though Slash was assigned to nights, he agreed to drop in at the law office around four that afternoon to review Erick Rackley's file. The way Cézanne had it figured she could catch a half-hour nap, shower, and blow dry her hair and still have fifteen minutes to spread the file out across the dining room table before he arrived.

An unexpected telephone call torpedoed the nap idea. Duty handed her the receiver and headed off toward the kitchen. The caller turned out to be Eunice, Bobby's secretary, phoning with bad news.

The sheriff was on his honeymoon.

Cézanne drew in a sharp intake of air. The room went out of focus. A shot of heat zigzagged between her eyes. The gut-cramping moment made her sway into the wall.

Duty yelled, "Can I bake cookies, Miz Zan?"

She covered the mouthpiece and affected a cheery tone. "Sugar cookies might be nice. Maybe you can decorate them?"

"That I can. I'll make sugar cookies shaped like 'Nigma. We can use chocolate chips for the spots."

Cézanne returned her full attention to Eunice. She carefully modulated her voice to conceal her despair. "Bobby's married?"

"That's what he said. You didn't ask for my advice, but if you did, I'd say getcha a bag of fresh limes, a bottle of triple sec, a good brand of tequila—preferably one with a great big worm—and blend yourself a giant margarita. Chug-a-lug it and pour yourself another. Nurse it 'til it's time to go to bed. Always worked for me."

Reason hung by a thread. A dozen *Whys?* circled inside her head, along with a few colorful expletives. Her voice trembled. The need to know bordered on masochism.

"Who is she? Is she someone he knew before me?"

Eunice's sigh carried through the phone line. "Only other thing I know is they're spending their honeymoon in Cabo San Lucas. Take care, hon. Goodbye and good luck."

Unable to lower the phone past her shoulder, Cézanne

listened to the buzz of a broken connection. Stricken, she stared into space.

Cabo.

She'd been to Cabo.

She married Shane in Cabo. The unconventional wedding, held on the beach with a sunset backdrop, was gorgeous. Three days later, her beloved Shane died in a scuba diving accident. Then came the mountain of red tape getting him out of a foreign country and back home—a nightmare experience she wouldn't wish on her worst enemy. That Bobby had wormed this information out of her the first night they spent together made matters worse. To learn he'd taken his bride to Cabo was tantamount to taking a right cross to the orbital bone, long distance.

With mind-numbing speed, she took a quick shower and blow-dried her hair. Duty picked out a lavender sweater made of angora and cashmere for her to wear, and she dressed without answering the girl's questions.

While inspecting her face in the mirror, Cézanne spoke to the girl's reflection. "Against my better judgment, I'm giving you your first assignment."

Duty's eyes grew wide. She straightened her posture as if that instantly made her a grown-up.

"I want you to take Mrs. Beaudoin's papers out to the Justice of the Peace and file them. While you're there, I'd like you to ask one of the clerks to have the judge call me about the bond."

"I'll be needin' the keys to yo' car."

"Velda can drive."

"Velda's old. She moves slow. It's rush hour traffic. Riding with Velda would be like riding in the official pace car. I can react faster." Duty grabbed an invisible steering wheel and jerked it hard right.

"Never mind. Bad idea."

"It's a great idea. Only you got the wrong driver. Velda's half blind. Have you looked real close at those beady eyes? I overheard her talkin' to the doctor yesterday. I heard her axe him if he knew whether she had two Cadillacs. She don't need to drive yo' car if she already has two."

"Cataracts."

"What's that?"

"It's where your eyes go bad, and you can't see."

"My point exactly. You're better off lettin' me drive."

"I don't think so. Tell Velda to look up the address of the sub-courthouse. And y'all don't cause any trouble out there because I'm not bailing you out." She announced her thoughts to the mirror. "You must've done something bad when you were little and now you're paying for it. Krivnek's right. Weird stuff doesn't happen to normal people. Only you. Why's that?"

Narrowing her eyes into a hard squint, she examined the arch of her brows. They might actually seem normal if she didn't let people get too close.

"You're not bad-looking," she reasoned with her reflection. "You've even been called pretty."

Her alter ego answered aloud. "Oh, sure, by drunks. What do they know? They see things in twos."

The monologue continued. "The police shrink thought you were nice looking."

"No, he didn't," she reminded herself. "He just wanted to get in your pants. Same with Driskoll. Same with Lieutenant Sid Klevenhagen. Well, shit, I guess I'd look damned beautiful to a sixty-two-year-old masher who had three pending cases for sexual harassment. Jesus, Cézanne, this is not normal."

Duty interrupted. "Miz Zan, when you say normal, do you think it's normal to talk to yo'self?"

"Normal means what's normal for you. For me, it's normal. For Velda, it's probably normal. For you? Well, you're still young.

But one day, God forbid, it'll probably be normal for you, too."

Duty stared at the floor. She traced the toe of her shoe over a hardwood plank. "You don't find it a little strange having conversations with yo'self? Is somebody else in there with you?" She looked up. Garnet eyes narrowed into slits. "How many people you got inside you, Miz Zan?"

"Shhh. You'll wake them."

Mercifully, Slash arrived early, putting an end to the designated driver discussion.

When Duty's Enigma-shaped cookies came out of the oven, they looked more like spotted buffalo. But Slash explained that even if they didn't hold their shape, they all looked the same inside the stomach. After gobbling down two to show he meant business, he picked up a third and studied it carefully.

"These are really good. Have you ever thought about becoming a baker?"

The idea intrigued her. Duty returned to the kitchen with the cookie sheet and transferred the rest of the shapeless treats onto a platter. While she hovered nearby, Cézanne and Slash sat at the table and conferred over mugs of hot cocoa. He moved his chair close enough to graze a thigh. At first, she accepted it as an accident. When it happened again, she wondered.

As they dusted crumbs off their hands and pushed aside their empty cups, she said, "You're too young for this," and sent Duty from the room.

Slash guided her attention to the crime scene photographs. "Check the position of the body."

Yvonne Rackley lay proned-out on the bed with her face contorted into a ghastly death mask and a bloody pillow over her chest. Eyelids coated with the dull glaze of death fell, half-mast, over dilated pupils. Her mouth sloped into a downward crescent. Pink froth bubbled at the edges.

"I knew Erick didn't kill her. Same way I knew you didn't kill that stripper at Ali Baba's."

They locked gazes. The Vaughn brothers had the same turquoise irises flecked with light blue specks. When he turned his face from the direct glow of the lamp, Slash's eyes darkened to match his mood.

"How'd you know it wasn't me?" Her words came out unhurried and deliberate.

"I can put it into words, but it probably wouldn't make sense. I've been doing this job so long that things I know about crime scenes have become ingrained in my personality."

"If Erick Rackley gets a new trial, you'll have to convince a jury he didn't do it. Why not start with me?" She selected another photograph and studied it. When she felt the depth of his stare, she returned his gaze. Her heart fluttered.

"It's hard to explain gut instinct. If you don't believe me, tell me the moment you first realized you were in love."

"I . . . it was his . . ." Her voice faltered, trying to recall. Slash's presence seemed to suck Bobby's memory right out of her. She shook her head to clear it and saw Bobby standing by the cattle guard with his arms slung across the gate and a boot heel hooked on one rung. "I liked the way he smiled."

"So the first time you saw a big, toothy grin you fell in love?" His lips curled at the corners. Searing eyes teased her.

"Not the first time. Lots of times. And the way he kissed. I liked it."

"So he kissed you, and you went head over heels?"

"There were other things . . . the way his eyes crinkled when he laughed. The way he looked at me."

"Describe that."

Her breath went shallow. "Like you're doing now."

The hard edge left his eyes. His pupils dilated like two charcoal briquettes. The overhead light reflected a tiny fire in the middle of each one.

An unexpected jolt zipped straight to her—

Ohmygod.

—and ricocheted through her body until it settled near the base of her neck. A million pinprick shards rained down inside her body. She spoke in a halting whisper. "I don't think we're talking about the same thing."

"I think we're talking about exactly the same thing." He leaned in so close that a hint of fabric softener in his shirt drifted up her nose. "You were telling me how you knew you were in love."

Deep sigh. "It just seemed right."

She shifted her chair enough to inch away. Not because she thought she saw him moisten his lips to kiss her, but because she half-expected to pitch over in a dead faint and needed more table space in case he did. Sitting within Slash's force field was dangerous—like standing at the precipice of one of those benign looking sinkholes in the Earth that sucked you in and burped before you realized you were a goner.

Not to mention Raven had a crush on him.

His mouth hovered within striking distance.

Raven would be devastated.

She should hop up. Should carry their empty cups to the kitchen. Shouldn't get within ten feet of him without her best friend in the room.

Too late, their lips touched.

She stayed deathly still, barely able to breathe. He parted his mouth and the heat of his tongue gently traced the contour of her lips. She felt a slight rush of air as he sucked in her breath. He cupped his hands to her face. Her eyelids closed as if the great weight of gravity had pulled them down. Images of tangled sheets and petal soft skin rubbing against each other played in her mind. She sensed the faint vibration of radar buzzing inside her head and knew if he didn't remove his mouth from the underside of her chin, she'd pitch over onto the floor in a limp heap.

And just like that, he stopped.

"I'm supposed to be engaged."

"Where's your ring?"

Guilt set in. "Raven's crazy about you. Why're you doing this? I already said I'd take the case."

He smoothed the hair from her face and tucked a fingerful behind each ear. "Get your coat. I'm taking you to see Erick Rackley's house."

"I already met the realtor and took a quick tour."

"With me, you get the unguided tour." He held up a key. She knew without inspection that it opened the lock box the listing agent secured to the door. "Don't look so worried. I have my sources." Slash grinned. "Grab your jacket. On the way over, you can tell me the first time you realized you were in love with me, and I'll try to work up enough nerve to tell you what you did to make me want you."

Chapter Fifteen

Getting Erick Rackley's case reversed on appeal had about as much chance as cutting a two-dollar steak with a feather. But curiosity got the better of her, so Cézanne decided to accompany Slash to Rackley's digs for several reasons. First, hearing the details about the magical moment he fell under her spell would shore up her battered self-esteem now that Bobby trashed her for what had to be a fast food worker or high school dropout; second, she intended to use the opportunity to tell Slash that such familiarity could never happen again. Not while Raven had any interest in dating him.

It probably boiled down to a dress.

Men loved second-skin cocktail dresses. She'd worn a skimpy little black number to the police banquet the previous year. Or maybe the narrow-legged leather pants and matching jacket she wore to the last police rodeo got his testosterone churning. Could've been the robin's-egg blue ropers. What was it with Texas men and their boot fetish? It was a cinch that she hadn't caught his eye after the shootout at Ali Baba's, the event that left one stripper dead and a bouncer on life support. She'd walked into the sniper's lair wearing a pretty blue Perry Ellis number and stumbled out looking like she'd been caught up in a hay baler.

At the mouth of the driveway to Erick Rackley's former home, Slash confessed.

"It was the eyebrow thing. When you wiped the face cream off."

She'd expected something more dignified than a pity crush. Like her stoic demeanor when the sector sergeant placed her under arrest for the stripper murder. Or the way she'd maintained her dignity when the Deputy Chief pushed her in front of the microphones and announced he'd put her in charge of the homicide unit even though she didn't have as much experience as the detectives she was expected to supervise. Or the way she didn't go to pieces at her partner's funeral when the Reverend Willie Lee Washington unexpectedly called her to the podium to deliver the eulogy.

"You're attracted to me because I looked like a fool?"

"I finally saw you in a vulnerable light. When you worked at the PD you put out bulletproof vibes. You were always conflict habituated and had to fight tooth and toenail to get respect. Mostly, you scared the hell out of people. Strong women usually do. My mother's that way.

"Teddy and I used to roughhouse when we were kids," he went on. "Things would get broken. Our mom would come into the room, plant her fists against her waist and stare until one of us caved."

"I scare people because I'm not a whiny baby?"

"When I was standing in your bathroom and you didn't have on anything but a towel and one eyebrow, it hit me—I'm crazy about this woman."

"You have a rescue fantasy. All cops have it. You just happen to like me better when I'm downtrodden."

"The word's vulnerable. Don't look at me that way. Besides, you're rescuing the Devilrow girl."

"No, she works for me. She's an employee. It's not personal. Her scumbag uncle abandons her periodically, and I don't want to see her fall in with dirtballs."

Big fat lie.

They got out of the truck, and Slash helped her step onto the curb.

He looked at her hand and said, "My mother has this saying: Never marry anyone with long fingernails—you'll never get any work out of them."

"Smart woman." She pulled free, and they stood in silence, peering down at the Rackley house.

With her thoughts free-associating, she wondered if she should bring up Raven again. Or to tell him it'd take a long time getting over Bobby Noah before she'd be ready to date again. But Slash didn't seem to require explanation. As they stood in front of the Rackley's former home, he hoisted a black FWPD duffle bag over his shoulder and made an unrelated observation.

"You'll be fine walking three sides of the property but the fourth requires a touch of mountain goat. As long as you're foot's still lame, we'll skip the east side."

But the section of property that bordered Bellaire Drive was exactly the part she wanted to see. It butted up against the road and formed a treacherous slope down to the creek. If an intruder could navigate such hostile terrain, it might explain how someone could've entered the house, undetected, to kill Yvonne Rackley.

"Can we at least shoot pictures from the street?"

"If you want to be road kill. It's a blind corner, and there's no shoulder."

He clasped her hand and tugged her into motion, leading her across the driveway to the west side of the house. Nothing unusual. Lots of trees. Even better, a chain link fence with a roll of concertina wire coiled at the top. According to Slash, investigators found no cuts or striation marks in the metal.

Same to the north. The only area an intruder could penetrate without notice was the east incline. The only other way in was the flagstone-and-railroad-tie incline leading down to the front door.

They retraced their steps to the mouth of the drive. Slash released her hand.

"Let's go." He gripped her elbow and steered her down the rocky path.

Opening the lock box with the steady hand of a safecracker, Slash swept her inside and took a detour to the left. With the authority of a museum docent, he narrated their travels through the kitchen, a small den, and onto an outside balcony. They descended several tiers of decking until they reached level ground overlooking the creek. He stopped next to a drained swimming pool landscaped on three sides by trees and shrubs. A thick layer of rusty brown leaves had collected in the deep end like a moist, cushy mattress.

Slash turned his face to the breeze. Shielding his eyes against the glare, he pointed out a couple of concave chips in the mortar below the aqua-blue tiles rimming the pool's edge. "Tell me what you see."

"Bullet holes."

"Erick's way of letting their houseguests know they'd worn out their welcome. Two nights before Yvonne died, the Rackleys threw a barbeque. They invited friends from her law firm and a slew of cops he used to work with. Everyone who attended agreed Erick got plastered. Witnesses said he had a knock-down-drag-out with one of Yvonne's co-workers and cranked off a few rounds."

"What was the argument about?"

"It was probably just a nasty rumor circulating at the time, but Erick thought Yvonne was slipping around."

"That's why people think he killed her? Because she had an affair?"

"No one pointed the finger. Her friend Rushmore—"

"Wait. Hollis Rushmore, the lawyer?" The news jarred her.

"Right. Rushmore testified Yvonne planned to leave Rackley because of his hot temper and the drinking binges."

She dug through her purse for a spiral notebook and pen. "When did she tell him that?"

"The night before the party. According to Rushmore, she decided to go through with the barbeque because the invitations had already been mailed out and Erick spent the day cooking fifty pounds of brisket. Come on." He gave her arm a playful swat. "Let's take a look around."

Back in the kitchen, Cézanne set her handbag on the ceramic countertop and leaned against the tiled edge. While inspecting the pink appliances to see if they were painted, she verbalized the elephant-sized thought rolling around in her head.

"If she did get caught with her thong down, that would go to motive."

"Except that he didn't kill her. I'm about to show you why."

They ended up in Yvonne Rackley's empty bedroom. Slash urged her to close her eyes.

"Visualize the layout: Queen mattress and box springs centered against the wall; no headboard or footboard. White spread, matching shams. Four pillows. On each side of the bed, a night table. French provincial, antique white. There's a Bible on hers. King James version. And a highball glass half-full of water. Two Alka-Seltzer packets lying off to the side, unopened. The closet door's closed. The bathroom door's open. Powder blue area rug on the tile floor in front of the pedestal sink. Battenburg lace shower curtain pulled shut. Fresh towels. Fresh washcloths.

"Yvonne Rackley's propped against the two pillows. She switches off the light. Then . . . boom."

Cézanne could see it all. The flash of the muzzle. Could hear the sound of footsteps pounding against the floor. She imagined Erick Rackley's horror as he flipped on the light and found his wife with a gaping hole in her chest.

She heard the sound of a metal zipper running along its track.

Her eyelids popped open in alarm.

Slash was digging through his duffle bag.

"What're you looking for?"

"I want you to see something." He closed the doors to the bathroom and bedroom. Then he pulled the drapes. Applying an aerosol spray on a section of wall above the area where the bed would've been, he said, "Hit the light," and flicked on the fluoroscope. The ultra violet lamp illuminated the wall with a purple glow. Iridescent green dots in varying sizes, previously invisible to the naked eye, seemed to pulse through the paint like a bad case of Martian measles.

Blood spatter.

"You can still see it," she said in surprise.

"You can clean it, you can paint it. But unless you put bleach or some other solvent on it to degrade it, blood spatter—like ex-wives and warrants—never goes away."

Slash explained the trajectory of the bullet and the position of Yvonne Rackley's body when she took the hit. He painstakingly ticked off plausible reasons why neither Yvonne nor Erick had gunpowder residue on their hands.

Cézanne studied his silhouette, backlit by a panel of UV light, and stated the obvious. "Seems to me Mr. Rackley could've passed the paraffin test because he had time to scrub the evidence off before the police got here."

"I can show you lots of cases where nobody has traces of gunpowder residue and it doesn't point to murder."

"There weren't any prints on the gun. He could've wiped them clean."

"I've worked a lot of suicides where the victim's fingerprints didn't show up on the grips." He switched off the fluoroscope. They stood so close she could smell his suede jacket. "You want to get the light?"

She didn't. She wanted to stay put. To have him take her hand again and feel the warmth of his skin.

"Cézanne . . . have you seen enough?"

Her pulse throbbed. Her breath went shallow. It was sick to stand in the same place where Yvonne Rackley died and want the man who worked her crime scene to make her feel desirable. To put his hand on her . . .

"Zan, are you all right?" He reached out and grazed her arm. Ran his hand over her sleeve to her shoulder and then to the base of her neck.

"Sure." Her voice dissolved to a whisper. Surrounded by darkness, she was glad Slash couldn't see her flush at his touch. She missed Bobby so much her heart ached. She thought of the petal softness of his mouth on hers. And how devastating it was to hear her fiancé was honeymooning in Cabo with his new wife. "I'll get the switch."

"Wait." Slash threaded his fingers through her hair. He let the fluoroscope touch the carpet, released his grip and allowed it to gently thud to the floor. The top of her head fit neatly under his chin. He inhaled the fragrance of her hair, then tilted her jaw up with his finger. In the dark, their lips sideswiped. He gobbled the area around her mouth until he found them again. Unhurried in his movements, he slipped a hand beneath her sweater. Her skin tingled with the coolness of his fingertips.

This was traitorous. They should leave.

"I want you." He peeled her sweater off.

Cézanne felt a lust so strong it whipped her breath away. Caught up in the heat of each other's bodies, they were halfway to stark naked when she froze in a mannequin-like pose.

"What?" Slash's husky whisper caressed her ear.

"Did you hear that? Someone's in the house." She wondered for a fleeting instant if it wasn't the sound of her stampeding heart.

"I locked the door."

But there it was, the creak of a hardwood plank underfoot.

She dropped to her knees and groped for her sweater. She'd left her purse in the kitchen. It had Raven's Chief Special inside.

Surrounded by darkness, Slash patted the floor for his gun.

An eternity passed between footsteps.

A loud pop sounded behind her and to the left. The scare was enough to liquefy her insides. Her squishy stomach tried to climb into her throat.

Slash whispered, "Get in the bathroom and lock the door."

"What about you?"

"I'm going after 'em. You have your gun?"

"In the kitchen."

"Lay low." He receded into the shadows.

She grabbed her bra, crawled to the corner, and tried to think of a story the emergency medical technicians might find convincing when they found her body—provided she was still conscious.

Slash yanked open the door, flooding the bedroom with light.

Gun blasts rocked the house. Slash returned fire.

He ducked behind the wall for cover. Chunks of drywall exploded inches from his nose. Snowflakes of chalk filled the air. Cézanne counted explosions . . . thirteen, fourteen, fifteen.

Probably a Glock with a seventeen-round magazine.

Please, God, make it time to reload.

She knew they shared the simultaneous thought.

Thundering footfalls hit the floor.

Slash sprang from his knees and gave chase. Beyond her view, the front door slammed. On the outside deck, drumming feet beat in cadence with her pounding heart.

She moved like a pissed-off snake. When she reached the kitchen, she experienced another a gut-wrenching moment. Her purse and its contents were strewn across the floor.

No gun.

No wallet.

No keys.

Minutes crept by—enough time to slip her lingerie back on and sort out what the hell just happened.

Who'd want to kill them? Oh, sure, Darlene had it in for her. But that didn't explain taking Slash out, too.

Could've been random. A home invasion. Happened all the time. An intruder could've seen them enter the house and planned a shakedown.

Yeah, you'd like that scenario a whole lot better, wouldn't you?

Not really. They all suck.

She dismissed the home invasion theory. In reality, someone wanted them both dead. Somebody who didn't want Erick Rackley's case reopened? If an intruder had staggered out holding a severed head by its ponytail, it wouldn't have shocked her more.

Boots pounded the two-by-fours. She scanned the perimeter for any useful weapon. Her eyes landed on the deadliest thing within reach—a retractable hose mounted in the kitchen sink. Now if she could just convince the intruder to bite down on an extension cord while she soaked him . . . yeah, that might work.

Slash called out, breathless. "Don't shoot." With his face beaded in sweat and his eyes darting furtively over the room, he slumped against the doorjamb. "Got your gun? I think they're still out there."

She shook her head. "It's gone. So're my wallet and keys." Panic set in. "Ohmygod. They know where I live. Think we were followed?"

His head drooped. His chin touched his chest. Except for a

thread of blood drying on his cheek, he seemed fine. He lowered his gun hand to his side and gave her a slow headshake. "Damn."

"Now what do we do?"

"You can start by putting your sweater on right-side-out and stop looking like a mental patient. I'll call Crime Scene."

Plenty of police officers managed to go an entire lifetime without getting shot at. Cézanne counted four times in as many months, three of them the product of Darlene Driskoll's poor marksmanship. But this time? This assailant nearly capped them both.

On the bright side, running gun battles served as a great contraceptive and came free of charge. Nothing like a firefight to curb her lust for Slash. Did she really care if he ever strip-searched her again? Not a whole lot.

They stood in the Rackley's former living room as witnesses, separated according to FWPD's standard operating procedure. The first line officer interviewed Cézanne; the day shift detective assigned to Crime Scene spoke with Slash.

Each told the truth, right up to the part where Slash fleeced her out of her sweater. And she neglected to mention how she damned near stripped the teeth off his zipper.

The investigating detective placed each shell casing in its own brown envelope and tagged it as evidence. Within earshot, Cézanne listened while the detective revealed his plan to run them through the Drugfire database.

He meant the FBI's stored information center.

The feds kept a file of shell casings from previously test-fired weapons that examiners across the country could use to compare questioned evidence to test-fired specimens. The database made it possible to link evidence in shooting investigations by using a comparison microscope to conduct a side-by-side observation of class characteristics. From this comparison, the examiner could tell whether a particular gun fired a particular bullet.

But that took time.

Meantime, the brother officer's best advice was to lay low.

Shortly after the police cleared out, Cézanne said, "Now what?"

"I'll take you home and come back over here so I can clean up after the search team. I'll also re-process the crime scene. See if they missed anything." He grinned. "I'm the best there is, you know."

She wasn't at all certain he was referring to the job.

"When I finish," he continued, "I'll have Crime Scene meet me at my house."

Her lip curled in confusion. "Why would they need to come to your house?"

"Because my mom's going to kill me when she hears about this. A unit should be there to process the scene before I get too ripe."

Slash had a way of lightening an awkward moment.

Thankful, Cézanne gripped his sleeve. "We were about to make a terrible mistake."

He nodded as if to admit they'd dodged more than one bullet that morning.

"I think the next time we get together," he said, "it should be at the prison. It's time you met Rackley and made up your own mind."

Chapter Sixteen

Long after the lipstick pink sunset melted into an indigo sky, Cézanne arrived back at the law office. The grandmother clock in the hall struck eight o'clock. She called out for Duty and Velda and heard the telltale sound of bunny slippers scuffing the hardwoods. Her nemesis shuffled in dressed like the organ grinder's monkey in her faded red Polynesian print and goofy mustard hat with the peacock plume.

"What's all the ruckus?"

"There's been a shooting."

Velda's downturned mouth tilted up. She flashed a Polygrip grin. "Anyone we know?" She looked Cézanne over, inspecting for leaks.

"This is serious. Slash and I were fired on. We need to get Duty in here so we can implement a safety plan."

"Praying's usually a good first step. You go to church?"

"Not religiously." Cézanne's glance ricocheted around the room. She didn't appreciate Velda's judgmental stare. "Excuse me. I happen to have a very close relationship with God."

"Using His name in conjunction with curse words doesn't constitute being on good terms with the Lord."

"You're one to talk."

"Fine. If you're on His A-list, why don't you ask Him to speed up my hair? I look like a cue ball. People at the courthouse were staring."

"Actually, your head looks more like a boiled egg. Where's Duty?"

"Outside with that horrible dog." Velda's eyes glimmered. Her face creased into a big smile. "Speaking of dogs, we have something to tell you."

"Not now." Cézanne went out the back door in search of Duty. In the yellow glow of the bug light, Enigma writhed on his back with his feet up in the air. His chops peeled back to expose a fine set of needle-teeth. A pink tongue the size of a Welcome mat lolled out of the side of his mouth. With her hands clasped tightly in front of her, Duty stood over him with her head bowed in reverence.

"Deuteronomy, what're you doing?"

The girl kept her eyes closed. "Shhhh, Miz Zan. You interruptin' a silent virgil."

"What?"

"We're havin' a silent virgil. For the fleas."

She thought she'd misheard and shook her head like she was trying to drain water from her hydrocephalitic skull through her ear. "Vigil. You mean vigil. You're having a silent vigil."

"Uh-huh. For the dead fleas."

"Come inside so we can talk."

Her eyelids popped open. "I'm askin' to be forgiven. It's not my nature to kill things." The cagey glance shifted as her voice went low and lethal. " 'Cept when I have to."

"Stop talking and come inside," Cézanne declared in the face of the girl's confession.

Velda appeared at the back door. "What in the cathair's taking so long?"

Duty said, "Give me a hand."

Velda clapped.

"Not that kind of hand."

The old woman ducked back inside and slammed the kitchen

door so hard the glass pane rattled.

Duty said, "Velda's a hoochie. Maybe while you're givin' me the word-for-the-day, I ought to be the one givin' you words-from-the-hood. You could use a lesson."

"I'm ethnically astute."

"What's a stute? I ain't a stute. Don't call me a stute."

"Jesus." Cézanne rolled her eyes. "Means I'm aware of your cultural diversity."

"No you ain't. I didn't go to no diversity, I'm a junior high dropout. And since I've been here, I've heard you talking ethnically to Slash. You say, 'Ethnically speaking, this is wrong. Ethnically speaking, we have a conflicting interest.' Why does everything have to be black or white? Can't we all just get along?"

"Conflict of interest. And it's ethically, not ethnically."

"Whatever." She snorted. "You still could use a word-from-the-hood."

"Fine. What's my word?"

"Study."

"You want me to study?"

"No, that's yo' word. It's from the verb 'to study.' It means pay attention to. When you hear me say I ain't studying yo' knobby-kneed old auntie that means I ain't giving that old sea hag the time of day."

"Are you mad at Velda?"

"Am I mad at Velda?" Duty glanced at the dog. She stood wordlessly staring off into space. "Am I mad at Velda? Let's see. Hmmmmmm." Finger to lips. "Am I mad at Velda?"

Enigma shook himself off, trotted across the yard to the flowerbed and promptly performed a breakdance-backspin in the dirt. When he stopped grinding potting soil into his spine, he shook himself off and joined Cézanne and Duty as they reconvened in the kitchen.

Velda padded in from the dining room and leaned against the doorframe.

Cézanne was halfway into the highlights of the shootout when a shadow appeared beneath the bar of light under the door leading into the hall. The story died in her throat.

She gave a low, throaty command. "Nobody move."

Velda and Duty stood inert.

She hissed, "Where's the bat?"

Velda answered in a stage whisper. "I'm not telling. I may have to use it on you."

Cézanne's eyes made a wild sweep across the countertop. She quietly sidestepped to a set of titanium butcher knives. "Someone's in the house," she hissed.

"There's nobody here, Miz Zan. 'Nigma woulda told us if there was."

Her heart beat triple time.

The shadow grew wider. Its unseen form bumped the door. Cézanne grabbed a knife handle, ripped it from its slotted space and produced—

A paring knife?

Velda hooted. She slapped her knee so hard her teeth nearly fell out. Enigma's tail thunked the floor. His mouth relaxed in a happy grin. Duty giggled.

Cézanne's face heated up. "What?"

"Oh, Miz Zan, you sho' are a sight with that little parer. There's nobody else in the house."

Another bump rattled the door but Duty showed no fear. "We got a surprise."

"You might even call it a new wrinkle." Unhurriedly, Velda opened the door.

Cézanne reared back with the knife.

Two of the ugliest, velveteen puppies she'd ever seen waddled into the room, their raisin eyes alert and twinkling behind multiple folds of skin; their faces serious and their necks pleated in fur the color of brown sugar. Bellies distended from gluttony.

"What the—?"

"I know, Miz Zan, ain't Miz Beaudoin's pups fine?"

Cézanne stared, speechless. She turned to Velda, expecting her to make sense of it. Her aunt nodded like a proud grandmother, and why not? They could have been her granddogs; they shared the same wrinkled hide.

One of the pups shaped himself into a horseshoe and hunched.

"No, no, no. Oh for God's sake. Who's going to clean the floor?"

"I think you should," Velda said.

"I'm not cleaning it up. You're the one who brought them here."

"You're right. I should clean up. After all, this is my house."

"It's mine. I'll clean it up."

"Like I said, I think you should be the one to clean it up."

Before she could unwrap the paper towels, the other Shar Pei sprang a leak.

Duty said, "I call the boy Cinnamon and the girl, Spice. We got our very own Spice girl right here."

One of the pups ventured too close to Enigma. A throaty growl sent it scampering in the opposite direction.

"Would somebody please tell me what's going on?" She looked to Duty for answers. "Did the judge waive the bond?"

"The judge didn't even wave bye-bye. What's a bond? Is it the same as bondage? 'Cause I know what bondage is."

Cézanne stared, mortified.

"Remember when I lived at yo' house, and we watched the naked videotape the Wild Orchid Society made of you?"

The very mention of those people made her hair stand on end.

"Stop talking." She turned to her aunt. Velda's partial plate had dropped onto her tongue. "It's not what you think. I was undercover."

"Undercover, my butt. You mean under *the* cover. I knew you were hooking the first time you came to this house. You're probably money laundering, too. This so-called law office bullshit's just a front." She whirled on one foot and stormed out at a fast clip. "I'm calling the cops."

Ohgod.

Cézanne grabbed Duty's shoulders. "Don't ever mention the Wild Orchid Society again. They could still come back."

"Yessum." The girl brightened. "Don'tchoo wanna hear about Cinnamon and Spice?"

When will it all end?

"What're these animals doing here? Did the Constable pick them up? Did the judge order us to keep them until the hearing?"

Duty's effervescence bubbled over. "Hearing? My hearing's just fine, thank you."

"A hearing in front of the judge. A court date."

"Don't need it. We got the dogs."

Ohgod.

Frustration rimmed her eyes with tears. "There has to be a hearing. To determine ownership."

"Miz Zan, you so funny. Even I know they's Miz Beaudoin's."

"Not until the judge says so."

"Well, you axe me, the judge don't know."

"The judge knows. That's why she's the judge. Because people thought she was wise and elected her."

"Well she don't know about Cinnamon and Spice unless she's clairvoyant."

Ohgod. These people are going to get me disbarred.

Cézanne's brows arched.

"I'm not as dumb as you think, Miz Zan. I know what clairvoyant is. Only my gramma, Corinthia, she calls it The Shine. Mostly black folk or people from Haiti got The Shine. I got it. I can see the future. And I see you're gonna come into big bucks from Miz Beaudoin for gettin' back her stolen babies."

Chills swarmed over Cézanne's skin. The buzzing of a thousand bees vibrated in her head.

"Technically, I realize me and your old auntie did all the work but since we work for you I reckon you can claim credit." Duty's teeth flashed white. "That Velda, she sho'nuff can drive. Reminds me of NASCAR the way that Caddy cornered on two wheels. Just like a gangsta getaway. You should've seen us, Miz Zan. Me and old Velda, we work good together."

Ohgod. A crime duo.

"Wait a minute." A horrible thought popped into mind. "You didn't file that writ?"

"I filed it. That I did. But the judge, she said we had to give the bond money up front, and I told her we didn't have it. She said you should come by tomorrow morning and talk to her. She's havin' an ex-party."

"Ex parte."

"Yeah. That. Only it's not nize to throw a party and not invite the person you're tellin' about it. I think I should be invited. I did all the work. Well okay, not just me. Ratty old Velda helped."

"It's not a party. It's a kind of hearing."

"Oh." Enigma nuzzled his owner's hand. He used his snout like a pry bar, shoving it under her palm and flipping it over his head until she stroked him. "Anyway, the judge told us we had to have more money. So me and Velda talked it over and decided it wasn't right to make Miz Beaudoin pay for her stolen babies twice. And Velda said she'd been readin' up on the law on account of she wants to put you outta yo' house. And she came across a statue."

"Statute."

"Is that like the Statute of Liberty? 'Cause I know about her. You can take an elevator up to her head and see for miles. I read it in a book."

"What?"

"Yo' auntie found the part that tells about retaking stolen property. Self-help."

"Ohgod." Puzzle pieces fell into place. Her eyes made a desperate scan of their surroundings. She needed a chair, and there wasn't one close by. "Ohgod."

Her knees turned to jelly. With her back pressed against the kitchen cabinets, she slid to the floor like a cartoon character. Mind-numbing words swirled in her skull. She shook her head from side to side in the faint hope they'd fall into an orderly combination.

"So me and Velda—she drove over but I drove the getaway car—"

Oh no. She actually referred to it as a getaway car.

"—and we got to the dognapper's house where Cinnamon and Spice were bein' held hostage. That's when Velda had a hissy fit, and we got into a spat."

"A spat?"

"Yessum. On account of Velda said no White woman would sell two high-dollar dogs to a little nig—to a girl like me." She balled up her fist and took a practice swing. "Miz Zan, you gotta do something about Velda before I slap her so hard she'll be able to buy new clothes in Hawaii once she stops rollin'." Duty rolled her eyes in the direction of the hallway.

Cézanne slouched limp as a ragdoll with her head against the jutting handle of the silverware drawer. It was brass, and it was pointed, and it hurt when she pressed the base of her skull near the brain stem against it. But she took great comfort knowing if

Duty's story didn't have a happy ending, she could always rear back and impale herself on it.

Armed with a quick and easy out, she concentrated on Duty's wild tale.

"So me and Velda was differin' in our opinions, and Velda said she'd go inside and say she was buyin' the dogs, only I said Velda looks like E.T. with her alopecia fuzz head. I said maybe we should both go since we drove up in a Caddy and the lady was bound to think we had money.

"I offered to playlike a ho, since hos are rich and I told yo' auntie to playlike a madam if the lady asked what we did for a livin'. We rang the bell, arguin', with Velda sayin' it wouldn't work and me sayin' it would. Next thing you know, there's the lady usin' her foot to keep Cinnamon and Spice from scramblin' out the front door."

"I need a bottle of aspirin."

"I may have a couple in my travel kit," Duty said helpfully.

"I don't want a couple. I want the whole bottle. And a cyanide cap to bite down on."

Duty slid open a drawer and poked through the contents with a skinny finger. "Does it have to be aspirin? We got anti-acid tablets. Is yo' stomach botherin' you 'cause you clutchin like it hurts?"

"No," Cézanne said weakly. "Hand me the whole bottle and get me a drink."

"Found it." Duty ran a glass of tap water. She opened the childproof cap. Without passing it to Cézanne, she popped an aspirin onto her pink tongue, chug-a-lugged the water, then returned the bottle to the drawer and the glass to the plastic dish drainer.

Cézanne blinked.

"As I was sayin' . . . me and Velda told her we saw the ad in the paper and came about the dogs. She invited us inside."

Oh please. Not inside the house.

"Me and Velda, we checked each other out, and Velda raised her eyebrows all cocky like, *Well, you heard her, go on in.*"

For a moment, she thought she felt her eyelids flutter, then realized it was just her retinas throbbing from dangerously high blood pressure.

"Please say you paid for the dogs."

The petite chandelier in the kitchen shined as bright as an interrogation spotlight. Cézanne shielded her eyes with a hand. She should start researching penitentiaries. Maybe she'd get lucky and the feds could get in on this little caper. Perhaps if she pled to racketeering she could serve her time in one of those cushy, minimum-security prisons with a golf course. She'd always wanted to learn to play the executive sport. With a long sentence she might even have a shot at turning pro.

"This constitutes burglary. Please tell me you didn't use force, did you? Because that's robbery. I don't think I'm good enough to get you both off on robbery charges." Cézanne's mind schemed. A glimmer of hope bubbled up. Brimming with excitement, she sat erect. "You're a juvenile. I could probably get the prosecutor to offer probation. But Velda's an adult. She could go to jail. We could say she corrupted you. Then I'd have this great house, and she'd get to live in the *big house.*" She craned her neck enough for a bird's eye view of the telephone nook. To amplify her voice, she cupped her hands to her mouth. "You go, Velda. Call the cops. You're the one going to jail."

Miraculously, her headache vanished. She turned to Duty with rapt attention. "So what happened at the woman's house?"

"It was a sight. Velda did most of the talkin'. She said we needed dogs, and the lady had dogs, and could we see the dogs up close so we could decide if they was the dogs for us. I said I wanted to hold one on account of dogs don't like me, which we all know's a big, hairy lie. But I figured I'd storied for a good cause so you wouldn't be mad.

"But Velda don't think nothin' of lyin' 'cause I was watchin' her mouth spinnin' yarns so fast it made me dizzy. And I don't remember all her fibs other than I did hear her say dogs love her which is also a big, fat, hairy lie, 'cause everybody knows 'Nigma can't stand her, and 'Nigma's just about the sweetest dog in the whole world." Shining like the royal rubies set in opals, her eyes rimmed red with emotion. She turned to the dog and cooed, "Isn't that right, 'Nigma?" With a *mwah, mwah, mwah,* she kissed the Great Dane on each cheek like a native European and placed the last smooch on his broad head.

Cézanne waited to see how the story turned out.

"I wanted to go in and so did Velda but Cinnamon and Spice wanted out. So I told the lady they probably needed to wee-wee. She must've agreed 'cause she said to keep an eye on 'em while she got her shoes on, and she'd step outside and talk."

Cézanne's mind rushed ahead with lightning speed. A giddy laugh crackled in her ears. "You didn't."

"I'd be lyin' if I said no. Velda snatched Cinnamon, and he peed on her. I nabbed Spice. She didn't wet on me, but she's got real bad breath and I think I mighta squeezed her too hard on account of she hurled. But we jumped in the car and sped off and that's my story. The end."

Cézanne found the strength to pull herself up off the floor. "We've got to stop Velda from calling nine-one-one." The woman they took the puppies from may've gotten the license plate.

Too late, her aunt hung up the telephone with a smirk and an attitude.

She braced her arms across her chest. "Kiss my ass. The law's on the way."

"Let me get this straight. You formed a conspiracy with child to steal a couple of show dogs valued at twelve hundred dollars each?"

"I planned to pay for the dogs with a check."

"You're telling me you intended to buy these puppies?"

"No. After we got the dogs, I figured I'd stop payment. Teach her a lesson."

Cézanne shook her finger in a no motion. "Your little caper resulted in swiping two Shar Peis."

"We stole them back. Self-help. Big difference."

"You corrupted a juvenile."

"Free will. Nobody asked her to tag along."

"You let a kid get behind the wheel."

"What's the big deal? It's not my car. Besides, I don't have a license either. Well I do, but it's revoked. They don't know what the hell they're talking about, either, because my vision's just fine."

"And you want to rat me off to the cops because you think I'm a call girl?"

"Whore."

"That's the story you intend to tell the police?"

"Pretty much."

Chapter Seventeen

The Blue arrived in record time. They used the distinctive cop knock followed by a persistent finger jamming against the bell.

She yanked open the door and was treated to the grim faces of the same two uniforms who mediated the window sign fiasco.

The one on steroids stood with his legs apart. Braced arms dropped to his sides, allowing her a clear view of his nametag. A.K. ELKHARDT. She decided A.K. stood for Ass Kicker.

"We're gonna need to have a look around."

Officer J.L. Flurry, the less scary of the two, watched her with the slow, deliberate blink of a salamander.

"I know," she said, anticipating the issue. "Crazy Aunt Velda phoned in a wild, imaginary tale."

"Crazy Aunt Velda?" Elkhardt asked.

She attempted to jar his memory. "The one who made the window sign."

"Oh, right. Your imaginary friend." Flurry, the crewcut cop, pulled his handie-talkie from its pouch. He turned away and radioed the dispatcher. "Who's the complainant?"

The answer from the communications center triggered an eye bulge. "Cézanne Martin."

"Ten-four." He unkeyed the mike, replaced the radio, and exchanged knowing looks with his partner. "Aren't you Cézanne Martin?"

"Yeah. But I didn't call for a unit."

"We're coming in." Elkhardt took over.

Oh, well sure. Be my guest. Mi casa es su casa. *And everyone else's casa.*

She stepped aside and allowed them to enter. "What's the nature of the complaint?"

"You ought to know."

"I already told you I didn't call."

Officer Flurry spoke. "So you're running prostitutes here?"

"Of course not. This is a law firm."

"Not much difference."

The Blue split off near the stairs. Elkhardt paused at the hallway, cocked his head, and listened to the left. His mouth curled up in a smirk.

Duty clomped down the steps modeling her lacy brassier, panties, and the garter belt holding up her silk stockings. "Miz Zan, come see my new threads. I'm ready for a date."

Cézanne flung herself between Duty and the uniform. "Put your clothes on."

Elkhardt said, "Let me get this straight. You're not running a brothel?"

She shouted for Velda who must've skipped out.

Duty's shoes hit the steps. She didn't stop running until the upstairs door slammed shut.

Officer Flurry unsnapped the leather case on his Sam Browne and pulled out a pair of handcuffs. He ratcheted the metal teeth through the aperture so fast it sounded like bones splintering. When the steel crescent swung free from its lock, he repeated the nerve-wracking cadence.

Cézanne pictured herself in jail khakis. "Look, fellows, Duty's a high school kid trying on new clothes. This girl doesn't have a date. She doesn't even know anybody here. Her uncle left her in my care to help me run my law office."

They obviously didn't believe her.

"I'm still having problems with Velda about the ownership of this house."

Duty bounded downstairs wrapped in a terrycloth robe several sizes too large. She crooked her finger at Elkhardt. "Mista Po-liceman, sir, could I see you for a second?"

He allowed himself to be pulled off to one side. Duty's hands fluttered like a moth near a hot bulb. Elkhardt glanced over his shoulder and nodded conspiratorially.

The girl spoke in a stage whisper. "We got a doctor to look at her. Mostly, she's pretty easy to deal with but Miz Zan can be a pill, too. Like the time I was cookin' a potion and she saw hair floatin' in the pot and thought I parboiled a dog."

"Duty, stop talking." Cézanne waved her arms. To Officer Flurry, she said, "There's nothing hinkey going on here. I'm a lawyer. I'll show you my bar card." She limped toward the sunroom with Flurry on her heels.

"Easy." While she dug out her badge case, his hand hovered above the butt of his .45. The police shield glinted in the sunlight. "You're a cop?"

"I worked Homicide. They let me keep my badge in case I come back to work in a few months."

Recognition flooded his cheeks bright pink. "Hey, Allen, we've got us a celebrity."

Elkhardt tromped into the room with Duty scurrying in behind him.

"She's that chick from Homicide. The one who capped all those people."

"I didn't shoot anybody. It was Darlene Driskoll."

"She solved the Carri Crane murder and the Dane Kissel murder."

"No kidding?" Elkhardt's grim expression turned to admiration.

Didn't anybody read the news? The local paper splashed her picture across the front page for three days before finally moving it to the Metro section for two more.

"Why'd you quit the force?" Flurry.

"I always wanted to be a lawyer. I finally got my law license and took a ninety-day leave to get my office up and running."

"You'd give up a captain's slot for this?" He opened his hands up to the pressed-tin ceiling and scoured it with his eyes as if he were searching for the secret portal to fame and riches.

"It didn't turn out exactly like I planned."

"No kidding." Flurry scowled at the Biedermeier. "So you're really an attorney?"

She dug the gold bar card out of her badge case and flashed it.

"There's no whorehouse?"

Cézanne shrugged.

Elkhardt held out his hand and she shook it. "Way to go, Captain. We won't bother you anymore." He balled up a fist and popped his partner's arm good-naturedly. "I hear that new burger joint down the street gives cops free food."

Flurry produced his business card, and she nodded her thanks.

With The Blue on the way out the front door, she caught snippets of conversation.

"Always wanted to marry a lawyer so I could spend the rest of my life fishin'." Flurry.

Elkhardt issued a warning. "Not this one . . . crazy as an outhouse rat."

Hearing the slam of car doors, Cézanne whirled on Duty. "What'd you tell that guy?"

"Nothing." Guilt got the better of the girl. She looked away. Up at the ceiling. Around the room.

A hunchback shadow fell across the staircase, startling them into silence.

Velda.

Cézanne yelled, "Where've you been?"

"I'm not giving away my hiding place." Wide-eyed and dragging the baseball bat like a tail, her aunt stepped into the room. "Did you really kill a bunch of people?"

"A bunch would be an exaggeration." She returned the badge case to her purse.

Maybe now Aunt Velda would consider her a threat instead a pushover.

Still infuriated at Velda for pulling such a dumb stunt, Cézanne sautéed pork chops for two, while Duty crushed homemade mashed potatoes. They sat on the Biedermeier with their plates balanced in their laps, watching TV and fending off Enigma as he periodically inspected each bone. The puppies waddled across their feet, tumbling over the rug and bumping into furniture. The dog viewed them with contempt.

Duty stripped the last of the meat off the chop. Enigma sat at attention, his piercing brown eyes following each motion as she spouted opinions, waving the bone like an orchestra conductor.

"Miz Zan, I think you should go out with Slash. If I was a white girl, I'd like him. That I would. Don't take much to see he took a shine to you."

"He's Raven's guy. Besides, I'm not dating."

"Is it because of Mista Bobby? 'Cause if it's what Mista Bobby done, I think you should get back at him. Best way I know of to get back at a man is to replace him with another man. You ought to call that no good scoundrel and tell him off. That's what I'd do. I'd phone him up and say, 'Kiss my raggedy ol' ass, you hypocrite.' "

Cézanne raised a stubbly eyebrow.

"New word. I looked it up, and I know what it means."

"I'm not calling."

Duty glanced around wistfully. "What do you s'pose she's

like, Miz Zan? That girl Mista Bobby ran off with?"

"Dunno."

But she did. Upon further reflection, she'd decided Bobby found a processed blonde with big breasts, an overbite, and a steady job at the Humane Society. She'd probably been married to her high school sweetheart. They'd had three kids, and it didn't work out, but it made a nice, ready-made family for the sheriff.

Enigma's ears twitched. He came up from his Sphinx-like pose. Growled low in his throat, then emitted an eerie whine. He lunged at Duty with such force that it knocked both of them to the floor.

The crack of a gunshot rang in Cézanne's ears and rocked her senses.

The front window exploded, propelling fragments of glass through the living room in a great white starburst.

On instinct, Cézanne grabbed Duty. Forced her head down onto the Oriental rug and shielded her with her body. Puppies yipped and squalled. Enigma made spooky sound effects and herded them into the sunroom. Footfalls receded. A car door slammed. Tires squealed against the asphalt. Velda bounded down the staircase with the bat resting on one shoulder.

Cézanne cried, "Stay down." She low-crawled to her purse and remembered she no longer had Raven's .38.

Duty yelled, "Call nine-one-one."

Velda dropped the bat. She sprinted for the phone and snatched it from its nook.

Cézanne crawled through broken glass and flicked off the light. Duty dashed for the drapes and pulled the cord, shielding them from view.

Ugly slashes of red streaked Cézanne's hands and knees. Duty insisted on doctoring the cuts with Merthiolate.

When she finished, Cézanne said, "Oh, great. I look like

something thawed out of Jeffrey Dahmer's freezer."

"Who's that?"

"A cannibal. He ate his victims."

"Hmmmmm." Duty stared thoughtfully at the ceiling. "Naw, that won't work."

The doorbell chimed.

Elkhardt and Flurry were the first uniforms on-scene. The crime scene detective Cézanne and Slash met earlier that afternoon also showed up. By shift-change, Slash rolled up, too.

The glass company refused to come out until the following morning so they waited in the kitchen until Velda's handyman arrived to board up the opening.

After everyone cleared out, Slash pulled Cézanne aside on a reconnaissance mission.

He rested a hand on her shoulder. "You're dangerous. My mother says you'll get me killed."

"You mentioned me to your mother?" Incredulous. "What'd you say?"

"I left out the part where you took off your clothes."

She stood in stricken silence, wondering how to muzzle him. Chills prickled the hairs at the nape of her neck. "Darlene did this. I think Doug told her how to find me."

"Why would Driskoll want you dead?"

"He's still mad that I transferred him to the auto pound."

The next notion she dismissed in her head as soon as the thought materialized. That maybe, just maybe, Doug wanted her back. And because he couldn't have her, he didn't want anyone else to either.

"He knows where I'm staying because I gave him my business card. Don't look at me that way. He said he'd refer me some clients. A guy showed up and creeped me out, so I didn't take his case."

"I have a Mossberg you can borrow. Tonight, when I'm not

dispatched to other calls, I'll pull close-patrol on your house and drop off the shotgun tomorrow. Three women under siege shouldn't be without serious firepower."

"Deal."

"You know," Slash said, "this should give you and your aunt an incentive to get along. After all, you're in the same leaky boat."

He was right. They might have to depend on each other in order to save their own lives.

With a sheepish grin, he invited her out. "Are you busy New Year's Eve?"

Chapter Eighteen

After Velda's handyman left, Cézanne and her aunt sat at the dining room table discussing their future in the dark. They kept their voices low as Duty brewed coffee.

"You could've gotten us all killed," Velda snapped.

"How do you know whoever did this wasn't after you?" Said defensively.

Velda snorted. "I think you should leave. I'll look after the girl."

"I'm not going anywhere. Neither is Deuteronomy. We're all staying here so we can watch each others' backs."

After Velda retired to her room, Duty came in with two cups of café au lait blended to perfection.

She fixed Cézanne with an accusing stare. "Why'd you say she could stay here with us?"

"I didn't have a choice."

"Consider it a self-inflicted wound."

Cézanne sipped from her cup. Her eyes went shrewd. "How would you have handled it, brainiac?"

"Brainiac." Duty tested the word. "I like that. I think that describes me. Hey, let's do rhyming words. Let's start with Velda. Velda's a maniac. Then there's my good dog, Enigma. Let's call him the Great Dane-iac. Then there's you. Insaniac. That's what you are for inviting her to stay."

"What was I supposed to do? The few times I saw her when I was a little kid, she wasn't so bad."

"You used to like Aunt Velda?"

This caused Cézanne to reflect on the notion. "I rather did, I suppose."

"Why?"

"She wasn't always an old crone. Back then she was beautiful and exotic and much taller." Her mood abruptly soured.

Heaven help me, I'm going to end up a shrunken old harpy just like Velda.

"She lived in Africa. I used to daydream of visiting her coffee plantation. I'd imagine how I'd take an airplane and travel by ship." She sank deep into her fantasies. "Bwana Mbugge would pick me up at the train station and we'd each ride our own elephant to the plantation. Aunt Velda and rich Uncle Oscar would serve tea and scones to me while I watched lion cubs frolic on the front lawn."

Duty fell, spellbound, into Cézanne's exotic tale. "What'd yo' bedroom look like?"

"It had a huge bed with a gauzy mosquito net hanging from the ceiling that covered all sides like a tent."

"A tent. Yes. I can see that. And do the windows have glass on them or can the monkeys just come inside and play?"

The thought of simians running rampant through open windows sheared the reverie. "This isn't real, you know," she reminded her glumly.

"Who's Bwana M . . . m . . . ?"

"A made-up name for the guide. Look, let's just forget it."

Duty reached out and grabbed her hand. She made serious eye contact and squeezed. "I don't want to forget it. I like doing playlike stuff. What was yo' elephant's name?"

No response.

Duty squeezed harder. "What was his name, Miz Zan? You rode him all the way from the train station. You must've known his name."

"Pewter. Because he was gray."

Again, Duty got caught up in breathless excitement. "Then what happened? Did you feed him peanuts?"

Cézanne's gaze floated, dreamily, to the ceiling. "Yes. Lots of peanuts."

"Peanuts that Bwana gave you so Pewter would take a shine to you?" Duty volunteered helpfully.

"Yes." Her thoughts strayed. "The way Velda used to care about me." She jarred herself back to reality. "Why doesn't Velda like me?"

"Well, Miz Zan, maybe she ain't her old self."

"Maybe." A horrible realization dawned. "Maybe . . ." she said, much louder. She felt her face contort into a grotesque mask of a spendthrift who'd just run up a half-million in debt, only to discover that her winning lottery ticket turned out to be fake.

"Whatchoo mean?"

Chills crawled the length of her body. "I'm not sure. But thanks." She lifted Duty's hand to her lips and gave it a peck. "Thank you a million times."

"What'd I do?"

"You inspired me. Do me a favor? Go upstairs and invite Velda to join us for a cup of hot cocoa."

"Are you outta yo' mind?"

"Hurry," Cézanne shooed her off.

Minutes later, Velda tromped downstairs wearing a purple robe with a gold turban wrapped around her head. Duty followed on her heels, twirling her index finger near her ear in the universal *Cuckoo* gesture.

Cézanne placed a cup of hot chocolate on the table and offered it to her aunt.

Velda eyed it with cold scrutiny. "You expect me to drink that?"

"If you like." She motioned the old woman into a chair. "Please join us."

"You poisoned it."

Cézanne's jaw went slack. "I didn't poison it. Why would I do that?"

"So you can take my house."

"A court will decide whose house this is," she said with smug certainty. "I'm extending the olive branch in an effort to be friendly."

Velda hollered for Duty. When the girl trotted in with Enigma sniffing the air, Velda collared her. "Drink that."

Cézanne torqued her jaw. "Who do you think she is, the King's taster? You're trying to see if she'll keel over, aren't you?"

Duty reached for the cup. She lifted it to her lips. Her eyes flitted from Cézanne to Velda and back to Cézanne. When the cup came within a hair of Duty's mouth, Velda yelled, "Stop. Give me my cocoa."

Duty stared, dumbfounded.

"It's okay. I need to talk to Aunt Velda. Grab a shower and get ready for bed. I'll be up to tuck you in."

Duty left dejected. Enigma slunk behind her with his tail drooping. When her footfalls receded upstairs, Velda said, "Give me your mug."

"I already drank out of it." Cézanne did an eye roll but she swapped drinks with Velda. She sipped from Velda's untouched chocolate, sat back in her chair and relaxed.

Her aunt left the table and returned with a fresh cup.

"What're you doing?" Cézanne said.

"I'm not drinking after you. Germs. Lord knows where your mouth's been."

Cézanne expelled a heavy sigh. "I don't remember you being this crazy but thanks for reminding me that lunacy isn't just confined to my mother's side of the family."

Velda mocked her with a huff. "I don't recall you being this selfish and hateful."

"I don't understand how you could change this much." Her eyes misted. "Remember the time you visited us on Thanksgiving?"

"Worst time of my life."

"I thought you enjoyed your visit."

"I didn't." The old woman spoke with a certain finality, leaving the impression she didn't want to talk about holidays or visits to the Martin house or anything else of historical evidentiary value.

Cézanne pressed harder. "Remember when my mother burned the apple pie and the kitchen filled with black smoke?"

"A terrible cook." Velda clicked her tongue, *tsk-tsk-tsk.*

A crushing weight formed in her chest. Bernice only had a few sterling qualities. Before mental illness ruled her life she'd been a devoted mother and a fabulous cook.

The pulse in her throat throbbed. "How come my mother burned our pie, Velda?" she asked with childlike innocence.

"The woman was horribly self-centered. She never paid attention."

"No . . . I mean . . . what caused it to burn?"

"She put the oven too high."

Wrong.

Even if Velda had the onset of early Alzheimer's she would've remembered the answer to that question. Bernice didn't set the temperature too high. She devoted herself to special events like holiday meals and the presentation and fanfare that went into them, especially if she was apt to be judged by a member of her husband's family—devoutly religious people who weren't exactly tickled pink that, of all the women the son of a Lutheran preacher could've married, Bob Martin had picked a Jew.

Duty padded downstairs dressed in pink pajamas, a wooly

robe, and fuzzy slippers. She waited awkwardly for a break in conversation.

Cézanne looked her way. "What?"

"I came to say good night." Duty turned away, dejected.

Cézanne turned to Velda. "Would you mind rinsing out our cups?"

Before the woman could balk, she pushed back from the table, caught up to Duty at the bottom of the stairs and slung an arm around the girl's shoulders. While Velda headed for the kitchen toting their empty mugs, Cézanne steered the aspiring Voodoo mambo to the front porch.

With the door closed behind them, Duty made an observation. "How come you're shaking? Want my housecoat?"

"That's not Velda. That shrew isn't my aunt."

"Whatchoo mean?" Duty's eyes slewed to the door. "You sure?"

"She would've remembered how the pie burned." The girl returned a blank stare. This would take some convincing. "My mother was a fabulous cook."

"Reckon it skips a generation?" Duty deadpanned.

"Knock it off. I need your help." Enthusiasm waffled between excitement and dread. "Don't you see?" She gripped Duty's shoulders and held on. "My mother's cooking was legendary. We ate a wonderful Thanksgiving dinner. But she tried this new recipe where you bake an apple pie in a brown paper bag. The sack caught fire in the oven and the place filled with smoke. While Dad—" she choked the word back down her throat "—my father put out the flames with a fire extinguisher, my mother locked herself in the bedroom and cried. Velda—the real Aunt Velda—would've remembered the chaos because she's the one who shepherded the kids outside until it was safe to come back in."

"Maybe her mind's slippin'."

"Don't think so. Some things you just don't forget. Like where you were the day the Challenger blew up . . . what you were wearing the day you totaled your first car . . . your sister's last words before she died. You remember," she insisted.

"Like when my cousin Nehemiah passed." Duty gave an enthusiastic head bob. "What're we gonna do?"

"I don't know." She gave the neighborhood a furtive glance. Her mind turned with ideas. "First, we've got to figure out who she is. What if she's dangerous? What if she wants this house bad enough to kill for it?"

"Maybe you're reading too much into this pie thing. I think you should give her another chance to be crazy ol' Aunt Velda."

Cézanne appraised her with a look of incredulity. "Do you now? Fine. I'm a good sport." Sarcasm bathed each word. "We'll find out if she's really my aunt and if she's not, I've decided to kill her before she murders me in my sleep. And you're going to help me."

"Deal." Duty stuck out her hand.

They settled the problem with a firm shake and went back inside knowing they didn't mean a word of it.

After everyone went to bed, Cézanne contacted the police dispatcher and asked for an officer to meet her at the bungalow. She needed to see if there was still at least one handgun left now that Raven's had been stolen but the idea of going back into that house alone made her flesh ripple.

The patrolman had already arrived when she drove up. From her vantage point, he appeared to be doing paperwork under the dome light. If Darlene had been there, he'd be a sitting duck—or a dead one.

Indoors, with the uniformed trooper at her side, she did a cursory search of her gun stash.

Gone.

The taser and survival knife were missing, too. She checked

the last place Darlene might've thought to look and held her breath as she opened the kitchen pantry and peeled back a section of linoleum. She lifted a couple of loose floorboards and found the loaded .38 caliber Colt Cobra that had once belonged to her father, wrapped in a bank deposit bag.

Her weapon of choice for a backup piece was a Smith & Wesson snub nose. She liked the five-shot Chief Special best because it was a gun she'd learned to shoot in the police academy and the one she felt most comfortable with. She never cared much for the Colt because the cylinder rotated in the opposite direction from the Smith and she wasn't that familiar with the way it handled.

But now, she developed an instant appreciation for the six-shot, two-inch barrel revolver with the blue finish. Removing the cover and tucking the Colt into her purse raised her comfort level.

She thanked the officer, locked the front door, and they headed off in different directions.

Tomorrow at the gun store she'd pick up a box of fresh ammunition—copper-jacketed hollowpoints—and buy a couple of new Smiths, one for herself and one to replace Raven's.

Chapter Nineteen

Door chimes rang, rhythmic and persistent.

Startled from dream-filled slumber, Cézanne's eyelids snapped open. In a moment of disorientation, she recalled Bobby Noah taking his mouth to her naked body in a thatch-roofed beach hut and wondered how she managed to awaken in a canopy bed. She wanted to smash the pillow over her face and finish the dream, but she checked the time—ten after nine—and heaved herself out of bed.

As best she could tell, Velda's routine began at six each morning; Duty shifted into gear by eight. Since neither housemate answered the door, she slipped into a red cashmere robe and reluctantly bound her swollen foot with the Velcro cast. By the time she tromped purposefully downstairs, scared, cranky, and spoiling for a fight, the uninvited caller abandoned the bell in favor of a series of loud, unrelenting knocks.

She peered out the peephole.

The sun was a bright orange thumbprint on the horizon and it bathed a blue MGB convertible parked at the curb in a peach glow. She sensed movement behind the door and continued to stare. A man moved into view, and she eyed him with cold scrutiny.

She took in his appearance in stages.

A felt beret cocked jauntily on his head earned entertainment points, which he promptly lost due to the sunglasses and trench coat. Only movie stars and thugs wore such amateur disguises.

And while he possessed the breathtakingly good looks of a leading man, the likelihood of a major motion picture star traveling to Cowtown and ending up on her veranda held about the same odds as her growing cone-shaped breasts and winning a Madonna look-alike contest.

She decided the stranger looked less like a cinematic VIP and more like a pop idol in those ratty blue jeans with the knees split-out and the T-shirt sporting a raunchy message.

White male, late thirties, around six feet. Wavy, flax-colored curls overhanging his collar. Neatly-trimmed moustache a shade lighter than his hair. Chiseled cheeks and full lips that had probably been breaking hearts since grade school. Handsome in a rugged sort of way, he was one of nature's cruel concoctions, with perfect skin that was too tawny for winter without the aid of a tanning bed or quick jaunt to the coast. And he was holding a small bouquet of daisies he no doubt purchased from the flower bum on the corner.

She called out to the man on her porch. "Who is it?"

"Is this a law office?"

"What do you need?" Could be a hit man.

Flower delivery for Cézanne Martin. Speaking of pushing up daisies . . .

KABOOM.

"Are you open to the public?"

"Just a minute."

She felt the magnetic force field of a drop-dead-gorgeous man sucking her in and padded into the sunroom bent on finding her crutches.

The better to bash his skull in.

He put one dark lens to the peephole and they stared at each other. When he pulled away, an inviting grin broke across his face.

She yanked open the door, standing far enough behind it to

make herself a smaller target. Or to wield a crutch.

He spoke with a roguish inflection. "May I come in?"

"Are you looking for legal counsel?"

"Not exactly."

"Whatever you're selling, we're not buying."

Behind her and off to one side, Velda screamed. Her upper plate dropped onto her tongue; her eyelids fluttered in astonishment. She made the sign of the cross with her hand before crumpling onto the floor in a wrinkled heap.

Now what?

Enigma's throaty growl vibrated through the house.

She tried to slam the door in the guy's face and hit the deck, but he braced a hand against the thick wood and pulled off his shades.

The Great Dane bounded in from the kitchen, teeth bared and snarling.

Cézanne's heart leapt to her throat. Reflexively, her hand went to her mouth and lingered in front of her gaping jaw. She saw what Velda saw. Recognized the unusual eye color—the same periwinkle blue as her own. For a split-second, her world stopped turning. The crutch clattered to the floor.

"It's me," he said. "Don't you even know your own brother?"

"Henri?" She experienced a polar shift and cried out for Duty to call off the dog.

The girl came flying into the dining room with an upraised butcher knife. " 'Nigma, sit."

The animal skidded to a halt. With muscles rippling, he froze on gangly legs and let go an unapologetic, "Woof."

No one moved, least of all Henri.

Duty glanced over at Cézanne's aunt. "Well, I'll be. If it isn't Ernest Borgnine. Oh, sorry . . . my mistake. It's Velda."

Cézanne ignored her frowzy-topped charge and welcomed her brother inside.

"Henri. It's really you?" She unabashedly flung her arms around him.

"Zannie."

For several minutes, they stood locked in each other's embrace, their tear-streaked faces buried in each other's necks, their shoulders wracked with sobs, their chests meshed together as if each held the matching half to the other's broken heart.

They heard throat-clearing rumblings from the little Voodoo mambo.

"Ahem. Miz Zan, I'm thinkin' now might be a good time to roll Velda onto the front porch and lock the doors."

Aw, Jeez. What to do with Aunt Velda?

The essence of Robin Hood-meets-Don Ho, decked out in her silly hat and flowered frock, lay splayed out on the floor with her skirt hiked past her cellulite and her ho-hum exposed.

"Lordy mercy," Duty said, "that woman's uglier than homemade soap. You don't reckon you'll end up looking like that someday, do you?"

The idea scorched her. "Not as long as I can reach my gun."

"Being ugly might actually work to your advantage," Duty said, egging her on with a bit of homespun advice. "My Unca Leviticus says if you go for the ugly early, you'll never go home alone."

"Bring me a wet washcloth."

"I was thinkin' more along the lines of duck tape."

"Duct."

Duty's shoulders hunched involuntarily. She raised her arms to shield her face.

"What're you doing?"

"Where I come from, when somebody shouts 'duck' you duck."

"Duct. Duct tape."

"That's what I said. Duck tape."

It gave Cézanne great pleasure smacking Velda back into consciousness.

With the three of them hovering over her, Velda cupped a parchment hand to Henri's cheek. "I thought you were Bob. For a second, it was like we went back in time. Like he never went away." She emitted a thin, eerie pitch that started low in her throat and climbed three octaves and hung in the air.

Duty started to sniffle. When Henri joined in, Cézanne broke down, too. Deep down, she wished they could all be a family again.

Leave it to Velda to zap them back into reality. Squinty eyes glowered with mistrust.

In a voice brittle with defiance, she said, "Listen, mister, you may be your daddy's spitting image, but you're, by God, not going to fleece me outta my house."

"Twenty years is a long time, Henri." Anger cast a pall over Cézanne's initial delight at her brother's return. "You could've called to let us know you were all right. But you roared off on your motorcycle and that was it. No word. Nothing."

"The only thing I regret is not taking you and Monet with me."

"Why didn't you?"

"On my bike? I might've squeezed one of you on, but I'd have had to choose."

"Well now you don't."

Henri bowed his head. Wiggled his toes inside the soft shoe leather. "She'd be alive today if . . ."

"Don't. Even now, I can't think of Monet without crying. It should've been me." Guilt eroded her resolve not to fall apart. She tightened her mouth to stop her chin from quivering.

She didn't want to relive how she and her twin were sick with pneumonia. That she was sleeping in a draft and getting sicker by the minute because her bed was located next to the window. Or how their parents' loud argument woke them up, and they heard their father storm out for good. She didn't want to tell him how Bernice came into their darkened room that night, deep in the throes of her illness, knowing she couldn't raise two kids on her own . . . and so one would be killed and one would be saved and their mother suffocated Monet with a pillow. She didn't want to go there because she'd have to tell him she'd asked Monet to swap beds, and that she'd been the one Bernice had chosen to kill.

He darted a look at Velda lurking in the hallway. "What's with the hag?"

"*Cruella De Velda?* She's just mad because we rescued the Dalmatians before she could have them stitched into a coat."

"She's bald." He chuckled. Velda flipped them the bird and stomped up the stairs. Fixing his gaze on the floor, he made a quiet inquiry. "How's our mother?"

"Committed to the state hospital for a year."

"I'll be gone before she's released."

"Where to?" For that matter where'd he come from?

His eyes danced. "Home. Back to the job."

"Where's home?"

"First things first." He clapped his hands together and glanced around expectantly. "Any coffee?"

She excused herself to the kitchen and encountered Duty.

"I already started a pot, Miz Zan. Is that man a movie star? What's he doin' in our livin' room? You have connections in Hollywood? 'Cause they don't have many black sisters, and I would make a good movie star. Watch this." She gathered her hair, crushed it against her head, and struck a pose. "This is whatchoo call vampin'. I'm vampin' for the camera, Miz Zan. The camera loves Deuteronomy Devilrow."

"You're glamorous. Stop pouching out your lips. That looks obscene."

She grinned a mouthful of teeth. "I'm puckerin' up for my leading man."

Cézanne thumbed in their guest's direction. "Henri's my brother. Are there any cookies left?"

" 'Nigma ate 'em. You sure he's not a famous actor? I'm pretty sure I've seen all his movies."

Cézanne closed the louvered doors, sealing off the kitchen from the dining room. She peered out through the wooden slats as her brother leafed through a tattered copy of *Field and Stream.* Duty joined her and the two of them eyed him through the slats.

"He's mighty handsome, Miz Zan."

He did have great skin. Terrific elasticity for a thirty-six year old man. And he was normal. Imagine—a brother who turned out to be a regular guy. Not eccentric like Velda or bizarre like their mother. Henri might just turn out to be the superstar in the family constellation. Someone she could actually slap a backwards-ballcap on and introduce to her friends.

Hi y'all. Meet my brother Henri. Let's all have a beer down at the Shamrock.

She caught herself nodding at the imaginary conversation playing out in her head.

Abruptly, Henri slapped the magazine shut, scrunched his eyes, and opened his mouth. Instead of yawning, he sneezed. He dug for a handkerchief, swiped his nose, and his mustache abruptly slid off.

"Ohmygod." Cézanne sucked air. Her hand tightened around Duty's wrist. "Did you see that?"

Any affinity she'd built up for him instantly turned to dread.

Duty's eyes bulged. "You think Darlene Driskoll messed with his shavin' cream? Maybe it's practice whiskers to see if it'll look good on him when he grows his own. Or he could be *in cognito.*" Long pause. "It means, 'in disguise.' Stop looking at me that way. When're you gonna learn I ain't as dumb as I play like? I watch TV."

Cézanne grabbed a knife handle and yanked out a vegetable peeler. What was she supposed to do with this? Skin his dick? She tossed it onto the counter and pulled out another. This time, she got the squatty little parer. With blood pounding behind both eyeballs, she shoved it deep into her pocket and pushed her way through the doors.

He stood when she entered the room.

"Who the hell are you?"

"I'm Henri." He looked down at the hairy caterpillar in his handkerchief. A sick smile curled his lips. "I can explain."

"Break out some ID." She held out her hand, palm-up, in demand.

He wiggled a finger into his back pocket and pulled out a wallet. She jerked the driver's license out of his hand and studied it with great interest.

Martin, Henri Matisse.

The little hairs on her arms stood straight up. She gave it back. "It's fake. So are you."

"No it's not."

Her hand went to her pocket. She tightened her grip on the handle. "Yes it is. Your given name is Matisse. You don't have a middle name. We only called you Henri so you wouldn't get the crap beat out of you at school. And your DOB's off by a day."

"The Department of Public Safety made a mistake."

"The DPS doesn't make mistakes. They sit at the right hand of God."

"Zan, listen . . ."

She took a backward step, whipped the knife from her pocket and brandished it. Henri's hands shot up in surrender.

"Calm down, I can explain. When I changed my name, I had to get a certified copy of my birth certificate." The cadence of his speech picked up. "I was born at eleven-fifty-eight on the twelfth, not on the thirteenth. Don't you see? It was Mother's idea. Remember how she used to set the egg timer when we were little so she could give us a kiss at the exact hour of our birth? Well I guess she didn't want to set the alarm for midnight so I always got mine at noon on the thirteenth."

It made no sense. Cézanne gave him a hard look. "I don't remember any birthday kiss."

"Of course you don't. You were too little."

This thing with Darlene trying to kill her was making her lose her composure. She did want him to be her brother. And unless she could coax him out onto the porch, stabbing him would make cleaning blood out of the Oriental rug difficult.

She returned the knife to her pocket without releasing her grip. "How come you're in disguise?"

"It seemed like the right thing."

"Why's that?" Her eyes narrowed to a squint.

"It's my job."

"Your job," she said dully.

"I have one of those jobs I can't really talk about."

Classified? A profession requiring top-secret clearance?

"You work at NASA?" She felt a drop in blood pressure. Her voice tapered off to a whisper. "Don't tell me you're in WITSEC. Are you in the witness protection program?"

"What if I am? Would you keep it quiet?"

Was it too much to expect this family to have one normal member?

A desperate thought plagued her. "You're not an assassin, are you?"

Wait a minute. An assassin motoring around in a classic car so blue and shiny that it may as well be outlined in neon flicker-lights? What was she thinking?

Henri grinned. It brought a certain amount of comfort to see that he had good teeth. Not like Velda's Polident grin floating in the water glass beside her bed.

"I'm an inventor. I invent things."

Her heart skipped. "What kind of things? Missiles? Nuclear warheads? Atomic bombs?"

"Nothing that cloak-and-dagger."

"Why can't you talk about it? I can keep a secret."

After a long pause, he leaned in close. His eyes lingered on her brows before flickering past her face to scan the room.

Cézanne tracked his gaze along the ceiling, around the crown molding, down the mitered walls, to the face on the grandmother clock. "What are you doing?"

"Looking for bugs. Mikes. Pin cameras."

"What kind of person would bug their own office?"

"Can't be too careful in my line of work." Henri took a deep breath. "I suppose I can trust my sister." In a voice raspy with intrigue, he said, "I invent cleaning products."

She thought her brain had short-circuited. She shook her head in the strained hope it would clear the cobwebs.

"Similar to the Swiffer sweeper." Purple irises glittered with excitement. "Only with the Abracadabra, you don't need to exert any energy. Instead of actually having to sweep or dust mop, I invented this giant, electro-magnetically charged cloth that you place in the middle of the floor. Head off to work, come home eight hours later, and . . . *abracadabra.* Dust-bunnies, lint, and dirt jump onto the micro-fibers. Gather it up—" hands leap-frogged through the air as he pantomimed the cleanup process "—throw it away. It's revolutionary. You'll never have to lift a finger to clean, ever again."

Speechless, Cézanne's mouth opened and closed like a big-mouth bass. Revolutionize housework? Could these family reunions get any weirder?

"I was in the middle of securing the patent for it when I learned about the old man."

"So you're here to help me get the house?"

"What house?"

"Daddy owned this place. Aunt Velda wants it. Of course you're welcome to stay as long as you like. You're going to help me keep it, aren't you? Isn't that why you're here?"

Henri hedged. "Actually, I need you to put me up for a few weeks. I have to lie low. I left work rather suddenly."

"You walked out on your job?"

"Left in a hurry, more like. That's why I need to borrow your digs. They'd never think of looking for me here."

She stared at him squinty-eyed. "Why would anyone be looking for you?"

"I sort of left with the formula." Henri avoided her gaze. "I took it for safekeeping. I didn't steal it; it's mine. I invented it."

Cézanne clenched her fists. She moved away from the boarded-up window and stood near the fireplace. A hail of bullets couldn't dent the fireplace. The 457th Fighter Squadron couldn't penetrate that fireplace. She made a mental note to purchase additional deadbolts.

Nix that. Wrought-iron bars. A tractor and wench couldn't can-opener the doors without alerting the neighbors.

She tried to keep the thickening dismay out of her voice. "These people you skipped out on . . . they wouldn't actually try to kill you, would they?"

"Oh, gosh no. They might hold me down and tickle me until they got me to reveal the contents, but kill me? No, they wouldn't kill me."

Her confidence tanked.

Ohmygodohmygodohmygod.

Anger pinched the corners of her mouth. She'd just offered

sanctuary to a corporate spy.

Duty waltzed in with Enigma on her heels. She glanced at Cézanne and made a quick observation.

"Yo' lips are tighter than a skeeter's ass in a nose dive. What's wrong?"

Chapter Twenty

While Henri unpacked in their father's study, Cézanne changed into a mint green angora sweater and matching wool slacks. She picked out one brown alligator mule guaranteed to call attention to the ace bandage binding her swollen ankle and stuffed her foot into it. She needed to pay Hollis Rushmore a visit to let him know Henri was present and accounted for. And to ask him about his involvement with Yvonne Rackley.

As she tossed a wool pashmina over one shoulder, she tried to make sense out of this scenario of unexplained events playing out in her head.

First and foremost, normal people didn't go out of their way to fly under the radar.

Second, if assassins were out to kill her brother, his presence would put Duty, Velda, and herself in harm's way. Not that this actually made sense. The guy invented cleaning products, for God's sake. Since when did Blue Chip companies send hit men to track down wayward employees? They sued the living daylights out of them; that's what they did. Drove them into the poor house paying legal fees.

Third, the people who were out to kill her would endanger Henri.

So no matter who shot at whom, they all made good targets. Which meant Henri had to go. Duty, too, to be on the safe side. As for Velda . . .

She conjured up a visual of Velda caught in the crossfire of a hit man's scope.

Duty's voice shook her from her reverie. "Miz Zan, whatchoo doin', bug-eyed and starin' at the ceiling?"

"Trying to figure out how to make Henri leave."

"I thought you liked him."

"It's complicated. I don't think he'll want to go. I may have to resort to guerilla tactics."

"What kind of gorilla tactics? Is that like monkey business?"

Cézanne shifted her gaze from a distant point in space. Slowly, her head rocked to one side. She studied the girl, flounder-eyed. "Monkey business?"

"I like him, Miz Zan. He's easy on the senses. Havin' a man around the house is good business. Maybe if we got us a man people would quit shootin' out our window panes."

"Maybe. I'm driving over to see the lawyer. I'll be back soon. While I'm gone, keep an eye out on Henri."

"I can do that. That I can do."

"Don't open the door for anyone."

"I can do that, too."

"And don't call unless you see blood."

In an effort to cut off two heads of the same snake, Cézanne set out for Hollis Rushmore's office.

Betty, the receptionist, was flitting around like a social butterfly filling clients' guest cups with coffee. As soon as Cézanne entered, she hit the intercom button and delivered what was obviously a coded message. "The vet just called. The dog died."

Cézanne bellied up to the desk. "I'm here to see Hollis."

"Mr. Rushmore's unavailable. He's having his prize Schnauzer euthanized."

"I don't care if he's having it stir fried. I'm going in."

"You can't see Mr. Rushmore without an appointment."

She said a mournful "Bless your heart," and wiggled her

fingers, *ta-ta.* With a "Goodbye, Betty," she sauntered back to Rushmore's private office.

She found him nursing a drink, slouched in his chair with the heels of his Bally's resting on the blotter and his ankles crossed. The scales on his bronze statue of blind justice were lopsided with paper clips and an ink stain from the Mont Blanc had bled through his shirt pocket.

"I'd fix you a scotch and soda but I wouldn't want to keep you."

"You were friends with Yvonne Rackley," she hazarded. "You testified at her husband's trial."

His glassy-eyed stare suddenly sharpened. The silence between them stretched a couple of beats.

He tented his hands on the desk. "I thought you came to talk about Velda. So how're things going at the house?"

"I want her gone. Her hair fell out, and she's scarier than ever. It's bad for business."

He touched a hand to the sparse bristles poking out from his scalp and smoothed them flat. His enthusiasm went as limp as his rumpled, cotton shirt. "She's not such a bad old lady. Velda's a sharp cookie. She loved her brother, and she didn't want to see anything happen to the things he held dear."

"Before we tune our violins and get misty-eyed, let's keep things in perspective, shall we? My father loved his house more than he loved his kids. *'Nuff sed.*"

"I think you underestimate the guy. If he'd wanted to cut you out of an inheritance, he would've left everything to his wife."

Cézanne bristled. "Let's discuss that, too. Where is the bereaved widow, anyway?"

"Probably retaining her own counsel."

Relatives were coming out of the woodwork.

Rushmore must've read frustration in her face. "That's where

Velda'll come in handy if you don't run her off. See, Velda thinks Aricella—"

"Who?"

"Your stepmother. Velda thinks Aricella's a gold digger. She's convinced the girl married your father for his money."

"Girl?" Cézanne's eyes scrunched in suspicion. "Just how old is she?"

"About your age. What are you . . . twenty-six, twenty-seven?"

"Thirty-two."

"Then Aricella's young enough to be your baby sister."

That scorched her. The old man wasn't only loaded, he was a cradle-robbing sex pervert.

"Your aunt Velda claims she has the dirt on her. She says Aricella's been riding the gravy train."

"She may've been riding the gravy train, but she's doing it on biscuit wheels. She's not getting my inheritance."

"We'll know for sure when we get to court."

"When will it all end?"

"When the judge rules. Provided Aricella doesn't appeal."

"You're saying if I want to keep the boudoir bandit out of our business I have to suck up to Velda?" Her mouth went slack.

"Could be worse."

Cézanne did some serious eye rolling. She remembered the real reason for coming here. "What was your interest in Erick Rackley's wife?"

"Yvonne came to me for help. She was trapped in a loveless marriage."

"I thought you only did probate law."

"Wasn't always the case." He stared into his glass and swirled the ice until it clinked. "Family law can be lucrative, but it's also draining. Nobody's ever happy. I quit doing divorces after the murder."

"Was she having an affair?"

"Where'd you get that information?"

"A hunch."

"Nobody would've blamed her if she was. Eric was a drunk. He loved guns more than he liked most people. Before the police department ran him off, Yvonne brought him to the office Christmas party. Showed him off to her friends and colleagues. He was a world-class asshole, and he didn't deserve her." He shook his head in disbelief. "Erick actually bragged about knowing how to commit murder and get away with it. We knew he'd killed Yvonne. He damned near got away with it."

She shifted uneasily in her chair.

"I used to tell her to leave him. I told her I didn't want to be called to testify at her murder trial. And that, by golly, is exactly what happened."

Cézanne dug through her handbag and pulled out a list of questions. "Were you at their home the night she died?"

Rushmore's rheumy-eyed expression didn't change, but she sensed she'd worn out her welcome.

"I only told you what I told you because it's already in the domain. Read the court transcript if you want to know anything else. The rest of your questions for me are protected by attorney-client confidentiality."

"She's dead."

"Our conversations are still protected."

"Don't you want to see justice done?"

He reacted with a frozen stare. Instantly, she wanted to instruct him to disregard, like in a courtroom.

"Justice was done. Let it alone." He stood on wobbly legs, teetering beside the desk until his equilibrium caught up. "Pity you can't stay longer, but I have a business to run."

He suddenly remembered he had a call to make.

She gathered her belongings and headed for the exit. At the door, she turned. "One more thing. Henri's accounted for."

The tension that had built up during their meeting left Rushmore's face. "I meant to call you. I found out yesterday. My condolences. I'll go ahead and set the hearing for the prove-up."

If she had to split the house two ways, she'd much rather share with Henri than Bob's child bride.

So why'd Rushmore offer his condolences?

Chapter Twenty-One

"Wear the red one." Duty held the slinky dress up to the light. "It's nize."

Upon closer inspection, Cézanne decided it had a spot on it. "I don't like any of them." She scanned the dresses fanned out over the bed covers and shook her head. "I shouldn't have agreed to go to this New Year's Eve party. Everybody I know'll be there, and I tend to draw mixed reviews. People'll ask questions about my job. They'll wonder why I'm not there showing off Bobby instead of going with Slash." She spoke the obvious. "Doug Driskoll will be there. I've never known him to pass up free hooch."

"Hooch?"

"Booze."

"Back home in Weeping Mary, we call it chock. White folks call chock moonshine. I say wear the black dress. Do these little sparkly things come off the straps?"

"They're rhinestones. Are you listening to me? I'm telling you I don't want to attend this soirée."

Raven should be going with Slash. Instead, she agreed to accompany Jinx Porter to a fundraiser at the children's hospital—Raven had a soft spot for kids—in what seemed like a trumped up way for the constable to get close to her again. But Slash and Raven talked it over: He'd escort Cézanne to protect her from Driskoll, and she'd be Jinx's date so he could continue to appear normal. Normal meaning since Jinx needed money for his re-election campaign, he could glad-hand, backslap, and politic to his heart's content as long as he had Raven at his side. Few people remembered Jinx after meeting him. Raven, they remembered.

"Here's the truth. I feel guilty going out with a guy my best friend is crazy about. And for some stupid reason, I feel like I'm two-timing Bobby, my fiancé who's on his honeymoon with another woman . . ." Cézanne blinked. A revolutionary thought occurred. "Why am I telling you this? I don't need your permission to stay home. You're not in charge here." She pitched the dress onto the bed. "That does it, I'm not going. I'll call and tell him I'm sick. Better yet, you do it. Tell him I'm too sick to talk to him. He'll believe you."

"Do your own dirty work, Miz Zan." Duty lifted the black dress by its hanger. "I think this one's real pretty. If we was to pin yo' hair up, you'd look like a movie star. What about yo' cast?"

"Tonight, I'm wearing shoes if it kills me." With her eyes scrunched tight, Cézanne squeezed her swollen foot into a low-heeled *peau de soie* pump.

"So you're going to the party?"

"Yeah, I'll go. But I won't enjoy it." A concession she'd make to absolve her of guilt.

She was still in the bathroom re-applying eyebrow pencil when the doorbell chimed. Slash had arrived. When Velda started quizzing him, Cézanne's heart fluttered.

Hobbling downstairs, she took in his appearance starting with his spit-polished shoes. Her attention traveled up the legs of his Dockers and settled on his—

"I'm ready," she said, and navigated the last couple of steps without looking down.

He held a clutch of miniature roses that Duty cheerfully extracted and bustled off to the kitchen for a vase. Enigma sat at Slash's feet radiating intelligence and curiosity. Giving the shoes an occasional sniff and a swipe of the tongue, he thumped his tail against the rug in loud, deliberate whacks.

Slash gawked. It was as if he wanted to speak, but the words slid back down his throat.

"Don't she look nize?" Duty returned and placed the flowers on the mantle.

Velda glowered from her place at the bottom of the stairs. "That dress is tighter than a tick, if you ask me."

"Nobody asked," Cézanne and Duty chorused.

"Looks like a sausage casing. I can see the pulse beating in your stomach. When you can see body functions taking place through a person's clothing, it's too damned tight."

"I like it." Slash presented his arm for the taking. "Ready?"

"Almost." Cézanne excused herself to the kitchen. She ran an inch of water into a glass and returned to the living room, sipping. Abruptly, she turned to her aunt. "Hold this, would you?" Without waiting for an answer, she shoved the tumbler into Velda's hand. "Tell me if my necklace is fastened," she said, and lifted her hair off her neck so Velda could see.

"Looks fine to me. Here—take this. I'm not your housekeeper." She shoved the glass at Cézanne, who cheerfully plucked it from her grasp and held it by the rim as if it contained something vile.

Henri ambled in munching a sandwich. He stopped short of the table and swallowed.

"Slash, this is my brother Henri. Henri, meet Slash."

They exchanged greetings. What started out as a brusque handshake ended up looking like a couple of jocks trying to take each other to the knees. She decided it was a man thing. The guys traded non-verbal, alpha male communications that filled the air and prickled the hair at the base of her neck with an unmistakable charge. Inwardly, she supposed there would always be macho stuff she didn't understand.

"Maybe Henri would like to go with us?"

Slash nipped the suggestion in the bud. "I'm sure he wouldn't be interested in hanging out with a bunch of strangers."

Henri begged off good-naturedly. "Business to take care of, don'tcha know?"

The Vaughn brothers swore by Chevy pickups. Cézanne dreaded hiking her dress far enough up to climb inside without an extra hoisting from her date so it pleasantly surprised her to see that Slash drove his silver Audi.

Beneath a porch light covered in bug husks, Slash said, "What's with your aunt?"

"She's just mad because a house fell on her sister."

Cézanne liked the way his teeth caught the light when he laughed. She loved the way he checked her out from the corner of his eye.

When they reached the passenger door, Slash made an observation. "You forgot to leave your water glass."

"I didn't forget. I want you to run the prints."

"Do what?"

"Run the prints through AFIS. That's not my aunt."

Slash cut his eyes to the house. "Who is it?"

"I expect you'll tell me."

Inside the car, he engaged the automatic door locks, and they seat-buckled themselves in. After backing out of the drive and merging into traffic, he made a suggestion. "We could skip the party."

"I'm okay." But she wasn't.

She dreaded the possibility of running into Doug Driskoll.

For fifteen years, Slash's sergeant threw a New Year's Eve party. He lived on a ninety-acre farm inherited from his grandparents and took great pride in the wood and fieldstone pavilion he built with the help of brother officers. This particular night, a local country-western band was performing a Hank Williams, Jr. tune when they arrived.

Cézanne elbowed Slash's arm. "Thought you said he lived in a log cabin. This is a lodge."

"I've never been here. I stay pretty busy. And if I'm not already scheduled to work holidays, I trade out with the married guys so they can be with their families. Sarge invited the crime scene unit out for Thanksgiving, but I had to work."

"You missed turkey?"

"I ate at my mom's. After working thirty-six hours straight on a double-homicide in Woodhaven, I passed out in the cornbread dressing. Boy was she pissed. She thought I was trying to get out of eating it. She puts celery in it, and I hate celery."

"I'll remember that."

"If my own mother doesn't care, why should you?"

She flashed a coy smile. "Maybe I like you."

"You love me. You just don't know it yet."

"I'm still weighing the pros and cons."

Slash provided the pros. "I'm clean, I own my house, and I'm not a Mama's boy. What're the cons?"

"Raven, for one. She's crazy about you. Erick Rackley, for another. You're obsessed with that case."

He took her hand and led her into the crowd.

She heard her name called out behind her.

In a far corner, Slash's brother Teddy waved them over.

With a "Be right back," Slash left her in his brother's protective custody and headed for the kegs. She gave Teddy a hug, and they exchanged small talk until his date ambled over, goat-drunk. Cézanne recognized her from the Sheriff's Office. The girl had urine-colored hair plaited into a long braid and more testosterone coursing through her system than most men.

Before Slash returned with their drinks, Cézanne excused

herself and headed up a stone path to the house. She found the powder room and was repairing her lipstick when she sensed she wasn't alone. On the other side of the bathroom, someone tried the locked handle.

"Just a minute." She smoothed a finger against her lip line in an attempt to even out the color. Returning the tube of gloss to her handbag, she snapped it closed and untoggled the lock. The moment she cracked the door, the bedroom light flicked off.

A hand came around the molding and pawed the bathroom switch, enveloping her in total darkness. Her first impulse was to slam the disembodied limb in the door.

Too late. Vise-grip hands forced her deeper into the bathroom. The lock clicked shut. She sniffed the vapors of Angel for Men and felt a chunk of granite where her heart should've been.

Driskoll.

He whirled her around and clamped a hand over her mouth, squelching a hysterical squeal. Grabbing her around the waist, he squeezed hard enough to deflate her lungs. With his lips pressed into her earlobe and hot breath reeking of liquor, she heard what he had to say up close and personal.

"You can't just walk out on me, understand? I'm a free man. The old ball and chain's not coming back so you can do this. You know you want to."

She tried to disabuse him of the notion, but her muffled protest got lost in his tightening grip.

Blood pounded in her ears. She went limp in the scant hope he'd loosen his hold. If he moved his hand even the slightest, she'd sink her canine teeth in so deep it'd take fifty stitches, a tetanus shot, and six months of rehab before he'd be able to qualify at the firearms range again.

"Accept it, babe. You're not gonna be with that asshole in Johnson County, and you're not gonna prick-tease me with a brother officer. Tonight, you're leaving with me. Got it?"

She plotted to drill a heel through his instep.

He let go of her waist and held her one-handed. The sound of his zipper grating along its track ratcheted up her heartbeat. Her eyes blurred with tears.

Where was Slash?

For that matter, where were the others? It was a party, for God's sake.

Driskoll tightened his grip on her face. She rose on tiptoes to keep from blacking out.

"Big Doug's missed you, babe. Kiss him hello."

She shook her head. The air was noxious with the smell of booze and testosterone. A primitive whimper escaped her lips.

"I remember a time when I couldn't keep you off me. It is gonna happen."

Driskoll had a way of immunizing her to indignity. He reached up the skirt of her dress, yanked down her silk bikinis, and pressed himself against her buttocks. She wriggled against his fumbling hand. The only way he'd ever get another piece of ass off her was if he sneaked into the Tarrant County M.E.'s Office and removed her cold, gray corpse from the cooler.

"Cézanne?"

Slash.

She wilted in relief.

"Cézanne, you in here?"

A strip of light appeared under the door.

"Change of plans, babe," Driskoll whispered. "The world hates a squealer."

He unhanded her mouth and flipped on the light switch. She yanked up her panties with such conviction they turned into a thong.

"I'm in here," she cried out, breathless and panicked.

She glimpsed her reflection in the mirror. Berry-stained slashes in the shape of Driskoll's fingers angled up the side of her face. Driskoll studied the remnants of lipgloss on his palm and smeared it across his mouth.

He opened the door, zipped his zipper, and stepped out into the bedroom.

Realization dawned on her—he wanted Slash to think they'd had sex.

"Thanks, babe," he called over his shoulder. "Hey, Slash, I didn't know you were here. This isn't what it looks like. I wasn't moving in on your territory."

The contours of Slash's face hardened. In three strides, he covered Driskoll like a skin graft, balling up a fist and cold-cocking him with an evil right cross. Sucking air, Driskoll crashed against the wood door's hollow core and crumpled, face-first, onto the Berber carpet.

Slash shook out his scuffed, red fingers and blew on his knuckles. "All-state boxing. You hurt?"

He offered his hand, and she took it. Sent him a wobbly smile of hope as she stepped over Driskoll's ragdoll carcass. At the last second, the devil on her shoulder goaded her. She whipped around, gave her former lover a well-placed kick in the ribs and left him bent at the waist like a sock monkey.

Let him explain the head imprint in the bathroom door.

Outside, thunder rumbled. Slash removed his leather bomber jacket and whipped it over her shoulders. He shuddered from the cold and picked up his gait.

Raw with humiliation, she caught up to him. "Driskoll wanted you to think this was consensual."

"I'd rather not hear any confessions tonight."

"Nothing happened. It might've if you hadn't come along when you did."

"Never did like that guy." He kept walking.

In an unguarded moment she took stock of her date. Slash, a few steps ahead of her, stopped abruptly and returned to her side. She clasped his hand, half-expecting to see the makings of a smile. Instead, he winced. Even in the blue glow of a security light she could see his fingers were bruised and swollen.

"Where to?" His breath turned to vapor when he spoke.

"Maybe we ought to go to the ER and get that looked at."

"I hate doctors."

"Then I know the perfect place."

Chapter Twenty-Two

"You again." Marvin Krivnek pushed the door closed. He slid the chain along its metal track until it fell, dangling, beneath the setscrew and reopened it. "What is it this time?"

"It's not for me. It's Slash. I was thinking maybe you could take a look at his hand as a professional courtesy."

Krivnek stepped back and let them inside.

She detected the smell of warm cocoa and cinnamon toast rising up through the air. Mouth watering, she darted a look at Slash.

"Wait in the den. I was making a cup of hot chocolate, and I need to take the milk off the burner. I have trouble sleeping; I can't imagine why."

He raked his fingers through high-voltage hair, padded past them in his Jiffies, and flipped on wall switches. As he walked toward the sofa where he wanted them to sit, her stomach growled with hunger.

"Listen, Marv, we didn't realize you'd be asleep." The apology was about as convincing as her fake eyebrows.

He gave them an uninvitingly blank look.

"We should leave," Slash said.

"Take a seat. You want a cup of cocoa? I know she does. We do this every so often," he said airily, as if she wasn't standing in the same room with them. "She comes over, wakes me up, badgers me until I do what she wants. People question why I never married. I'd rather jump barefoot into a fifty-gallon drum full of porcupines. Women come with more baggage than American Tourister, but this one's a walking, talking ten-piece set. Marshmallows?"

They shook their heads. "No, thanks," they said in unison and watched him shuffle off.

Deep in the kitchen, cups clinked. They glimpsed him behind the kitchen pass-through. He worked over the stove like a mad scientist hunkered over the pan in his robe with his whisk whipping.

"I thought you were smarter than this," Krivnek called out.

Slash elbowed her. "He's talking to you."

"No, he's talking to you." She gave a gusty sigh. "I'm pretty sure it's because you're with me."

Krivnek leaned beyond the pass-through. "I can hear you, Zan. I'm talking to Wolf. This lady's quicksand. You don't recognize it on sight, and it looks pretty benign until you walk into it and sink up to your gills. Next thing you know, you're a goner." He smoothed over the harsh words with a bit of verbal lubricant. "And yet you can't help yourself."

"Thanks for the endorsement, Marvin. I brought him here because if we go to the ER, the on-duty cops will have to fill out a report. Nobody wants to end up in IA."

"IA?" Krivnek padded out gripping two mug handles in one hand and one in the other. He distributed them with minimal fanfare. "I won't provide cover for misconduct."

Slash said, "It's not like that, Marve. Doug Driskoll overstepped his boundaries. I just reminded him where they were. You might call it defense of a third party."

"Driskoll's got a ten-gallon mouth. Never did like him." Krivnek set his mug on an end table and reached for Slash's injured hand. His eyes flickered to Cézanne. "She can take care of herself better than you can, my man." He manipulated the knuckles, squeezed fingers, and made his diagnosis. "Doesn't appear to be broken but you won't be able to flip anybody off for a few days. It wouldn't hurt to put a couple of splints on these blue ones. They're an over-the-counter drugstore item." He let go, retrieved his cocoa, and directed his next comment to Cézanne. "I take it your foot healed?"

"I thought I'd give shoes a try."

"How'd that work out?"

"I re-injured my toe driving it into Driskoll's ribcage."

Krivnek shook his head. "Occasionally, when I have nothing better to do, I imagine how you'd look caring for young children. Unfortunately, I can't seem to keep the image in my head more than a few seconds before an act of violence occurs. Manual strangulation, generally. I imagine it's even more true with boyfriends." He locked Slash in his stare. "Do not underestimate this wolverine in sheep's clothing."

Cézanne switched gears. "Speaking of violence, you're familiar with Yvonne Rackley's case?"

Slash stared, his face unreadable.

"I've only autopsied about three thousand bodies to date. I'm sure I can remember whichever one interests you," Krivnek said sarcastically.

"Ex-cop's wife, GSW to the chest, Erick Rackley, tried for murder?"

"Ahhhh." The M.E. grew quiet. "We ruled it undetermined. The DA wouldn't touch, it so the family found a hired gun to take it to the grand jury. They indicted the fellow."

"That's the one."

"I don't remember anything about it."

His words carried a bit of hang time. One corner of his mouth turned up. He returned her stare with a look of fake surprise.

"What? You think you're the only one around here who can make jokes?"

★ ★ ★ ★ ★

At three-thirty in the morning, Cézanne expected to walk into the house, trot her sleep-deprived body up the stairs, and fall into bed. It didn't happen.

Duty, flipping oversized picture cards, sat at the dining room table with a plush towel wrapped, turban-like, around her head. She resembled the carnival fortune-teller with Henri seated across from her, scrutinizing each upturned card.

"The ace of pentacles is in a good position. Gonna get money. I see the two of wands. It's in the reverse position so that means a surprise."

Cézanne suppressed a loud intake of air. "What's going on here?"

"Quiet, Miz Zan. I have to concentrate." Duty scrunched her lids shut. She put her fingers against her temples as if to summon a spirit from the netherworld.

"Are those Tarot cards?"

Her eyes popped open. "Yessum. We're seeing if Mista Henri should return to work."

"You're not serious." Flabbergasted, she turned to her brother. "You don't actually believe this hooey, do you?"

Without giving him a chance to answer, Duty rose from the table and fixed her gaze on some distant point beyond Cézanne's shoulder. "Tarot cards can lead you to discover your spirit guides. My gramma, Corinthia, she learned to read Tarot when she was a baby livin' in the bayou. Her mama, Galatia, my great-gramma, she came from Haiti. She could do runes. I inherited this gift, and I have to use it or lose it."

She plopped back down into the chair. Her lips thinned. She tapped a card with her fingernail to get Henri's attention. "This here's the six of swords. There was a trip, but you didn't go. I know because I'm lookin' at the magician card."

Henri's mouth had a hard edge. "What else do the cards say?"

Duty turned up two more cards. She sucked in a loud breath. "I see the ten of pentacles in the reverse position. Somebody's a liar."

Henri stiffened. "Who?"

"Lookie here. Just what I thought. Nine of discs, reversed. This is about money, only this money comes from tainted sources." She leaned inches from his face. "Either you know the source of this sudden wealth or you suspect it. You have to consult yo' conscience on whether to accept it or not."

Henri winked. "Sit down, Sis. Let her tell your fortune."

Duty scowled. "It's a readin', not fortune-tellin'."

Henri pulled out a chair. "C'mon. Sit. It'll be fun."

"That's exactly what the gynecologist said last time I went in." Cézanne gave him the evil eye and reluctantly scooted onto the seat.

Enigma got up from Duty's side and inserted himself between Cézanne and Henri. A low growl vibrated in his throat.

"Duty, your dog's making spooky sound effects again."

"Quiet, 'Nigma. Everybody stop talkin'. I'm almost finished. Uh-oh, this is bad, Mista Henri. You got someone close to you . . ." Her voice broke. "Let's just say they know what you're doin' here. You need to be extra careful."

Duty gathered the cards and started over. "Uh-oh. Here's that Darlene Driskoll. She can't be trusted, and she's emotionally unstable. See, this is the queen of cups and it's reversed. That's bad. Okay, here we go."

She turned up two more cards. "Listen here, Miz Zan. I'm showin' you the six of cups. You're still tryin' to escape into the past 'cause you think it's happy and beautiful. But you gotta stop wallowin' in self-pity and realize yo' ambitions are in the here and now. Oh, look what we've got."

Cézanne glanced at Henri and rolled her eyes.

Duty overturned more cards. "King of cups. You got a friend givin' you unreliable advice. Don't screw up yo' piddly eyebrows, Miz Zan. It ain't talkin' about me. This is a man-friend. You ever lucky enough to get advice from Deuteronomy Devilrow, you need to take it.

"Don't look now. Page of cups. Pay attention. This represents an intense person. They have a controlled exterior maskin' a volcano of emotions lyin' within. You need to watch out for this person."

"Man or woman?"

"Could be either."

"Oh, yeah. I see where this is going. That gives you a hundred percent chance of being right."

"Don't kill the messenger. Cards speak the truth." She tapped a fingernail against the queen of wands card. "It's upside down so you're gonna come in contact with a jealous, insecure woman."

Cézanne and Duty exchanged looks. They piped up at the same time. "Velda."

Duty turned over the next card.

"Death." Words tumbled out in a rush. "It ain't what you think, Miz Zan. It ain't about physical death. This card means the end of a cycle. You need to re-evaluate yo' life and change yo' consciousness."

"Well, that's reassuring. For a second I thought Velda might do me in."

Unexpectedly, Duty gasped. She stopped dealing and scooped up the cards with a broad sweep of her hand. "Session's over."

She pulled the towel off her head and shook it out. With the grace of an Egyptian queen, she rose and glided to the hallway where the hem of her ill-fitting housecoat formed a train that disappeared up the stairs.

Beleaguered, Henri scratched his chin. "Where'd you find this kook?"

Deep sigh. "Long story."

"Do we really need her here?"

"I don't have a choice." Cézanne glanced around and did a visual inventory. It happened each time she entered a room. Police academy teachings died hard, she supposed. "Besides, I've kind of gotten used to having her around." She took a deep breath and weighed the decision to express a thought that had woven itself into her short-term plans. "I'm actually thinking of inviting her to stay once she finishes school."

"Big mistake."

"Really?" Cézanne smiled. "I know she seems peculiar, but the truth is I've grown fond of her. I like teaching her to be more cosmopolitan. She has style." With that, she pushed away from the table and headed upstairs. "Turn out the light when you're done."

Over the next two days, the winter weather went through three distinct changes: freezing, to warm, to miserable and wet. Cézanne made the most of a biting rain by sitting at the telephone tracking down more jurors in Erick Rackley's murder trial. When Duty brought the morning paper inside, Cézanne shook out the Metro section, flipped through looking for local news, and did a double take.

Pearlie Gray's name appeared in the obituaries. Cézanne copied down the address of the funeral parlor and called out for Duty.

"Put on something nice. We're going to a wake."

"I'm already awake. 'Nigma's still asleep, though."

"Not awake. A wake." She spelled it for her. "Look it up."

Duty returned with the dictionary open and her finger pressed to the page. Her eyes bulged so much the whites encircling her irises resembled Saturn.

"We're seein' a dead person? 'Cause I don't like to be around people who've passed."

"I was under the impression your people view death differently." Cézanne matched Duty's unblinking stare. "I thought these services were supposed to be a celebration of life in your culture."

"Who're you kiddin'?" The girl swatted the air between them. "Dead's dead. It's all just a big put-on."

"Regardless, I need you to go with me so I don't stick out like a sore thumb."

"Who're we seein'?"

"Pearlie Mae Gray."

"How do you know Pearlie Gray?"

"I don't."

"Miz Zan, don'tchoo think goin' to a stranger's funeral is kinda weird? I could see why you'd wanna hob-knob with her kin if she was famous, but to go see a dead woman just 'cause she's dead . . . that's sick."

"It's not sick. Besides, it's not her I'm there to see; I want to talk to her family."

"Go to her house. I don't wanna see no dead lady."

"I don't know where she lived. But I know where she is now that she's dead as a herring."

"I don't know nothin' about her hearing, but I reckon now all her senses are dead. Dead eyes, dead smell, dead to the touch, taste buds're dead."

Cézanne shook her head. "I'm not even going to try to explain. Get dressed."

Duty slammed the dictionary shut. "Lemme get this straight, Miz Zan. You'd be wantin' to go see some dead woman who you don't know, at a place where you never visited, and don't know her kinfolk, and you wanna do this 'cause why?"

"She was a juror in a case I'm working on."

"The Rackley case?"

"Exactly. Since I can't interview her, I want to talk to her family to see if she ever revealed anything to them about her experience sitting on the jury. I don't want to go by myself because, in case you haven't noticed, I'm white. Pearlie Gray was a black lady. You're black," Cézanne pointed out, despite the girl's complicated heritage. Deuteronomy Devilrow, with her café au lait skin, might've passed for Caucasian had it not been for the texture of her dark hair, full lips, and those spooky, garnet-gemstone eyes. "So I'm taking you with me to Pearlie Gray's wake so we'll blend in."

Duty appeared thunderstruck. "So I'm your ticket into the wake?"

"Exactly."

"So I should pretend I knew Pearlie Gray?"

"Might help."

"I can do that. That, I can do." Duty punctuated her opinion with a curt nod. Her eyes thinned. "I could work a lot better if you was to let me wear that pretty red dress."

"You don't wear red to a funeral. It's considered bad taste."

"I don't have to touch her, do I? 'Cause I won't touch a dead person."

"You don't have to lay a finger on her."

"Well, anyway," Duty went on in her animated way, "I didn't say I was gonna wear it to see my poor dead friend, Pearlie Mae. I'm sayin' it's what I'm gonna wear when you take me to dinner at the Fort Worth Club. And we're gonna invite yo' brother. On account of I'm sweet on him." Duty ducked her head. Her cheeks rounded like plums. "I deserve to have this as my reward even if you don't have a boyfriend. On account of I did such a good job scammin' people at the funeral parlor."

"This isn't a scam. We're not scamming anybody."

Duty fixed her with a stare. "Miz Zan, you can paint a cow purple, but that don't make it an eggplant."

Chapter Twenty-Three

Cézanne was no stranger to Reverend Willie Lee Washington's House of the Celestial Dove. The Reverend Washington, a self-ordained minister and irreverent blowhard, buried her partner Roby Tyson a few days before Thanksgiving. Almost none of the mourners wore black. And during the service, people would erupt from their seats and scream their lungs out for no good reason. A few ladies even fainted.

Among Washington's trademark services, one stood out from the rest of the city's morticians—the release of five hundred doves into the heavens at the end of the ceremony. That, and coffins iced down with Schlitz Malt Liquor in the back room.

In the crowded parking lot, Duty patted a small yawn. "What'd Pearlie Mae do for a livin'?"

"Retired school teacher."

"Oh. Good. If I'm asked how I know her, I'll say I was a student."

Cézanne wheeled the Cadillac into a space near the curb and cut the engine. With one hand on the steering wheel and the other gripping Duty's shoulder, she laid down the law.

"The one thing I learned in my years as a police officer that's become etched into my brain is what gets people sent to prison: Talking too much," she explained, enunciating her words in a loud, slow voice as if they'd never met and English was Duty's second language. "The penitentiary's full of people who aren't deaf and dumb. So don't start blabbing about stuff that can trap you. We don't want to stand out."

"You know that's right, Miz White-lady-in-a-black-dress-at-a-black-funeral-parlor."

Distress puckered her lips. "The less said the better. We'll walk in and pay our respects, maybe hang around and listen to what other people have to say about Pearlie, okay? Don't start spinning yarns that'll get us kicked out."

"I'm a good listener. Nobody ever said Deuteronomy Devilrow couldn't lend an ear." The girl pinched her index finger and thumb together, put them to her lips and twisted them, counterclockwise, in a tic-a-lock gesture. She even pitched the invisible key over her shoulder.

"Here's the plan. Whoever speaks to us first, you say you came to see Pearlie Mae. Only you should call her Mrs. Gray. If anybody presses for more information you say you knew her from school. Let them do most of the talking." As Duty head-bobbed, Cézanne checked her makeup in the rearview mirror. "Ready?"

"Ready as a racehorse." The girl popped the door handle and swung out a leg. Cézanne couldn't be sure, but she thought the kid's lithe, sinewy gait had something to do with the silk stockings and garter belt from Cox's. Either that, or the violet angora sweater and black leather skirt the girl conned her out of made her feel grown up and important.

A set of steps leading up to an entry of carved double doors awaited them. A few feet shy of the stairs, intuition took over. Cézanne froze. The plan had too many holes. She should've drawn up a contingency plan in case they were chased down the street by a mob of angry black people.

"Duty, wait. Maybe we shouldn't—"

But Duty trotted ahead with spring in her step.

Cézanne caught up. Inside, she found the kid bending the ear of a creaky old gentleman in a charcoal pinstripe suit and silver ascot. As she approached, Duty let out a scream loud enough to clot blood. Three pints of O-positive settled in Cézanne's feet.

"Lawd, I can't believe she's gone. Tell me how it happened so I can sleep at night."

The old man glanced in Cézanne's direction. His face bore the expression of a host who'd ushered his party guests out onto the patio only to find a turd floating in the swimming pool. Duty must've noticed, too. She threw her arms around the man's middle and buried her face in his shirt.

He patted the soft curve of her shoulder. "Would you like to see her?" He thumbed down the aisle in the direction of an iridescent pink casket.

Duty sniffled. She pulled away and snapped to attention like she didn't even notice the fawn-colored oval face print her makeup left on his shiny satin ascot. "Not yet. There's someone I wantchoo to meet. This is Miz Zan. I'm her wart."

"Ward."

"That's what I said."

Cézanne extended her hand. The old man engulfed her hand in gnarled, calloused fingers. "I'm so sorry for your loss."

Tears jeweled his eyes. They teetered along the rims like glass beads each time he glanced over expectantly at the front door.

"If you don't mind," Duty said, "where was Mrs. Gray when the chariot swung low?"

Cézanne stood, marooned, half-expecting to be escorted out but the man indulged Duty's brazen ways. "She was asleep. I rolled over and said, 'Gee baby, get up and turn on the heat. You're as cold as ice.' "

"And stiff as a flagpole, too?"

Inwardly, Cézanne swooned. "Pardon us, we don't wish to intrude upon your grief." Before Duty could balk, she grabbed her elbow. "We'll pay our respects now."

The girl put up a slight resistance. Cézanne strong-armed

her, and they started off down the aisle like a herd of turtles.

"Didn't I tell you not to talk so much? And what the hell? 'Was she stiff as a flagpole?' I never saw such bad manners. A civilized person doesn't go around reminding a grief-stricken man that his wife's dead—what's wrong with you?"

"I think he already knows, considering she's laid out in her Sunday best with a big smile frozen on her face, and there's a backhoe with a front-end loader diggin' a big hole outside."

A sturdy man who appeared to be in his forties walked their way. Cézanne sensed danger lurking beneath his feral smile and felt a thrill of terror. She hissed, "Let me do the talking."

"I thought that's why you brought me."

She tightened her grip on Duty's arm and the girl fell silent.

The man blocked their path. "Did you come to see Mama?"

They chimed simultaneous answers: Cézanne, "Yes." Duty, "No."

Duty contorted her face until she resembled a crime victim in a grade-B horror flick. "I can't bring myself to look at her. I want to remember her the way she was." She faked a crying jag.

"You'll have to excuse her. She's overwrought."

The son's eyes went shrewd. He had a menacing presence, towering over them and breathing heavy didn't help. "And you are?"

"Deuteronomy Devilrow. I loved yo' mama. She was a breath of fresh air. She was sunlight on a rainy day. She was—"

"Supposed to be quiet," Cézanne said through gritted teeth. She forced a smile. "I think we'll just have a seat for a few minutes until Deuteronomy composes herself."

She hip-checked the girl into the nearest pew. The front doors swung open, moving a shaft of sunlight over the room like a lighthouse beacon. A cluster of people entered, and the man excused himself. He ventured forth to console the newcomers.

"Are you trying to get us thrown out?"

"I'm helpin'."

"Well don't help so much." Cézanne rose. "You wait here. I'm going to pay my respects to the deceased, and then I'm going to mingle."

She stepped away and braved the walk to the open coffin. She surmised Pearlie Mae Gray had been a good cook judging by her plump cheeks and robust girth.

She sensed a presence behind her. Three puffy-eyed ladies bellied up to the casket.

"Mmmm, mmm, mmm," said the one dressed in a hot pink taffeta dress two sizes too small. "Reverend Willie Lee's people sho' did ruin her hair. Don't you think they ruined Pearlie's hair?" When she moved, her pink felt hat cut the air like a flying saucer. "Looks like she's been dragged through a knot hole backwards."

Cézanne ad libbed. "It's certainly . . . different."

"She woulda never had her hair like that. Woulda passed on the spot if Merdelene down at the Clip Joint woulda handed her a mirror and showed her this hair. Whatchoo think, Imagene? Think Pearlie woulda liked this hair?"

"Mmmm, mmm, mmm," said a woman wearing a bright blue suit whose own shellacked "do" looked like a cockatoo crest and had an unnatural blue streak running through it that matched her clothes. "Wait'll Oolong and Chai see this."

"Who?" Cézanne inserted herself into the conversation.

"The twins, Oolong and Chai." Blue suit slid her friends a sideways glance.

"Interesting names." Cézanne wanted to whip out her spiral notebook and jot this information down. "How's that spelled?"

"Girl, don't start me lyin'," said purple pantsuit, who'd remained quiet up until now. "All I know is Pearlie Mae's son married a half-wit named Takisha—"

"You's just callin' Takisha a half-wit 'cause she tried to trifle with yo' sister's husband," said pink dress.

Purple pantsuit took offense. "I'm callin' Takisha a half-wit 'cause she is a half-wit. And if you was twice as smart, you'd be a half-wit on account of you don't even realize Takisha's over there rubbin' on yo' man."

Pink dress' eyes bulged. She let out a yip and strode up the aisle, straight for a slender black woman with a brassy streak down one side of her hair.

Blue suit said, "I told LaZelda not to wear that shiny pink dress. Her ass is so big it looks like two Buicks fightin' for a parking place."

Cézanne bit the inside of her mouth to keep from hooting. She liked blue suit.

"Oolong and Chai?" she prompted. "How'd you say those names are spelled?"

"I didn't. On account of I don't know for sure. When that triflin' Takisha needed baby names she went to the pantry, opened it up, and saw a stack of tea boxes on the shelf. That's where the names of her babies came from."

Oolong and Chai were named after tea? And nobody thought to name one Earl Grey?

Cézanne thumbed in Duty's direction. "I didn't know Mrs. Gray. I brought my little friend to pay her respects because she isn't old enough to drive." She glanced back over where the girl should've been and nearly slipped into shock.

Duty had abandoned her post and was conversing with a group of elderly folks on the opposite side of the room.

"Would you excuse me?" Cézanne asked sweetly. Halfway up the aisle, she watched helplessly as Duty flitted off to interrogate the next set of survivors.

Cézanne sashayed up to a group of women and cut to the chase. "Mind if I ask you ladies a question? Wasn't Mrs. Gray a juror on that murder case?" She snapped her fingers near her ear as if it would help her recall a lost thought orbiting a confused mind. "Erick Rackley."

Eyes turned cagey. "Are you a reporter?" one asked.

"No, but I read the newspaper. Things stick with me."

"Lawd, yes, child. Pearlie never did think that boy did it. She said he was too good-lookin'. Said a man that attractive wouldn't have to kill his wife if he'd wanted to get rid of her. A man that handsome could've had any woman he set his cap for."

"Mmm-hmmm," said another of Pearlie Mae's friends. "You know that's right. After it was all over, she felt real bad they sent him away. She even wrote a letter to the judge tellin' him she made a big mistake goin' along with the others and could Mista Rackley please get another chance? Even when that man came around a few days ago tellin' her not to say nothin' to nobody if somebody was to come around askin', she told him to shove it."

"A man came to see her?"

"Did. Brought a nize box of chocolates and told her, 'Don't say nothin' about nothin'.' But Pearlie, she just took the candy and said maybe he ought to mind his own business, thank you very much, and sent him packin'."

Another lady in the group piped up. "That's not the way I heard it. Wendell said she took after him with a broom."

Cézanne broke in. "Do you know the man who came to see her?"

"She said it had somethin' to do with the trial. And then she asked Ella and me if we wanted to come for tea and chocolates that afternoon. But Ella here has an allergy, and I shouldn't be havin' candy on account of I'm trying to reduce. And Lulu here has diabetes, and she ain't supposed to have sugar even though she gobbles it down like the hog she is. So Pearlie ate that whole box herself. I guess it was too much because later, she called

Ella here and said she had a bellyache that wouldn't quit."

Heads bobbed all around.

Cézanne's blood ran cold. She didn't want to suspect Pearlie Gray had been poisoned, but what else was she supposed to think? "We wanted to stop by the house, but Duty couldn't remember how to get there."

"Pearlie's place is in Stop Six off Avenue J. Wendell wouldn't leave that house for nothin' even though we told him a man who just got a hundred thousand dollars insurance money ought to spend some of it on a better house."

A streak of purple caught Cézanne's eye. Deuteronomy was sprinting toward the nearest exit with a string of angry mourners in tow.

"It was good to speak with you. Please let me know if I can do anything." She pressed a business card into the nearest palm and headed for the front doors.

Duty was nowhere in sight. Cézanne hurried to the car. When she reached the driver's door she heard a noise.

"Psst."

"Duty?"

"Miz Zan, open up."

Cézanne gave the parking lot a furtive once-over. "Where are you?"

"Over here."

She still couldn't pinpoint the girl's location.

"Miz Zan, I need you to get in the car and open my door. Pull up to the end of the drive and toot the horn."

Friends of the deceased milled around the steps. Judging by the animated hand gestures, Duty stirred up the ant bed.

Cézanne slid behind the wheel and fired up the engine. When she reached the mouth of the drive she tapped the horn. Duty erupted from between several cars and raced for the door. She yanked on the handle and threw herself into the seat.

Cézanne floored the Cadillac and the door slammed shut. They breezed through a yellow light before she demanded details.

"I used one of my new words, and they thought I said somethin' bad."

Her stomach clenched. "What'd you say?"

"That for such a fancy place, they was sure niggardly choosin' that cheap-ass casket."

Cézanne whipped the Cadillac into the parking spot reserved for the M.E.

"How come we don't park where it says visitor?"

"Because it's farther away. I need to keep an eye on you."

"You still stewin' over what happened at Pearlie's visitation?"

Cézanne cut the engine and twisted in her seat. "I'm not accustomed to fleeing from angry mobs." Duty looked out the window. "I'll thank you to take this lecture seriously. If you're going to work for me, we can't have pissed-off people popping up like coffins in a Savannah rainstorm."

Duty grinned. "You askin' me to stay on after my visit runs out?"

The muscles in Cézanne's face relaxed. "Maybe. I think we need to enroll you in a regular school so you can get a diploma someday. A sheepskin's more impressive than a GED certificate."

"And just as effective," Duty said with some authority. "My cousin Nebuchadnezzar uses the sheepskin ones even though his wife Debra says to use the ones made outta latex on account of they're stronger. But 'Nez claims latex gives him the itch and sheepskin's just as effective. I know 'cause one night I heard 'em arguin'."

Nice.

Cézanne powered down the windows a few inches. "Wait in

the car and keep the doors locked. I need to go in and talk to Dr. Krivnek."

"Who's that?"

"Assistant Medical Examiner."

"Is he the one who cuts people open? 'Cause if he is, I don't wanna be knowin' him."

With a curt, "Stay put," Cézanne left Duty unattended. On the way inside, she dreamed up a story to use on the M.E.'s receptionist.

Krivnek came out of the lab in an autopsy suit made of Mylar, still wearing his hood and clear plastic faceplate. With his head bent in concentration, he was tagging a vial of blood as he walked. When he penned the finishing touches on the label, he glanced up.

"Oh, hell. What now?" He had the look of a man who'd just swallowed a putrefied oyster. Before he could chastise the receptionist, she grabbed her coffee mug and excused herself. He remained cordial but detached as he spoke. "I want a picture of you."

Gulled by his sudden shift in demeanor, she flashed a smile. "Why, Marve, that's so sweet. A small one for your wallet?"

"Three-by-five or larger. I want to post it at Charlotte's desk so she'll recognize you on sight and call security to have you removed."

"You don't mean that."

"If you don't give me one, I'll ask one of my friends at the PD to get me a copy of your driver's license photo. I'll have it blown up and tape it to the front door."

Her mouth gaped. Krivnek played dirty pool.

His eyes gleamed stubbornly. "You're not a cop anymore, Cézanne. I don't have to put up with your shenanigans."

"I want to talk to you about poison."

His brow knitted with skepticism. "Did you ingest it or

administer it? If you ingested it, I'm not going to tell you. If you administered it, I'll see what I can do if it's not too late."

"I think Pearlie Mae Gray was poisoned."

"Who?"

"A juror in Erick Rackley's murder trial. She's dead. Somebody didn't want her talking about that case, and they killed her with chocolates."

"Death by chocolate? I can think of worse ways to check out."

He wasn't taking her seriously. She planted a fist on one hip. "They're burying her tomorrow. I want you to come to the funeral home and do something."

"What would you have me do? Snip off a finger? Maybe lift her blouse and make a Y-incision while the family looks on?"

"If I'm right and they bury her, she'll have to be exhumed."

Krivnek pivoted on one foot and headed off in the opposite direction. She trailed him into the lab and watched as he placed the vial of blood in a refrigerator.

"What is this prurient interest you have with digging up the dead? Did your mother not let you play in the sandbox during your formative years? Didn't you bake mud pies like regular kids or were you the neighborhood ghoul who dug up your pets so you could monitor the natural process of decomposition?"

Wounded, Cézanne clamped her teeth together so hard a jolt of pain went through a couple of molars. Tears blistered behind her eyeballs. Krivnek didn't know her mother was crazy. He had no way of knowing Bernice buried Kitty-Kitty's babies alive in a tow sack rather than adopting them out. She felt a sudden prickle in her nose. Her eyes welled.

He shut the door to the cooler and stood helpless, arms limp at his sides. "I'm sorry. That was inappropriate. I haven't had much sleep lately. People keep dropping by my house at night, waking me up. Sit down. I'll get you a soda, and we can talk."

She shook her head and hid a sigh. "I left Deuteronomy in the car. She's a teenager I agreed to take care of for a few months."

"Not the girl who stole the police car?" he asked by way of confirmation.

"They were shooting at her. What was she supposed to do, take a bullet?"

"I'm not the enemy. You don't have to snipe at me. Come. Sit. Really." His eyes flickered to the wall clock. "I've got a few minutes."

Reluctantly, she poured out the story of Pearlie Gray and the unidentified man who left a warning with his box of candy.

When she finished, Krivnek said, "You're about to talk me out of having a crush on you."

"You don't have a crush on me. You'd settle for any woman who can drive at night. The reason you like me is because you see a bit of yourself in me. Are you going to help, or not?"

With his face bathed in the glow of the computer screen, he banged out a few keystrokes and waited for the information to pop up.

"We didn't autopsy Mrs. Gray because she'd been under the care of her family doctor within the previous twenty-four hours." He noted a history of cardiac problems on the death certificate. "Pearlie Gray had an enlarged heart and could've gone to Canaan anytime. There's no poisoning and no mystery."

Cézanne disagreed. "Her fingernails were blue."

Krivnek laid a hand on her shoulder. Compassion lurked behind his thick lenses. "My dear, you don't have enough to go on to start trouble like this."

Maybe not right this second but she would.

And when she had what she needed she'd be back.

Chapter Twenty-Four

Urging sleep upon Deuteronomy Devilrow wasn't a difficult sell. Cézanne returned to find her lying across the seat, snoring like a harp seal.

As soon as she opened the driver's door, the girl sat up at attention.

"I didn't do it. It wasn't me." She glanced around, disoriented.

"Do what?"

"Nothin'. I had a vision." Duty jerked her drowsy head. She blinked herself into full consciousness. "Must've been catnappin'. Where're we goin'?"

Cézanne started the engine and wrenched it into gear. "To Pearlie Gray's house."

"Jesa." Duty corkscrewed herself into her seat. "Miz Zan, didn't you learn nothin' at the Reverend Willie Lee's?"

"Pearlie Mae was poisoned."

Reflexively, Duty's hand fluttered to her chest. "For real?"

"One of her sisters told me a man came to see her. He tried to convince her not to talk about the Rackley case. He left her a box of sweets. Poisoned candy."

"I swanee."

They merged into traffic, and Cézanne punched the accelerator. For all she knew, poor Wendell threw out any remaining candy or, God forbid, served it to bereaved friends and family.

Duty said, "You wanna take that candy to yo' friend, Mista Krivnek?"

"Something like that."

"How we gonna do it?"

"People eat at wakes. We'll drive down Avenue J until we find the house with the most cars parked in front of it. If they let us in, we'll scope out the food until we locate that box of candy."

Duty patted herself on the shoulder. "Of course I predicted this."

"What?"

"Saw it in the cards, remember?" Garnet eyes glittered stubbornly. "Page of cups? Things're turning out just like I predicted. You're supposed to watch out for a person who's intense, with emotions waitin' to erupt like a volcano. That's what I said. Gloss it over and call it hooey, but the cards don't lie."

"You're not actually taking credit for this . . ."

"I know what I saw." Duty braced her arms across her chest and turned away.

It wasn't hard to find Wendell and Pearlie Gray's place. Cézanne watched people in their Sunday best filing in and out of the white clapboard house and parked a half-block down. She cut the motor and twisted in her seat.

"We're doing things a bit differently this go-round. I'll do the talking. You'll be seen and not heard."

"Whatchoo mean? I don't get to speak? What if I have somethin' important to say?"

"Save it until we get to the car."

Duty snorted in disgust, protesting all the way up the sidewalk to the front door. Cézanne tried the knob. It gave way when she pushed it, and the two stepped inside. The room was lit by a thin sliver of light filtered through a dirty window. Smells of ham and greens filled the air.

Several ladies sat around the dining room table, hunkered over and whispering. When they looked up and took stock of the interlopers, Cézanne gave a little finger wave.

"We came to pay our respects."

The women went suddenly quiet. Like waiting to see who'd claim the albino in the herd. She felt an unpleasant lurch in her stomach.

Then she saw it—a candy box. She wasn't conscious of having crossed the room, but when she reached the kitchen the front door lay behind her.

One lady who was slumped mournfully over the stove stopped what she was doing and dried her hands on a cup towel. With her forehead stippled with perspiration, she came over and introduced herself.

"I'm Ida June. Fix you little dahlin's a plate?"

"No, thank you. We only have a few minutes."

Duty thought otherwise. "I don't see why we can't eat. I'm hungry. On account of you don't feed me enough, and you always buy the wrong things. I'm used to stuffin' myself on greens and ribs, and you been feedin' me White food. I want Soul food." She turned to Ida Mae. "Hi. I'm Deuteronomy Devilrow, descendent of the Shreveport Devereaus. I would very much like to dine here. Got any chocolate?"

Easier than taking candy from a corpse.

By the time they said their goodbyes, Duty was walking around as bloated as a balloon in the Macy's Thanksgiving Day Parade while Cézanne was plotting the fastest way back to Krivenek's office.

Krivnek, still in the lab tagging tissue samples, peered over his glasses and scowled. "You want me to what?"

"Test the candy." Cézanne pinched a tissue against one corner of the box to keep from transferring her prints.

"Do you realize the expense you're putting me through? For starters, I'm not letting you ramrod me into one of your deep-sea fishing expeditions. I realize I only have to be ten percent smarter than the equipment I'm using, but we still need to know what poison we're testing for. You can't even be sure the woman ingested any toxins. This is one of your wacky, sixth-sense hunches."

"If I'm wrong—" she gnawed her bottom lip and mentally debated her options "—I'll sleep with you."

Duty's eyes protruded. Krivnek's almost pole-vaulted out of his skull.

"There won't be any unbridled sex. I'll throw a pajama party and invite all my pretty friends. You'll be the only man there, and we'll all sleep in the living room. Or if I'm wrong, I promise never to bother you again. Your choice."

Duty flung invisible sweat from her brow.

Krivnek said, "Keeping you away from me is like trying to herd cats."

"Look, Marve, I'm not asking you to test the whole box—only the ones that appear to have a break in the chocolate shell. Like that one." She pointed. "And that one. And this half with the teeth marks that somebody—maybe even Pearlie Gray—threw away."

Krivnek's attention shifted to Duty. "I know you. You're the girl who stole a police car and parked it on the Trinity River bottom."

"Borrowed."

"Tell me, what's your involvement in this little caper?"

"I got 'em to give me the candy. And I read it in the cards."

"Pardon me?"

"Tarot cards. Only I didn't realize it was poison at the time. But it was the page of cups card and in the olden days, people drank poison in cups so that makes sense. Really, the poison was Miz Zan's idea. But I'm inclined to think she may be onto something 'cause these pieces have needle holes in 'em and you know that ain't right."

"Hmmmph." Krivnek locked eyes with Cézanne. "What about your chain of custody?"

"I called Slash at home. He's driving in."

"Bet he'll appreciate losing a day's rest. Give me the box."

"We need him to check it for prints. It should have Duty's and Pearlie's and the killer's. And God only knows who else's."

"Put yourself to good use." He handed her a triplicate form, then plucked a fresh pair of latex surgeon's gloves from their carton. Carefully, he extracted the chocolates and placed them on an unadulterated workspace. "Fill out that report while I get the camera."

Cézanne wanted confirmation. "Can you enlarge the pinpricks?"

"They'll look like rabbit holes when I'm through. If eight-by-ten glossies are what turns you on, I'll make copies."

"It's not a turn-on, Marve."

"No?" Krivnek grinned his big, toothy smile. "I bet a close-up of the ridge prints I'm looking at, melted into the shell, will be. Especially if they don't come back to Mrs. Gray."

Duty retold the story at the dinner table that night.

Henri seemed particularly intrigued. "You know about poisons, Sis?"

"I'm not an expert, but I know enough to make trouble."

Velda ran a bony hand over the peach fuzz sprouting across her scalp. "If you had any here, I'd drink it."

Forks hovered inches from their mouths. Everyone gave Velda blank stares.

"You people make too much noise. I can't remember when I had such a pitiful night's sleep."

"Nobody made noise," Cézanne said.

"Yes, you did. Wandering around, opening doors, closing doors. Can't you be quiet?"

"Nobody was walking around."

"The guilty party doesn't want to own up to it, but I heard the floors creak."

"It's probably the house settling," Cézanne said, and went back to eating. Duty had prepared shrimp gumbo from her grandmother's secret recipe, and they all wanted a shot at seconds.

Henri made an observation. "Could've been the dog."

Duty took offense. " 'Nigma don't make noise, do you, 'Nigma?"

"Hypothetically," Henri began.

Duty sat up rigid with her bottom lip curling into a pout. "Don'tchoo call me pathetic. I ain't pathetic. You're the one's pathetic. You and yo' miracle dust cloth."

"It's not a dust cloth. It's the Abracadabra."

"Abracadabra, don't that grab-ya? If that invention's so hot, why don'tchoo get off yo' rusty-dusty and put one out tonight, so I don't hafta clean tomorrow?"

Velda's queen-in-heat screech redirected everyone's attention. "Did you hear me say they were opening doors? I don't like the dog, and I never thought I'd take up for him, but unless the damned dog has thumbs, it was one of you people." Velda settled her slitty-eyed glare on Henri. "I blame you."

"Colonel Mustard in the dining room with the knife." Henri joked.

Cézanne bit her lip to keep from laughing.

Duty's eyes darkened. "Maybe this is a haunted house."

"Haunted-schmaunted. Tonight, if any of you cretins wake me up again," Velda cast a wicked glare, "I'll brain you with my bat."

Chapter Twenty-Five

During the night, deep intuition triggered by a rustle of fabric jerked Cézanne awake.

In a moment of confusion, she was naked behind the wheel trying to talk the motor jock out of a traffic citation. In fact, the shrill she'd incorporated into her dream came from the coyote wind howling outside, not a police siren signaling her to pull over.

A blue slice of moonlight cut through a slit where the drapes met.

Once her eyes adjusted to the dark, the silhouette of Henri seated at the foot of her bed came into sharp focus. He'd somehow slipped in without her hearing.

Her brother was fully clothed. Fingers toyed with the sash of her robe slung over the back of a nearby chair. He moved his free hand up her thigh and caressed her skin. The gentle scrape of his nails sent chills climbing her ribs. She propped herself up on one arm and fisted sleep from her eyes.

"What's wrong?" She stifled a yawn, huffing a breath that could use a handful of mints. Instinctively, she reared back her head so as not to offend him.

On second thought, she could use some garlic and a cross. She glanced down and saw that her gown was cockeyed with the hem hitched up, as if she'd dressed in a hurry or somebody tried to sneak a peek. Self-conscious, she readjusted the fabric. Suddenly, the room seemed colder than a mother-in-law's love.

Henri said, "I heard a noise outside and thought I'd investigate. Probably just a cat. Do we have a cat?"

"No. What time is it?"

"Three-ish. Didn't mean to wake you. I still can't believe I'm here."

She patted his hand. "Stay as long as you want."

He entwined his fingers with hers. "I'll be leaving soon."

She came fully awake. "You're going to help me get the house, aren't you? It's half yours."

"I was hoping you could buy me out. How much do you think it's worth?"

"Velda wants a hundred and fifty thousand dollars. I don't have that kind of money or believe me, that old harpy would be running out of here like her feet were on fire and her ass was catching."

Henri slid his hand up her arm. She felt the strength of his squeeze as powerful hands kneaded her muscles.

"How much could you pay me if I signed over my half? I wouldn't expect full value, of course. You'd be doing me a favor."

"You need money that badly?"

"I can't get to my bank accounts."

"Why not? There are lots of banks in this town. Wire yourself some money."

"It's not that simple. By now, they've probably contacted the bank, watching for activity."

This time, she sat bolt upright. "Henri, what kind of trouble are you really in?"

He moved his hand up her shoulder. His fingers tickled her hairline and wrapped around the back of her neck. In the shadows, his eyes took on a hard look and his face, a blank, scary expression.

Unexpectedly, Enigma head-butted his way through the door. With a low rumble in his throat, he trotted in with Duty behind him. Henri drew back his hand and rested it in his lap.

"Miz Zan, there's somebody knocking downstairs. Should we answer?"

Henri said, "I'll take care of it."

"Stay put. It's my house." Cézanne threw back the covers and shrugged into her robe.

On the other side of the peephole, Slash shifted on his feet. When Cézanne cracked the door, she saw that he had on his work clothes—black SWAT pants and a long-sleeve polo shirt with the FWPD badge emblazoned where a pocket should've been.

"I was driving by and noticed your porch light out."

"That's odd. I'm sure I turned it on before we went to bed." She flipped the switch. A creamy yellow glow washed over him. "At least the bulb's not out. What gives?"

"I parked across the street to finish a burglary report. The upstairs light came on. I figured you were awake."

"Must've been Henri. He woke me up, too. Want to come in?"

Slash hesitated. He seemed to be contemplating an idea. "When's the last time you saw your brother?"

"I was twelve. Twenty years ago."

"Does he look like you thought he would?"

"Much better." She caught herself smiling. "When Velda came out of the woodwork I figured she'd fallen out of the ugly tree and hit every branch on the way down. I'm not even vaguely interested in my own family's genealogy. Why would I want to unearth more people like Velda? But you wonder how you're going to look when you're that age, and I was starting to get depressed. Then Henri showed up, and he's a hunk. So there."

"Where's he been all these years?"

He ruffled a defensive feather. Slash didn't ask questions just to make conversation. He was a watcher and a listener.

"Can't you be happy for me?"

"I want to be." He shifted his focus to the driveway. "He put a car cover over the MGB."

"So what?"

"It's like he doesn't want anybody to know he's here. You don't think that's strange?"

"It's a classic car. He's protecting it from the elements."

"I'm not trying to pick a fight, but something about your brother bothers me."

"You don't understand because you've got a big family, and y'all are crazy about each other. My family's just crazy. And we're precariously close to extinction. For the first time in twenty years, I've reconnected to blood kin who shared the same experiences with me, and I have to tell you, I slept better the last four hours than I have in years."

He forced a smile, then reached around the doorjamb and lifted the sawed-off, twelve-gauge shotgun with pistol grips he'd propped up against the bricks. "Take the Mossberg. It's locked and loaded, and it'll cut a man in half. Make sure you keep it in your room where nobody else can get to it."

She assured him they'd be fine. Thanked him for dropping by. Tried to close the door but Slash stayed it with a hand.

"Get your credentials in order. I got us an appointment at the prison. Day after tomorrow, we're driving down to see Erick Rackley." Before the door sealed him off from view, he dropped a bombshell. "Take care of yourself, Zan. I'm crazy about you."

Early morning, Cézanne realized she must've fallen into a deep sleep because she could've sworn she was giving a press conference after getting Erick Rackley's murder case reversed on appeal. She tried to incorporate the high-pitched squeal filtering up from downstairs into her dream, but the noise sounded like it came from Duty, and Deuteronomy Devilrow had no place at her press conference.

Blinking her surroundings into focus, she grabbed her robe, wrangled into each sleeve, cinched the tie closed at the waist and hurried down the steps.

A cloth approximately four feet square lay in the middle of the living room and Duty was dancing the Watusi around it. Henri stood in the kitchen doorway, eyeing her up as he bit into a sandwich.

"Look, Miz Zan, look. Mista Henri's Abracadabra really works."

Cézanne went slack-jawed. It had dust bunnies the size of tumbleweeds in the center of it and sprinkles of dirt all around. She shifted her attention to the edge of the Oriental rug. Apparently, some of the fuzz didn't make it onto her brother's electromagnetically charged invention and the baseboards still had a layer of dust where they met the wall.

She pronounced sentence on his invention. "The floor's dirty."

He sauntered in chewing a mouthful of food and swallowed hard. "It's not through its cleaning cycle yet. I put it out after your boyfriend left. It hasn't had time to finish doing its job."

"Slash isn't my boyfriend."

Duty broke into a childhood rhyme. "Miz Zan and Mista Slash, sittin' in a tree . . . k-i-s-s-i-n-g."

"That's enough." She was about to suggest maybe Henri scattered the mess over the cloth himself but the chime of the bell sheared her attention.

Duty ran to the door, flattened her palms against it and stuck her eye up to the peephole. "It's Miz Beaudoin. Cinnamon and Spice's mama." Her grin evaporated. "You don't think she's here to take 'em home, do you?"

"Let her in and round up the puppies."

"Can't we keep 'em?"

"No." She hustled upstairs and hurriedly dressed. When she trotted back down, Doretta Beaudoin was standing near the door, all smiles, hugging her squirming animals and speaking pidgin-Shar Peis. Dejected, Duty bit her lower lip.

"I can't thank you enough, Ms. Martin," Doretta said.

"My pleasure. If you know of anyone who needs a lawyer, please refer them to me."

"You know I will."

While Cézanne and Duty stood on the porch waving goodbye, Enigma paced the length of the veranda like a member of U.S. Customs preparing to inspect the next shipment.

Duty blinked back tears. "Wish we could've kept 'em."

The fake smile Cézanne fixed on her face slipped away. She slung an arm around the girl's shoulders. "Did I tell you what a great job you did, getting those puppies back? Not that I condone stealing."

Duty sniffled. "What's condone mean?"

"It means I'm not excusing stealing."

"Oh. 'Cause for a minute I thought you wanted to have a talk about sex."

They went back indoors and found Henri pawing through the refrigerator. He pulled out a container of milk and drank directly from the carton. Cézanne grimaced.

Duty stomped over to a drawer, dug out a black marker and handed it to him. "Might as well write yo' name on the box, 'cause nobody's gonna want to drink after you."

"You think I have cooties?"

"If you get enzymes in the food, the enzymes break down the proteins. So you not supposed to put yo' mouth on stuff where spit touches it." Garnet eyes cut to Cézanne. "I ain't as dumb as you think."

Velda, who'd gone from card-carrying shrew to genteel plantation owner ever since Henri's arrival, stomped downstairs wearing a neon orange robe that brought out the peach in the fuzz sprouting out of her scalp. She'd returned to her natural state. "I've been robbed."

Cézanne said, "What're you talking about?"

"Somebody stole me blind in the night." Scalded, she shot Duty an accusing glare.

"Don't look at me."

"One of you's a thief."

Cézanne said, "Don't look at me."

Henri gave her the universal palms-up, shoulder shrug. "Ditto."

Velda's cloudy eyes sharpened. A spray of spit sputtered out when she spoke. "When I find out which one of you went through my purse, I'll cut off your hands."

Cézanne made out the day's schedule by setting back-to-back appointments with two more jurors.

Juan Guzman lived in a wooden tract home off Eighth Avenue a few miles from the hospital district in an area cops referred to as Short South. Chester Willoughby lived deep East, not too far from Pearlie Gray's house.

She called ahead and found that Guzman and Willoughby were both at home, and since Willoughby lived the farthest away, she decided to contact him first about the Rackley case.

In the area known as Stop Six, Chester's wife Irene, a heavy-set woman with skin the shade of Honduran mahogany, answered the door of what amounted to a lean-to.

"Pardon me if I don't shake yo' hand but I'm in the kitchen bakin' biscuits, and I got flour up to my elbows. But you c'mon in, and I'll bring Chet out."

Bring Chet out? Where'd she keep him, in the attic?

Cézanne gave the ramshackle living room a furtive once-over. A stale odor of indeterminate origin blanketed the room. When she spied a silver dollar sized hole chewed through the rough-hewn floor along with what appeared to be rat droppings in the corner, she opted to stand rather than accept Mrs. Willoughby's offer to take a seat on the lumpy, threadbare couch.

Her ears pricked up. A mechanical, rusty-bedspring squeak repeated itself at five-second intervals. A wheelchair rolled into view with an elderly black man slumped over to one side.

"Pumpkin, this is Miz Martin, the lady I told you about." Mrs. Willoughby shifted her tired eyes. "He don't talk much since the accident, but I understand him fine. If you want to ask a question I can help. Go ahead."

Cézanne did a visual check. Drool oozed from one corner of Chester Willoughby's mouth, and he had a tremor in his left hand.

"Don't be scared, lady, just have a seat so he can watch you when you talk. Speak nice and slow, and I'll tell you what he says. Have at it."

"Accident?"

"Why, yes. Chet had a bad wreck last October. A car crossed the highway. Hit him head-on. Liked to killed him. Killed the boy in the other car. The po-lice said that boy never knew what hit him. I s'pose not since he had gold paint all over his nose and mouth. If Chet hadn't been driving our old truck, probably would've killed him, too. Ain't that right, baby? Chet says, 'That's right.' "

Actually, Chet said nothing. The man didn't blink, didn't grunt, didn't do anything but slobber and shake his hand uncontrollably. She stood in dead silence digesting the news.

"I came to talk to him about Erick Rackley. Does he remember sitting on the jury?"

"Don't ask me, baby. Ask Chet." She raised her voice and shouted into his ear. "She wants to know if you remember sittin' on the jury. He says, 'Yes.' "

It didn't take a brick upside the head to realize the interview was over. "This isn't going to work."

"Sho' it is. Chet understands. He wants to do the right thing, don't you, baby? Chet says, 'Yes.' "

"I'm sorry to have bothered you. I'll show myself out."

"Would you like to come back tomorrow morning, early? He's a lot spryer at dawn. I could fix biscuits and gravy and you could have breakfast with us if you'd like. Chet says, 'That'd be nice.' "

Seated behind the wheel of the Caddy, she crossed Mr. Willoughby off her list.

The interview with Juan Guzman turned out to be even more challenging. His wife, Rosa, led Cézanne into the kitchen. She couldn't see Guzman's face, only viewed the wiry Hispanic from the knees down to his steel-toed boots. The rest of his body seemed to be folded under the sink. A filthy hand groped for a wrench.

Rosa Guzman announced her presence in a thick, Mexican accent. "The lady's here to see you."

Cézanne bent at the waist for a better vantage point. She spoke to his pants pockets. "I'm the one who called about the Erick Rackley case."

"I'm stuck." He pressed the switch on his snakelight and a weak wash of yellow light illuminated his grimy environment. He rolled onto his back where she could see a Pancho Villa salt-and-pepper mustache drooping past the corners of his mouth. Sweat poured over his grease-streaked face.

"Stuck?"

"My hand."

Rosa chattered in Spanish. Juan outshouted her in their native tongue. Cézanne stepped aside to keep the water pooling near her feet from soaking her shoe soles.

"Maybe I should come back another time."

Guzman writhed in discomfort. "We need to call nine-one-one. I have a heart problem. I'm having trouble breathing."

Rosa ran to the telephone and stabbed out the number.

He said, "What'd you want to ask me?"

"Are you having a heart attack?"

"No, but I need help getting loose." He pulled his knees up and rested the soles of his boots on the linoleum. "Ask me whatever you came for."

"What made you vote to convict Erick Rackley?"

"He killed his wife."

"You believed that?"

"Not at first. At first I thought maybe she killed herself. But the prosecutor had an expert."

"But Rackley's lawyer called the PD's crime scene investigator to testify. He called it suicide."

The bulb on the snakelight dimmed. Guzman turned off the switch and placed it within reach. His voice sounded as cold as the shadows engulfing him. "I was supposed to vote that way."

The faint sound of car tires braked to a stop.

Cézanne said, "I think the police are here."

"Good. I don't feel so hot. My chest hurts."

Footfalls thundered across the plank flooring. A babyfaced female police officer strutted into the kitchen with Rosa in tow.

They were all appraising Guzman when Cézanne whiffed the vapors of Angel For Men. Her skin crawled. She heard a voice behind her and to the right.

"Look what the cat dragged up."

Doug Driskoll. With his eyes ringed purple from Slash's New Year's Eve thrashing.

She almost hyperventilated. "What're you doing here?"

"Checking up on you," he said with a leer. He was dressed in plainclothes which meant he was either working in the detective division or he'd hitched a ride with his uniformed squeeze.

The female officer gave her a guarded look, then dropped to one knee and peered at Guzman. "What's up?"

"Chest pains. Can't get out."

Her brown eyes shifted to Driskoll and a telepathic communication seemed to pass between them.

Driskoll said, "There's not a problem in the world I can't solve. Be right back."

Cézanne knew she should leave. Nothing short of the jaws-of-life would get Juan Guzman out of his predicament, but she stayed. Watching Driskoll fall on his face in front of his latest conquest would go a long way toward boosting her self-esteem. A minute passed before the womanizing scumbag swaggered back into the kitchen.

"Outta the way, ladies." Driskoll dropped on his knees and wedged himself under the sink as far as his shoulders allowed.

Guzman said, "What the hell?"

"Pipe down. You want out, don't you?"

Rosa made the sign of the cross and launched into an Ave María.

The female officer glowered. Cézanne recognized that look. It was how Driskoll's successor victims usually reacted toward the competition. She wanted to slap Driskoll so hard his whole family would vibrate.

Abruptly, Juan Guzman pulled free. Backing out from under the sink, Driskoll banged his head. He grinned big and held up a tube of contraceptive jelly. She should've known he was probably the only cop in the world who carried a tube of lubricating gel as standard issue equipment.

Cézanne arrived home as the mailman zoomed off. Inside the house, she weeded out letters addressed to Occupant and ripped open an envelope from the bank. It contained an overdraft notice, along with a surcharge.

Doretta Beaudoin's check bounced.

Chapter Twenty-Six

Long before sunrise on the morning of the prison interview, Cézanne met her aunt in the dining room.

"All right, Velda, here are the delinquent accounts. Call these people and tell them to bring in money and zero out their bills." Cézanne slapped a handful of invoices on the dining room table. Doretta Beaudoin's topped the stack. "I'll give you ten percent of whatever you collect."

"I want half."

"I'm not splitting fifty-fifty. I did all the work."

"Since you're so good at doing all the work, why don't you hound these people yourself and keep it all?"

"Fifteen percent."

"Forty." Velda's nostrils flared.

"Twenty."

"Thirty."

"Deal."

Velda snatched the papers and padded off to the kitchen in her flip-flops.

"Be nice when you call. Just ask how much they can bring in this week and schedule their appointment."

"Why do they need an appointment?"

"So you'll be here when they come by."

"Where would I go? Sister, I don't have a car."

Duty sashayed in on the tail end of the conversation, still wearing bedclothes and heading for the breakfast cereal. "I can drive you wherever you want to go while Miz Zan's gone."

"No, you can't. That's a rental car, and I'm responsible for it. Which reminds me, Velda, while you're at it, why don't you check with the insurance company to see why I haven't gotten a check for the Mercedes?"

Velda whipped around, eyes glinting. "You drive a Mercedes?"

"Not anymore."

"I want half of what they send you."

"Forget it. Tend to the bills, and I'll see you later. Remember—don't be ugly to clients. As my agent, you're a reflection on me."

Teeth clicked behind Velda's prune-like mouth.

Slash, who'd been squirming on the Beidermeier, watching the dick-dance without comment, rose and adjusted his FWPD ball cap against his forehead. "Ladies, we'll be back late tonight. Don't wait supper."

Fretting, Duty followed them to the door. She clutched the sleeve of Cézanne's suede jacket. "Miz Zan, have you seen 'Nigma? I let him out for just a minute, and he didn't come back."

"He'll turn up."

"It ain't like 'Nigma to be gone so long. Can't you help me look?"

Cézanne shifted her gaze.

Slash shook his head. "Our appointment's at ten. We barely have time as it is."

Cézanne pressed Henri into service. "He'll help."

Footfalls pounded the stairs. As if on cue, her brother appeared in a pair of plaid flannel boxers and a Notre Dame sweatshirt with the sleeves pushed up to his elbows. At the sight of Slash, the smile died and his eyes turned hard. "What gives, Sis?"

"We're meeting a client. Duty can't find Enigma. Could you help her look? Velda's going to be on the phone squaring away my delinquent accounts, so if you've got any calls to make you'll have to coordinate it with her." She turned to Slash. "Ready?"

He opened the front door and sliced his hand through the air in the traditional *After you* gesture. As she stepped into the cold morning air, Henri called her back.

When Slash moved to follow, Henri balked. "Not you, dude."

Off to one side of the living room, her brother lowered his voice to a whisper. "We've got a problem."

"What kind of problem?"

"An environmental problem. I hate to tell you because I know how much you love this house."

"Tell me what?"

"I think we've got black mold."

"What?" For a house, black mold was the kiss of death.

"Shhhhh. I don't know for sure, and we don't want to panic anyone."

"Where?"

"The bathroom. But I found it in the walls, too."

She glanced frantically at Slash, who seemed to be receiving invisible daggers flung at him from Henri's amethyst eyes.

The investigator tapped his watch crystal.

"Okay, Henri, here's what you do. Call the insurance company and have them send out an adjustor. The number's in the kitchen drawer with Dad—" she caught herself "—Bob's other papers. I won't be back until late, but you can brief me first thing tomorrow morning."

"Gotcha." Henri flashed a reassuring smile and gave her a pat on the shoulder. Unexpectedly, he slipped a firm hand around Cézanne's waist and pulled her to him. With Slash looking on, he planted a lip lock on her mouth.

Dumbstruck, she pulled away. Slash had turned into the Firestone tire of confidence and seemed to be losing tread with each passing second.

Henri said, “Take care and hurry back.” To the crime scene investigator, he said, “Don’t do anything I wouldn’t do.” His mouth angled up in a smirk.

Duty trotted up and gave her a goodbye hug. “What’s my word for the day? You been givin’ me easy words. I need a hard one.”

Don’t we all.

Slash glanced through the living room window at Henri, flopped on the Beidermeier with the remote in hand, and came up with Duty’s word. “Charlatan.”

Duty touched her lip thoughtfully. “I don’t know that one.”

“I’ll bet by tonight, you will.” He took Cézanne’s arm and steered her to the door.

The sun popped up like a big orange thumbprint. After Cézanne and Slash had been on the road for an hour, the conversation turned to Henri.

Slash said, “What was he so anxious to talk to you about?”

“He thinks the house has black mold.”

“Black mold, huh? So you might have to move out?”

“Unless I wake up and it’s growing on me, I’m not leaving. Henri knows that.”

Slash flipped the Audi’s turn signal and changed lanes. A neon sign for the Bluebonnet Café flickered in the distance. After a quick breakfast of sausage, eggs, buttered wheat toast, and coffee, they got back onto the highway. The drive to the Briscoe Unit in Dilley, Texas would’ve bored her to tears if Slash hadn’t groped behind the seat and pulled out a plastic sack with a bookstore logo on it. The bag contained a textbook on forensics written by the state’s expert who testified in the Rackley trial.

"What's this?" Distracted, Cézanne flipped it over and let her eyes drift over the back.

"Hot off the press. My gift to you." He teased her with his eyes.

She scanned the table of contents. When she saw what he wanted her to see, her eyes got big. She jerked her head in his direction.

"Exactly." Slash grinned big. "Read what he wrote about expirated blood. He totally contradicts his testimony. Now he's saying to be damn careful when investigating a case because expirated blood in a suicide can mimic a homicide. And vice versa." Slash's voice escalated in volume and pitch. "He can't have it both ways."

Cézanne felt a lightheaded rush. She'd seen a photograph similar to the blood-spattered T-shirt used in the book among the Rackley crime scene photos. Instantly, she understood. The state's expert testified Rackley murdered his wife based on bloodstain analysis. Two years later, he'd written a treatise that indicated how blood spatter from expirated blood could also point to suicide.

"Do you think this could be a picture of Rackley's T-shirt?"

"I know it is."

This qualified as newly discovered evidence, and it flew in the face of the expert's testimony.

The paid expert had whored for the state.

Her confidence buoyed. "How long have you known about this?"

"I heard rumblings within the crime scene community last year. Now that it's in print, he clearly contradicted himself."

Conversation turned to the interview with the prisoner.

Slash said, "Do you want to talk to Erick in the attorney's room or in a booth?"

"What's the difference?"

"Space, for one thing. There's a camera in the attorney's room and a table and chairs. It's soundproof, but a good lip-reader could crack your code. In the booth, it's just you, a phone, and a Plexiglas partition."

"Where'll you be?"

"If you pick the room, I can go in as your investigator. Any questions?"

"Think he'll notice my eyebrows?"

Slash laughed. "That shade of brown goes with the yellow bruise on your ankle. He'll think you're color-coordinated."

She gave him a long, hard look. "Anything else I should know before we go in?"

Slash glanced over, uneasy. "Don't stare at his scar."

The prison holding Erick Rackley looked like any other penal institution peppering the state: dust-colored bricks, concertina fences, and towers with guards dressed in Confederate-gray uniforms who had orders to shoot on sight anyone trying to scale the wicked coils of razor-wire strung across the tops.

Slash pulled up even with the entrance. A uniformed prison guard stepped from a kiosk with a clipboard in hand and his bottom lip distended from a pinch of smokeless tobacco. Two guards appeared out of nowhere. They fanned out like dueling chefs with huge spatulas and visually swept the Audi's undercarriage using long poles with mirrors connected to the ends.

The detective badged the guard. "Wolfgang X. Vaughn. Fort Worth PD. Here to see an inmate. This is his lawyer, Cézanne Martin."

She passed her bar card across the seat. He scraped it with his thumbnail, flipped it over, and scrutinized it.

Slash leaned forward. "We have a ten o'clock appointment."

The man's eyes drifted over the clipboard. Midway, he penned a small checkmark on the page. "Pop the trunk."

Slash hit the button. The lid sprang open.

The guard bent over and peered past the detective, at Cézanne. "That your briefcase?" When she nodded, he said, "Got any firearms, explosives, knives, contraband, or anything else that could present a danger?"

"Extra-Strength Midol."

"Open it. Now pass it over so I can see it."

"Don't read my papers. Attorney-client privilege."

"Then remove them."

He laid the briefcase on the hood. It seemed to appease him, picking at the leather, checking for false bottoms that didn't exist, and scrutinizing the analgesic against the light.

She glanced at Slash. "What's next? A strip search?"

"Only for you." He grinned and relaxed against the seat.

The guard returned to the driver's window. "You wearing boots?"

A nod.

"Back-up piece?"

"Not today."

The guard moved around to the passenger side again. He pecked on the glass with his pen. "Step out."

She did a ventriloquist impression with her teeth clamped shut. "Now what?"

"Just do it, honey. Some of them are so crooked they'd have to screw on their socks. We should appreciate the ones who take pride doing their jobs."

"Pride ends with the proctology exam."

He called her honey. Heat flamed her cheeks. She shuddered from the tickle zipping up her neck.

The guard gave her a thorough going-over with the wand-shaped metal detector and ordered her back into the Audi. He handed Slash a pre-printed permit and motioned where to park.

"You'll go through a series of metal detectors inside. After you check in with the warden, the grays will show you where to go. And here's a list of what not to do if you want to get invited back."

Erick Rackley padded into the attorney conference room with leg irons chaining his ankles together and an appreciative grin spreading across his face. He wore prison whites, socks, and flip-flops and bore only a faint resemblance to his mug shot. For one thing, his face looked thinner and more rawboned. For another, he'd bulked up the muscles in his upper body. Long hours in the welding shop could do that to a person. And he had a scar.

"Am I glad to see you." Rackley's eyes welled.

Slash made introductions.

Rackley stared at the ceiling. His dark hair caught the light, shining like a thousand filaments under the fluorescent glow. "Thank you, Lord Jesus." Clear brown eyes settled on Cézanne. "I never thought anyone would take my case. I can't pay you, you know. My sister has a little money, but she's got kids. Did you get heckled coming in?"

"A couple of hoots and a cat call."

"The screws are bad here." He thumbed at a corrections officer and shook his head. "The inmates are as bad a lot as I've ever seen. I'm in a unique position having been a cop. The only good thing about this whole sad deal is they know I'm in here for murder. Which sets me up to be feared, I suppose. Baby rapers have it the worst. They're locked away from the rest of the population. But murderers, armed robbers, burglars? Nobody much cares. None of these assholes committed their offenses. They all used the SODDI defense—some other dude did it. We're all a bunch of sorrys waiting for a break."

"Jail break?"

"A break on our appeals."

Cézanne and Slash took seats opposite Erick Rackley. While a jolly-faced guard stationed beyond the bars pretended to be a deaf mute, Cézanne opened her briefcase and removed a legal pad. She poised her pen to write.

"Once again, from the top. Don't leave anything out. Start two days before your wife's death and if you lie to me—even so much as a white lie—I'm off the case."

Chapter Twenty-Seven

Erick Rackley claimed to remember nothing about the night of the party he and his wife threw other than guzzling beer all day while he barbecued brisket, shooting up the swimming pool, and waving the gun bye-bye at the guests as they ran screaming into the night.

In fact, nothing in Erick Rackley's narration blipped on Cézanne's internal radar until he told a story about the night following the barbeque.

"We went dancing at Jim Bob's honky tonk. There was a—"

"Who's 'we'?"

"Me, Yvonne, Hollis, and Fran. By then, Hollis and Fran were the only friends we had left who were willing to put up with me."

"Who's Fran?"

"Françesca DiPaolo. Hollis's wife."

"Rushmore's married?"

"Wasn't at the time. Fran was his girlfriend. Yvonne didn't like her, but that's okay. Fran didn't much care for Yvonne, either."

Rackley combed his fingers through his hair and slouched against the chair back. "My wife didn't think Fran was the right woman for Hollis. She was pretty vocal about it, and it got back to her. I told Yvonne to butt out. It wasn't her business who he tied up with. But Vonnie wouldn't let it go. She said Hollis deserved better."

Cézanne stopped scribbling. Put down her pen. Leaned in across the table and watched for a reaction. "Did you ever cheat on your wife?"

Rackley sat up straight, slamming his back, hard, against the chair. His eyes ignited. "Who said that?" The sudden act of violence caught Cézanne off guard. Her breath went shallow as she glimpsed the hatred of the inner man. His voice went strident. "Did that come from Hollis? Sorry son-of-a-bitch. He was fucking my wife."

The guard lowered his copy of *Guns and Ammo* enough to peer over the top. "It ain't soundproof if you yell, dickweed."

Rackley said, "Sorry, boss."

Slash gave him the A-okay wave, and the three of them hunkered in closer.

Cézanne locked gazes with the inmate and steered him back on track. "How do you know they were having an affair?"

"I caught them." His voice went strident. "Yvonne told me I should dance with Fran, so I did. It was a two-step, and it was nearly half over by the time I got her out on the floor, so we waltzed to the next tune. When we got back to the table, Hollis and Yvonne had disappeared."

"Where'd they go?"

Rackley's eyes blazed. His cheeks turned as red as the florid face of a hard drinker. "The women's restroom. Did they think people wouldn't notice the man's shoes showing beneath the handicap stall? He was performing oral sex on my wife, who by the way was straddling the commode seat. I know what you're thinking—did she see me come in? Hell, no. She was plastered, and they got caught up in the moment. Her eyes rolled back so far into her head she could've counted the ceiling tiles."

Jaw muscles flexed. Veins plumped at his temples. She took in the essence of an angry Erick Rackley and knew, at once, he had the capability and motive to murder his wife.

She tried to vanquish the ugly visual playing out in her mind . . . the smoldering beauty, legs splayed, with a white-knuckled grip on the metal safety bars, oblivious to anything but her own pleasure. In a businesslike voice, she prompted him to finish. Forcing details out of Rackley was like applying the screws—painful to watch, shocking to hear, and almost cruel to be a part of. "Then what happened?"

"It was like a knife in the gut. After adjusting to the initial shock, I left. If I'd wanted to kill her, I would've done it right then, don't you think?"

Cézanne played devil's advocate. "Maybe you didn't have your gun with you."

"Sure, I did. Stuffed down my boot. Could've pulled it out and plugged them both."

"Why didn't you?"

"Because I loved her more than I hated him."

Cézanne formed a scenario in her head. Would she have slinked off without commotion if she'd walked in on Bobby with another woman? Not likely. "What kept you from yelling, 'Hey, scumbag, get away from my wife?' "

Rackley blinked back tears. "I didn't want a showdown. She might've told me she wanted a divorce. He could've said they were making plans to be together. I couldn't deal with hearing that—not right then."

"Believe me," Cézanne said, "there's no good time to learn you've been dumped."

He took a deep breath and smashed his fingertips into his eyes, as if to punish them for what they'd seen.

"I think, on some level, I made a pact with myself to do better. To be a better mate. I knew Yvonne and her family thought I'd turned into a big disappointment. I was between jobs, you know? The PD ran me off a few months before—I'm sure Slash told you the story."

"I'd like to hear it from you."

"They thought I had an alcohol problem and offered me rehab. I told them to get bent, and they showed me the door. I was too arrogant to admit I had a problem. I went on my merry way, kept on drinking, and didn't have a steady income. I was struggling to get my realtor's license. What choice did I have? If I'd confronted Yvonne and Hollis . . . if she told me to pack my shit and get out, where would I have gone?

"I'd pissed off most of my friends—ask anybody on the force. Yvonne would've gotten the house because she was the only one working and the only one who could've afforded it. She was my sole support. How crazy would I have to be to kill the goose that laid the golden egg?" His eyes took on a distant gaze as if he were staring at a big screen TV, watching an instant replay of that miserable part of his life. "No, my only choice was to win back my wife."

"So what'd you do?"

"Backed out of the bathroom and retraced my steps. Returned to our table and ordered Fran and me another Coors."

"Did you tell her what you'd seen?"

"No. That would've brought the friction to a head, and I already told you I didn't want that. We drank a few more beers, and she started coming on to me."

Cézanne could see why. Before prison, before the nasty scar that started near his ear and ran the length of his jaw, Rackley must've had the kind of looks that got actors on the cover of *People*.

"Did you want her? Rushmore's girlfriend?"

"Ms. Martin, when it's two in the morning, and you're a drunken, out-of-work bum slamming back longnecks, a spindly little Italian chick with a double-A chest and a pierced tongue wiggles a great piece of tail."

On break, Cézanne finished drying her hands in the guards' restroom. When she exited the door, Slash was waiting in the common area just outside the attorney conference room.

"I don't like him," Cézanne announced without preliminary.

"You don't have to like him to be able to represent him. Do you believe him?"

"So far."

He took her by the hands. "He was a drunken cop. You knew that, Zan. It's what got him kicked off the force. Doesn't make him a killer. Look at him when he talks to you. That man's in pain."

"Yeah—from alcohol withdrawal. Did you notice the gleam whenever he mentioned booze?"

"Good call."

"Did y'all polygraph him?"

"Inconclusive. He had the DTs, and they couldn't get a good read." Slash had a different take on lie detector tests. "You can always find some Voodoo doctor that comes up with a new way to tell whether someone's telling the truth. Want to know if someone's telling the truth? Sit them down in front of their parents." He glanced at the clock. "Fifteen minutes left. Maybe he's pulling the tough-guy act because I'm in there. Finish up alone, and we'll talk on the ride back."

Grudgingly, she returned doing a mental inventory. Hollis Rushmore screwing Rackley's wife; Rackley screwing Rushmore's girlfriend. The whole sordid mess reeked.

The convict behaved differently without Slash there. He stood when she walked in, remained at attention until she sat, and never raised his voice above a low-level hum.

"Did you have sex with Françesca that night?" She moved uneasily under his intent regard.

"In the parking lot. In my truck."

She closed her eyes and gave him a slow headshake. When she opened them, he had the mournful look of a broken hound beaten into submission by a cruel owner.

"Did Françesca tattle?"

Rackley snorted in disgust. "I doubt it was that memorable. I sure don't remember it. I passed out, and that's where my wife found me . . . asleep on the seat with my withered little pecker poking out past my zipper."

A smile angled up one side of her face. He was trying to be funny. To make her laugh. They'd broken him, and he still had a sense of humor. "Do you think your wife suspected anything between you and Hollis's girlfriend?"

"No way. She thought I'd come out to take a leak."

"Where was Françesca?"

"Beats the hell out of me. A few days after Yvonne shot herself, a detective told me to come back down to the police station. Françesca was sitting outside one of the interrogation rooms. When she saw me, she looked away."

"Embarrassed?"

"I suspect she thought I murdered my wife. She didn't come to the house to offer her condolences, and that was strange. I heard she went back to the Western Riviera for a while. Her family owns a fish market in Arenzano. That's in Genoa. The next time I laid eyes on her, she showed up at my trial married. No 'Good luck, Erick'; no crossed fingers or thumbs up; no 'I'll pray for you.' She went from sweetness and light to my face, to daggers and slander behind my back. The Rushmores are the most cutthroat couple I know."

"I have this gift," Cézanne said carefully. "It's similar to a sixth sense only it has to do with deception. I'm like an ocular lie detector." Rackley blinked a salamander eye-blink. "Look me in the eye. I want to know if you killed your wife. If you did,

just say so. She was cheating on you, and you killed her. If you tell me you caught them in bed together, I'll understand and we'll go from there. Just give me something to work with."

"I didn't kill her. The night of the party, after I cranked off a couple of rounds into the swimming pool, Rushmore went inside. He told Yvonne to pack a bag. She did, but she didn't leave with him. I suspect he disabled a window so he could get back in later. There was no forced entry, you know." A tear popped up in one corner of his eye and sluiced down his cheek. Brown eyes clouded over as he held her in his stormy gaze.

"Instead of shooting up our pool, I should've pumped those rounds into that shyster and used the *Because-he-needed-killing* defense. I wouldn't be here today."

"You're scaring me."

"I loved my wife. You've got to believe me."

But that's where he was wrong; she didn't have to believe him.

The cop part of her brain needed a fresh squirt of lubricant.

Prisoners were called cons for a reason—it wasn't merely an abbreviated form of the word convict. The terms con artist, con man, and confidence games also came to mind. The longer the prison sentence, the more practiced the con. So what kind of tricks had Rackley learned here?

"I don't know who killed my wife. Slash says she committed suicide. I wonder. But why would she take her own life? She had everything going for her: Big-time lawyer with a chance to make partner, lots of friends and family. We had dogs. She'd made an appointment to take them to the vet the next day for their shots." His forehead wrinkled. "Why would she bother to make that appointment if she was planning to kill herself?"

"Slash believes it was an impulse suicide. That something set her off, and she summoned the courage to do it."

"It'd be real easy for me to play along with his theory, being

that I'm locked up. Only I don't think she killed herself."

"Why not? You said she was miserable. That your marriage was falling apart."

"The shower."

Cézanne did a double take.

"When we got home that night from Jim Bob's, she headed straight for the shower. I went straight to the kitchen and put on a pot of coffee. I splashed water on my face and tried to sober up. I downed a few cups of strong coffee and met my wife in the shower. At first, she acted surprised to see me. But as I started touching her, her anger toward me seemed to wash down the drain along with the soap suds."

"What happened in the shower?"

"The same thing that happened in the bathroom stall with Hollis." Rackley's cheeks flushed beet red. "I couldn't get it up, so I did the next best thing. When she was done, I cried. I told her I loved her and to please not leave me. That I'd be a good husband. That I'd go to AA meetings. I promised to do anything she wanted."

"What'd she say?"

He scrunched his eyes closed. Tears leaked out as the muscles in his face hardened. His shoulders heaved with silent sobs. Momentarily, he went rigid. Took a deep breath and inhaled the stale, fear-laden air. His lids popped open. He'd composed himself in the blink of an eye.

It was an *ah-ha* moment.

He leaned in close. His voice dropped to a whisper. "If the guard tells anybody I cried, I'm as good as dead. If you show any kind of weakness, if word gets around you're not so tough, they'll be on you like dried blood on a white shirt. I have enough trouble keeping the bigger guys away from me in the shower. I'd rather be dead than be turned into one of their bitches."

"Tell me what Yvonne said when you made those promises."

Rackley drew in a ragged breath. "I begged her for another chance. At first, she didn't want to give it to me. But then she said, 'Straighten up and fly right. Get yourself into AA tomorrow and work the program. Concentrate on being the best realtor you can be. Take pride in yourself and give me back the Erick I fell in love with. If you screw up again, I won't be here.' "

"Then what happened?"

"I was on my knees. I told her I loved her again; she said she loved me, too. That moment was filled with such promise. She was so happy the next night when I showed written proof that I'd gone to my first AA meeting. I don't know why she'd kill herself. One thing I know as sure as I'm sitting here for the next twenty years, that jury was rigged."

"Walk me through what happened on the day your wife died, starting with when you woke up."

"I tried to make love to her, but I was still too hung over so I did the next best thing and that made her happy."

She didn't have to ask.

"Then I cooked us breakfast, kissed her goodbye, and went off to show houses to a couple of prospective buyers."

He didn't remember the clients' names, only that they seemed interested in several properties and they were solid investors and that put him in on an emotional high for the rest of the day. Late afternoon, he called Yvonne at her office and told her to meet him at a chain restaurant for dinner. They ate a nice meal, toasted champagne glasses in celebration of their renewed commitment to each other, and he followed her home when they left around ten-thirty that night. They hadn't even argued about the champagne because he'd pulled out a sheet of paper and shown her proof that he'd gone to his first AA meeting. Yvonne seemed to be enjoying his company.

The rest of the evening was uneventful—until they arrived home.

"Doug Driskoll said you were drunk when the police arrived at the scene."

Rackley's gaze dipped. He drew in a long breath and let it out slowly. "We pulled into the driveway around ten forty-five. I told her she should get naked because I wanted to make love to her. She went straight to the bedroom, and I went straight to my office to check the answering machine to see if either of those buyers had called." He looked up hopeless and brokenhearted. "I won't lie to you. I had a bottle of Vodka stashed in the bookshelf and I drank myself into a stupor. When I heard the gunshot, I thought it was a burglar. I grabbed my shotgun and went to protect my wife. The rest, you already know."

The guard slapped his magazine on the desk and stretched in his seat. "Two minutes, counselor. Make the most of it." He rose from his chair, turned his back to them and faced the barred windows. With the sunlight behind him, his head and shoulders almost vanished into the bars.

Cézanne gathered her notes. "Anything else?"

"Yes. A favor."

She gave him a wary look.

"You're wearing Victoria's Secret. That was Yvonne's perfume."

Did he want her to send him a bottle?

He seemed to read her thoughts. "That's not the favor. It's been a long time . . . since I touched a woman. I was wondering . . ."

Did he want her to let him feel her up? That wasn't about to happen, not in a million years, buddy.

His chin rippled. He drew in a deep breath. "I was wondering if you'd . . ."

She thought her heart would beat right through her chest. The guard still had his back to them but the man could whip around any moment. He checked his watch and her pulse shifted into double-time.

"If I could close my eyes just this once—pretend she's still here and tell her goodbye—I could do another six years, swear to God."

Cézanne's heart raced. "What're you asking?"

"Let me kiss you."

"There's a no-contact rule. It's listed on the prohibition sheet."

"See the guard? It's why he turned away. I bribed him with a week's worth of cigarettes on a chance."

The guard shifted his weight. "One minute."

"Please, I'm almost out of time," Rackley said and closed his eyes.

Chapter Twenty-Eight

Of the top ten items on Cézanne's list of things not to do, swapping spit with a convicted felon hovered around number three.

"You've been awfully quiet, Zan," Slash said. The countryside rolled by like tan blankets unfurling. Strains of Fleetwood Mac presided over their conversation. "Everything all right?"

"Yes." She moved uneasily under his intent regard.

"Want to talk about it?"

"No." Recalling the slam of the big iron door made her wince.

He broke his concentration on the open road enough to check the rearview mirror. "I promised you a nice dinner. Where'd you like to go?"

"I'm not hungry."

"Want to swing by and pick up Deuteronomy, maybe catch a movie?"

"No." She slipped further down in her seat, shut her eyes, and got assaulted by a vision of Bobby and the new bride. Only in this scenario, the lady was a country music star who popped onto the scene long enough to perform a couple of shows and whisk Bobby into the bright lights of fame.

Ridiculous. She shook off the visual and decided to psychoanalyze herself to find out how she managed to make so many bad choices when it came to men.

They traveled under a dreary sweep of sky. By the time they returned to Fort Worth, a light snow blanketed the city. At the house on University, they were treated to the sight of Henri waiting on the porch with cigarette smoke snaking out of his nose.

The detective pulled up even with the curb and walked her to the door. "I had a nice time."

With Henri standing nearby, smirking, they stood in the spectral gray air in a haze so thick it left a bad taste in her mouth. Slash gave her a hug. He fisted a handful of her hair and held on tight, then pressed a kiss onto her forehead.

"Go on inside. I'd like a word with your brother." Abruptly, he let go.

Anger hardened the corners of Henri's mouth. He stared at them with a degree of censure.

Cézanne let herself into the house half expecting Enigma to saunter out and cold nose her. As a concession to the pressure on her injured foot, she kicked off her shoes and stowed her briefcase in the sunroom. Henri's Abracadabra was lying in the middle of the floor clean as a whistle.

Idiot.

Duty was seated at the dining room table turning up Tarot cards. With her eyes nearly swollen shut, it was a wonder the kid could see the pictures at all.

"Miz Zan, he's gone," she cried. " 'Nigma's gone. What'm I to do? I've checked the cards over and over but I can't find him. The cards say he's here. But if he's here, why don't he come out?" She flipped over another card. Tears that had been building up spilled over her cheeks. "There it is. Nine of swords. Means great pain and unhappiness. Miz Zan, I'm so sad without 'Nigma I may just up and die."

"He'll find his way home."

Half crazed with worry, Duty flipped over a card. "Lordy mercy. King of cups, reversed. It warns, Don't take advice from a friend. You're my friend."

She gathered the deck and shuffled it while questioning the

air. "Am I gonna find my good dog 'Nigma?" She belted out a mournful wail. "Eight of cups. Says I have to let go. 'Nigma's dead. I know it. A thousand times today, I heard him crying. But I went outside and he never showed."

Cézanne pulled up a chair and slung an arm over the girl's shoulder. "Come on upstairs, honey. We'll find him tomorrow."

Duty stared through sorrowful eyes. "Promise?"

In her own bed, beneath the satiny gold glow of a banker's lamp, Cézanne re-read her notes from Rackley's prison interview. With questions of guilt-innocence vibrating in her head, she yanked the pull-chain and extinguished the light. Barely breathing, she lay in bed with her thoughts.

Almost asleep, she rolled over and scrunched a pillow to her. For no good reason other than instinct, the skin-crawling feeling she wasn't alone prickled the hairs on her neck.

"You in love with that guy?"

She jumped at Henri's voice.

Transfixed, he stood next to the bed, blued by a shaft of moonlight slicing through the break in the curtains. He was stark naked, a perfect male specimen. And his—she knew it was scandalous to stare but his alter ego was sticking up like a divining rod and the sheer size of it was amazing.

She glanced down to see what he was looking at and her stomach went hollow.

"Sorry." She untwisted her nightgown's silky fabric and covered an exposed breast. "Henri, what're you doing in here? Is something wrong? And where are your clothes?"

"I just got out of the shower." He dropped his hand, shielding himself from closer scrutiny. Only he wasn't shrouding it so much as as he was . . . well . . . *touching* it. "Look, I didn't mean to alarm you, but I found a cut window screen. I thought you should know."

She hoisted herself up on one elbow. "Which one?"

"Downstairs bathroom. I made sure the lock's secure, but I think someone tried to get in. The dust on the window sill's been disturbed."

"Darlene. She's back." Her eyes darted around the room. Little hairs on her arm stuck straight up. With the Mossberg hidden in the closet, she considered her chances for success if Driskoll's wife got in.

Henry seated himself on the edge of the bed. "What's so great about him?"

"Who?"

"That detective." He snagged the belt from the robe tossed over the chair and wrapped it around his fingers. "He's a friggin' neat-freak. He scooped up the cigarette butt I flicked into the yard and said, 'Don't mess with Texas, pardner.' I told him to go fuck himself, that it's biodegradable. He's OCD."

Cézanne grazed his arm. "If anybody has obsessive-compulsive disorder, it's you. Remember your collection of matchbox toys all parked in a straight line, grouped into colors."

Henri forced a laugh. "I used to be particular about my little cars. Hell, I used to be particular about all my stuff, but I've mellowed."

Not cars. Motorcycles. His little cast aluminum motorcycle collection. Why'd he say cars?

"That guy's no good for you. You need somebody smarter. Somebody like me."

Her brother's words acted like a harpoon to the brain. She must've misheard. He must've said, "Somebody *more* like me."

"Slash is borderline-genius. He's the finest crime scene detective in the whole state. Criminals run scared from him. If you're guilty, he'll nail you."

Henri stretched the robe sash tight. He fixed her with an emotionless stare and addressed her in an eerie monotone. "I haven't done anything."

"I didn't mean you, personally. I'm talking generically."

"I knew that." He dropped the belt. His hand relaxed and tension seemed to slide off his shoulders. "You have sex with him?"

She yanked the covers up to her chin. "That's personal, don't you think?"

"Didn't mean to piss you off, Sis." His face creased into a broad smile. They sat in an atmosphere heavy with memories. Without warning, he scrunched his fingers into her gown and hauled her so close their lips almost touched. "You turned out so beautiful, Zan. I wish we weren't related." When he released his grip his hand skimmed her breast.

Her stomach tensed.

No accident.

Something dead up the creek.

Cézanne thought fast. She forced a smile and made light of the situation, pushing him away with a flirty hand swat. "Oh, Henri. You always were such a hoot."

"Think you would've recognized me if you'd run into me on the street?"

"No. But I would've wondered about the eye color. Nana's mother had eyes like ours. I've never seen anyone else with irises shaded the same." She wanted to ask him if he wore purple contacts, but that would tip her hand.

Henri's hand hovered near his crotch. "If you saw me on the street and didn't know I was your brother . . . if I asked you on a date, would you have gone out with me?"

"You'd have gotten my attention."

His mouth tipped at the corners. But for Cézanne, the icky feeling returned.

She said, "Remember when we were kids, and you caught me and Monet playing in your room? And you told Monet to get milk and Oreos for us and then you locked her out? We had fun, didn't we?"

Henri's breath quickened. "Yes."

Cézanne entwined her fingers with his. Saw the stirring beneath the small section of sheet he'd covered himself with. With a shudder climbing her ribcage and her breath in her throat, she kept her eyes firmly averted.

"Remember the time we played . . . well . . . you know . . ." She thought fast. Ducked her chin and gave him a sly smile. ". . . doctor?"

Henri's breath went shallow. "Yes."

She unhanded him. Slid him a sideways glance and hooked him by the crook of his arm. His breathing seemed labored. His muscles tensed. Her insides were screaming, but she gave him a playful push.

"What do you remember most about it?"

"You were hot." Her brother's voice quivered.

"Was that the first time for you to . . . well . . . you know?"

"Yes." Heavy breathing.

"Good night, Henri. Sleep tight."

He did a subtle lean-in to kiss her. She braced herself for a peck on the cheek, but his tongue forged its way into her mouth.

"Let's do it," he panted.

"Good night, Henri." She gave him a dismissive flick of the wrist and wiggled further beneath the covers. She'd given him a simple test, and he flunked it.

Now she wanted to sleep with the Mossberg under her pillow.

With blood pounding in her ears, she watched him walk out. He gave a half-hearted wave before closing the door. Her heart thundered so loud it muted his footsteps. The hardwoods creaked underneath his weight. She wasn't satisfied he'd really gone until she heard a prolonged squeak coming from the door to his bedroom.

There was no doctor game.

No milk and Oreos.

No matchbook cars. Henri collected cast-aluminum motorcycles. Her brother had a bike fetish.

She threw back the covers and tiptoed to the closet. Behind her clothes, propped in the corner, she felt the cold steel barrel of the sawed-off shotgun. She grabbed it by the throat and lifted it out.

Whoever the guy in the next room was, it wasn't her brother.

Even sadder, the real Henri probably ended up on the wrong side of the grass in an anonymous grave in a third-world country.

She slipped to the door, carefully twisted the knob and opened it enough to stick out her head and look the length of the hallway. All clear. She paused at the threshold. Her ears pricked up with the intensity of bat radar. The braces in the attic moaned under the fresh weight of snow blanketing the roof. The ribbon of light under Henri's door went out.

With Mossberg in hand, Cézanne started the trek down the hall. Outside Duty's room, she paused to listen. A soft, rhythmic cadence came from behind Henri's door.

Cézanne disappeared inside Duty's room. Her eyes focused on an empty bed.

"Duty? Are you in here?"

No response.

She spotted the girl huddled in the corner with her knees tucked under her chin and her arms wrapped around her legs.

Cézanne whispered, "Shhhhhh," and put a finger to her lips. "Get your clothes on. Now. We have to get out of here."

"What's wrong?" The girl yawned into her sleeve.

She shushed her again. "Try not to make noise."

"What about 'Nigma? What're we gonna do about 'Nigma?"

"We'll come back for him." She reached out her hand and pulled Duty to her feet.

"Somethin' awful's gonna happen, Miz Zan. I saw it in the cards."

They were already downstairs when they heard footsteps moving toward the landing. They froze less than twenty feet from the front door.

Cézanne said, "Hide."

Duty whispered, "Kitchen?"

"What if he's hungry?"

"Sunroom closet."

"Not enough room."

"Think small."

They barely got the door closed when a strip of light shined under the door.

Cézanne's heart thundered. Duty gripped her arm tighter than a blood pressure cuff. Ratlike noises came from inside the sunroom. They listened carefully, trying to make out the origin of sounds.

Duty whispered, "You gonna shoot him?"

"Shhhh."

Her heartbeat slowed. She took measured breaths. It sounded like . . . whisking. Sweeping.

Duty clutched Cézanne's wrist and dug in her fingernails. "I've gotta pee."

"Hold it."

"Do I look like a camel?" She bounced at the knees.

The noise stopped. The light under the door went out.

Hardwood planks popped under the weight.

Footfalls receded in the direction of the stairs.

Believing they were alone, Cézanne opened the closet. She stepped out with Duty behind her.

Even in the shadows, she could see the pyramid of dirt dumped in the middle of the Abracadabra.

"What a charlatan." Duty shook her head in disbelief.

She gripped the girl by the shoulders and pulled her nose-to-nose. "When we reach the car, get behind the wheel. Put the gearshift in neutral. I'll see if I can push it into the street."

"You can push a big Caddy like that?"

"I've got enough adrenaline running through me to shove the Statue of Liberty off its base."

They crept to the front door and let themselves out. Wind whipped their faces.

Cézanne said, "If you still need to use the restroom, do it in the bushes."

"I only need to go when I'm under pressure. I'm not under pressure."

She wanted to laugh. They'd gotten out safely. But her stomach dropped two levels when she saw the Catera blocked in by the MGB.

She looked at Duty knowing they shared a simultaneous thought.

Holy smoke.

"We can probably pick up that little car and carry it out to the street," Duty offered helpfully.

"That little car weighs as much as a tank."

"Why don't we just borrow the MGB, Miz Zan?"

"Do I look like I have a key?" She heaved a sigh and watched the exhale turn to vapor.

Duty toed the ground. "I don't exactly have a key, but if you was to say it's an emergency and bless it, I could do a little hot-wirin'."

Cézanne's jaw gaped. "These criminal thinking errors that are coming out in you . . . it's disturbing on so many levels." Then she wised up. "Okay."

They peeled back the car cover with care.

Raspy-voiced, Duty factored a new problem into the equation. "What about Velda?"

"What about her?"

"She took in a lot of money for you today."

"She did?"

"Over two grand."

That really gored her ox. Here she'd thought Velda was so useless if she'd had a third hand, she'd need another pocket to put it in. Then Duty set the record straight. Velda had a talent for debt collecting. God only knew Cézanne needed money.

"Dammit." She stopped short of kicking a tire.

"You gonna let her stay in there with a strange man?"

"They deserve each other."

"What if he kills her? Reckon it's hard getting blood out of a rug?"

"Harder than getting it out of a turnip," she said, springing up like a yard onion. "Stay put."

"So you're going back for her?"

Cézanne cringed. "I'd sooner wear white shoes in February and drink unsweetened tea. But you're making me feel guilty."

Duty squeezed under the steering wheel. Skinny fingers probed beneath the column. "I'll be sittin' right here when you come back, doing a few alterations on the car."

Upstairs in Velda's room, Cézanne propped the shotgun against a chair and crept over to the bed. Velda was snoring like a walrus.

Float like a butterfly, sting like a bee.

She pounced on the old lady. Clapped a hand over toothless gums. Got her in a chokehold and hissed in her ear.

"Don't move a muscle or I'll snap your neck like a pretzel. You hear me?" A nod. "We've got to leave the house." Velda stiffened. Resistance swelled. Cézanne jutted her chin in the direction of Henri's room. "We're in danger. I don't know who that guy is in there, but he's not my brother. Understand?"

Velda went limp.

"He came into my room. He wrapped the tie to my robe around his fists. I'm pretty sure he was about to strangle me."

Velda's eyes widened, saucerlike. It wasn't a *Bless your heart, you got away* look of relief. More of a *Damned the luck* kind of look.

"Don't be so anxious to get rid of me, Velda. I may be the only thing standing between you and certain death." She got a nod of understanding. "I'm going to let go. But just so you know I mean business—" she pulled her aunt within view of the shotgun "—don't make a peep or I'll shoot you both and let the cops think it was a murder-suicide."

Big head bob.

"It's cold outside," she continued in a whisper. "You'll need shoes. There's no time to dress so get your coat. I'll find your purse. I'm letting go now." She released her grip.

"Over my dead body," Velda snarled. "I'll get my own purse."

"Fine. Duty says you brought in a lot of money today."

Another nod.

"Good. You'd better be quieter than a gnat peeing on silk."

Chapter Twenty-Nine

Cézanne came out of the house gripping the Mossberg in one hand and hauling Velda by the wrist with the other. She propped the shotgun against the MGB, threaded her fingers to make a stirrup, and stared pointedly at her aunt.

Velda screwed up her face. "What?"

"I'm hoisting you over the door."

"Why don't we just open it?"

"Because we're trying not to make noise. Now do it."

"Do I look like the head tightrope walker for Barnum and Bailey?"

"There's an easier way," Cézanne admitted, clenching her jaw. "I could grab the loose skin around your neck and pitch you in."

Velda hiked up her sheer cotton gown. "You don't have to get snotty." With one hand on the car, she steadied herself.

Cézanne gave her a leg up and heaved the old woman over the side.

"My head's cold. Go get my hat."

"For God's sake, Velda, put a lid on it." Cézanne, straddling the door, pulled her leg inside. "Duty, start the car."

"I ain't ridin' next to Velda."

Velda scowled. "What's the hell's your problem?"

"You stink."

"Do not."

"Zip it, both of you. The idea is to get out of here in one

piece." She grabbed the shotgun by the throat and pulled it into the car.

"I ain't sittin' next to Velda. And I'm the only one who can start this bad boy. So you better switch, Miz Zan."

They needed to exchange places before Henri heard the commotion. Cézanne hiked up her leopard print gown and crawled over Velda.

"You smashed my toe." Velda again, tuning up with a new indictment.

"Try moving your carcass."

Duty shot the old lady a wicked glare. She let out a prolonged, "Eeeewwww. Velda's got green stuff on her arm."

"Do not."

"Do, too."

"Let's see." Cézanne grabbed her aunt's gnarled hand and tugged. She sucked air. "Black mold."

Velda glanced down. "What the hell?" She studied her arm.

Duty leaned around the steering wheel and touched two wires together. The engine caught. She gunned the accelerator and twisted in her seat. "Now what, Miz Zan?"

"Shift it into reverse and let's get out of here."

"How do I do that?"

"You don't know how to drive a stick?"

"I only promised to hotwire it. I never said I knew how to shift."

"Ohgod. Ohgod." She thought fast. "Okay, leave your foot on the clutch."

"What's a clutch?"

Velda cackled.

Cézanne elbowed her in the ribs so hard she gasped. "It's the pedal next to the brake. Don't take your foot off it." She shifted the stick. It made an ugly clunk. "Give it a little gas."

Duty stomped the accelerator and the MGB shot out into the street.

Tires screamed against the blacktop. While Cézanne rammed the stick shift into first gear, her eyes flickered to the house. A light came on in the upstairs hallway. Her heart raced. "Give it the gas and let out easy on the clutch."

The car lurched forward. Metal ground against metal.

"Clutch, clutch." She pulled the gearshift into second. An eerie whine came from under the hood. "Give it more gas. Step on the clutch." She dropped the gear into third.

The MGB streaked through the intersection, never mind the red light.

Duty headed north on University. "This is pretty cool, Miz Zan. You're my co-pilot." She turned on the radio.

"My head's freezing." Velda rode with her hands on her scalp. The wind blew the wrinkles back from her face, making her look like she was sitting on the wing of an F-16.

"I'm gettin' the hang of it." Duty topped Cézanne's hand with her own, stripping cogs on the way to overdrive.

Cézanne directed her into a residential subdivision.

She pointed to an antique wrought-iron mailbox illuminated by a street lamp. "Pull up to that house and stop."

Duty took her foot off the clutch. The car stalled out with a jerk.

Three women trooped up to the porch like Charlie's Hellions on a mission.

"Whose house is this?" Velda, still acting contrary, shivered beneath the flimsy cloth of her nightie. "I like this house. I wouldn't mind living in this house."

Pumped into fearlessness after listening to an Alanis Morrisette tune on the radio, Cézanne rang the chimes. She stepped back from the door in anticipation and watched the light come on in the upstairs corner window. Seconds later, a wash of color illuminated the stained glass windows. She sensed movement behind the big Tudor door. The porch light flickered on. A shadow fell over the peephole and a slew of colorful expletives filtered out.

The door opened up to reveal the unsmiling face of Marvin Krivnek.

She gave him a little finger wiggle. “Hi, Marve. We need your help.”

“Oh, good. I see you brought your gun. Who wants to be first?” The M.E. stepped aside and allowed them to file in. They followed him into the living room, seating themselves without invitation as he walked past switching on lamps.

Velda smoothed the front of her gown. Crossed her legs and made eyes at the back of his PJs and plaid robe.

Krivnek flopped into a leather recliner opposite them. He pulled the footrest lever until it snapped into place, crossed his legs at the ankles, and steepled his fingers. “Why’re you here?”

Cézanne took a deep breath. “How fast can you do a DNA test?”

He rested his hands in his lap and eyed her warily. “To determine paternity? You need child support?” Said nastily.

“Ha.” She cracked up, barely able to suppress an extended donkey bray of a laugh. “I’d need a donor first. No, this is much more serious.”

“Save your breath. Detective Vaughn dropped by earlier. He brought me a cigarette filter and a hunk of your hair. Suspects your brother isn’t really your brother.”

Duty said, “I never liked Henri. Too pretty. And that Abracadabra? He put dirt on it himself.” Her eyes widened. She gave a little gasp. “Velda, look what you did. You got green stuff on Mista Marvin’s white sofa.”

Eyes moved in a collective shift. Sure enough, she’d left a moldy imprint on the armrest.

"It was already there," Velda insisted in an exaggerated Southern drawl.

Duty stared through shrewd eyes. "No, it wasn't. Henri said our house has black mold. Henri said it'll make us sick and die. Henri said sometimes it grows on old folks 'cause they don't keep themselves as clean as young people—"

"That's a bald-face lie." Velda hopped up and disappeared into Krivnek's kitchen. She returned with a wet paper towel, sponged off her arm and unceremoniously deposited it in the M.E.'s lap. "There. Test that, too."

Krivnek stared, emotionless. He pushed his glasses up over his weathered, picket-fence hair and rubbed the pink dents they left in his nose. "Wolfgang and I went to my lab. He thinks you're in danger. Says you got your window shot out the night before this man showed up at your house, and prior to that, someone tried to pick you off at Erick Rackley's former residence."

He let the footrest down, then rose and retraced his steps, switching off lights as he moved through the room.

Cézanne hopped up from her place on the couch. "What do we do now?"

"I'm going to back to bed. You'll find fresh towels in the linen closet upstairs." He studied them like thugs in a police lineup. "Please do not get on my phone and start making long distance phone calls."

The women traded awkward glances. Krivnek headed for the stairs.

Duty called out, "How many bedrooms you got? Can I have my own? Because I don't wanna share no room with Velda."

He held up his hand and splayed his fingers.

Duty said, "Dibs on first pick."

They watched the back of his head disappear, then his shoulders, and finally the heels of his brown Jiffy houseshoes. A door slammed and the lock snicked shut.

Velda smoothed a hand over her wrinkled neck. "He's about my age, don't you think?"

Duty craned her neck enough to peer into the kitchen. "Reckon Mista Marvin's got chocolate ice cream?"

Around six o'clock the following morning, Cézanne awakened to the smell of bacon frying. After making the bed and tidying the room, she slipped into a paisley silk smoking jacket she found looped over a brass hook in the guest bathroom. Downstairs, she discovered their host hunkered over a large bowl whipping eggs.

Krivnek spoke without looking up. "You eat migas?"

He was talking about tortilla chips over scrambled eggs and shredded chicken, topped with melted Monterrey jack cheese.

"Sounds fabulous. I think Aunt Velda's sweet on you."

Krivnek stopped whisking and corkscrewed an eyebrow. "I'm single, not desperate."

"If you'll let her move in, I'll consider giving you half of my inheritance."

"I'd sooner take a spoon and carve out an eyeball." He turned the knob on the gas stove and dialed down the flare on the burner. "I don't suppose you were the one who licked the tub of ice cream clean?"

She winced. "Sorry. Duty has a thing for chocolate."

He dropped a pat of butter into the skillet. It danced across the Teflon bottom. In went the eggs, popping and sizzling. Marvin Krivnek was a food magician.

"Why are you doing this . . . being so nice?"

"Damned if I know. You want to pour us a cup?" He pointed her to a cabinet where she took out four mugs and ferried them to the coffee pot. "I know what that substance was on your aunt's arm."

Cézanne stopped lightening her coffee and set down the carton of half-and-half. "Black mold?"

Krivnek smiled. "If it was, would you move in with me?"

She brushed off the invitation with a playful swat. "Seriously. What is it?"

"You obviously don't cook. It's filé."

"What?"

Duty appeared in the doorway, patting a small yawn. "Filé. It's a Cajun spice. Looks like ground up sphagnum moss. Goes in shrimp gumbo and other dishes." Almond-shaped eyes twinkled. "I ain't as dumb as you think, Miz Zan."

Krivnek handed Cézanne the spatula and headed for the refrigerator. He'd no more opened the door before he slammed it shut and walked, zombie-like, to the window.

"I don't suppose you'd know why the police are out in my front yard?"

Duty fessed up. "I might've hotwired Henri's car."

Krivnek let out a sigh that sounded like a punctured tire. "You stole it." His gaze flitted over the room. "I'm harboring fugitives. We're all going to jail."

Duty said, "I did it. I'll handle it."

"It's my responsibility." Cézanne took off, but Duty beat her out to the curb.

She sidled up to a black officer with a shaved head and struck a pose. "Help you, officer?"

"Is this your car?"

"My car? You think this is my car? That's so funny, you thinkin' this is my car."

"We had a report of a stolen car. You wouldn't know anything about this, would you?"

"Nosirree. And might I add how nice it is to see a big, strappin' man patrolin' our neighborhood."

He lifted one eyebrow. Cézanne rolled her eyes.

Duty moved close enough to graze a skinny finger down his forearm. "If I was to apply for a job at the po-lice department, how would I do that?"

"Call Recruiting. Get an application."

Duty placed her hand on his sleeve. "Really?" Breathless. "That would be nize. I'll do that."

He eyed her pointedly. "You know anything about this car?"

"Why yes. This is an MGB. It's an English car. I don't think this is the original color though, 'cause it's a shade or two off from Tahiti Blue. Seems like the owner would've kept the integrity of the vehicle by paintin' it the same color. But maybe he didn't care 'cause he added aftermarket products that made the brakes notoriously bad, and I wouldn't think anybody would want to own a car with faulty brakes." Cézanne watched in stunned silence. Duty turned her way and muttered, "My cousin Ezekiel owns a chop shop." With her voice dripping syrup, she turned back to the officer. "What makes you think it's stolen?"

"The owner called it in. It has a GPS."

"Oh," she said dully.

Nobody'd counted on the MGB having a global positioning system.

She chatted on, as if she had a pull string hanging out of her neck and didn't have sense enough to stop yanking it. "Have you run the LP to see if the license plate matches the person who called it in? 'Cause it may've been a prank. I've never seen this car around here." She assumed a wistful visage. "Although we do get a lot of kids racing down the street. I suggest you begin your search at the high school."

Cézanne hip-checked her out of the way. "I'll take it from here."

The black officer said, "You live here?"

Before Cézanne could answer, Duty pulled her string again. "Live here? Do we live here?" She hooted. "You think a proud black woman can't live in a neighborhood like this?" She slapped him playfully on the wrist and changed the subject without answering his question. "Say, if I was to come down to the police station, you think I could ride around in the po-lice car and you could tell me more about how to get that job? 'Cause right now, I'm just a legal assistant, and I would like to get out of the business 'fore it makes me crabby like Miz Zan."

Cézanne headed back to the house. They were all going to jail. May as well see if Krivnek would arrange for clothes.

Inside, the forensic pathologist was sitting across the table from Aunt Velda with his hair sticking up like wires in a currycomb. Velda was making a fool of herself mooning over him.

Krivnek took one look at her and anticipated the problem. "I'm not posting anybody's bail," he announced to the dining room at large.

Exasperated by the circus, she waved him away and started for the stairs. Momentarily, Duty burst in through the front door.

"Miz Zan, Mista Henri's on his way. Roland says—"

"Roland?"

"The nize lookin' one I have a date with tonight."

"No. There's no date. You can't date until you produce a birth certificate showing your true age."

But Duty brushed her off with a hand-flick. "Let's cut and run before Henri shows up."

They left out the back way with Krivnek chauffeuring them in his big black Mercedes. At the house on South University, the occupants breathed a collective sigh of relief. Henri had cleared out his belongings and wiped down his room. And even though Cézanne called Slash to stop by and dust for prints, she didn't expect his efforts to yield any.

For now, discovering Henri's true identity would have to wait.

Chapter Thirty

While Cézanne finished preparing a writ of habeas corpus to get Erick Rackley benched back to his court of conviction, Duty lounged on the Biedermeier, glued to the TV, enumerating reasons why she should be able to go out with Roland. With her feet propped on a pillow and a plate of chicken salad balanced on the flat of her stomach, she announced in no uncertain terms that she was practically an adult and should be allowed to date.

"You can hang with boys up to two years older. You may not see a man twice your age." Cézanne hunkered over a volume containing prototypes of legal forms and double-checked her document.

"How'd you know he's twice my age? He might only be a few years older. Then you'd let me go, wouldn't you? 'Cause I don't get to meet many eligible black men in Weeping Mary who are worthy of me, and I was thinkin' this would be a good time to start so I don't end up like you."

"Like me?" Cézanne's startle reflex kicked in. She stopped reading, stiffened with fury and turned. "Like me?" Her voice corkscrewed upward. "And how is that?"

"Bucked from the bronco of love."

Cézanne seethed. "I'm sitting here listening to a Voodoo practicing, Tarot card reading teenager from the sticks tell me how fucked-up my life is?"

"I never said the f-word. If I'd used the f-word at least you'd be gettin' some."

"You don't know anything about my personal life."

Duty's eyes cut to the window and back. "I know you ain't got one."

"Oh, yeah? If you're such a great fortuneteller, why didn't you predict the future by figuring out who Henri was?"

"Already did."

"Yeah? What the hell's my future, huh? I'll bet you can't tell me what's going to happen in the next fifteen minutes, much less the rest of my life."

Duty directed her attention out the window. "If I predict it right, can I go out with Roland?"

"If your prediction's correct you can marry the bastard."

"Let's not go that far." Maroon eyes shifted. "I'll predict your immediate future. Then I get to date."

The house echoed with moody sounds. Cézanne rose from her chair. Braced her arms across her chest and waited for pearls of wisdom to spill out of Duty's mouth.

"For the next couple of seconds, I need complete quiet." Duty pressed her fingertips to her temples and closed her lids. When she spoke, her voice dropped an octave. "I see a black man coming into your life."

"Bull . . . loney. You don't have second sight."

"Silence. This man'll be bearing gifts. His presence'll change yo' life."

"What'd you do, tell Roland to bring me candy and flowers so I'd let you go out with him?"

"Hush. A lady's pushin' him."

"You're predicting I'll get hired to defend a domestic violence case?"

"Not exactly. But if I'm right about the black man getting pushed by the lady, I get to go out with Roland, right?"

"Fine."

"Excellent." She punctuated her good fortune with a nod.

"Get the door."

"What?"

The bell chimed. Inertia kept Cézanne in place.

"Miz Zan, get the door."

Sun slanted through the wood Venetian blinds. Glancing over made her eyes smart. She angled across the room as Duty stuffed the last bite of chicken salad into her mouth and headed to the kitchen with an empty plate.

"Where do you think you're going?"

"Gotta get ready for my date."

Cézanne opened the door. She couldn't have been more surprised if a dozen Indians galloped up on horseback and shot arrows at her.

Chester Willoughby sat in his wheelchair with his chin tucked into his chest and his wife Irene behind him. He glanced up, blank faced. A gossamer thread of drool oozed out of one corner of his mouth. Then his eyes abruptly cleared, and she saw recognition kick in.

"Miz Martin? Chet asked me to drive him over. He has something special he wants to give you."

Her gaze dipped to Chet's lap. "You brought me a book?"

"Not just any book. Chet says it's a journal. He was savin' it for the right person, isn't that right, Chet? Chet says, 'That's right.' " Irene Willoughby beamed. Large teeth appeared even whiter against the backdrop of blue gums and a fuchsia tongue. "Open it."

"What's in it?"

"Chet says he kept it during that trial. Says you'll know what to do with it. Isn't that right, Chet? Chet says, 'You know that's right.' "

Chet didn't say anything. But his lips trembled like he wanted to. A tear slid out of the corner of one eye and sluiced down his cheek like a raindrop on the windowpane to his soul.

"We'd best be letting you get back to work. Chet wants me to drive by the zoo so he can hear the monkeys chatter. It'll be time for the zookeepers to feed them, and they always get riled up just before they eat, isn't that right, Chet? Chet says, 'That's right.' Let's go, baby."

Chet focused on something behind her, and his expression changed. It was the sort of response a man confronted with the sight of his daughter on her wedding day might have. Cézanne turned and caught Duty giving the old man a tentative wave from foot of the stairs.

Decked out in the borrowed red cocktail dress, she looked beautiful with her hair up-swept and her marble-smooth, café au lait face powdered.

"We'll be going now, Miz Martin. If you need anything, just call. The number's in the front of Chet's journal. He'll gladly answer any questions if you don't understand."

Roland rang the doorbell a few minutes after six. Duty jockeyed for position, but Cézanne won. She opened the door wide, saw the bouquet of carnations, took the nosegay, and handed it off to Duty. As the girl wandered off toward the kitchen in search of a vase, Cézanne launched rapid-fire questions.

"How long have you been on the PD? Do you intend to make rank? How old are you?"

He stammered out answers. "Two years. I'd like to be chief someday. I'm twenty-three."

"You're too old for her."

"I know." Roland gave her a toothy grin. "That's why I brought my nephew along. He's twelve. I figured they'd hit it off."

"Duty'll be furious when she finds out you're just the chauffeur."

"I knew she wasn't old enough to be asking me out. Besides,

Elkhardt told me not to get crosswise with you."

She could imagine that conversation. "Duty's my ward, which makes me responsible." She inclined her head toward the kitchen, listening for the sound of running water. "Just so we understand each other, I'm on a first name basis with the lieutenant in Internal Affairs." To raise her comfort level, she moved to the window. Sure enough, a kid sat in the front seat of the truck. "I want her home by ten."

"The movie's not until eight. It's a two hour flick."

"Then you'll have to drive Code-Three, won't you?"

Cézanne was waiting in the dark on the veranda when Roland's pickup coasted into the driveway with seconds to spare. When Duty didn't climb out right away, she slipped inside and turned on the porch lights, including the directional beacons illuminating the trees. The yard lit up like a space-shuttle drop zone. When Duty didn't come right in, she looked through the window trying to vector her location and saw only one silhouette.

That put the rock in the snowball.

She stepped onto the welcome mat, pulling the door closed behind her.

From some distant place, Duty screamed, "Tire iron." The ungodly shriek pierced the night. With neck hairs prickling, Cézanne dashed back inside.

"Dial nine-one-one," she yelled to Velda then grabbed the shotgun from its place in the corner and limped outside.

"Duty, where are you?"

Neighbors' lights flickered on.

Roland yelled, "Back here." His voice came from the right, toward the rear of the house.

She rounded the veranda with the Mossberg leveled waist high. Sobs built in her throat. She couldn't imagine having to explain to Leviticus Devilrow that something horrible had happened to his niece.

A lie.

This wasn't about being accountable to her con-wise handyman.

She loved that kid.

There. Truth was out.

She'd been given the chance to help an impoverished black child and had screwed it up. A shrill whine shriveled her fear. Pure instinct kicked in. She eased off the safety and leaped around the corner ready to cut a man in half.

The man marked for death turned out to be Duty.

She was on her belly wrangling with a . . .

. . . with a . . .

. . . large man . . . or a small horse.

Cézanne fired a warning shot into the ground. Exploding dirt-clods freeze-framed the moment.

Roland took cover and cowered behind a pecan tree in the shadowy recesses of the back yard. The cellar door gaped open.

Cézanne watched her red cocktail dress turn black as Duty dragged Enigma from the cellar. He stumbled and collapsed, unable to stand on gangly legs.

"What the hell?"

" 'Nigma." The girl turned to Cézanne, her face bathed in tears, her hair like Brillo pads stuck to the side of her head. "Mista Henri did it, Miz Zan. Put my good dog 'Nigma in the cellar and locked it. 'Nigma could've died. We need to get him to the dog hospital."

She started to protest. To say he just needed water and maybe food. But the effect of the shadows made his ribs look like stair steps, and she no longer cared about the frickin' dress or the late hour or the fact that Enigma needed a veterinarian.

Duty was safe. That's what mattered.

Sirens pealed in the distance.

Velda had called nine-one-one.

Cézanne turned to Roland. "Can you drive us to the animal clinic?" This meant one of them would have to ride in the truck bed with Enigma. She suspected it'd be her.

"If you don't mind, we'll be on our way." Saucer-eyed, Roland fished for his keys. "If you don't have to, please don't mention my name . . . I called in sick tonight. I could get fired."

She hollered at Velda for water. Her aunt hobbled down the back steps, wrenched the faucet on, and picked up the plastic garden hose by its middle. The sprinkler head twisted and squirmed, effectively dousing Cézanne.

Enigma's tongue flicked out like a mud flap on an eighteen-wheeler.

Halfway to hysterics, Duty screamed at Roland. "Pick him up. Be gentle. 'Nigma don't like being held that way. You're not gonna make him ride in the truck bed. Gimme my dog."

Roland reluctantly accepted his new role as ambulance driver. After badgering him into letting Enigma ride in the cab, Duty squeezed in, and they took off.

While Cézanne sat on the veranda dripping water and waiting for the police to arrive, three pervasive thoughts controlled her feelings.

First, Roland and his nephew were history.

Second, the red cocktail dress and her water-soaked Ferragamos were history.

Third, she'd be going to jail for discharging a firearm in the city limits.

Officers Flurry and Elkhardt were first on-scene. They trundled up the porch steps followed by Slash, who'd heard the call on his handie-talkie as he reported for duty. Three more units screeched up to the curb. Strobe lights and overheads lit up the neighborhood like the mothership had landed.

Elkhardt pulled a spiral notebook from his shirt pocket. "Who's dead?"

"Nobody."

"Good." He keyed his shoulder mike, dipped his chin, and radioed the dispatcher. "Code-Four. Cancel Homicide. It's the Signal-thirteen's house." Signal-thirteen was FWPD's code for a demented person.

Flurry said, "You sure nobody's dead?"

"Not yet."

"We made a bet on the off chance your imaginary friend turned out to be real. I put fifty dollars on the old lady killing you."

"Glad you lost. You can go now."

"Not until we see the old lady. If she's dead, Elkhardt wins."

"Who fired the shots?" Elkhardt.

She invoked her Fifth Amendment right against self-incrimination. "It'd be kind of stupid to answer that, now wouldn't it?"

"Nobody's dead?"

"Not this time."

"Anybody see you pull the trigger?"

"What makes you so sure it was me?"

"You just seem good for it. And we'll be canvassing your neighbors. They're not real happy with you, in case you didn't know." Elkhardt turned to Slash. "You wanna take over here? Don't let her leave."

Slash stood, grim-faced, completing the pissed-off cop stance with his arms braced across his chest. "She's not going anywhere."

"Let us know if she shot the old lady. Otherwise, it's shift-change, and I've got a T-bone at home with my name on it."

"Definitely." Slash again, fighting a smile.

Upstairs, Velda raised the window and poked out her head.

"What the hell's going on down there? Can't you skullbusters keep quiet? You're wakin' up the dead."

Elkhardt keyed his mike and gave his call sign. "Hold me Ten-eight." To Flurry, he said, "Looks like we both lose."

Flurry radioed the dispatcher and went back in service.

Slash keyed his hand-held. "Hold me out at the scene."

"Ten-four," came the calm, capable voice of a female dispatcher.

Chapter Thirty-One

The biggest surprise for the Martin Law Firm came the following week.

Never in a million years did Cézanne figure the appeals court would review her writ of habeas corpus so quickly, much less order an evidentiary hearing and remand the case back to the trial court. But she hadn't counted on Rackley's case being such a political hot horseshoe until Special State District Judge Pittman was called in from retirement to hear the matter.

So when Slash's brother Teddy happened to be testifying at the Justice Center on an unrelated matter and heard the news from an angry prosecutor, he telephoned Slash. According to Teddy, it turned out Yvonne's parents had connections in the Governor's Office. Judge Pittman declared the retrial an APE case—acute political emergency—and was having his clerk issue a bench warrant to bring Rackley back for the hearing. Before the clerk even finished typing it out, Slash showed up and asked Pittman to let him serve the papers instead of sending deputies from the Tarrant County Sheriff's Office.

Now the crime scene investigator stood in the foyer of the law office with warrant in hand, running down the game plan. He'd checked out a brand new unmarked patrol car and was heading down to the Briscoe Unit to serve the warden, pick up Erick Rackley, and transport him to jail.

"This is great news," Cézanne said about Judge Pittman presiding over the case. The old judge had sworn her in when she passed the bar, and he had a reputation for honesty and fairness.

As for Slash's trip to the penitentiary, she said, "I'll tag along," and held up her hand before he could argue. He'd gotten her into this mess, and she used it as leverage when she insisted on riding shotgun. "Besides, since I'm having to learn all this legal stuff in the trenches, who knows when I'll have this much time to talk to him? I still have to make a living taking dogshit cases. It's not like the Rackley case will make me rich and famous." The words popped out before she realized she'd been thinking them.

Slash challenged her. "I offered to pay. I *will* pay you," he said and vetoed her request. She was a civilian now, not a cop. She could see Rackley after he got booked into the Tarrant County jail.

Understanding his reluctance, she mounted a good argument. "I'm still on the FWPD payroll. I have my badge and ID. You asked me to take him on as a client, and this'll be a good opportunity to use the dead time to interview him."

He dismissed her with his eyes and checked his watch. If she could be ready in ten minutes he'd take her along.

"Bring your gun and creds," he reminded her as she headed upstairs. It wasn't until they were on the highway that he brought up a concern. "Word leaked out—well, okay, it didn't exactly leak out. The prosecutor turned into the town crier and spread the word about your motion. Now all the lawyers in the Metroplex are screaming bloody murder that you're a traitor. I wouldn't expect to get hired by the DA's office anytime soon. You're too controversial."

The countryside tended to be flat to slightly undulating, with light-colored loam and plenty of brush and prickly pear, and it wasn't long before Cézanne felt herself being seduced into sleep by the lackluster terrain. She slipped on her sunglasses and flipped down the visor and snoozed. The jarring sound of gravel hitting the cruiser's undercarriage roused her from her nap. She felt the car brake, and when she opened her eyes, Slash had stopped on the road's shoulder. With the Briscoe Unit looming in the distance, he turned to face her.

"We need to talk." He took a deep breath. "The judge was afraid this little jaunt might turn into one of those Clint Eastwood deals where we'd get ambushed." He let the gravity of the situation soak in.

"So I'm the designated decoy?" she said with a pout of defensiveness.

"I let you come along because at this point, I don't trust anyone else to back me up."

At the prison gate, they went through the usual security clearances. As soon as they got the warden served and the inmate safely loaded into the cage of the unmarked car, Erick tuned up like a divo. He carped about the clothes, which had been donated from a local church and were several sizes too large, and he whined because Slash put a belly chain around his waist and handcuffed his hands in front.

"Why do I need bracelets? I'm not going anywhere."

"We're doing this according to SOP," Slash said, and quoted the PD's standard operating procedure manual.

"You don't trust me."

Slash ignored him. When they hit the highway, he turned on the stereo and volumed it down low. As Cézanne used the drive time to ask Rackley questions, a Charlie Daniels tune leaked out of the speakers.

Deep into brush country Slash reached over and flicked her knee. She stopped in mid-sentence and turned.

His eyes flickered to the rearview mirror. He twisted the stereo knob, shifting the music to the back speakers so their cargo wouldn't overhear. "Tighten your seatbelt. We're being followed."

"How do you know?" She wrenched in her seat to see past Rackley's shoulder and noticed a black pickup. Bobby's truck had an intimidating grill guard like that. When she turned back around, Slash's jaw torqued. "Maybe they just want to pass us."

"Maybe," he said without conviction. But he unsnapped his holster and placed his .45 caliber on the seat between them.

The truck closed in. "What do you want me to do?" Cézanne's stomach gave a nervous flip.

"Get your gun." The veins in his neck plumped up. He slapped off the stereo and tightened his grip on the steering wheel. Rackley had been singing along with the FM radio; now he strained to look out the back windshield.

Slash gradually increased his speed. They were doing ninety in a sixty, and the truck was gaining on them. She took the new stainless steel Smith & Wesson .38 out of her handbag and wrapped her fingers around the Pachmeyer grips.

"Maybe they're just in a hurry," she said hopefully. But she was thinking *Maybe it's Bobby* and wondered if Slash might pull over so she could talk to him.

"Maybe," Slash echoed. Intensity hardened his lips. He inclined his head to the left where he could monitor the vehicle from his side mirror. "Brace yourself."

He braked hard. Steel-belted radials laid down tread, screaming against the blacktop. Smoke darkened the air behind them. The driver and passenger shot past and disappeared into the horizon.

Erick said, "Jeez, you almost gave me a heart attack."

She looked at her client hard, but he didn't get the message. Neither she nor Slash said anything, but they both watched the inmate carefully; Slash, through the rearview mirror; she, through the thick wire mesh. He slumped miserably against the back seat with his eyes focused, saucer-like, on the dome light.

Tires droned on the asphalt.

She moved in close and lowered her voice. "See? I told you it was nothing." Then she leaned against the headrest, relaxed her grip on the Chief Special and closed her eyes.

She'd barely drifted off to sleep when Slash finger-flicked her thigh again. Her lids slitted open. For no reason other than instinct, she shifted her attention out the front windshield and saw the red smear of brake lights in the distance. The same black truck that had careened past them five minutes earlier now sat on the shoulder of the highway. Something moved at the limits of her vision.

Slash braked to a stop. They studied the scene from afar.

"Binoculars?" Cézanne whispered as the engine idled and the heater circulated warm air through the compartment.

He kept his focus straightaway. "Now do you believe me?"

"Move closer. I can't see what they're doing." She glanced into the back seat. Rackley, who'd been in and out of their conversations ever since he'd gotten into the cage, was fast asleep with his mouth agape, stirring up a racket with his snoring.

Slash took his foot off the brake. The patrol car crept forward.

"Is that a woman or a man? Ohmygod, he's on the ground. Is that guy doing CPR?"

"We're not stopping."

"We have to stop. It's the PD motto: 'Dedicated to protect.' I'm not saying we should get out. We can just let them know we'll call for help."

The cruiser inched ahead. It took several minutes for the squad car to ease close enough for them to start making out facial features.

"See? Told you they needed medical attention," Cézanne said in a stage whisper.

They drove within ten car lengths.

Slash powered down the passenger window. "We're out in the boondocks. There's nothing in sight. It's not like they hit a tree. Could be a trap."

"Probably braked for a deer." She took his arm confidentially and started to cup a hand to her mouth. Slash focused on something past her shoulder, and his expression hardened. She turned toward the open window and shouted, "Need an ambu—"

The rest of the words died in her throat.

Two bearded men pulled ski masks over their faces. The one who was street-proned sat up. The other took cover behind the truck bed. Up came their guns. The motorists opened fire.

"Setup, setup, setup." Slash's yell rent the air.

Bullets rained over them like a Biblical scourge.

He stomped the accelerator, gunning the big V-8 engine forward. The squad car shot past as Rackley's window shattered and the inmate came fully awake.

Cézanne traded the .38 for Slash's semi-automatic. She hung out the window and drove the men back until the clip emptied and the slide hung in the re-load position. She ducked back into the cruiser and felt the car pulling Gs. Rounds whistled overhead and grooved the roof.

Lead pierced the car in a blast of firepower; the firefight had the potential to liquefy their brains.

Rackley sat bolt upright and screamed, "What the hell?"

She grabbed the .38 and made it halfway out the window when Slash yanked her back by the scruff of the neck.

"Too far away," he said. "You okay?"

"Yes," she lied, suddenly understanding how the daredevils of Niagra Falls felt when their barrels popped up from the undercurrent. "They tried to kill us. Go back." She was shaking now.

"I'm not turning back."

"But they tried to turn us into organ donors," she said understanding his reluctance. Then, the narrow escape sunk in, and she saw red. "We can't let them get away with that. We can re-load. Give me an extra clip. You just drive. I'll do all the work."

He was right, of course. Still, the thugs who tried to kill them deserved to experience the pucker power of a real firefight. If they had an extra gun, they could give it to Rackley, and the three of them could—

She shook her head violently. What was she thinking? Maybe those men weren't trying to *kill* her client. Maybe they were trying to *free* him.

Suddenly, she wanted to slap Rackley so hard he'd be coughing up bones.

"Who knew you were leaving besides the warden?"

"My cell mate. The screws knew. And my sister. I called her in case she wanted to come to the hearing. Wait a minute—" feral toughness tightened his face "—you think I did this?"

"Let's just clean the whole fish right here. If I find out you cooked up that gun battle to bust out of here, I'll kill you myself."

"Hey, I've got an idea," he said with sugary sweetness, "why don't we swap positions? You sit back here trussed up like the Christmas turkey and dodge shrapnel while I put on lip gloss and pretend I'm a damned princess."

Wanting to inflict pain, she now understood how the Rackleys' petty disagreements could've escalated to murder. The only thing she couldn't figure out was why Yvonne didn't kill him instead of herself.

"I ought to fire you," she said, scorched. "You're such a jerk."

"That's the nicest thing I've been called all week, princess."

Humiliation crept over her. She could use a charm school class.

Slash slid her a warning look. He kept his voice even and metered. "See if you can find an intercity channel." He dislodged the dash mike from its prongs and passed it to Cézanne. "Ask for DPS. They're bound to have a highway patrolman out here. If they don't, then ask for a Texas Ranger. We may need a convoy to get this guy back." Then he spotted a mile marker and gave her the number to call in their location. "Tell the dispatcher what happened. Ask for directions to the sheriff's station."

"I want a gun," Rackley shouted. "I'm a sitting, fucking duck."

Cézanne flipped through channels calling, "Officer needs assistance, Ten-eighteen."

"Did you get a tag number on the plate?" Slash wanted to know.

Was he kidding?

"Gee, I'm afraid not. I was too busy trying to remember last night's lotto numbers while my life was flashing before me," she said sarcastically. Caustic humor often functioned as a personality bonus during life and death emergencies.

Rackley was still speaking in tongues. He curled up on the seat like a cocktail shrimp.

They simultaneously turned. Cézanne, who'd lost patience with getting shot at and didn't like to think assassins might be gaining on them, snapped, "Shut up," but the inmate wasn't about to have his monologue interrupted.

Slash ground his molars. He slid Cézanne a sideways glance.

"Did you recognize them? Could one have been Darlene Driskoll?"

"I'm pretty sure those were men wearing fake beards. I thought one looked like your brother."

"Why would Henri want to—"

"Who's Henri?" Rackley chanted through the mesh divider. "Henri who?"

Slash caught the prisoner's eye in the rearview mirror and spoke in a deep, roughly textured growl. "If I hear one more peep out of you in the next ten minutes, I'll jerk you out of this car and handcuff you to a fencepost."

For Cézanne, he softened his voice. "Did you notice anything useful?"

"I don't think Henri would shoot at us."

"No? I took one of his cast-off cigarette butts and gave it to Krivnek to test for mitochondrial DNA. He couldn't spare the time, so he turned it over to a friend of mine in the FBI—"

"You have a friend in the FBI?" This genuinely puzzled her. You didn't befriend those guys any more than you'd take home a rattlesnake and turn it into a pet.

"—who ran it through the DNA database. The guy calling himself your brother is definitely not your brother."

A wave of nausea washed over her. "I just remembered something better than a license plate. One of those men resembled Gary Oakes, the jury foreman on Erick's case."

"But why would . . . ?" Rackley's eyes went wide. He seemed to be slipping into shock.

The police radio crackled to life. Cézanne gave the Frio County Sheriff's Office a rundown on what happened. The dispatcher sent a couple of deputy sheriffs and a state trooper to intercept them and in a matter of minutes, the cavalry arrived and led them to safety.

At the SO, they each gave written statements while a perturbed Erick Rackley sat shackled to a metal bench. A deputy reloaded Slash's magazine with fresh ammo, and the sheriff himself escorted them to the county line. A couple of highway patrolmen took the handoff in a kind of bizarre human relay and multiple law enforcement officers from each successive county made ready to lead them to safety.

Everyone except FWPD.

At the Tarrant County line, a lone patrol car merged into the convoy. At the next exit, DPS peeled off like the Thunderbirds and disappeared onto the frontage road.

"A single unit," Cézanne said, "that's all they sent us?"

"One Ranger, one riot," Slash said, playing off an old adage.

One of the crime scene investigator's greatest talents was his ability to carefully modulate his voice to conceal his fear. She suspected this was one of those times.

Downtown on Belknap Street they passed lawyer row—a strip of legal firms that included Hollis Rushmore's—and were within three blocks of the jail when she finally took a deep, relaxing breath. She rotated her head to work the kink out of her neck, thankful they were almost done.

For no good reason the back window exploded.

Rackley screamed. He keeled over onto his side and hunkered down in the floorboard bleating like a tethered sheep.

Cézanne's mouth rounded into an "O," and she looked at Slash. They exchanged eyebrow-encrypted messages that telepathically suggested booking Erick into the Tarrant County jail might not be such a hot idea after all.

He shouted, "Hit the deck."

She dove, face-first, into his lap and felt her insides flip like they did on the double-upside-down rollercoaster ride at Six Flags. Slash jerked the wheel, hard left. Brakes screeched. Horns blared. She instinctively knew by the rough jolt and the scrape of shrubs against the car's undercarriage that he'd careened over the median in a mid-block U-turn. For a few seconds they headed in the direction where the shot had come from, and she wondered why he'd drive them into the jaws of death. With a turn of the wheel, hard right, he stomped the accelerator.

"You can get up now." He toggled the emergency lights and

siren and accelerated through the red traffic signal Code-Three. "You all right?"

"Never felt more alive." Sitting erect, she oriented herself to their location. They traveled down Houston Street, under cover of skyscrapers, at a high rate of speed during the busiest time of day.

"You hurt?" Slash called back over the headrest. Rackley was making spine-chilling noises into the floor mat. "Check on him, will you?"

Still caught in the hang time of a stunned stupor, Cézanne unbuckled her seatbelt, did a 180-degree turn and pressed her hands against the wire mesh for a better look.

"He's okay. Now what?"

"We ditch the car and head for someplace safe."

Normally, sanctuary would've meant heading for Bobby's house, but Bobby and his new wife probably wouldn't approve of an ex-fiancée showing up unannounced wanting to bunk over with a convicted murderer and a guy whose hair was sticking up like a zebra's mane. Instead, she placed her head in her palms, massaged her headache, and thought of the next best thing.

They entered the morgue to the sight of everyone ricocheting off each other trying to leave for the day. In the mad scramble, Krivnek burst forth from the double doors dressed in casual clothes and skidded to a halt. The trick would've been to backtrack slowly and hope no one noticed, but Cézanne glimpsed his eyes telescope back into their sockets and called out his name.

He looked anxious and vaguely resentful, eyeing up Rackley who was still in shackles. With dozens of wrinkles fishnetting his face under the harsh fluorescent lighting, Krivnek crossed his arms in a standoff.

"Charlotte," he directed the receptionist, "call the police."

"We are the police," Slash reminded him.

Charlotte, who'd raised an eight-by-ten glossy to the light and was comparing it to Cézanne, dropped the photo and picked up the telephone.

Cézanne depressed the button, disconnecting the call. "I wouldn't do that if I were you," she said, drawing out the words to prolong the agony.

The young lady glanced at Krivnek for new instructions.

"Disregard. No cops." His whole body seemed to sigh. "I've spent the better part of a month plotting the perfect murder. Your visit will give me the opportunity to test my theory."

Cézanne gave him a bland smile. "Thanks, Marve, you're a pal."

He showed them into his office and closed the door with an authoritative clunk. She followed his eyes to the clock on the wall, then surveyed the coffee pot and saw it was half empty with the cord unplugged. The furniture was motel Danish with blond wood and clean lines, and when the M.E. sat, he swung around in his chair to face the exit as though contemplating escape.

"We need your help." She pictured him having a psychotic break.

"Of course," he said affably, but his face said *No way.* Steely eyes coolly narrowed.

She ran down the problem in short, abbreviated bursts, giving him details on trading gunfire with hit men that morning and getting sniped at three blocks from the jail that afternoon. As she clued him in, his vision was most of the time cast to the floor, never looking her directly in the face. Without invitation, she moved to the credenza, poured herself a cup of cold coffee and gulped it down, speeding caffeine into her system. She paused and considered her empty cup.

"Let me guess." Krivnek looked up from behind stubby gray

lashes and folded a stick of cinnamon gum into his mouth. "You thought you'd drag me into your little caper by asking me to zip Mr. Rackley into a body bag and transport him to the county lockup in the meatwagon."

Actually, that wasn't what she thought at all, but she had to admit he'd come up with a light bulb idea, the perfect solution. One look at Slash confirmed her thoughts.

"You're a genius, Marvin," she said.

The part about the body bag drew fire from Erick. "The only way you're zipping me in a body bag is if I'm dead."

She sliced a finger across her throat to indicate a violent accommodation, and Rackley piped down. When she looked back over at Krivnek his thin lips were bracketed by laugh lines.

"So you'll help us get him to the jail in one piece?" she said through a smile so forced she felt her jaw go numb.

Thanks to the M.E.'s adventuresome spirit, Erick Rackley traded his civilian clothes and belly chain for a cell in I-block with a jumpsuit and ugly plastic slides to wear. By midnight he had nothing to worry about but stamps, envelopes, commissary, and the upcoming hearing.

Chapter Thirty-Two

The morning of Rackley's hearing began with a brilliant sunrise that quickly turned to an overcast sky followed by pellets of rain. It was the perfect metaphor.

Cézanne walked into a packed courtroom for the nine o'clock hearing before Judge Pittman. At first, she thought there might be a docket call because of the packed gallery. Then she noticed a scattering of plainclothes cops, some obvious civil attorneys, and a couple of tight-jawed spectators whose glares suggested they'd like to get her in the crosshairs of their scopes. She signed in with the bailiff, asked about Rackley, and was told he was being kept in a holding cell beyond the courtroom. A fresh wave of anxiety washed over her. These could be Yvonne's angry relatives and colleagues, come to watch her fail. This was a serious case, and she was a baby lawyer about to get her ass kicked.

She could be sued for malpractice whether she got paid or not. The last thing she needed in her legal career was to be labeled incompetent, but the kiss of death would be getting disbarred. She reminded herself that nobody else would take Rackley's case. That she was his last hope. And when you've fallen overboard into a sea of sharks, you don't really care whether the life ring is fully inflated—you just want to grab on and hope the rope doesn't break while your rescuer tows you up.

The mental pep talk vanquished her jitters.

She barked out a relieved laugh, and all the lawmen twisted

around to see if she was a lunatic.

Without warning, everything changed.

The entryway leading out into the corridor banged open and a handful of prosecutors rode in on their egos like a band of marauding Goths. She took in the men in one dismissive glance. It wasn't as if they were hell on wheels. She let out a sigh and felt the tension drain from her shoulders.

Then the double doors banged open again, and her heart slipped into defib mode. Sheer panic made the air unbreathable.

Helena Lindner strutted in on a burst of energy. The DA'd pulled out his big gun. Cézanne knew the chief prosecutor by reputation and took in the sight of her in increments: the severe navy suit, the impenetrable, unreadable brown eyes, the processed blonde hair, the dolly she dragged effortlessly behind her with three huge boxes marked RACKLEY stacked on top of each other . . .

I'm screwed.

Helena, all brisk and efficient, consulted her Blackberry and bossed her lackeys from her seat at the prosecutor's table.

Cézanne walked over and introduced herself in an unstable voice.

Instead of a handshake, Helena scowled. "Exactly why are we here?"

"Uh—" finger to lips in the thinking position, she paused reflectively before dripping sarcasm "—maybe because I'm a defense attorney?" Yikes. Lindner would probably blame an elephant for having a long nose.

"Your hero's exactly where he needs to be. If you were smart, you'd drop this hot potato. You'll never get a new trial; you'll just look inept."

The state's attorney was probably right. Expecting to get Rackley a new trial was like asking for a pot of gold at the end of the rainbow and getting a crock of those fake chocolate coins wrapped in a gay pride flag.

So why'd the woman have to act so nasty? Cézanne cracked a smile. Maybe she had good reason to worry. Maybe two of those boxes were nothing but empty props wheeled in to intimidate her.

Judge Pittman swept in with his black robe flowing, and the bailiff called the court to order with an authoritative, "All rise." Everyone stood then dropped back onto the pews when the judge said, "Be seated."

He spoke in a raspy, three-pack-a-day voice. Ancient and dignified, not a lock of white hair out of place, Pittman had skin the shade and texture of old Samsonite luggage. and his face was a phalanx of wrinkles. And like the subject in an ancestral painting, his deep, fathomless eyes seemed to track everyone in the room whether they happened to be looking at him or not.

The attorneys took their places behind their respective tables.

Bailiffs brought Erick Rackley in from the holding cell. He was wearing a bright orange jumpsuit, and he entered the room belly-chained and shackled. She discreetly eyed him up. He wore two beige plastic sandals, two white socks, two black eyes . . .

Judge Pittman looked him over, flinty-eyed. "Well, son, did you win?"

"Not this time, Judge."

"What happened?"

"Ran into a door."

"Ah, yes . . . the blue wall of silence. I'm familiar with it. Very well, let's move on."

As the raptor-eyed jurist nodded at the court reporter and announced the case on the record, Cézanne did a conspiratorial lean-in. "What really happened?"

"Forgot to tell you. Yvonne has a cousin at the SO. He's a wheel."

"He beat you up?" she whispered.

"Nobody likes a snitch. I ran into a door." For a guy who'd gotten the stuffing knocked out of him, Rackley sounded unassailably indifferent. "Let's just leave it at that."

Her mind went through a series of cruel mental gymnastics that grew more pronounced the longer she thought about it. They'd put him in I-block for a reason. Ex-cops didn't get locked up with the rest of the population. So much for protective custody.

Rackley sheared her thoughts. "Nice legs." He looked past her to the prosecutors' table. "Who's she?"

"Helena Handcart." Her eyes slewed to her client. "Which is exactly where you're going since you're unlucky enough to get her as opposing counsel."

"Maybe they sent her because we have a good case."

Bless his heart. He was either the stupidest man on Earth or the most trusting. Either way, what he said inspired confidence. She was actually starting to warm to him now that they'd shared the bond of a near-death experience.

Then he added, "That skirt's short enough to keep the waxer in business."

Knock it off she tried to tell him telepathically.

Judge Pittman must've said something because the room got deathly quiet. He settled his falcon-eyed stare on her.

For the better part of a day, she moved through the motions to get Rackley a new trial, alternately listening to Helena Handbucket's brain-dulling tripe as she unpacked files and made furious objections and making her own objections while sliding sideways glances to see if the prosecutors were mocking her. When each side finished, Judge Pittman received Chester Willoughby's journal into evidence along with the expert witness's textbook on blood spatter. Without preamble, he announced he'd take the matter under advisement, dismissed them for the afternoon, and stepped down from the bench.

Cézanne turned at the sound of Helena Lindner's voice.

"Not half bad for a rookie," the chief prosecutor said, halfway to gloating as her minions packed up cartons, "but you're still going to lose."

"And if I don't?" She tried to keep her voice light and convincing.

"We'll just convict him again."

The next day dawned with a butterscotch sunrise. While the rest of the household slept, Cézanne was in bed with the lights off, running on adrenaline and trying to organize her racing thoughts. She was lying there shrouded in gloom when she heard the shrill of the phone and dragged herself out of bed on a yawn. Judge Pittman's coordinator was on the line. Pittman wanted the lawyers back in court.

This time, Rackley showed up with a split lip.

Everyone waited with anticipation for the judge to breeze in. The chief prosecutor, still brimming with confidence, discreetly consulted her Blackberry; Cézanne picked at her cuticles until they bled; and Erick Rackley sat with his eyes downcast and his hands under the table, pressed together in the prayer position.

Somebody summoned the television reporters—probably Helena Haute Couture since she'd dressed for the red carpet—and the big stations had sent their celebs to cover the story. After all, sex and death were two of the four media food groups, and the broadcast journalists were there to put together an all-you-can-eat smorgasboard for the six-and-ten newscasts.

Judge Pittman swooped in, cut his eyes to Rackley, and did a double take. "Door getcha again?"

Cowed, Rackley nodded.

The judge signaled ready.

Camera lights brightened the room. With hostility crackling all around her, Cézanne's stomach gave a nasty flip.

When the old judge announced his ruling, it was as if the air pressure had changed.

A collective gasp filled the room.

Cézanne blinked, slow on the uptake. It wasn't until Rackley grabbed an arm and shook her like a ragdoll that realization dawned: She'd won him a new trial.

Her eyes bounced around like pinballs. Every camera shifted in her direction as the inmate planted an enthusiastic kiss on her cheek. She recoiled as if scalded.

Helena Lindner looked around as if scoping out the room for a place to hang herself. She noticed a camera trained on her and gave a brittle smile. With a determined expression on her pale, alabaster face, she suddenly remembered she had calls to return. She was out of her chair, dragging the hand truck behind her like a dog with its tail tucked, when the judge gaveled down the noise.

"If there's no other business on the matter, counselors," Pittman turned to his bailiff, "you may escort the defendant back to jail."

"Wait." Cézanne sprang to her feet. "Your Honor, we'd like a bond set."

Helena Lindner had paused at the bar until officially released. She unhanded the dolly, reclaimed her seat, and opposed Rackley's bail with the vengeance of a Biblical plague.

Cézanne mounted a valiant counter-argument, ticking off reasons on her fingers one, two, three. "My client's not safe in jail. He's been bloodied up twice. And a couple of thugs tried to assassinate us on the ride back from the Briscoe Unit, and a sniper tried again when we were within three blocks of the jail. We ask the court to set a reasonable bond so we can find Mr.

Rackley a safe place to stay."

Pittman granted the request—a cash bond in the amount of a hundred thousand dollars.

They were treated to a view of Helena Lexus with her eyes bungee jumping back into their sockets. Cézanne turned at the sound of shuffling feet coming from the corridor as the doors opened wide. She saw a slew of angry attorneys filing in and considered retreating to her office to dig a foxhole.

But Judge Pittman had more to say.

As a concession to the state's attorney's conniption fit about Rackley being a flight risk, the judge came up with the perfect house arrest solution.

If Rackley made bail, he'd have to wear an active monitoring GPS ankle bracelet. His movements would be tracked, in real time, by global positioning satellites, and the information would be submitted every few minutes by cell phone to a tracking center. And if he wanted access to an automobile while he was out on bond, he'd be required to have an AVLN installed. That way, the automatic vehicle location navigation system would function as a backup to track Rackley's whereabouts if he left the house.

A peal of laughter came from the prosecutor's table. It had a jarring effect, like an alligator coming up from the sewer. Helena Lindner was yukking it up, secure in the knowledge that nobody in their right mind would post Rackley's bail and reveling in the notion that the defendant had no money to bond himself out.

Then Judge Pittman set a trial date that extinguished everyone's grin.

Rackley's re-trial would start in two weeks.

Chapter Thirty-Three

If anyone had predicted Erick Rackley would be sitting on the Biedermeier two weeks after the prison interview, Cézanne wouldn't have believed it. But there he was, dressed in Slash's "free world clothes," taking in the sights and smells of a grand old home. Upon leaving the jail, he'd been fitted with a three-ounce, top-of-the-line, tamper-proof GPS ankle monitor that also established baseline levels for alcohol consumption. The state-of-the-art monitor submitted information every few minutes by cell phone to a tracking center so Rackley couldn't make a move without the authorities knowing about it.

In the corner near the front door, Enigma slept on his side. He was chasing rabbits in his sleep and making whimpering sounds. He must've caught a jackrabbit because he let out a yip that startled him awake. With paws outstretched and his brown eyes alert, he did a full body stretch and looked around with his pointy ears functioning like independent satellites.

Cézanne set a tray of Duty's chocolate chip cookies on the coffee table and offered Rackley a cup of Jamaican fine grind.

"I'd rather have a Coors."

She scowled. "Isn't that how you got into this mess in the first place?"

"You're right. Coffee's fine. Black. No, wait. Got any real cream?"

Duty, who'd been watching from the kitchen, gave him the thumbs-up and disappeared from view.

Rackley took a cookie and held it up to the light. "If I owned a house like this, I'd never leave."

"I don't intend to."

From the vicinity of the back porch, Velda yelled, "We'll see about that."

By way of explanation, Cézanne said, "Long story. Hatfield-McCoy. We're all staying here until it crumbles down around us or the probate judge awards it to me, whichever comes first."

Rackley bit into the cookie. Intense brown eyes pierced her. He lowered his voice to a whisper. "That day in the attorney room . . . I shouldn't have . . . but I never thought I'd see daylight again."

"I'd feel more comfortable if we could forget it." She averted her eyes. "Who posted your bond?"

"Who cares?"

"Not that many people have a hundred thousand dollars in cash to throw around and even fewer want to throw it at you. Aren't you just a little bit curious? I am."

"The smell of a jail and the smell of freedom is very distinct. I'm free. That's what counts."

"I'll look into it," she said uneasily. Honestly, grilling Rackley on a topic he didn't want to talk about was like shouting into a box canyon.

"I want to explain about the kiss." Rackley polished off the cookie, wiping remnants of chocolate off his fingers with a napkin. "I didn't think I'd ever be able to touch a woman again. That hellhole eats away at you. You're convinced you'll die there. Horrible stuff goes on behind bars, and the guards don't do anything to stop it." Flashes of anger meshed with true fear. "That day I knew if you'd let me—"

Duty came in balancing the silver coffee service and good china. "Are you a friend of Miz Zan's?"

"I hope so."

"I'm Deuteronomy Devilrow. Of the Shreveport Devereaus. I work for Miz Zan, but I'm her ward, too. I like bein' her ward better 'cause Miz Zan can be stingy sometimes. Like when I want chocolate milk at the store, she says we don't have enough money and put that back, it'll make you fat. Okay, if you're gonna get it anyhow, get an extra half-gallon 'cause me and Velda don't wanna eat after you. That's Miz Zan talkin'." She turned. "Oh, by the way, my word for the day is duplicitous."

Cézanne dismissed her with a glare. She spoke to Rackley in cryptic sentences. "I understand. Let's forget it." In a dismissive move, she headed for the sunroom and located her briefcase.

She was pulling out copies of Chet Willoughby's journal and the expert witness's textbook when she realized Rackley had joined her. The weight of his hand fell heavy on her shoulder.

"Thanks for everything."

He positioned himself behind her. She sensed him sniffing her hair and stepped beyond his reach.

She pointed to the newly discovered evidence. "This is what's getting you a new trial, not me. I think we should go over these so you'll know what happened."

She led him back to the Biedermeier. When they sat, he sandwiched her hand between his.

"Nobody knows how much I loved my wife." Wulfenite eyes, impassioned and unyielding, captured her attention. "I didn't deserve to be convicted of murder. I would never hurt her. Ever."

Listening to smooth talk numbed her senses. He was handsome in a rugged sort of way, and she found herself wondering how he got that scar and where he acquired a tan that made him look as if he'd spent a week in Acapulco on a party boat.

"It's important you believe me."

"I believe you," she said without enthusiasm.

"You don't. You're doing my case because Slash asked you.

But to me it's imperative that you accept this as the God's-honest truth."

"I can defend you whether I believe you or not." With a pointed look, she slipped from his grasp. "My job is to protect your rights, not to create facts."

"After you left the prison, you're all I could think about. I hardly slept that night. The next day, I was working in the carpentry shop and almost cut my finger off remembering the way your hair smelled. I thought about the strange color of your eyes. The way you looked into my soul when you spoke. I did the right thing kissing you. But I did it for the wrong reason."

Her heart raced. If Erick Rackley was telling the truth, what happened to him was a consequence of human tragedy. But if he'd murdered his wife, then she was sitting on the sofa letting herself be seduced by a killer.

She creased open the textbook to the section on expirated blood. "This speaks for itself. Notice anything weird?"

"That's my shirt." Confused, he traced a finger over the photograph.

"Here's our ace in the hole." Leafing through Willoughby's journal, she found her place mark. She kept her tone business-like as she summed up the first few pages of documentation.

"Mr. Willoughby began this entry on the day he was called for jury duty. He didn't expect to be picked, and it says so right here." She fingerpointed. "But he did get on the panel, and when he learned he was sitting in judgment of an accused murderer, he stopped off on his way home and bought this book. He kept a running account of the day's events each night. His wife Irene said he'd lock himself in the bathroom and write. He was a good man. A decent man."

Rackley's unblinking stare unnerved her.

"Remember, the judge instructed them not to talk about the case to anyone. Every night, Chester Willoughby wrote for hours using the back of the commode as a desktop. That way, he'd have privacy and not break the rules."

Rackley barely breathed. She sensed he'd become spellbound by the tenuous hope that hung on the diary of a wheelchair-bound black man with a closed head injury and shoestring drool draining out of the side of his mouth.

She flipped to an excerpt earmarked with a Post-It note and showed him the childlike scrawl. He frowned; she knew without asking that he was straining to decipher Willoughby's ragged script, the same way she'd done the first time through. To make things easier she paraphrased the entry.

Gary Oakes, the jury foreman, took the women aside individually and woodshedded them. When it came to Willoughby, Oakes told him they were all in agreement to find Rackley guilty and wanted to know if they were going to have any trouble with Willoughby's vote.

"That was one week into a ten-day trial. According to this journal, they'd already found you guilty. What we need to know is why Gary Oakes would lobby for a guilty verdict for a man he didn't even know before all the evidence was in?"

Rackley shrugged. "You're talking conspiracy? I was railroaded."

"It's almost like somebody on the outside got to him. Or he was a plant."

Rackley sat lost in thought with his head bowed and his fingers meshed.

"Who had the most to lose if you went free?"

"Hollis Rushmore. He was screwing my wife."

There was no delicate way to ask the next question. "Did you ever catch them in bed together?"

"When we were first married, Yvonne would come home and make lunch. Our house was on my patrol beat. I'd take a Ten-seven at the house, we'd get frisky, and I'd go back on duty thinking I was the luckiest man on Earth to have a wife with such a healthy sexual appetite. Those were the early years. Things soured. She said I drank too much, and I suppose I did. She stopped coming home, took lunches with her partners, and I ate at fast-food joints with guys on my shift."

"Just guys?"

"There was a female . . ."

"You had an affair?"

"Didn't mean anything. And I didn't stray until I knew for sure Yvonne was fooling around."

"You had the most to gain from her death." She watched Rackley through insightful eyes. "There was an insurance policy. One hundred-fifty thousand dollars. You were the beneficiary."

"Believe me, if you're going for the money angle, she was worth more to me alive than dead. To be crude, Yvonne was my cash cow. Why would I kill her for a lousy hundred-and-fifty-K when she could make that in a year?"

"Let's talk about why she'd fool around with Hollis Rushmore."

"What's the point? It's over. Neither of us has her."

Was he kidding?

Somebody went out of the way to ensure he got convicted of a horrible crime he claimed he didn't commit. If everything had been on the up-and-up, twelve unbiased people would've listened to the evidence and returned an untainted verdict. But according to Chester Willoughby they were twelve blind mice.

So who was the rat behind the conspiracy to swing a guilty verdict?

"If she didn't commit suicide, and you didn't do it, then who did?"

Before Rackley could answer, the crack of a high-powered weapon exploded the front window into a million shards of glass.

Chapter Thirty-Four

At first, Cézanne thought she'd been shot. The impact of Erick Rackley nailing her to the floor in a flying tackle forced the air from her lungs. When he didn't move until tires squealed against the asphalt, she thought he'd taken a bullet. With her chest burning from oxygen deprivation, she pushed against his shoulders and rolled him off.

Rackley shouted, "Stay down," at the top of his lungs.

Duty.

Velda dashed into the dining room with mime-loud face cream that made her head look like a moonscape. She had hair bleach smeared across her upper lip and the baseball bat balanced on one shoulder. She stood in the bullet's trajectory camouflaged in a chartreuse muumuu with red birds of paradise that practically dared the shooter to scream *Bonsai!* and crank off more rounds.

Cézanne yelled, "Hit the lights." Velda flicked off the nearest switch.

Duty scrambled downstairs hunkering close to the wall. She grabbed the phone from the hall nook, stabbed the keypad three times and shouted, "Miz Zan's been fired on. Come quick," before slamming down the receiver.

A moment later the telephone rang.

Duty affected a dignified tone. "Law office, may we help you? Why, yes. Somebody shot out our front window. Miz Zan's on the floor. Mista Erick's next to her. No, there ain't nobody else here."

Velda shouted, "What about me?"

Duty covered the mouthpiece. "What about you?"

"You didn't tell them I was here."

"Are you still here?" she said with a touch of sarcasm. "I'm sorry to say Aunt Velda's still here. Although we wish she wasn't. But you might check her birth date against yo' computer, maybe see if she don't have warrants. By the way, is Roland workin'? 'Cause I forgot to tell him what a nize time I had on account of 'Nigma got found and we had to take him to the animal hospital. You heard me, I said 'Nigma. I did not call you a bad name. What's the matter with you?" She pulled the phone away from her ear and banged it against the wall a couple of times before yelling into the mouthpiece. "Is you or is you not gonna send a squad car? What's my name?"

Cézanne did a combat belly-crawl to the hallway. She jerked the phone out of Duty's hand. "I'm Cézanne Martin. We had a drive-by at my law office on South University." She gave the physical address, asked for crime scene, hung up the phone, and flipped off the last of the light switches.

With the rest of the bulbs extinguished, she directed Duty and Velda to pack an overnight bag. No way were they spending another night here.

No damned way.

"You're coming to my house," Slash said after the crime scene investigator packed up his gear and left. He set his drill bit gaze on Cézanne. "No arguing. A witness sighted Darlene Driskoll about an hour ago at a gas station in Burleson. It only takes twenty minutes to get to Fort Worth, so she would've had plenty of time to make it over here."

Rackley said, "You didn't tell me you had enemies."

She appealed to the detective. "Take Erick and the women. I'll stay here."

Velda said, "You ask me, you people are in cahoots. You orchestrated this sideshow in order to scare me outta my inheritance."

Duty whined, "I don't wanna go unless Miz Zan goes."

Slash said, "Everybody's going. Now pile into the car." To Cézanne, he said, "Give me a key. I'll stick around until I can get the window boarded up. Shouldn't take long."

Velda balked at leaving. "Nobody's driving me out of my home."

"Fine." Cézanne headed for the stairs. "Feel free to stay. I'd planned to hire the Limón brothers to bump you off, but this'll make it easier."

In a velvet voice, Slash appealed to Velda. "You really should come. At least for the time being. You can stay the night, and if you still feel like returning tomorrow, it's up to you."

"Since you put it that way . . ."

A half hour later, they arrived at Slash's. The ranch house was situated on a one-acre tract surrounded by a split rail fence made of rough-hewn posts. Five miles outside the Fort Worth city limits, the stars shined brighter without the glow of streetlights and the air smelled fresher with the absence of traffic.

Velda scratched the peach-fuzz cropping up on her scalp. "You have a pool?"

"Hot tub."

Duty said, "I read in a magazine that old people shouldn't get in hot tubs. They can have a heart attack. It would be bad if you had a heart attack, Velda, out here in the boondocks and no hospital for miles. You axe me, you should take a nize, hot shower and call it a night."

Velda mocked her. "Nobody axed you." She took her bat and a change of clothes to the first bathroom off the hallway and twisted the lock shut.

"I guess that just leaves Mista Erick and Miz Zan and me." She clapped her hands together. "Who wants to go hot-tubbin'?"

"It's past your bedtime."

"Miz Zan, I'm practically a grownup."

"Don't argue. Tomorrow's a big day."

Duty snorted in disgust. Velda must've had her ear to the wall because she let out one of her irritating cackles.

At the front door, Slash dug in his pocket and pulled out his keys. He turned to Erick. "Look after her, will you?"

"I'd feel better if you left me a gun."

"No gun. She can have one, but you're a convicted felon. No point making it worse."

Erick took the bad news in stride. He picked up the television remote control, studied it a few seconds, and powered on the television.

Duty glided over and gingerly slipped the remote from his grasp. She channel-surfed until the forensics network popped up. "Whatchoo want to look at, Mista Erick? This okay with you?"

"I'd watch the TV test pattern if it meant I didn't have to sit in jail."

Cézanne followed Slash out the door. "Thanks for letting us take over your house."

"You'd have done it for me."

"That's just it . . . I wouldn't have. Why're you being so nice?"

He winked. "I already told you."

She touched his sleeve. "Wish you didn't have to report in to work."

"Me, too." He snaked an arm around her waist and drew her close. "Take my bedroom. There's a nine-millimeter sandwiched between the mattress and box springs. Lock yourself in and sleep with it under your pillow."

"What about the others?" She meant Deuteronomy. For all she cared, Velda could get caught in the crossfire.

"Nobody's trying to kill the others." He cradled her head and pressed a kiss into her hair. Then he kissed her for real.

In a few seconds it was over. But the magic of Slash's lips lingered long after he backed his truck out of the driveway and his taillights receded into the gauzy night air.

When she went back inside the living room lights were out and the TV, off. From the strip of light under the bathroom off the hallway, she suspected Velda was still using up all the hot water and that Erick and Duty had found their respective bedrooms. In Slash's room, she found a chest of drawers filled with T-shirts, underwear, and socks organized by colors. She selected a black "T" and disrobed. Clad in Slash's shirt and bikini panties, she checked to make sure the hallway was clear before tiptoeing into the kitchen to nose around in the refrigerator.

She found an open bottle of Italian rosé, a wine stem, and a half moon of Colby-Jack cheese. With a box of crackers and cheese tucked under one arm and the wine and goblet in hand, she made her way outside to the hot tub.

Soaking in the whirlpool with the jets dialed low, she poured a glass of truth serum. She settled into one of the molded seats where she could keep an eye on the fence and rested her head against a vinyl bolster. Chilled rosé slid down her throat like icy fire. For a long time, she stared at the velvety sky in search of the North Star. She drained the stem and poured another. By the third empty glass, she forgot about the cheese and crackers and savored the idea of a decent night's sleep—even alcohol-induced slumber. With her back to the French doors and the soothing hum of water jets pulsing near her ears, she closed her eyes and let the white noise wash over her.

"Nice, isn't it?"

Cézanne's heart jumped. Her eyes fluttered open. She sat erect, splashing water over the sides. In a moment of disorientation, she thought she was seeing twin Ericks. She scrunched her eyes. When she opened them again, her double vision pulled her client into a single shape.

"You scared me."

"Wouldn't want to do that. You and Slash are the only people who've been civil to me in the last five years."

Wearing only boxers, he carried four Coors Lights threaded through his fingers. One was half full. He took a long pull from the bottle before setting the empty on the patio floor.

Cézanne glanced around. "Where's my wine glass?"

"It was about to slip out of your hand. I set it on the picnic table."

"Wait." She realized he was about to join her in the spa and gestured to the ankle monitor.

He said, "Waterproof," as he lowered himself into the swirling cauldron and seated himself directly across from her where he could keep an eye on the door.

They surveilled the perimeter in the way of veteran cops, with each looking past the other's shoulder, bird-dogging their self-assigned turf to make sure nobody got the jump on them.

He came up out of the churning froth enough to reach his arm over the redwood frame. He corralled another beer from his stash, tossed the twist-off cap over the side and took a sip. The hardest part of having Erick Rackley out of prison, she decided, might boil down to keeping him off the sauce.

They made idle chat with the inmate discussing the pros and cons of swimming pools and hot tubs while reminiscing about material possessions he no longer had.

He cut his eyes in her direction. "You look beautiful tonight."

A wet T-shirt, no makeup, and waterlogged, chicory-colored

hair wasn't exactly seductive. She sent him a wobbly smile across the water and looked back up at the sky. A water jet pulsed against her lower back. She savored the lightheaded tingle as the last of the wine worked its magic. Foam bubbled near her ears. She relaxed against the padded edge and allowed her weightless feet to float up from the molded fiberglass bottom.

Rackley touched her foot. Her instinct to pull away, to mumble "Sorry," and draw back, ended when he cradled her heel with both hands and began kneading her instep with his thumbs. The sensation went beyond good. It bordered on heaven.

He lifted her other foot and balanced it on his knee. The force field of his touch sucked her in. She wondered if this was how astronauts felt in the absence of gravitational pull and realized she'd placed herself within her client's.

She knew she should put an end to it, and she would—as soon as he finished massaging both feet.

In the moonlight, he bore a striking resemblance to Doug Driskoll. And he smooth-talked her the way Doug used to before gunshots rang out and Darlene's killer instinct took over. By the time she realized the philandering cop wasn't divorced and had never filed the paperwork to get one, he'd already selected a new victim from the latest cadet class.

Rackley worked his way up her ankles. She made a mental note to thank him for making her feel like a pampered diva. To grab her empty wine glass and head inside. When he reached the backs of her knees, she became aware he had eased himself between her thighs and knew she should stop him. Her heart did a little tap dance.

She didn't think he would go farther.

She didn't think, period.

In an unguarded moment, he slid his hands up under the tee

and gently cupped her breasts. The rush of his touch electrified her body. Too much wine dulled her sense of shame. Her eyelids popped open. In stunned silence, she watched his strong muscles tense. Her shirt bloused out. He pushed it up and exposed her nipples to the night air. When he took his mouth to her, his skilled tongue almost made her forget . . .

. . . he'd been convicted of murdering his wife.

She fisted his hair and pulled savagely.

"Erick, don't."

His mouth came off her breast and attached itself to her neck. Her heart bounced wildly from the raw, animal pleasure of his bite. His hands slid down to her waist to her buttocks and crushed her against his erection.

"Stop it. This is wrong. I'm your lawyer."

He covered her lips with his, hungry and desperate and tasting of beer. For one delirious, out-of-focus moment, her eyes flickered to the spotlight of a full moon. Unbelievably, she caught herself responding, powerless to stop.

A few seconds more and I'll quit.

"Yvonne, don't leave me. I'll make it up to you."

What?

"He doesn't love you like I do."

Holy cow. Guy's off balance.

"Erick, listen to me." He was peeling off her panties. In a one-handed grab, she hiked them back up. "I'm not Yvonne. I'm not her."

He pressed his nose into her hair. During the insanity of it all, she remembered she'd spritzed herself with Victoria's Secret. Hot breath and a wet tongue acted as a narcotic against her ear. Chill bumps danced across her neck, up her head, down her body.

The moment had gotten out of hand.

She tried to push him away, but her fingers glanced off the

hard curve of his shoulder. With her upper body strength compromised, a wet hand against his skin was as slick as a marble on glass.

He devoured her neck. Whispered words too soft for her to hear. Licked her chin. Sucked her lips into his mouth. Caressed her nipples. When his hand slid between her legs and he found her secret place, she responded with the enthusiasm of a junkie.

She wrapped her legs around his waist, inwardly convinced that by doing so he couldn't complete the act.

"Make love to me."

In her head, she heard the lean, hungry demand of Doug Driskoll and knew she had to make it stop.

"I'm not Yvonne."

"You could be for right now." Eyes closed, he kissed her face. His tongue slithered over her mouth and snaked between parted lips. "You smell like her. You feel the way I remember her. Please just be her. Just for tonight. Just for the next ten minutes. Tell me you love me. That you want me more than him. That he could never do for you what I do. Tell me how each time you made love to him you were thinking of me. Wishing it was me inside you. Say it, Yvonne."

The words sent a chill through her heart. The thought occurred to her—if he murdered his wife he might try to kill her all over again. Could drown her right here, replace the spa cover, and take off.

He'd managed to slide out of his shorts. His penis stirred beneath her buttocks. He was staring, glassy-eyed, at the sky. She sensed his desperation as he massaged one breast and drew in great intakes of air.

Carnal panic set in.

"Tell me you love me."

Breathless and suddenly sober, she waited for an opportunity to flee. To dive over the side like a slick, flopping fish.

Considered her chances of success. Inwardly muttered curses for being so caught up in the moment she didn't realize Erick Rackley had lost touch with reality.

"Say it, Yvonne." He caressed her face. "Say you love me, too." His hand slid to her throat.

She gambled on what to do and chose to play the role of Yvonne.

Her voice cracked with the effort of speech. "I love you."

It was a concession to desperation, and it worked like an antibody.

He closed his eyes and heaved a sigh. The anger he displayed seemed to follow it out. Tension dissolved in his body. As he took in air by way of slow, deliberate breaths, he relaxed his hold on her. Unexpectedly, his eyes scrunched in a tight seal.

"I'm sorry," he cried. "I'm so sorry. So God-awful sorry. Can you ever forgive me?"

He buried his face in her neck and sobbed out a small child's anguish.

Instead of pushing him away, Cézanne held him tight . . .

. . . and wondered if he'd apologized to her, or to Yvonne.

Chapter Thirty-Five

Cézanne never heard Slash's locked bedroom door open; it was the uneven distribution of weight on the edge of the bed that roused her to consciousness. The sudden presence of an intruder sent her grappling for the 9mm beneath the pillow.

Hands clamped around her wrists in a vise grip and forced them against the bed.

"Zan, it's me. Stop. It it's me."

Her heart was still defibrillating when Slash unhanded her. She sank into the stash of pillows, halfway to hyperventilating, and tried to keep her insides from crawling into her throat.

"How'd you get in?"

"Loided the door." Cop slang for celluloid. He'd used a credit card. "I finished my reports and told the sarge I was calling it a night."

"You scared the hell outta me. Do you realize I could've killed you?"

He leaned across and kissed her on the forehead. "Got room for me in there?"

"I suppose you intend to exercise your proprietary rights as the homeowner?"

"Is that a problem?"

"Not as long as your rights only extend to the bed. Nothing else. Raven's my best friend, and I don't want to hurt her."

She listened to the rustle of clothes in the dark. In the faint green glow of the clock's digital readout, she watched him move toward the bathroom. She'd almost drifted back to sleep when he slipped between the covers.

"You're making too much of this Raven thing, by the way." He lopped an arm over her side and nuzzled her hair. "It's not like I'm pussy marked because I slept with her. We had four dates. I only took her out in the first place because you asked me to after the spook dumped her at the altar."

He was talking about the CIA agent Raven almost married. She felt the sudden need to defend her friend. "Raven didn't get dumped. She dumped him. I had a front row seat, remember? It was so horrible it's probably on YouTube by now."

Slash chuckled. "Raven's still hot for Jinx Porter no matter what she says. The spook was just the rebound guy when she and the constable broke up. Then I became the rebound guy after the wedding to the spook cratered. Believe me, it's a go-nowhere relationship." His voice trailed.

He made it sound so reasonable. Deep down, though, she knew Raven wanted more.

Maybe she should call her and flat-out ask. Sit up and speed-dial the number. Make sure she didn't end up with two crazy women hunting her down like a dirty dog.

Something like: *"Hiya. I'm in bed with Slash. That's not a problem, is it?"*

Strong arms and warm skin felt good to the touch. His presence left her with the secure feeling that whoever had tried to kill them would never find them here. She listened to Slash's breathing, rapid at first, then longer breaths and finally the remnants of a thin snore.

She rolled over to face him. Placed a soft kiss on his cheek. Such a brave man.

He pulled her close, cradled her in the nook of his arm and tucked his chin against the top of her head. For a few moments she lay pressed against his chest, lazily caressing the curve of his shoulder before realizing he'd come to bed naked.

She closed her eyes. Took in the scent of his aftershave.

He stirred beneath the covers.

She placed a hand on his cheek and gave him another kiss. Slash's mouth twitched.

Thoughts of Erick Rackley careened back, along with the electric jolt of his touch.

Slash was probably right—Raven was still in love with Jinx. And it wasn't as if Yours Truly was still in a relationship. Talk about getting ditched—how many women got an engagement ring for Christmas and found out later that their fiancé had eloped with another woman? If she didn't move on she'd end up just like Raven—chasing an illusion.

He pressed his lips against hers, and she responded.

He pulled at the T-shirt. She maneuvered out of it, and he discarded it over the edge of the bed. As he grazed a hand across her breasts, she felt the tickle of a thousand grains of sand spill over her. Eyes closed, he rolled onto his back and pulled her upright.

She sat astraddle, staring at the shape of Slash's face backlit by the glow of the alarm clock. His hands rode up her hips to her breasts; she savored the caress of work-roughened hands against the smoothness of her skin.

Bobby Noah's disapproving face flashed into mind. The unexpected image almost shocked her into retreating.

What if it wasn't true? The Bobby she knew was a man of great character. Would he really take off with someone else without releasing his hold on her?

Her nipples hardened beneath Slash's fingers.

She should stop. She hadn't heard the news firsthand from Bobby. Only the disembodied voice of a sultry-sounding female purring through the line. What if it had all been a bad joke?

But the mental picture of Bobby's face was no match for

Slash's hands exploring her ears, neck, breasts, and navel. Before she could act on the impulse to undo what she'd started, he raised her hips enough to guide himself inside her.

Chills fluttered over her body like a thousand butterfly wings. At first, he rocked her gently, then with more force. With every inch of friction, her body cried out for more.

"Tell me you love me.

"That you want me more than him.

"That he could never do for you what I do."

Her body responded like a flash fire. Slash tensed beneath her weight.

"Tell me you were thinking of me when you made love to him.

"Say it, Yvonne."

He gripped her buttocks, dug in his fingertips and forced himself deeper. The sting of his nails made her want more.

"Say it, Yvonne. SayitYvonnesayitYvonne."

Slash groaned. His body went rigid.

"SayitYvonnesayitYvonnesayitYvonne."

For what seemed a glorious eternity, he squeezed her breasts while her body bucked above his perfect frame. She neared her crescendo hearing the echo of Rackley's words.

"Sayitsayitsayitsayit."

Felt his fiery release, slick between her legs.

Comets streaked across her field of vision.

"Sayitsayitsayit."

Her body exploded in chills.

"Say it."

"I love you." She collapsed forward. Wrapped her arms around him. Melted into his embrace.

And as she rolled off and watched him panting, drifting into dreamless slumber, she wondered which of four men she'd just made love to.

Chapter Thirty-Six

Cézanne didn't know exactly what time Slash took a blanket and pillow and moved to the sofa in the den. She only knew he'd done so before the others awakened. She sat up and threw back the covers, dressed quickly, and found him in the dimly lit room talking in hushed tones to Erick Rackley.

"Don't let me interrupt." She walked in brimming with a curious mixture of playfulness and guilt and slid onto the couch next to him. He'd creased open the copy of Chester Willoughby's journal to the entry regarding the verdict.

"Just buffing up on the hearing next Friday," he said.

Rackley sat across from them in utter bewilderment. "Didn't any of these people go to the judge after it was all over and tell him what happened?"

"Some thought they'd done the right thing for the wrong reason," she said pointedly. "Others thought they'd get in trouble for being sheep."

"What're my chances?"

"It's obviously a compelling case, otherwise you wouldn't be getting a new trial. But Chester Willoughby's close to a vegetative state. We'll need his wife to sponsor the journal. Pearlie Gray won't be much help in that she's dead, unless the M.E. ties her poisoning to someone affiliated with this case. I don't expect the other jurors to talk, but you never know. I subpoenaed every last one of them, including the state's so-called expert. I'll bet there are thirty thousand copies of that textbook in the publisher's warehouse waiting to ship to the distributor. He can either tell the truth about the expirated blood spatter patterns—that they mimic high velocity blood spatter—or he can perjure himself and scuttle that book deal. I'm betting he'd rather autograph books."

Slash got up, folded his blanket, and gave her a sly wink. He was wearing his work clothes from the night before, and it warmed her knowing he'd moved into the den to protect her reputation.

"Y'all want breakfast?" he asked. "We have bacon, eggs, sausage . . . there's a can of refried beans and a jar of chiles if you want a Mexican omelet."

Rackley looked dreamy-eyed. "The last time I saw a real egg was five years ago."

"I'll be in the kitchen." Slash turned to Cézanne. "Care to pitch in?"

Away from her client, they plotted strategies. They'd have to keep him off booze. He'd need a proper suit for court. And they'd have to keep him out of sight until the hearing.

He confided another detail. "I had AVLNs installed on the Audi and my truck."

The impact of his words soaked in. "You don't trust him."

"Judge Pittman thought it'd be a good idea. Don't mention it to Erick. Look, he says he wants to be exonerated, but let's face it . . . just because he gets a new trial doesn't mean he'll be acquitted. He may get to thinking about that and rabbit on us. I would if I was him. The outcome of this case is too close to call." Slash cracked six eggs against the edge of a cast iron skillet and watched them spread across sizzling butter. In a whiskey voice he asked the million-dollar question. "Who put up his bond?"

"I already asked. He acted pretty cavalier about it. I intended to look into it when the drive-by occurred."

"He has a sister."

"If she had that kind of money she'd have hired him a good lawyer."

For no good reason Slash called over his shoulder. "Who posted your bond?"

"A frog."

They exchanged awkward looks. For several seconds, they stared at each other in quiet assessment. Butter bubbled, turning the edges of the eggs brown. Slash dashed a teaspoon of water into the skillet and slapped a lid on tight.

Cézanne poked her head around the corner. Rackley was thumbing through the TV guide.

"Did you say frog?"

"Frog. Frenchman. Foreigner. Fag with a foreign-sounding name." Rackley shrugged. "Maybe he's one of those do-gooders who thinks I'm innocent. Or a rich guy with nothing better to do."

Or a killer trying to bump you off before the hearing.

She took a slow, deliberate breath. "Tell me his name."

"Some dude named Henri Matisse."

Why would Henri post Rackley's bond?

Lost in thought, Cézanne drove Slash's pickup along Airport Freeway with the window rolled down and the air streaming through her hair.

Deuteronomy, riding shotgun, piped up. "Whatchoo gonna do at Mista Rushmore's? Did you bring a gun? I should be there in case you need an alibi. I'll say I saw the whole thing."

"Stop chattering. I'm trying to think." Cézanne twisted the knob on the radio. A Michelle Branch tune wound down, followed by Dido. The back-to-back hits were enough to inspire fearlessness. "Listen to the music and don't interrupt."

"I know just whatchoo mean, Miz Zan. I can see yo' mind

turnin' like a whirligig. Same as when I'm channeling spirits, I need to be able to concentrate. Like right now, I can hear the voice of yo' dead daddy sayin' you made a big mistake not bringin' Mista Slash with you."

"Slash has to find another place for Mr. Rackley to stay until we figure out why Henri would post bail. Hollis Rushmore's the only connection to Rackley. I'm the only connection to Henri. But I'm connected to Hollis Rushmore, too. And leave my dead father out of this."

"I only repeat what he says."

"Yeah? Well give him a message. Tell the son-of-a-bitch if he'd really wanted to help, he would've left a will."

Duty got real quiet. "Did."

Cézanne snorted in contempt. "Then ask him where he hid the damned thing."

"Says it's all part of yo' growth process. To make you stronger. Says it'll make you more compassionate—he's right, Miz Zan, 'cause you so irritable most of the time nobody but me and 'Nigma can stand to be around you. Right now, I'm preferrin' Mista Erick's company to yours."

Twenty years of pent-up rage hardened her lips. "Tell him I said to go fuck himself."

"He heard you." Duty's eyes thinned into slits. "Now don't kill the messenger, Miz Zan, but he says he's fucked, all right. On account of he's dead."

She started to protest. To make another smartass comment but the distant sight of Henri's MGB in Hollis Rushmore's parking lot whipped the air right out of her.

"Look yonder, Miz Zan. It's Mista Henri's car. I'm goin' with you. Maybe you should let me carry the gun. I like guns. I know all about 'em on account of Roland let me touch his. Well, not right away. I had to convince him on account of he said you'd skin his dick if he showed me. His gun. Not what else yo' thinkin'. I didn't see that. I'm a nize girl like you, Miz Zan."

She stopped the truck and yanked up the emergency brake. "Sit tight."

"Lemme come. I'd be real quiet. I'll play *The Quiet Game.*"

Cézanne twisted in her seat. Looked Duty square in the eye. "If I don't come back in fifteen minutes—" she handed over Slash's cell phone and jotted his pager number on a scrap of paper "—call Slash and tell him Henri's at Rushmore's."

Chapter Thirty-Seven

The chime to Rushmore's office signaled Cézanne's entrance. Betty wasn't behind the counter, so Cézanne slipped into the bathroom off the hall and waited. As she carefully closed the door, Betty emerged from the copy room and glanced around.

"Anybody here?"

Cézanne played mute. She checked her watch and noted the time. Thirteen minutes left before Duty called for help. She pulled the door open a sliver, heard the mechanical thump of the copier collating pages, and looked the length of the hallway.

No Betty.

Next-door, in Rushmore's office, a heated argument took place. Angry voices traveled through the vent. She couldn't identify the woman but Henri was there.

"I'm telling you I've seen that old hag before," Henri said. "It'll come to me."

"That's highly unlikely, Jake. She probably resembles a familiar face." The woman again.

Jake? Who the hell was Jake?

"I'm positive about this. It's bugging the hell out of me." Frustration mounted in Henri's voice.

"Then take care of it." The lethal quality in her command prickled the hair on Cézanne's neck.

"Want me to kill her, too?"

Rushmore came alive. "Stop saying shit like that. You can think it, but don't speak it."

"What if they throw in together?" The female's deadly soprano shot up in the annoying whine of a spoiled brat.

Henri barked out a laugh. "Those two couldn't agree on how to cut up a bar of gold to share between them. If we're patient, they'll probably kill each other."

"You said it'd be over, Hollis. You said Jake would get a cut of Bob's estate and we'd be out of here in a few weeks. Now it's all buggered up. We have nothing."

"Not *nothing,* Aricella." Rushmore, infuriated.

Aricella. Bob's widow.

"Pigs get fat; hogs get slaughtered. Don't get greedy, Aricella. You and Jake'll split half of the six hundred thousand and a share of the house. I can probably convince the daughter into taking less money if Jake signs the property over to her in full."

"She'll sign. She's eaten up with that goddam house. You should see the way she babies the furniture. Stares at the crown molding. Worships that bedroom. I've watched her when she thought I wasn't looking. She loves that house." Henri again, filled with contempt.

Cézanne squelched a shriek.

Henri was Jake.

She wondered how long she could eavesdrop before Betty left the copy room. Eight minutes had already passed.

Aricella spoke. "What if the real Henri shows up?"

"He won't."

"How do you know?"

"If I can't track him down, nobody can. I've got friends on the force saying Henri Martin doesn't exist. If by some strange coincidence he does show up, you'll be living it up in Rio de Janeiro or basking in a place where there's no extradition treaty Then it won't much matter, will it?" Rushmore, facetious. "Tr Genoa. My wife's from there."

"You should've killed the bitch when you had the chan

Jake." Aricella again, spewing venom. "I don't understand how you could live in the house with her for five fucking days and not have a single opportunity to get rid of her. I'll bet you were hoping to screw her, weren't you?"

"Don't yell at me. Believe me, I tried. It was that old woman and the black chick. I couldn't get her alone without one or the other of them walking in. If you want to send me back, Hollis, I'll do it."

"Your window of opportunity's closed."

"What about the old woman?" asked Aricella. "Velda."

Rushmore said, "She'll be cut out once Henri and Cézanne get their respective shares. Only way she'd inherit is if the two of you screw up and Bob's daughter falls off the planet."

"Which is what should've happened," Aricella snapped. The sound of flesh slapping flesh stung Cézanne's ears. Henri, rather, Jake, yipped in pain. "You should've drop-kicked that old lady down the stairs. Should've strangled the daughter like I told you to."

Cézanne's thoughts rushed back to the night Henri sat on her bed stretching the sash of her robe between his fists like a garrote. She felt a block of ice where her heart should've been.

The doorbell jingled. When Cézanne peeked out, she was treated to a bird's eye view of Duty stumbling into Rushmore's office. Betty came out of the copy room and walked down the hall. With the receptionist's back to her, she caught Duty's attention and executed orders with her eyes.

Go away.

"May I help you?" Betty said.

"Why, yes. I've been in a little accident and I got a bad bump on my head. The man drove off without helping—"

I'm screwed.

"—and I need to sit a spell while my headache goes away."

"You poor thing. Did you get a license plate number?"

Cézanne rolled her eyes. Flattened herself up against the wall next to Rushmore's door and tried to listen.

Duty said, "The plate fell off in the road. Can you help me find it? 'Cause then we could call the po-lice and give it to them. But my head hurts so bad I'm seein' things." She looked past Betty's shoulder and made eye contact. "I'm seein' a man's face, and he's sayin' to get outta here. He's talkin' about danger, and I'm feelin' kinda faint."

"How about a cup of water?"

Duty's words spilled out in a hyperventilating rush. "No ma'am. We need to get that license plate in a hurry. You can help me. My vision's gettin' bad. I can't see. Maybe you could walk me outside . . ."

Inside Rushmore's office, accusations flew.

"You're positively inept, Jake. You couldn't do in Bob's daughter. You couldn't do the job for Hollis . . ."

"Hey, it's not my fault the place was crawling with cops."

Rushmore banged on the desk. "Stop it, both of you. It's almost over. You'll get part of the money when Rackley's dead and the other part when the estate's settled."

Jake's voice came out melodic and taunting. "What's the matter Hollis? Things getting a little uncomfortable? How long you think it'll be before Cézanne finds out I'm the bondsman?"

She heard the sickening snap of broken bone and recognized it as the unmistakable sound of a semi-automatic being ratcheted back.

"Take this. Go back to the house on South University and wait. I'm not paying you to do the daughter. The daughter's your problem. Rackley's mine. I want him taken care of before the hearing on Friday, and I don't care how you do it."

"Oh, what a tangled web we weave."

"Shut up and don't come back—either of you—until I say. Got it?"

Cézanne peered through a horizontal window no bigger than two loaves of bread stacked end-on-end. Outside, Betty angled back across the parking lot with Duty close behind. The girl's hands fluttered faster than a chimney sweep's. From the look of desperation on her face, something had gone terribly wrong. Now would be a good time to get outta Dodge.

She made it as far as the door handle when the lock on Rushmore's office clicked open. Her heart thudded. She ducked into an empty stall and waited. Duty had a bladder the size of a pea, especially under stress. She'd likely head this way. If the girl created a distraction . . .

The attorney paused in the hallway and directed his guests out a back exit.

Bob's widow excused herself. "I'll just be a moment."

Without warning, the bathroom door flew open. The metal door on the stall next to hers banged against its partition and a pair of small, expensive shoes came into view. Jimmy Chius by the looks of them.

Aricella.

She wanted to charge in and fit her hands around the widow's scrawny neck. Wanted to squeeze until the gold digger's eyes popped and then shake her back into consciousness. Make her say what happened to Bob Martin. Make her tell how she got Rushmore to cooperate with their plan and then choke her again.

"Betty? Is that you?" Aricella called out through the splash of a telltale trickle.

"Sorry, wrong person."

"Could you pass me some tissue?"

"Sure." Cézanne thrust the roll under the partition.

The fingers of a small hand with a French manicure and a big-ass diamond wiggled. The paper disappeared beneath the shared metal wall. "Thanks."

"No problem." Her heart beat so loud she was sure Aricella could hear it.

Water flushed. The door banged open and the Chius took off. For the longest time, Aricella ran the faucet. She hummed in a seductive soprano. Cézanne recognized the tune: *How Lucky Can You Get?*

She stepped out of the stall. Stood several feet behind the petite lady and watched her apply fresh lipstick in front of the mirror.

Dark, billowy curls cascaded down Aricella's back. Her olive complexion and chiseled face gave her an exotic look, while huge onyx eyes with spidery lashes hinted at mystery. Her breasts seemed almost grotesque in proportion to her tiny frame, making Cézanne wonder if Aricella moonlighted as a topless dancer when she wasn't scamming old men out of their hard-earned fortunes.

"Thanks for the tissue."

"You're welcome," Cézanne said in a zombie voice. "You're chipper. Good news?"

"The best. I'm inheriting from my dead husband's estate. Big mess, you know. Greedy little bitch, that daughter of his."

"Sorry to hear about your husband," she lied, feeling suddenly colder. "You must be devastated."

"*Ha.* If things got any better, I'd have to hire someone to help me enjoy my good fortune." Aricella took a deep breath. Her chest swelled to capacity, and she heaved a sigh. "It was a blessing. I knew when we married he didn't have long."

"Children?"

"You'd have to have sex for that to happen. Besides, I'm not the mothering kind." She scrutinized her reflection, then pulled out a comb and feathered her hair until it stood out from her head like a tumbleweed. "What is it with you Texas ladies," she asked, "always teasing your hair until it's as tall as a skyscraper?"

"Blame it on the oppressive humidity. If we didn't rat it to a fare-thee-well and spray the tar out of it, it'd hang limper than noodles."

Aricella did a slow head turn. Slanted eyes studied her. She gave Cézanne a brittle smile. "That's funny," she said uncomfortably, as if an internal warning system had activated inside her head, "you talk like my dead husband. He used to say his first wife sprayed the tar out of her hair."

"Well bless your heart," Cézanne said, all molasses and Southern and quick on the drawl. "Aren't you just the cutest thing now with your big hair? If it weren't for that hair, why, you'd have to stand up twice just to cast a shadow. Bless your heart."

"I don't get it." Aricella wore a vacuous bovine expression on her face. "You Texans sure have a strange sense of humor."

"Well don't worry if you don't understand us. We don't understand you, either." She stared into impenetrable eyes, predatory and flat. "You're not from around here, are you?"

"No, thank God." With a determined expression on her tan marble face, Aricella studied her reflection.

Cézanne forced a smile. "Where are you from?"

"Passing through on my way out of the country. By the way, what's with the Stockyards? We partied out there last night. I never saw so many drunken cowboys in my life. Please don't take this the wrong way," Aricella said in a stage whisper, all fake-chummy and with a flick of her diamond-braceleted wrist, "but I'm so sick of slow-walking, slow-talking Texans I'll be glad to leave this inferno and get back to the jetsetter lifestyle I'm accustomed to. As my dead husband used to say, 'Texas is so hot the seat belt makes a good branding iron.' "

"I hope you find someone who deserves you." Cézanne meant it.

"I already have," her stepmother sing-songed. "Jake."

"Well butter my butt and call me a biscuit." Cézanne swatted Aricella's arm, a little too hard . . . almost unfriendly. "What does Jake do for a living?"

"That's uncanny." A deep crease formed between the woman's fathomless eyes. "My dead husband used to say that, too. Used to drive me up a wall with all those witty ditties. Do they send you people to school for this kind of stuff?"

"We pick it up at home when we're little. You were talking about your new love interest . . ."

Aricella took out a goldstone compact and touched the powdered sponge to her nose. "He's independently wealthy. Or will be soon. Here, I'm through." She snapped the compact shut. "Go ahead."

Cézanne moved to the sink. For a few seconds they stood side-by-side. Aricella rummaged through her Louis Vuitton handbag and produced a gold ring.

"Want to buy it?" She held it out for closer inspection. "It belonged to my dead husband. Jake insisted I get rid of all his stuff."

"How much?"

"A hundred?"

"I think I have a ten."

"Sold." She placed it on the counter, plucked the cash and snapped her bag closed.

"Well, bless your heart. That's sweeter than a tumbler full of sweet tea on a hot summer day." Cézanne held her father's ring up to the light and studied the inscription: *'Til death do us part.* "How long were y'all married?"

"Three weeks—two weeks and six days too long if you ask me." With an exaggerated sway Aricella prissed to the door.

A raw, creepy feeling started in Cézanne's neck and worked its way across her skin. Had they killed Bob Martin? "Thanks for the ring." She wiggled her fingers, *toodledoo.* "We'll be seeing you."

"Highly unlikely. Thursday I'll be on a plane bound for Rio."

Like I said, we'll be seeing you.

Cézanne's smile went flat. "Hold up," she called out after her. "Mind if I give you a piece of friendly advice?" Aricella paused with her fingers on the handle and arched one carefully shaped brow. "You may think people talk slower here. People also walk slower here. But it can be a serious mistake to believe they think slower here and a far graver mistake to say so."

Chapter Thirty-Eight

Cézanne hooked up with Duty outside Rushmore's office, and they scrambled to the pickup. She fired up the engine, let off the emergency brake, shifted gears, and floored it.

"Give me the phone."

"It's not good to dial and drive, Miz Zan. I could operate Slash's truck while you use the phone."

"Stop talking." She tapped out Slash's home number and listened for a trill at the other end of the line. "Should've picked up by now," she mumbled.

"Maybe he went somewhere with Mista Erick."

"He said they'd wait on us. That we'd go back to my law office together."

The truck raced down the highway. The silence between them grew long. At the cut-off to the ranch house, she tapped the phone back on and pressed the redial button.

She handed Duty the phone. "Give it back if he answers."

Within a half mile of Slash's house, Cézanne crested the hill. The sight of emergency lights strobing atop two sheriff's vehicles put her heart in her throat. Sirens screamed toward them.

She took in the scene in a glance.

In the distance, Velda stood on the front porch wringing her hands. Her pleated face contorted into a hideous mask. Her green floral muumuu seemed to blend into the scenery. Her head looked disembodied floating in the growth of vines creeping up the wire trellis, camouflaging Slash's front porch. Rackley, dressed in Slash's clothes, hunkered over a body on the grass.

"Ohmygod," she screamed at Duty. "Get the gun outta my bag. Lay it on the seat."

"Want me to use it? I could shoot somebody if I had to."

"Don't point it at me," she yelled, truly frightened.

Cézanne skidded the truck to a stop. She jammed the gearshift into park, grabbed the back of Duty's neck and forced her, face-first, onto the seat. "Stay down. Don't get up until I come back for you."

She snatched the gun off the seat, leaped from the truck, and sprinted toward Rackley. He was holding Slash's semi-automatic.

He stared up in horror. "She's dead."

Cézanne stared at the face—what was left of it.

Darlene Driskoll.

With her head stained crimson and her eyes half-closed, Darlene lay on her side with her legs in a scissor-like position. A Glock 9mm rested a few inches from her gun hand.

The wail of sirens closed in. Rackley dropped the .45 caliber and stood.

Carnal panic showed in his face. "There's nothing I can do here."

"What're you saying?" She clutched his wrist, but he shook her off and took a backward step. "Where's Slash?"

"She fired through the back windshield. I grabbed his gun and bailed out. Velda called for an ambulance. There's nothing left to do." He grabbed her shoulders, hauled her close, and kissed her hard on the mouth. "I've gotta go."

Cézanne's voice climbed two octaves. "You can't leave. This is a crime scene."

He bolted for the truck. "I'm not going back to prison."

She ran for the Cadillac. Called out, "It was self-defense.

There are witnesses. You won't be convicted."

"That's what the last lawyer said."

"I think Hollis Rushmore killed Yvonne," she shouted. "Whatever you did that last night, whatever you said to her . . . it worked. She picked you, Erick. Hollis couldn't accept that. Give me a chance to clear you."

"I can't go back to prison."

Her skin crawled at the sight of the gaping hole and spider web cracks in the Catera's windshield. She yanked open the driver's door. Slash was slumped forward with his cheek against the steering wheel. Lifeless eyes stared. Lids fell to half-mast. A thin thread of blood stained the corner of his mouth.

Ohmygod.

She thought it was me in that car.

This happened because of me.

The pickup's engine roared to life.

Carnal panic set in. She screamed, "Erick, don't leave us." But the truck lurched forward and careened out of sight. She looked to Velda for help. "Don't just stand there! I need you."

Duty stood in the driveway trembling. She shrieked gibberish into the cell phone as she gawked at Darlene's body. Velda came off the porch step, ripping the skirt of her housedress into strips.

Cézanne dropped to her knees. Wrapped her arms around Slash's waist and moaned, "Please don't die."

His cheek felt clammy against her neck but the sensation of a shallow breath against her skin gave her hope. Her vision tunneled. Her ears muted the wail of sirens speeding up the road. For the moment, the driver's compartment of her rental car contained her entire universe. Nothing existed beyond the three-foot radius she shared with Slash. Her eyes saw only the detective. Her heart sensed him slipping away.

Paramedics swarmed the drive. Strident voices filled the air.

"Step back, lady. Let us through." Said with authority.

Someone pulled at her arm. She kissed Slash's cheek as a deputy pried her off. She got up on shaky legs and stumbled out of the way. For the next few minutes she watched, helpless and shaking.

Deputies and paramedics communicated with each other as if she wasn't there.

"Aw, Jesus. It's Teddy Vaughn's big brother. We went to school together."

"BP's dropping."

"Hang on, buddy, we'll take care of you."

Emergency medical technicians eased him onto a gurney. Her stomach dropped at the sound of ratcheting metal when they raised him waist-high. Wheels clacked as they steered him to the back of the ambulance.

Cézanne's heart thudded. "I'm going with him," she announced to the group.

But paramedics were jockeying for position, and the deputy held her firmly in place.

Wimpering, Duty moved to her side. Her arms snaked around Cézanne's middle, and she hung on for dear life. The deputy let go.

"Miz Zan, is Mista Slash gonna make it?"

Her voice trembled. "I don't know." But intuition and desperation told her otherwise.

With the brim of a cowboy hat pulled low over the deputy's forehead, he stared through a gunslinger gaze. "What happened?"

Numb, Cézanne shook her head. Slash was dying or dead. The rest no longer mattered. She stared at the body of Darlene Driskoll. A man wearing a windbreaker with Deputy Sheriff silk-screened on the back in bright yellow letters snapped pictures of the corpse. She noticed the matted grass where Erick

Rackley knelt and wondered if the crime scene investigator saw it, too.

The deputy squinted fiercely at Duty, who came close to slipping into shock. "What happened?"

"We just got here."

Velda was standing by the hood of the Cadillac holding strips of fabric in her hands. Cézanne assumed she'd ripped her clothes to make a tourniquet. The women locked gazes.

Cézanne's skin tingled.

She sensed something extraordinary was about to happen.

With her beady-eyed glare focused on Cézanne, Velda addressed the Sheriff's men. "We were leaving to check on my brother's house. I forgot my bag and came back inside. Detective Vaughn started the car, and I was locking the door when that crazy woman jumped out of the bushes and fired through the back windshield." Velda pointed to Darlene, now covered with a Mylar sheet. "I ran to the car—"

Cézanne's eyes widened. Velda stopped her with a look.

"—got Detective Vaughn's gun and shot her."

Cézanne stared, transfixed. Velda had just reinvented herself as the heroine.

"Dropped her right there, dead in her tracks. Ever since she escaped from your jail, she's been gunning for my niece. Reckon she mistook Detective Vaughn for Cézanne since that's her car."

Cézanne's mouth gaped.

Duty whispered, "Quiet Miz Zan. Don't say nothin'. Velda did a good thing. Let it ride."

"But—"

"No, Miz Zan. We didn't see nothin'. Let Velda say what she has to say."

"I can't let her do this." Spoken in a zombie slur.

"Yessum, you can. Mista Erick didn't kill his wife. You said so yourself. Now let it go."

But the deputy had other ideas. He rocked on his boot heels like he smelled a dead rat. "How'd you two get here?" he asked, and she knew he'd started to poke holes in Velda's story.

Cézanne said, "The truck."

Duty said, "Walked."

The deputy's eyes glinted. "What truck?"

"I swanee. This'll jar your preserves. Would you look, Miz Zan? Somebody stole Mr. Slash's wheels."

Two hours passed before deputies released Cézanne from questioning and gave her a ride downtown.

Inside Our Lady of Mercy Hospital she bargained with God on the sprint down the corridor. Outside the doors marked Surgery, she scanned the faces in the waiting room. Teddy Vaughn slouched against the wall with his shoulder propping him up. When he saw her, his turquoise eyes rounded into spheres. The color in his face had drained ghostly pale. A matronly woman Cézanne took to be in her late sixties sat slumped to one side in an overstuffed chair with her forehead resting in her hand.

Mrs. Vaughn.

The North Star in the Vaughn brothers' family constellation.

Except for the cinnamon tinge in her champagne hair, she bore little resemblance to the ten-foot-tall Zeus-woman the Vaughn brothers described when they spoke of her zero-tolerance ways. Especially with her apron still on and a dusting of flour on her hands.

"Teddy." Cézanne's voice came out in a whisper.

He gave her a slow stare. Horror flooded his face. "Zan. What the hell happened?"

She hadn't expected to be treated with hostility and suspicion, but his eyes dulled when he saw her shirt covered in his brother's blood and she knew, on instinct, that he blamed her.

"Teddy, I'm so sorry."

"They said a woman shot him. Was it you?"

On the brink of tears, she shared what she knew about Slash borrowing her car and Darlene Driskoll firing through the tinted glass.

"I guess she thought it was me. I wouldn't blame you if you hated me."

Their mother looked up and caught Teddy's attention. By way of a weird familial telepathy, she commanded him with her eyes.

He stepped away with an, "Excuse me," and strode down the hall to check on his brother.

Her first instinct was to drop into a chair, tuck her head between her knees, and take deep breaths until someone happened by with a canister of pure oxygen. Her second was to taunt the nearest hospital cop until he shot her.

With great hesitation, she ventured over to Slash's mother. "Mrs. Vaughn?"

In a clipped German accent, the woman said, "Not now," and dismissed her with eyes cold enough to freeze-dry everything in the room.

Well into the fourth hour, a ragged surgeon in sweaty scrubs barged through the double doors and pulled a mask from his face. Dark hollows beneath his eyes told of a long night's work ahead of him. When he grazed a hand over his head to remove his cap, his gray hair stayed matted against his scalp.

"Mrs. Vaughn?"

"Yes?" Jaw muscles flexed. She wiggled her fingers, come-hither, and Teddy romped to her side. He draped a protective arm over her shoulder to steady her.

"The bullet shattered your son's jawbone and severed the nerves on one side of his face. We've called in a plastic surgeon."

"Good."

"He's not out of the woods yet. Once he is, he'll experience a great deal of pain."

"Good." Mrs. Vaughn bobbed her head.

"We're doing all we can. If he pulls through, he'll require a great deal of reconstructive surgery to the right side of his face."

"Good."

"He'll probably have permanent hearing loss in the right ear."

"Good."

The physician developed an edge. "Mrs. Vaughn, this is not good. This young man's in very bad shape. I'm not certain you understand the gravity of his condition."

"I understand perfectly." Nostrils flared. Hazy blue eyes rimmed red. "What you've told me is wonderful news. If he's in pain, it's because he can feel. You could've said he had no pain; that he couldn't feel from the neck down. You could've told me he was dead."

Everyone understood.

The doctor's face uncreased. His eyes cut to Cézanne. "Are you his wife?"

Mrs. Vaughn flinched.

"Close personal friend and colleague."

"I see." He let out a long sigh. "All right then, ya'll know as much as I do at this point. If you have a relationship with God I suggest you capitalize on it."

Teddy caught the surgeon as he turned to leave. "Did he say anything?"

"Two things. He told me to tag the bullet as evidence and turn it over to crime scene."

Teddy's eyes welled. He bit his bottom lip.

"And he kept repeating something that made absolutely no sense."

Mrs. Vaughn waited in angst. "Did he ask for me?"

"He said he wanted sand. 'Find sand. I want sand. Get sand.' I have no idea what that means."

But Cézanne knew.

While the others were scratching their heads, she headed for the ladies' room for a private cry and a talk with the Big Guy.

Chapter Thirty-Nine

Velda was still at the SO giving a statement when Teddy dropped Cézanne and Duty off at the house on South University. While Duty tended to Enigma, Cézanne climbed the stairs and flopped onto her bed. She couldn't remember a scarier day, not even when Darlene broke in and pulled a gun on her. To think she could trace all this misery back to her rookie days on the PD, back to the time she recovered a stolen car owned by Doug Driskoll . . .

She realized she'd drifted off when Enigma's snoring jolted her awake. He'd fallen asleep at the foot of her bed with his paws draped over the edge. Groggy, she pushed herself up on one elbow and blinked. Duty was sitting in the rocking chair with a quilt covering her legs and the Mossberg resting across her lap.

"What're you doing?"

"Pullin' guard duty. Waitin' for you to wake up."

"That's spooky. Why aren't you in your own room?"

" 'Cause we need each other right now. Nobody knows where Mista Henri is—"

"That degenerate's not my brother. His name's Jake."

"—and yo' daddy's still sayin' you need to look for his will. While Velda's out, I was thinkin' maybe we should tear this place apart. You think they'll lock Velda up? I wouldn't. What if she has a heart attack? Does the sheriff have to pay Velda's medical bills if she strokes out in jail?"

Cézanne mashed her fingers against her eyes until red and gold comets arced behind her lids. When she opened them, the chatterbox was still there.

They spent the first hour pawing through every shred of paper in Velda's room. They finished searching Bob's bureau and came up empty-handed.

Duty hatched an idea. "What'd yo' daddy do for a livin'?"

"Postman. After he ran out on us, he got a job as a merchant seaman."

"What's that?"

"Sailing on ships. Docking in foreign ports. Hanging out in exotic places."

Duty stared at a speck on the wall, pursed her lips, and mused aloud. "If I was a sailor and I had important papers, where would I put 'em?"

Cézanne huffed in frustration. "Let's finish looking through these drawers and call it a day. I want to get back to the hospital."

Duty gently massaged her temples. "Where would I put 'em?" Maroon eyes bugged. "I'd put 'em where it wouldn't be easy for a thief or a burglar to get to, but where I had excess—"

"Access."

"—access to 'em."

"I give up. You make me weary. Just cut the drama and tell me where you want me to look."

"Attic."

The trap door to the attic came down with a yank of the pull string. Duty handed Cézanne a cheap plastic flashlight and stood by while she tugged at the folding stairs. When she climbed through the opening, she saw that a small section of rough-hewn planks played out just beyond the central air conditioning unit. If she wanted to traverse the length of the house, she'd have to balance on the crossbeams with the flashlight clamped between her teeth.

Beams groaned under her weight. In the space above Velda's bedroom, she stepped onto an area floored-in with two-by-fours. Dust shimmered up from her feet, filling the phantasmal ring of light with flecks of gold.

A fire safe positioned next to a sea captain's desk caught her eye. She tried to lift it but it wouldn't budge. And when she opened the latch on the portable desk, she found no will, only letters.

The flashlight dimmed to a ghostly sphere.

Not much time. She grabbed the bundle of letters and started for the steps. They'd need a safecracker for the rest and she knew just who to ask—the lieutenant in Internal Affairs, an old-timer familiar with all the city's criminal population.

Duty's voice sounded like it came from the inside of a well. "Did you find it? 'Cause yo' dead daddy's sayin' it's up there."

"Yeah? Tell the son-of-a-bitch to give us the combination to his safe."

Ten feet from the ladder the light faded out. What a perfect metaphor to end a suck-dog day.

"Careful, Miz Zan. Don't fall through the floor."

She descended the steps covered in cobwebs. Duty was there to brush them off.

"Whatchoo got? Did we get money? 'Cause he didn't say nothin' about money . . . just that you'd be surprised."

"If you want me, I'll be in my room."

"Lemme stay with you while you read. I can go through yo' cabinets. Maybe we can find a key to that safe."

"I have an idea. Why don't you take Enigma for a walk?"

"I'll be real quiet. I promise."

Cézanne caved.

Duty tiptoed into the bedroom. She sat at the bureau and rifled through drawers while Cézanne took a spot on the bed and thumbed through envelopes. There were twelve in all, postmarked from Seattle and addressed to her mother. Each had been returned unclaimed. She found the one with the earliest postmark, slit the envelope and read:

Bernice,

You should've told me about Monet. I would've returned. You know I love my kids more than anything. What kind of woman would prevent a good father from having a relationship with his children? A bitter, spiteful, mean-spirited one.

When Henri was small, you said you didn't want more children. I know you had the girls because you thought it was the only way to keep me. But I loved those babies more than life, itself.

I gave you everything. I made sure you had plenty of money to care for the kids. Why didn't you tell me they were sick? Why didn't you take them to a doctor?

Soon, I'll have stockpiled enough money to fight you for Henri and Cézanne. You're an unfit mother, and I'll wrench my wonderful children from your evil grasp or die trying.

May you rot in hell for neglecting our girls.

Bob

Cézanne's eyes misted.

He did want them. So what kept him from returning?

She read six more letters before her father's venom diminished. In the seventh, Bob tried a different approach.

Dear Bernice,

What did I do to deserve such loathing and hatred from you?

I fell in love the moment I saw you. I knew in time you'd love me, too. Our parents tried to keep us apart because of our religious backgrounds. You said you wanted us to marry in spite of the fact you're Jewish, and I was committed to the Lutheran church. I knew we'd have a rough go of it but you convinced me we could make it work.

I blamed you for the affair with the cantor, but I would've stayed if you'd promised to stop seeing him.

Bernice, what happened to that girl at the lake? You used to be so gracious and kind. It's hard to believe you turned into the woman you are today. It's even harder to believe that, in all these years, I never stopped loving you.

For your own sake seek help.

For our children's sake, please let them see their father. Whether you believe it or not, they need me.

Bob

Down to one letter, she read:

Dear Bernice,

My health is poor. Doctors say I don't have much time. A month at best. Please put me in contact with Henri and Cézanne, and I'll have my attorney draw up papers to leave you my estate in its entirety, to use as you see fit.

Bernice, I must have your answer soon. Please, I beg of you. Grant my dying wish so that I may know my children again before I go.

I wish you peace and happiness.

Bob

Cézanne's eyes watered. He'd loved them all along. Her mother may've been mentally ill, but even on medication her cruelty knew no bounds.

Duty sat ramrod straight. "I found somethin'. It's a fortune cookie fortune. Why would yo' daddy keep a fortune cookie fortune?"

She brushed away a tear. "Maybe he played the lotto using those numbers."

Maybe it's the combination to the fire safe.

Velda walked in. Duty fisted the paper.

Cézanne studied her aunt in awe. "I can't believe you tried to protect Erick Rackley. They'll find out. They always do."

"Poppycock. You said yourself Slash was the best crime scene investigator in the whole wide world. If he's not around to speak up, who else is good enough to figure it out?"

There was still Marvin Krivnek. It wasn't his job to initiate reports, but he could certainly tell if a crime scene was staged, starting with the trajectory of the bullet.

Depleted, the old lady flopped down in the rocker. She eyed Cézanne through a beady squint. "What's that?"

"Letters from my father to my mother."

"You've been in the attic."

"You knew they were there?" She looked aghast. "But why didn't you tell me?"

Velda shrugged. "No slave builds his master better chains."

CHAPTER FORTY

To no one's surprise, Erick Rackley missed his hearing the following Friday.

The judge forfeited the one hundred-fifty thousand-dollar-cash bond posted by Henri Matisse Martin and issued a warrant for Rackley's arrest. Installing an AVLN on Slash's truck turned out to be a good idea. The pickup was recovered at the bus station downtown with the engine running and the key left in the ignition. The steering wheel had been wiped clean, but Rackley's thumbprint was found on the rearview mirror, and a fingerprint from his left hand was recovered on the seat adjustment mechanism.

Nobody believed Rackley boarded the bus. The lead investigator thought he hitched a ride to DFW Airport, but he could've easily ridden the Trinity Railway Express to Dallas and disappeared.

The following week, doctors released Slash from the hospital. With his jaw wired shut, he spent that afternoon convalescing at Cézanne's on the Beidermeier. Velda was airing out the kitchen, railing away at Duty for stinking up the place with one of her Voodoo potions. When the girl defended her Cajun cuisine, Velda's rant turned the occupants of the house into a hostage situation.

"This smells worse than a dirty diaper. Why can't you cook normal stuff?"

"This is normal. Normal for me."

"I'm talking about cooking food we can eat."

"Me and Miz Zan are tryin' to get rid of you." A kitchen utensil clanged against a pot. "Here, Velda, taste this."

"Get back." The back door banged open and directly slammed shut.

Duty chuckled the triumphant "hee-hee-hee" of an old lady. She had an infectious laugh, and Cézanne couldn't help smiling.

She turned to Slash. "Velda has no room to complain about the chow around here. She couldn't make a decent batch of biscuits if she had her mother's family recipe in one hand and a copy of *Southern Living* in the other, bless her heart." She unpacked Slash's overnight bag as she spoke, searching for the prescriptions he asked her to have filled and the list of nutritional supplements the doctor ordered.

He'd lost ten pounds slurping down hospital gruel, and his face was still swollen and badly bruised. In a month or so, the plastic surgeon would make another attempt to reconstruct his jaw and later, to remove the ugly scar running along his shattered jawbone. In the meantime, he was relegated to liquids.

"Do you want soup? I can make a milkshake. Just tell me what you want."

He shook his head. "Henri?"

The mention of her brother caught her off guard. She blinked hard, looked at the sunlight slanting through the wood blinds and willed herself not to cry.

"He's probably on the wrong side of the grass," she said. "It's been more than twenty years since he left on his motorcycle in the middle of the night. I no longer have any illusions that he's alive. The man who claimed to be my brother's an imposter. His name's Jacob Tierney. Jake."

She told him about the connection between Jake and Aricella. That she suspected they were husband-and-wife con artists. And that until the Seattle law firm produced a marriage license proving her father had married the slip of a brunette, she wasn't convinced Aricella was really her stepmother. But the cruelest part of their con game had been to make her believe her brother had returned.

"To think I almost gave that hustler money in exchange for his share of the house." She sighed.

"Sit," Slash did a quick hand pat to show he wanted her beside him. "If Velda comes in . . ." His tongue moved clumsily behind the confines of his teeth. To assist with the ventriloquism, he spooled his finger in a *Speed it up* gesture. "Get your gun."

"We're peacefully co-existing. She's pretty good at bill collecting. And she only threatened one of my clients with her baseball bat. I may actually hire her to work for me after the judge awards me the house. In a way, I almost feel sorry for her. I'm not sure I can throw her out."

But that was only part of the problem. Slash still didn't know Velda had done the noble thing, taking the rap for Erick Rackley—that, alone, was enough to keep them shotgun married for awhile.

The doorbell rang, and she got up to answer it. The postman had a package delivery for Velda and needed a signature. She scrawled out her name, accepted the box with the rest of the mail, and closed the door. She dropped the parcel on the dining room table and angled over to Slash while sorting the day's mail.

The sight of a postcard halted her in her tracks.

She studied the beach scene on one side. Then she flipped it over. The Barcelona postmark and postage stamp from Spain—a country that had no extradition treaty with the United States—was enough to make her heart flutter. It contained no message.

Erick Rackley.

She crumpled the card and thrust it into the back pocket of her jeans.

Slash pointed toward the kitchen. "Not who you think she is."

"Who? Velda?" She nodded, slow on the uptake. "Her temper's a lot nastier than I remember as a kid. I suppose it's old age making her crotchety."

"Remember the glass?" Mush-mouthed, he lifted his hand, gripped an invisible tumbler, and took an invisible swig.

"You want water?"

He shook his head.

"Sweet tea? Cola? Coffee?" All out of ideas, she spread her hands, palms up.

"Fingerprints. From water glass. AFIS."

She thunked her forehead with the heel of her hand. "Of course. The prints. You ran them?"

He nodded. "Not Aunt Velda."

A lance of fear went straight to her heart. Her blood ran cold. Primal fear wrenched her gut. Duty's strange comment about bad vibes upon meeting Velda for the first time came rushing back to her.

"The air around her turned violet . . . well, waves of violet. Like heat snakes on the road."

She listened painfully as the Spam hit the fan.

According to Slash, the fingerprints belonged to a jailed hot check writer from New Orleans, Louisiana who'd escaped during Hurricane Katrina when corrections officers emptied the jail and moved prisoners to safety.

Cézanne's so-called aunt had active warrants out of Orleans parish.

Nausea settled in. Tears percolated. She'd already lost Henri. Now Aunt Velda turned out to be a fraud.

"I feel sick. How can a person turn your life upside down

and they don't even know you?"

The back door banged open. They could hear the old woman's scuffy houseshoes slapping against the floor as she schlepped inside. Cézanne rose from the sofa. She dashed into the sunroom and returned with the .38 stuffed in the back waistband of her jeans and a new cell phone in her hand.

"What's her name?"

"Delilah Meade." He talked like he had a mouthful of marbles. After pronouncing it for the third time, he wrote on his hand and held up his palm.

Like the mad cow in the herd, Velda needed to be culled. Cézanne tapped out nine-one-one. After a short discussion, the dispatcher agreed to send a unit for a prisoner transport. She tapped off the wireless and turned to Slash for input. He shook his head. This time, she was on her own.

"Don't look at me that way. What else am I supposed to do? She's a criminal."

He shrugged. "Call her in. Let's hear her side."

"What if she bolts?"

Slash did an eye roll. "She's seventy-five. How far do you think she'll get loping down the street in a flowered tee pee?"

"Muumuu." Cézanne cupped her hands to her mouth. "Velda, get in here." She made eye contact with the dog who acknowledged her with a couple of tail thumps.

Velda shuffled in with the remnants of a cinnamon roll mortared between her dentures. "What?"

"Sit down. We need to talk."

"What do we need to talk about? Can't you see I'm busy?" Fist to hip, testy and rude. A burst of red flamed her cheeks as crimson as the heavy coat of rouge she troweled on each morning before breakfast.

Slash spoke through teeth wired shut. "Mrs. Meade."

"Can't say I did. I supposed I should've missed you, being as you've become a fixture around here lately. But I can't say I have." Velda cocked an eyebrow. "I am sorry what happened to you, and I do hope you get better soon . . ." she raised her voice in case they'd gone deaf ". . . so you'll get out of my house and stay out."

She turned to leave but Cézanne called her back. "You're not too busy to hear this . . . Delilah. Or should I call you Mrs. Meade?" She whipped out the .38 and aimed it at her.

Delilah Meade froze in her tracks.

Color drained from Fake Velda's face as if she'd powdered her skin with flour. With a heady sigh, she went limp and sank into the nearest chair. With her eyes downcast, she gave her flip-flops a bland smile.

Delilah Meade spoke in the hushed tone of a funeral director. "How'd you find out?"

"You exploited my family."

"Stop looking at me like I just shot off your big toe. You should be grateful. I'm the closest thing to a relative you have."

"You're a grifter." She cocked back the hammer. The unnerving sound of a lightning-split oak echoed through the room. Slash instinctively stiffened. Deuteronomy walked in, took in the showdown through protruding maroon eyes, and suddenly remembered she had something better to do.

Cézanne grew angrier by the second. "Start talking before I shoot off your big toe."

Fake Velda talked fast.

After the jail escape, she'd assimilated into the free world population by boarding a bus loaded with Katrina evacuees headed for Texas. She took a seat near a young couple who'd flown in from Seattle to spend their honeymoon in the French Quarter. She didn't start out planning to eavesdrop on their conversations, but the pretty brunette's second husband had recently died without a will and left a huge estate up for grab

The couple spoke in conspiratorial whispers, ignoring the old woman in the seat behind them—them in their fancy clothes and her with a scarf draped over her head to cut out the light, the noise, and the unpleasant smells coming from four-dozen sweaty bodies.

Slash riveted on her story. He must've realized Velda was about to confess because he uttered, "Miranda," in a low, throaty ventriloquism.

With an almost imperceptible headshake, Cézanne declined Slash's advice. She wasn't about to Mirandize this faker. By not reciting the Miranda warning, she might learn things of interest to use as leverage against Fake Henri and his scheming wife, Aricella. Once she delivered those Constitutional rights, Delilah Meade would clam up tighter than an unshucked oyster.

The woman she knew as Aunt Velda went on with her story.

The couple had a copy of the Texas Probate Code. They took turns researching it to see where the wife stood in the hierarchy of heirs. By the time the bus reached Shreveport, the man chose to play the role of the deceased's son in case his wife couldn't inherit his estate.

"That's when I decided to be the dead man's sister. I figured we'd be about the same age. What the hell? I realized it could work. Lord knows I needed a place to stay. I couldn't go back home since my house washed away. When the man kept talking about the lawyer, Hollis Rushmore, I figured if I beat him to the table that nice Mr. Rushmore might let me live in my dead brother's home."

Cézanne ground her molars. "Were you the one who vandalized it?"

"Throwing rocks through the windows was the only sure-fire way to convince him to let me move in. As caretaker, you understand. Just until he found you."

She looked at the floor as if ashamed, but Cézanne caught

the glint in her eyes. "Save it. If I hadn't found out I had a house coming to me, you'd still be trying to bilk me out of it." She wagged the gun. "Continue."

After Fake Aunt Velda conned Rushmore into believing she was an heir, she seized control of the house. Instead of sitting around all day watching mindless talk shows on TV, she went through file cabinets full of papers and boned up on the Martin family's history.

"I did my homework," she said with an aristocratic sniff. "I think I made a good aunt. You should be thankful."

"Thankful?" Cézanne practically hyperventilated with rage. She thumbed at Slash. "You're the one who should be thankful you have a witness who's preventing me from tattooing a widow's peak on your forehead with .38 hollowpoints. How could you?"

"I'm not a bad person." The old woman stared through eyes that were uninvitingly blank. "I ran out of money after I found out I had breast cancer. That's the reason I wrote those bad checks. When the hurricane hit, I ran. It's not easy being an evacuee. I did what I had to." She eased halfway up from the chair.

"Where do you think you're going?"

"Jig's up. You caught me fair and square, so you can put that bazooka away. I won't run. I want to show you something. I have what you've been looking for."

"Just so you know, I have no qualms about shooting a fleeing felon."

She followed Fake Velda into the kitchen with the gun aimed at her back and watched in disbelief as she lifted a section of linoleum inside the pantry and removed a couple of floorboards—imagine that. Seconds later, the scammer pulled out an accordion file labeled ESTATE and grudgingly handed it over.

Wordlessly, Cézanne marched the chiseler back into the living room and waved her into the chair with the gun muzzle.

While Slash looked on, she pulled the tie string, lifted the flap, and removed two envelopes embossed in gold script from the law firm of Roselli, Hudson and Foster. Both bore Seattle postmarks.

Cézanne rested the pistol in her lap and locked gazes with Delilah Meade. "Don't give me a reason to cap you."

"So does this mean you're not scared of me anymore?" Delilah asked hopefully.

"No. It means I'm faster than you."

Her hands trembled as she opened the envelope with the earlier postmark. Because her mother's name and address had been marked through with *Return to sender* written in Bernice's angular script, and since the envelope had been re-sealed, she assumed her mother had read it.

She slid out the paper and saw the stationary had been torn into pieces—probably her mother's handiwork—and subsequently retaped, probably by a legal assistant. It read:

Dear Mrs. Rosen-Martin,

It is with great sorrow that we notify you of the death of our client, Bob Martin. In order to settle his estate, it is imperative that we locate any surviving children.

Please furnish their names and addresses upon receipt of this notice. We regret any inconvenience.

With every good wish, I am

Very truly yours,
Mitchell Q. Roselli, Esq.

A week later, the lawyer wrote a follow-up letter that had been returned to the firm unopened.

Dear Mrs. Rosen-Martin,

We're now in possession of the signature card from the certi-

fied letter we sent on the 26th of November informing you of your ex-husband's death and asking your cooperation in locating his children, Cézanne and Henry. Inasmuch as we have now verified that you're alive and residing in Fort Worth, Texas it's our duty to proceed in accordance with the terms of our employment agreement with Mr. Martin.

In the event you disregarded his dying wish; in the event we were able to locate someone other than you who has knowledge of the whereabouts of your children, we are contractually obligated to inform you of Bob Martin's deathbed message to you. These words are Bob Martin's, not ours:

"Tell Bernice to disregard my letter," *and,* "Tell her I said to go fuck herself."

With every good wish, I am

Apologetically yours,
Mitchell Q. Roselli, Esq.

Cézanne glanced out the window. A smear of white sheared her attention. She heard two car doors slam and suspected the uniforms had arrived. When she craned her neck and inclined her head for a better view, Officers Elkhardt and Flurry were angling up the walk and sliding their batons into the rings on their Sam Browne belts.

A mind-numbing police knock rattled the front door.

Fake Velda seemed to know, on instinct, what was about to happen.

Duty slinked in from the kitchen, licking brownie batter off a big wooden spoon. Her eyes slewed to the front window, to the patrol cars parked at the curb. "Is Velda finally going to the pokey? Do we get our house back?"

Cézanne opened the door and looked up at their unsmiling faces. "Come in, gentlemen." She made a sweeping gesture toward Fake Velda. "This is Delilah Meade, con artist extraordinaire. She has outstanding warrants out of Louisiana."

When she turned to look, everyone was eyeballing an empty chair.

The sound of a revving engine startled Cézanne into action. She ran to the window in time to see the jailbird fly the coop in Slash's pickup. If Elkhardt hadn't chased her into the yard and wrestled the revolver from her grip, she would've been sprinting down the road cranking off rounds until she was dry-firing an empty weapon.

It took awhile to convince the patrolmen that Delilah Meade was a real person. It would've happened sooner, but Slash had trouble making himself understood.

"She boogied out the back door," Duty said helpfully. "Let's round up a posse and go after her. You can't miss her. Pink fuzz sprouting out of her head, beady eyes, red rabbit-fur flip-flops with rhinestone clips on the sides, wearing a green flowered tow sack with ugly red flowers on it . . ."

Scorched to the gills that nobody stopped the crook from taking off out the back door like a fat rat with cheese, she turned to Slash. "For a man who just had his truck stolen, you don't look very worried."

"I'm not." Relaxed humor showed on his face. "The AVLN's still attached."

Chapter Forty-One

After the officers left, the trio of friends were still sitting in Cézanne's living room when the doorbell chimed.

"If it's a client," she said to Duty, "this isn't a good time. Tell them to make an appointment."

Duty opened the door, took a backward step and let out a delighted squeal. "Mista Jinx. As I live and breathe. Look Miz Zan, it's Mista Jinx Porter and Miz Raven, come to visit."

Constable Jinx Porter and Raven stepped into the living room. Duty closed the door behind them. Jinx, a man in his mid-fifties, removed his gray Stetson to reveal a bad sunburn coloring the top of his bald head. Wire-rimmed glasses with thick, coke-bottle lenses dented his nose and magnified his asymmetrical, gray-green eyes until they looked like nickels. He stared at Cézanne, grim-faced.

Raven didn't look any happier. Fleshy, berry-stained lips tipped down at the corners. Pewter-gray eyes that normally sparkled had turned as dull as lead slugs. She didn't remove her Lady Texas High Roller as a sign of respect like Jinx did and she didn't advance any farther than the doormat the way Jinx did, either.

Cézanne searched her face for signs of anger—did she know about the overnight with Slash? But Raven only looked frightened.

"Duty, go watch TV," she said in an attempt to shoo the girl out of the room.

Jinx, who shared a strange bond with the odd teenager, shot down the suggestion. "Don't turn on the television." Three feet from where Cézanne sat, he dropped to one knee. Put his hat over his heart as if he were about to propose. "I'm sorry to have to tell you this."

Raven closed her eyes and slumped miserably against the doorjamb. She looked as if she might start wailing.

Cézanne hoped they'd come to tell her Fake Velda had tried to hijack a lowrider full of gang members and had been shot dead in the middle of the street. As quickly as the idea occurred to her, she shook off the ugly visual and hoped the car thief was fine. That authorities had tracked her through the navigation device. That she was cooling her hocks in the Tarrant County Jail.

The ugly reality was she needed Delilah Meade to help make a case against Jake and Aricella.

Jinx was talking. He'd said something important, and she'd missed it.

"They're both dead. I'm sorry, Cézanne, really so sorry for your loss."

Raven burst into tears. "Tell me what to do for you. Tell me what I can do."

Her body tingled with dread.

These people made no sense.

She settled her gaze on Slash who was staring with such intensity that his lips parted like a dog with bared fangs. Her eyes drifted over to Duty, weeping into her hands, keening like an Irish mourner.

"What?" Her eyes played leapfrog with each of her friends. Nobody uttered a peep. Numbed by the sudden display of grief, she grabbed Jinx by the shirt collar and hauled him up, eye-level. "What?"

"They're dead. Both of them. It's all over the news. Raven

insisted we come here as soon as the Teletype came into the precinct. She killed them."

"Who?"

"Darlene Driskoll."

But Darlene was dead. How could she kill anyone now?

"Killed who?" she asked, with the sort of dumbfounded confusion one might expect from someone who'd just dodged a meteor screaming to earth.

"Sheriff Noah and his father."

Cézanne's eyelids fluttered open. White squares turned into ceiling tiles as she careened back into consciousness from her place on the floor. When the men lifted her to a sitting position, the room tilted on its side. She focused on Duty's plate-sized garnet eyes as Jinx and Slash hoisted her up by the arms and deposited her onto the Biedermeier. Raven and Duty slid in beside her like bookends, balancing her upright.

After her grief roared out, she spoke with the monotone and cadence of a robot. "He didn't leave me for someone else?"

"He didn't leave you for someone else." Raven squeezed her hand. "He loved you."

"He didn't get married and fly off to Cabo with his new wife?" Her voice sounded tinny and distant as if she were in another room listening to a fifth-generation echo of herself.

"No, sweetie. We think Darlene answered the Noahs' telephone and made up that bogus story so you wouldn't come looking for Bobby."

"It didn't sound like Darlene." She gave the room a slow, doom-filled headshake.

Raven remained patient. "Who else could've done it? They found my Chief Special at Bobby's house."

"I bought you a replacement," she said, heaving a great sigh and wiping a tear away with the back of her hand. "It's in my bedroom. I didn't want you to be angry with me."

"I could never be mad at you." Raven kissed her cheek and hugged her tight.

As best Cézanne could tell, this was the third time they'd had this same conversation. The first two times took on all the characteristics of a closed head injury with short-term memory loss.

Hearing the devastating news was like getting a shot of Novocain to the brain. Initially, she didn't fully appreciate the way her mind shut down in order to insulate her from such a massive shock to the system. But now that the tragic event had fully registered, any self-protection powers had started to wear off, allowing the beginning of serious grief to seep in.

"How long?" This turned out to be a new query for her. On some level, her sluggish mind told her not to ask more questions than she could deal with. It was enough having to process her fiancé's death in increments. She wasn't prepared to hear the gory details.

The doorbell clanged. Jinx, who'd commandeered the chair she'd been sitting in before the collapse, got up to answer it.

A small but imposing silhouette stood in the doorway. Haloed in a backdrop of bright sunlight, he seemed to blend into the landscape. Then the haze wore off and Marvin Krivnek came into sharp focus.

He joined her on the couch. Duty moved closer to make room.

The dull ache of grief held her in its grip. She'd have to remind herself to put one foot in front of the other in order to get through this.

"What brings you here, Marve?" she asked, stupefied.

"We're friends. I came to tell you how sorry I am." He sandwiched her hand between his. For a short little fellow in a job that required precision, they felt surprisingly large and comfortingly warm.

She didn't remember much about the visit, only that he kissed her hand when he went away. After everyone left except Duty and Raven, Cézanne laid in bed for hours before sleep finally put her out of her misery. She awakened to a light knuckle rap on the bedroom door. Duty had come to tell her she had a walk-in client.

"Tell him to go away." She pulled the pillow closer to her face and shielded her head with the covers.

"He axed, can you do an expungement? I told him this is a bad time, but he insisted on seeing you. I told him if he wanted an expungement, why didn't he go back to the doctor that left the sponge in and get him to take it out?"

It was the only time she could remember smiling that day. Cézanne whipped the sheet back from her face. "Come here."

Duty tiptoed in.

"Sit down." Cézanne gave the bed a little hand pat. "I know you think I'm tough on you but I want you to know I'm glad you're here."

"Me, too."

"Things happen for a reason even though I don't always know why."

Duty nodded knowingly. "Like what happened to Mista Hollis Rushmore, right?"

She hoisted herself up on one elbow. "What happened to Hollis Rushmore?"

"A po-lice lady came by earlier. You were asleep; she said don't wake you. Said she had information you might like to know if you were still working on Mista Erick's case."

"What police lady? What's her name? Did she leave a business card?"

"All she said was Mista Rushmore got what he deserved. Said there was something the newspapers didn't report after

Mista Rushmore got arrested. Said Mista Rushmore's wife walked out on him the same day Mista Erick left. She told me to axe you, do you believe in coincidences?"

Chapter Forty-Two

Thousands turned out for the funerals of Bobby and his father, but only a few dozen close friends attended the graveside service on their dairy farm at the family cemetery overlooking the oak-dotted countryside.

Unlike Bob Martin, Bobby Noah had a will. In it, he left everything to Cézanne—or so his attorney disclosed when he introduced himself and offered his condolences.

As they trudged through a muddy field on their way back to the car, Cézanne linked arms with Raven and Duty. Jinx and Slash followed a respectable distance behind; not too close to eavesdrop, not too far away to be called upon if needed. Enigma romped beside them, snapping the air and letting out throaty *woofs*.

"What am I supposed to do with a dairy farm? I'm a city girl." She spoke in the grief-stricken voice of a survivor.

Raven offered words of comfort. "You don't have to do anything with it right now."

"I like cows, Miz Zan. I could help with the cows. What kind of cows do we have? Are these Oreo cows?"

"Holsteins."

"Holsteins," Duty said, trying out her new word. "I like the sound of that. I like Holsteins on account of they look like 'Nigma, all black and white and polka-dotty."

Cézanne ignored her. Her mind raced with thoughts of Erick Rackley. She felt inside her coat pocket and fingered the latest postcard, this one from Italy. It had a crude drawing of a proned-out silhouette lying face down with a chalk outline around it. The text was printed in pencil: *I promised I wouldn't tell.*

He was messing with her. She remembered what he'd said at the hearing.

"Nobody likes a snitch."

She pulled out the card and passed it to Raven. "What do you make of this?"

Lost in thought, visions of Erick Rackley danced in her head. She needed to contact him. To ask more questions. Without Erick's testimony, Hollis Rushmore might get off scott-free. Not only that, the case still haunted her. And there were holes in it.

She didn't believe, for an instant, Erick's theory that the lawyer had hidden inside Rackley's house and surprised Yvonne when she went to bed that evening. The windows were too small for him to have crawled in. Hollis wasn't exactly a long drink of water. Bless his heart, you had to wonder how the man squeezed out of the shower once he got all the soap rinsed off.

Raven handed the postcard back. "You don't suppose it's his way of confessing, do you?"

A skin-crawly feeling crept over her. "I think he's pointing the finger."

Françesca DiPaolo.

She recalled what Erick had said about her the night they went dancing.

"Yvonne didn't like her. But that's okay. Fran didn't much like Yvonne either."

She replayed his conversation in her head.

"Ms. Martin, when it's two in the morning and you're a drunken, out-of-work, bum slamming back longnecks, a spindly little Italian chick with a double-A chest and a pierced tongue wiggles a great piece of tail."

Françesca DiPaolo could've easily slipped in and out of the Rackley's windows.

Could've eliminated the competition.

Raven sucked air. "You think Hollis Rushmore's wife murdered Yvonne Rackley."

It was as though Jinx's deputy had telepathically tapped into Cézanne's thoughts.

"Worse. I think Françesca and Erick are together now." She clapped gloved hands to her cheeks, covering her ears and stretching the skin back from her face until her eyes took on an Asian slant. "I'm so stupid. What if Slash is wrong? What if it wasn't suicide? He didn't kill his wife, but he must've known all along who did. The only way to get back at Hollis for rigging that jury was to steal his wife and hope he took a murder rap."

Raven halted. From the looks of things, the cogs in her investigative mind had revved up into the danger zone.

The nice thing about involving her best friend in the Rackley case, Cézanne admitted inwardly, was that the minds of two intuitive, calculating females were better than one.

"Yvonne was screwing Hollis to get back at Erick for being an emotionally bankrupt husband and an unemployed drunk. But once he decided to fight for her, Yvonne played Hollis. Then Hollis played Erick at the trial. Once the writ of habeas corpus worked, Erick played Hollis by stealing his wife. But Françesca DiPaolo played them all. I think she's the one who got away with murder."

"What happens now?"

"My bar card's on the line. I filed the writ. I represented certain things to the judge, and I'm not about to get disbarred after working so hard to get my law license."

"You won't get disbarred," Raven said comfortingly, but the wild look in her eyes was far from convincing. "You may have to work off the stigma of being gullible and naïve, but the judge wouldn't hold that against you, would he?"

They exchanged looks that said *The hell he won't.*

"What are you going to do?"

"I'm calling Interpol."

Raven paused expectantly. "Then what?"

"We're getting on a plane."

"Who's 'we'? You and your tapeworm? Or is this like the queen's 'we'?" She affected a British accent. " '*We are not amused.*' "

"Me and you. Pack your bags. We're going on an adventure."

Raven rested a hand on Cézanne's arm. "Pardon me," she injected syrup in her tone, "but you seem to be under the misapprehension that I have tons of money to scatter around for a scavenger hunt."

"As it turns out, I have tons of it. I'll pick up the tab."

Sugar turned to sarcasm. "I see. Now that we've surmounted that hurdle have you forgotten Jinx Porter?" Jinx, a great admirer of the managerial skills and work ethic of Joseph Stalin, would do more than balk at the request for a leave of absence. "The man'll screech like a tree full of Chinese monkeys. He'll never let me take off work to go globetrotting across the United States with you."

Raven had apparently missed the card's postmark. He'd mailed it from the next town over, Cogoleto. But the picture of the fish on the front of the cheap postcard was a close-up of the shingle overhanging a restaurant.

Frutti di mare del Rikky.

Translation: Seafood by Erick.

"We're flying to Italy. To Arenzano, on the Western Riviera in the Province of Genoa. If Jinx threatens to fire you, we'll take him with us."

Cynicism made way for irony.

"Perhaps you've forgotten, but I've placed a DNR on my

personal relationship with Jinx. Do Not Resuscitate," Raven explained for Duty's benefit. "We're not breathing life into that dead-end. I've spent the better part of a year trying not to place myself in the path of Jinx Porter's alter ego, if you know what I mean. I'm not sure it's in my best interest to be near him in any country where romance languages are spoken."

"You don't have to get chummy with him. This is a business trip."

"When have I ever been able to resist that man? Remember the night of the hospital fundraiser? I'm afraid I had a little too much to drink and . . . never mind. Let's just agree this is a suck-dog idea."

"If I'm wrong, we'll have a nice vacation. If I'm right, I know just where Rackley and DiPaolo are."

Raven's voice spiraled upward. "They'll never come back on their own. And the United States has no extradition treaty with Italy. Face it. They're safe."

Cézanne suspected Raven's concerns had less to do with finding two fugitives and more to do with not falling back in love with Jinx Porter.

"True, we have no extradition treaty with Italy. Double-true, they're not likely to return on their own."

"Then what's the point of going over there?"

"I'm not exactly sure how to put the best spin on this. I'd like you to open your mind and view this scenario in the most favorable light," Cézanne said, watching Raven's expression. "I thought we'd bring them back without going through the government."

"You mean kidnap them?" Raven barely suppressed a shriek.

"That's a harsh word." Cézanne placed her hands over Duty's ears. "Think of it as cutting through the bureaucratic red tape."

"I was thinking more along the lines of you duct taping their mouths shut, poking air holes in a crate, and mailing them back to us *Par Avion.*"

A huge smile transformed Cézanne's gloomy face into radiance. "That's a wonderful suggestion." The idea gained momentum. Thoughts careened out of control. She visualized them throwing tow sacks over their quarry's heads, stuffing them into a Fiat, and speeding off into the night to some undisclosed location where Jinx Porter would carefully crate them for shipping. "We should practice on someone before we leave."

She gave Duty a scary glance.

"What about me?" Duty shook free. "Don't even think about ditchin' me. I'm what you call a loose end. I might spill the beans if you go off and leave me."

"You're going, too," Cézanne reassured her. "We'll get you a passport."

"What about 'Nigma?"

The dog heard his name and bounded over. He stared up through soulful eyes.

"Enigma isn't going. He can stay at the dairy farm. I'll hire someone to keep him fed."

"Who? Who's gonna feed 'Nigma?" Duty demanded, clearly reluctant to entrust the care and feeding of the Great Dane to just anyone.

"Maybe we can just empty a couple of forty-pound bags of chow in a trough and free feed him," she suggested and then immediately rejected the idea. Enigma was a binge eater. They might return to find him doubled in size. She came up with another plan. "Delilah Meade. I'm sure we can work something out with her probation officer. Like assigning her to do community service at the law office. And feed your dog."

"Have you taken leave of your senses?" Raven's eyes went wide. "This is certifiably crazy."

"I know. So, are you in?"

"I'm in." She looked skyward. "Heaven help us."

In the way of best buddies, the ladies entered into a three-way hug, making the upcoming caper official.

ABOUT THE AUTHOR

Laurie Moore was born and reared in the Great State of Texas where she developed a flair for foreign languages. She's traveled to forty-nine U.S. states, most of the Canadian provinces, Mexico, and Spain.

She majored in Spanish at the University of Texas at Austin where she received her Bachelor of Arts degree in Spanish, English, and Elementary and Secondary Education. She entered a career in law enforcement in 1979. After six years on police patrol and a year of criminal investigation, she made sergeant and worked as a District Attorney investigator over the next seven years for several DAs in the central Texas area.

In 1992, she moved to Fort Worth and received her Juris Doctor from Texas Wesleyan University School of Law in 1995. She is currently in private practice in "Cowtown" and lives with a jealous Siamese cat and a rude Welsh Corgi. She is still a licensed, commissioned peace officer and recently celebrated her 29th year in law enforcement.

Laurie became a member of DFW Writers Workshop in 1992 and is the author of *Constable's Run, Constable's Apprehension, Constable's Wedding, The Lady Godiva Murder, The Wild Orchid Society,* and *Simmering Secrets of Weeping Mary~A Deuteronomy Devilrow Mystery,* a young adult novel she wrote using the pseudonym Merry Hassell Frels. Writing is her passion. Contact Laurie through her Web site at www.LaurieMooreMysteries.com.